# In The Spotlight:
# Runway to Romance

SHARON KENDRICK

MELANIE MILBURNE

DANI COLLINS

MILLS & BOON

All rights reserved including the right of reproduction in whole or in part in any form. This edition is published by arrangement with Harlequin Enterprises ULC.

This is a work of fiction. Names, characters, places, locations and incidents are purely fictional and bear no relationship to any real life individuals, living or dead, or to any actual places, business establishments, locations, events or incidents. Any resemblance is entirely coincidental.

Without limiting the exclusive rights of any author, contributor or the publisher of this publication, any unauthorised use of this publication to train generative artificial intelligence (AI) technologies is expressly prohibited. HarperCollins also exercise their rights under Article 4(3) of the Digital Single Market Directive 2019/790 and expressly reserve this publication from the text and data mining exception.

® and ™ are trademarks owned and used by the trademark owner and/or its licensee. Trademarks marked with ® are registered with the United Kingdom Patent Office and/or the Office for Harmonisation in the Internal Market and in other countries.

First Published in Great Britain 2026
by Mills & Boon, an imprint of HarperCollins*Publishers* Ltd
1 London Bridge Street, London, SE1 9GF

www.harpercollins.co.uk

HarperCollins*Publishers*
Macken House, 39/40 Mayor Street Upper,
Dublin 1, D01 C9W8, Ireland

In The Spotlight: Runway to Romance © 2026 Harlequin Enterprises ULC.

*The Ruthless Greek's Return* © 2015 Sharon Kendrick
*A Contract for His Runaway Bride* © 2021 Melanie Milburne
*Married for One Reason Only* © 2021 Dani Collins

ISBN: 978-0-263-42108-8

Printed and Bound in the UK using 100% Renewable Electricity
at CPI Group (UK) Ltd, Croydon, CR0 4YY

# In The Spotlight

September 2025
**Fame's Temptation**

February 2026
**Runway to Romance**

December 2025
**Chasing Stars**

March 2026
**Desired Melodies**

January 2026
**Written in Passion**

April 2026
**Prescription for Love**

# About the Authors

**Sharon Kendrick** started storytelling at the age of eleven and has never stopped. She likes to write fast-paced, feel-good romances with heroes who are so sexy they'll make your toes curl! She lives in the beautiful city of Winchester – where she can see the cathedral from her window (when standing on tip-toes!). She has two children, Celia and Patrick and her passions include music, books, cooking and eating – and drifting into daydreams while working out new plots.

**Melanie Milburne** read her first Mills & Boon book at age seventeen in between studying for her final exams. After completing a Bachelor's and then a Master's Degree in Education, she decided to write a novel, and thus her career as a romance author was born. Melanie is an ambassador for the Australian Childhood Foundation and is a devoted owner of two cheeky toy poodles who insist on taking turns sitting on her lap while she's writing.

When Canadian **Dani Collins** found romance novels in high school, she wondered how one trained for such an awesome job. She wrote for over two decades without publishing, but remained inspired by the romance message that if you hang in there, you'll find a happy ending. In May of 2012, Mills & Boon bought her manuscript in a two-book deal. She's since published more than forty books with Mills & Boon and is definitely living happily ever after.

# THE RUTHLESS
# GREEK'S RETURN

**SHARON KENDRICK**

This book acknowledges with grateful thanks the help and inspiration given to me by Piero Campomarte, patron of the Citera Hotel in Venice.

Thanks also to one of the Citera's most famous and favoured guests – Dennis Riddiford.

# CHAPTER ONE

SOMETHING WAS DIFFERENT. Jessica felt it the moment she walked into the building. An unmistakable air of excitement and expectation. A rippling sense of change. She felt her throat constrict with something which felt like fear. Because people didn't like change. Even though it was about the only thing in life you could guarantee, nobody really welcomed it—and she was right up there with all those change-haters, wasn't she?

Outwardly the headquarters of the upmarket chain of jewellery stores was the same. Same plush sofas and scented candles and twinkling chandeliers. Same posters of glittering jewels spilled casually onto folds of dark velvet. There were glossy shots of women gazing dreamily at engagement rings, while their impossibly handsome fiancés looked on. There was even a poster of *her*, leaning reflectively against a sea wall and gazing into the distance, with a chunky platinum watch gleaming against her wrist. Briefly, Jessica's gaze flicked over it. Anyone looking at that poster would think the woman in the crisp shirt and sleek ponytail inhabited a life which was all neat and sorted. She gave a wry smile. Whoever said the camera never lied had been very misguided.

Glancing down at her pale leather boots, which had somehow survived the journey from Cornwall without being splashed, she walked over to the desk where the receptionist was wearing a new blouse which displayed her ample cleavage. Jessica blinked. She was *sure* she could smell furniture polish mingling with the scent of gardenia from the flickering candles. Even the extra-large display of roses sitting on the fancy glass desk looked as if they'd been given a makeover.

'Hi, Suzy,' said Jessica, bending her head to sniff at one of the roses and finding it completely without fragrance. 'I have a three o'clock appointment.'

Suzy glanced down at her computer screen and smiled. 'So you do. Nice to see you, Jessica.'

'Nice to be here,' said Jessica, although that bit wasn't *quite* true. Her life in the country had claimed her wholesale and she only came to London when she had to. And today it seemed she had to—summoned by an enigmatic email, which had provoked more questions than it had answered and left her feeling slightly confused. Which was why she had abandoned her jeans and sweater and was standing in reception in her city clothes, with the cool smile expected of her. And if inside her heart was aching because Hannah had gone…well, she would soon learn to deal with that. She had dealt with plenty worse.

Brushing fine droplets of water from her raincoat, she lowered her voice. 'You don't happen to know what's going on?' she said. 'Why I received a mystery summons out of the blue, when I'm not due to start shooting the new catalogue until early summer?'

Suzy started looking from side to side, like someone who had been watching too many spy films. 'Actually, I do.' She paused. 'We have a new boss.'

Jessica's smile didn't slip. 'Really? First I've heard about it.'

'Oh, you wouldn't have heard anything. Big takeover deal—very hush-hush. The new owner's Greek. Very Greek. A playboy by all accounts,' said Suzy succinctly, her eyes suddenly darkening. 'And *very* dangerous.'

Jessica felt the hairs on the back of her neck prickle, as if someone had just stroked an icy finger over her skin. Hearing someone say *Greek* shouldn't produce a reaction, but the stupid thing was that it did, every time. It wasn't as bad as it used to be, but she could never hear the mention of anything Hellenic without the sudden rush of blood to her heart. She was like one of Pavlov's dogs, who used to salivate whenever a bell was rung. One of those dumb dogs who expected to be fed and instead were presented with nothing but an empty bowl. And how sad was that? She stared at Suzy and injected a light-hearted note into her voice.

'Really?' she questioned. 'You mean dangerous as in swashbuckling?'

Suzy shook her mop of red curls. 'I mean dangerous as in oozing sex appeal, and knows it.' A light flashed on her desk and she clicked the button with a perfectly manicured fingernail. 'Something which you're just about to find out for yourself.'

Jessica thought about Suzy's words as she rode in the elevator towards the penthouse offices, wishing they could have swopped places. Because the new boss would be completely wasted on her—no matter how hunky he was. She'd met men who'd oozed testosterone and she'd had her fingers burnt. She stared at her reflection in the smoky elevator mirrors. Actually, it had only been one man and she'd had her whole body burnt—her heart and soul completely fried—and as a consequence she steered clear of *dangerous* men and all the stuff which came with them.

The elevator stopped and the first thing Jessica noticed was that things were different up here, too. More flowers, but the place was deserted and oddly quiet. She'd expected a small delegation of executives or some sort of fanfare, but even the usual rather scary-looking assistant who guarded the inner sanctum was missing. She looked around. The doors to the executive suite were open. She glanced down at her watch. Dead on three. So did she just walk in and announce herself? Or hang around here and wait until someone came out to find her? For a moment she stood there feeling slightly uncertain, when a richly accented voice brushed over her skin like gravel which had been steeped in honey.

'Don't just stand there, Jess. Come right in. I've been waiting for you.'

Her heart clenched and at first she thought her mind was playing tricks. She told herself that all Mediterranean voices sounded similar and that it couldn't possibly be him. Because how could she instantly recognise a voice she hadn't heard for years?

But she was wrong. *Wrong, wrong, wrong.*

She walked into the office in the direction of the voice and stopped dead in the centre of the vast room. And even though her brain was sending out frantic and confused messages to her suddenly tightening body, there was no denying the identity of the man behind the desk.

It *was* him.

Loukas Sarantos, framed by the backdrop of a London skyline—looking like the king of all he surveyed. Big, and brooding and in total command. A mocking half-smile curved his lips. His long legs were spread out beneath the desk while his hands were spread-eagled on the expansive surface, as if emphasising that it all belonged to him. With a shock she noted the expensive charcoal suit which hugged his powerful frame and more confusion washed over her. Because Loukas was a bodyguard. A top-notch bodyguard with clothes which made him blend in, not stand out. What was he doing *here*, dressed like that?

He had been forbidden to her from the start and it was easy to see why. He could intimidate people with a single glance from those searing black eyes. He was like no one else she'd ever met, nor was ever likely to. He made her want things she hadn't even realised she wanted—and when he'd given them to her, he'd made her want even more. He was trouble. He was the night to her day. She knew that.

The room seemed to shift in and out of focus, blurring at the edges before reappearing with a clarity so sharp that it almost hurt her eyes. She wanted the sight of him to leave her cold. For him to be nothing but a distant reminder of another time and another life.

Some hope.

He was leaning back in a black leather chair, which gleamed like the thick hair that curled against his neck. But his half-smile held no trace of humour—it was nothing but an icy assessment which seemed to hit her like a chill wind. His eyes bored through her and for a moment Jessica felt as if she was going to faint, and part of her wondered if that might not be a good thing. Because if she crumpled to the floor, wouldn't that give her a let-out clause? Wouldn't it force him to ring for medical assistance, so that his potency would be diluted by the presence of other people?

But the feeling quickly passed and a lifetime of hiding her emotions meant she was able to look around the room with nothing but curiosity on her face and say almost casually, 'Where's the assistant who's usually here?'

A flicker of irritation passed across his face as he leaned forward. 'Eight years,' he said softly. 'Eight long years since we've seen each other—and all you can do is ask me some banal question about a member of staff?'

His confidence unnerved her almost as much as his appearance, because the brashness of yesteryear seemed to have disappeared—along with the beaten-up leather jacket and faded jeans. Yet even in his made-to-measure suit, he still exuded a carnal sexuality which nothing could disguise. Was that why the almost forgotten aching had started deep inside her? Why she suddenly found herself remembering the burn of his lips pressing down on hers and the impatience of his fingers as he pushed up her little tennis skirt and…and…

'What are you doing here?' she questioned, only suddenly she didn't sound quite so calm and she wondered if he'd picked up on that.

'Why don't you take off your coat and sit down,

Jess?' he suggested silkily. 'Your face has gone very white.'

She wanted to tell him that she'd stay standing, but the shock of seeing him again really *had* affected her equilibrium. And maybe fainting wasn't such a good idea after all. She would only find herself horizontal—and imagine just how disconcerting it would be to find Loukas bending over her. Bending over her as if he wanted to kiss her...when the reality was that he was looking at her as if she'd recently crawled out from beneath a stone.

She walked over to the chair he'd indicated and sank down, letting her leather bag slide noiselessly to the ground as she lifted her gaze towards the empty blackness of his. 'This is a...surprise,' she said lightly.

'I imagine it must be. Tell me...' his eyes gleamed '...how it felt to walk into the room and realise it was me?'

She lifted her shoulders as if there were no words to answer that particular question, and even if there were she wasn't sure she'd want him to hear them. 'I suppose there must be some sort of...explanation?'

He looked at her unhelpfully. 'To what, Jess? Perhaps you could be a little more specific.'

'To you sitting here and behaving as if—'

That half-smile again. 'As if I own the place?'

She swallowed, thinking how arrogant he sounded. 'Well, yes.'

'Because I do own it,' he said, suddenly impatient. 'I've bought the company, Jess—I should have thought that much was obvious. I now own every one of the Lulu outlets, in cities and airports and cruise ships all over the world.'

Shock rippled over her skin. Stay focused, she told herself. You can do it. You were trained in the art of staying focused.

She kept her voice casual. 'I didn't realise—'

'That I was rich enough?'

'Well, there's that, of course.' Her smile felt as if it were slicing her face in two. 'Or that you had an interest in jewellery and watches.'

Loukas touched the tips of his fingers together and stared into eyes which were the exact colour of aquamarines. As always, not a single strand of her blonde hair was out of place and he remembered that even after the most strenuous sex, it always seemed to fall back into a neat and shiny curtain. He looked at the pink gleam of her lips and something dark and nebulous whispered over his skin. Jessica Cartwright. The one woman he'd never been able to forget. The woman who had unravelled him and then tied him up in knots. His pale and unexpected nemesis. He expelled a slow breath and let his gaze travel over her at a leisurely pace—because surely he had earned the right to study her as he would any other thing of beauty which he'd just purchased.

As usual, her style was understated. Classy and cool. A streamlined body, which left the observer in no doubt about her athletic background. She'd never been into revealing clothes or heavy make-up—her look had always been scrubbed and fairly natural and that hadn't changed. He had been attracted to her in a way which had taken him by surprise and he'd never been able to work out why. He noticed how her white shirt hugged those neat little breasts and the subtle gleam of pearls at her ears. With her pale hair pulled back in a ponytail, which emphasised her high cheekbones, he thought how remote she seemed. How *untouchable*. And it was all a lie. Because behind the false ice-maiden image, wasn't there a woman as shallow and as grasping as all the others? Someone who would take what they wanted from you and then just leave you—gasping like a fish which had been tossed from the water.

'There's plenty you don't know about me.' His mouth hardened and he felt the delicious rush of blood to his groin. *And plenty she was about to find out.*

'I don't understand...' She shrugged her shoulders and now her aquamarine eyes were wide with question. 'The last time I saw you, you were a bodyguard. You worked for that Russian oligarch.' She frowned as if she was trying to remember. 'Dimitri Makarov. That was his name, wasn't it?'

'*Neh.* That was his name.' Loukas nodded. 'I was the guy with the gun inside his jacket. The guy who knew no fear. The wall of muscle who could smash through a plank with a single blow.' He paused and flicked her a look because he remembered the way she used to run those long fingers over the hard bulge of his muscles, cooing her satisfaction as she touched his iron-hard flesh. 'But one day I decided to start using my brains instead of just my brawn. I realised that a life spent protecting others has a very limited timescale and that I needed to look towards the future. And, of course, some women consider such men to be little more than *savages*—don't they, Jess?'

She flinched. He could see the whitening of her knuckles in her lap and her reaction gave him a rush of pleasure. Because he wanted to see her react. He wanted to see her coolness melt and to watch her squirm.

'You know I never said that.' Her voice was trembling.

'No,' he agreed grimly. 'But your father said it and you just stood there and agreed with every damned word, didn't you, Jess? You were complicit in your silence. The little princess, agreeing with Daddy. Shall I remind you of some of the other things he said?'

'No!' Her hand had flown to her neck, as if her fingers could disguise the little pulse which was working frantically there.

'He called me a thug. He said I would drag you down to the gutter where I came from, if you stayed with me. Do you remember that, Jess?'

She shook her head. 'Wh—why are we sitting here talking about the past?' she questioned and suddenly her voice didn't sound so cool. 'I dated you when I was a teenager and, yes, my father reacted badly when he found out we were...'

'Lovers,' he put in silkily.

She swallowed. 'Lovers,' she repeated, as if it hurt her to say it. 'But it all happened such a long time ago and none of it matters any more. I've...well, I've moved on and I expect you have, too.'

Loukas might have laughed if he hadn't felt the cold twist of rage. She had humiliated him as no woman had ever dared try. She had trampled on his foolish dreams—and she thought that none of it mattered? Well, he was about to show her that it did. That if you betrayed someone then sooner or later it would come back to haunt you.

He picked up a gold pen which was lying on his

desk and began to twirl it between his thumb and forefinger, his eyes never leaving her face.

'Maybe you're right,' he said. 'It isn't the past we should be concentrating on, but the present. And, of course, the future. Or rather more importantly—your future.'

He saw her shoulders stiffen. Did she guess what was coming? Surely she realised that anyone in his position would set about terminating her contract with as little fallout as possible.

'What about it?'

He heard the defensiveness in her voice as he twirled the pen in the opposite direction. 'You've been working for the company for—how long is it now, Jess?'

'I'm sure you know exactly how long it is.'

'You're right. I do. I have your contract here in front of me.' He glanced down at it before looking up again. 'You joined Lulu right after you gave up your tennis career, yes?'

Jessica didn't answer straight away because she was afraid of giving herself away. She didn't want to show anything which might make her vulnerable to this very intimidating Loukas. Given up her tennis career? He made it sound as if she'd given up taking sugar in her coffee! As if the thing she'd devoted her entire life to—the sport she'd lived and breathed since she was barely out of nappies—hadn't suddenly been snatched away from her. It had left a great, gaping hole in her life and, coming straight after her break-up with him, it had been a double whammy she'd found difficult to claw her way back from. But she'd done it because it had been either sink or swim, and very soon after that she'd had Hannah to care for. So sinking had never really been an option. 'That's right,' she said.

'So why don't you tell me how you got the job, which I understand surprised a lot of people in the industry, since you had zero modelling experience?' He raised his eyebrows. 'Did you sleep with the boss?'

'Don't be stupid,' she snapped, before she could stop herself. 'He was a man in his sixties.'

'Otherwise you might have been tempted?' He leaned back in his chair and smiled, as if he was pleased to have got some kind of reaction from her at last. 'I know from my own experience that sportswomen have particularly *voracious* sexual appetites. You in particular were pretty spectacular in bed, Jess. And out of it. You could never get enough of me, could you?'

Jessica willed herself not to respond to the taunt, even though it was true. She felt as if he was toying with her, the way a cat sometimes toyed with a dragonfly just before its sheathed paw finally stilled the chattering wings. But for the time being she would play along. What choice did she have when the balance of power was so unevenly divided? Flouncing out of here wasn't an option, because this wasn't just about survival—it was about pride. She might have got the job by chance, but she'd grown into the unexpected career which fate had provided by way of compensation for her shattered dreams. She was *proud* of what she'd achieved and she wasn't going to toss it all away in a heated moment of retaliation, just because the man asking the questions was the man she'd never been able to forget.

'Do you want an answer to your question?' she

asked quietly. 'Or are you just going to sit there insulting me?'

A hint of a smile tugged at the edges of his lips, but just as quickly it was gone. 'Carry on,' he said.

She drew in a deep breath, like one which used to fire her up just before she began a service game. 'You know I tore a ligament, which effectively ended my career?' She stared into his face, but any sympathy she might have been hoping for was absent. His cursory nod was an acknowledgment, not a condolence. There was no understanding in the cold gleam of his eyes. She wondered if he knew that her father had died.

'I heard you pulled out on the eve of a big tournament,' he said.

'I did.' She nodded. 'Obviously, there was a lot of publicity. I was…'

'You were poised on the brink of international success,' he interjected softly. 'Expected to win at least one Grand Slam, despite your precocious age.'

'That's right,' she said, and this time no amount of training could keep the faint crack of emotion from her voice. Didn't matter how many times she told herself that worse things had happened to people than having to pull out of a career before it had really begun—it still hurt. She thought of all the pain and practice. Of the friends and relationships she'd lost along the way. Of the disapproving silences at home and the way her father had pushed her and pushed her until she'd felt she couldn't be pushed any more. The endless sacrifices and the sense that she was never quite good enough. All ended with the sickening snap of her ligament as she ran across the court for a ball she was never going to reach.

She swallowed. 'The papers ran a photo of me leaving the press conference after I'd been discharged from hospital.' It had become an iconic image, which had been splashed all over the tabloids. Her face had been pale and edged with strain. Her trademark blonde plait falling over the narrow shoulders on which a nation's hopes had been resting.

'And?

His bullet-like interjection snapped Jessica back to the present and she looked into the rugged beauty of his olive-skinned face. And wasn't it a mark of her own weakness that she found herself aching to touch it again? To whisper her fingertips all over its hard angles and hollows and feel the shadowed roughness of his jaw. Couldn't he blot out the uncomfortable way she was feeling with the power of one of his incredible kisses and make everything seem all right? She swallowed as she met the answering gleam in his eyes. As if he had guessed what she was thinking. And that was a mistake. It was the most important lesson drummed into her since childhood, that she could never afford to show weakness, not to anyone—but especially not to Loukas. Because hadn't he been trained to leap on any such weakness, and exploit it?

'Lulu noticed in the photo that I was wearing a plastic wristwatch,' she continued. 'And it just so happened that they were launching a sporty new watch aimed at teenagers and thought I had the ideal image to front their advertising campaign.'

'Yet you are not conventionally beautiful,' he observed.

She met the dark ice of his gaze, determined not to show her hurt, but you couldn't really blame someone for telling the truth, could you? 'I know I'm not. But I'm photogenic. I have that curious alchemy of high cheekbones and widely spaced eyes, which makes the camera like me—at least, that's what the photographer told me. I realised a long time ago that I look better in photos than in real life. That's why they took me on. I think they were just capitalising on all the publicity of my stalled career to begin with, but the campaign was a surprise success. And then when my father and stepmother were killed in the avalanche, I think they felt sorry for me—and of course, there was more publicity, which was good for the brand.'

'I'm sorry about your father and stepmother,' he said, almost as an afterthought. 'But these things happen.'

'Yes, I know they do.' She looked into his hard eyes and it was difficult not to feel defensive. 'But they wouldn't have kept me on all these years unless I was helping the watches to sell. That's why they keep renewing my contract.'

'But they aren't selling any more, because you are no longer a teenager,' he said slowly. 'And you no longer represent that age group.'

She felt a beat of disquiet. She told herself to forget they'd been lovers and to forget that it had ended so badly. She needed to treat him the way she would any other executive—male *or* female. Be nice to him. He's your sponsor. *Charm him.* 'I'm twenty-six, Loukas. That's hardly over the hill,' she said, managing to produce a smile from somewhere. The kind of smile a woman might use on a passing car mechanic, if she discovered her car had developed a puncture on a badly lit road. 'Even in these youth-obsessed times.'

She saw the flicker of a nerve at his temple—as if he was aware of her charm offensive. As if he didn't approve of it very much. She wondered if she came over as manipulative but suddenly she didn't care, because she was fighting for her livelihood. And Hannah's, too.

'I don't think you understand what I'm saying, Jess.'

Jessica felt her future flash before her as it suddenly occurred to her why she was here. Why she'd received that terse email demanding her presence. Of *course* he had her contract on his desk. He now owned the company and could do anything he pleased. He was about to tell her that her contract wouldn't be renewed—that it only operated on a year-to-year basis. And then what would she do—a burnt-out tennis player with no real qualifications? She thought about Hannah and her college fees. About the little house she'd bought after she'd paid off all her father's debts. The house that had become their only security. About all the difficulties and heartbreak along the way, and the slow breaking down of barriers to arrive at the workable and loving relationship she had with her half-sister today.

A shiver whispered its way down her spine and she prayed Loukas wouldn't notice—even though he'd been trained to notice every little thing about other people. Especially their weaknesses.

'How can I understand what you're saying when you've been nothing but enigmatic?' she said. 'When you've sat there for the entire time with that judgemental look on your face?'

'Then perhaps I should be a little clearer.' He drummed his fingertips on the contract. 'If you want your contract extended, you might want to rethink your attitude. Being a little nicer to the boss might be a good place to start.'

'Be nice to you?' she questioned. 'That's rich. You're the one who has been hostile from the moment I walked into this office—and you still haven't told me anything.' There was a pause. 'What are you planning to do?'

Loukas swivelled his chair round, removing the distraction of her fine-boned face from his line of vision and replacing it with the gleam of the London skyline. It was a view which carried an eye-watering price tag. The view which reinforced just how far he had come. The space-age circle of the Eye framing the pewter ribbon of the river. Jostling for position among all the centuries-old monuments were all the new kids on the block—the skyscrapers aimed at the stars. A bit like him, really. He stared at the Walkie-Talkie building with its fabled sky garden. Whoever would have thought that the boy who'd once had to ferret for food at the back of restaurants would have ended up sitting here, with such unbelievable wealth at his fingertips?

It had been his burning ambition to crawl out of the poverty and despair which had defined his childhood. To make right a life steeped in bitterness and betrayal. And he had done as he had set out to, ticking off every ambition along the way. He'd done his best for his mother, even though... Painfully, he closed his eyes and refocused his thoughts. He'd made the fortune he'd always lusted after when he'd worked as a bodyguard for oligarchs and billionaires and seen their lavish displays of wealth. He'd always wondered what it would be like to carelessly lose a million dollars at a casino table and not even notice the loss. And he'd discovered that he used to get more pleasure from the food he'd been forced to steal from the restaurant bins when his belly was empty. Because that was the thing about money. The pleasure it was supposed to give you was a myth, peddled by those who were in possession of it. It brought nothing but problems and expectations. It made people behave in ways which sickened him.

Even when he'd been poor he'd never had a problem finding women, but he'd often wondered whether it would make a difference if you were rich. His mouth hardened. And it did. Oh, it did. He felt the acrid taste of old-fashioned disapproval in his mouth as he recalled the variety of *extras* women had offered him since he'd become a billionaire in his own right. Did he like to watch? Did he want threesomes? Foursomes? Was he interested in dressing up and role play? It had been made clear to him that anything he wanted was his for the taking and all he had to do was ask. And he had tried it all. He would have tried anything to fill the dark emptiness inside him, but nothing ever did. He'd cavorted with women with plastic bodies and gorgeous, vacuous faces. Models and princesses were his for the taking. So many things had been dangled in front of him in order to entice him, but he had been like a child let loose in a candy store who, after a few days of indulging himself, had felt completely jaded.

And that was when he had decided that you couldn't move on until your life was straightened out. Until you'd tied up all the loose ends which had threatened to trip you up over the years. His mother was dead. His brother was found. Briefly, he closed his eyes as he thought about the rest of that story and felt a painful beat of his heart. Which left only Jessica Cartwright.

His mouth hardened. And she was a loose end he was going to take particular pleasure tying up.

He turned his chair back around. She was still sitting there, trying to hide her natural anxiety, and he allowed himself a moment of pure, sadistic pleasure. Because he wouldn't have been human if he hadn't appreciated the exquisite irony of seeing how much the tables had turned. How the snooty tennis prodigy who'd kept him hidden away like a guilty secret—while he *serviced her physical needs*—was now waiting for an answer on which her whole future would be decided.

How far would she go to keep her job? he wondered idly. If he ordered her to crawl under the desk and unzip him and take him in her mouth—would she oblige? He felt the hard throb at his groin as he imagined his seed spilling inside her mouth, before changing his mind. No. He didn't want Jess behaving like a hooker. What he wanted—what he *really* wanted—was for her to be compliant and willing and giving. He wanted her beneath him, preferably naked. He wanted to see her eyes darken and hear her gasp of disbelieving pleasure as he entered her. He wanted to feed her hunger for him, until she was dependent on him. Until she couldn't draw a breath without thinking of him.

And then he would walk away, just as she'd done.

The tables would be turned.

They would be equals.

He looked into her aquamarine eyes.

'You're going to have to change,' he said.

# CHAPTER TWO

JESSICA'S HEART WAS pounding loudly as she looked across the desk at Loukas, who in that moment seemed to symbolise everything which was darkness...and power. As if he held her future in the palm of his hand and was just about to crush it.

He had begun removing the jacket of his beautiful suit. Sliding it from his shoulders and looping it over the back of his chair and that was making her feel even more disorientated. He looked so...intimidating. Yet the instant he started rolling up his sleeves to display his hair-roughened arms, it seemed much more like the Loukas of old. Sexy and sleek and completely compelling. Her thoughts were skittering all over the place and suddenly she was having to try very hard to keep the anxiety from her voice. 'What do you mean—I have to change? Change what, exactly?'

His smile didn't meet his eyes. In fact, it barely touched his lips. He was enjoying this, she realised. He was enjoying it a lot.

'Everything,' he said. 'But mostly, your image.'

Jessica looked at him in confusion. 'My image?'

Again, he did that thing of joining the tips of his fingers together and she was reminded of a head teacher who'd sent for an unruly pupil and was just about to give them a stern telling-off.

'I can't believe that nobody has looked at your particular advertising campaign before,' he continued. 'Or why it has been allowed to continue.' His black eyes glittered. 'A variation of the same old thing—year in and year out. The agency the company have been using have become complacent, which is why the first thing I did when I took over was to sack them.'

'You've sacked them?' Jessica echoed, her heart sinking—because she liked the agency they used and the photographer they employed. She only saw them once a year when they shot the Lulu catalogue but she'd got to know them and they felt *comfortable*.

'Profits have been sliding for the past two years,' he continued remorselessly. 'Which isn't necessarily a bad thing—because it meant I was able to hammer out an excellent price for my buyout. But it does mean that things are going to be very different from now on.'

She heard the dark note in his voice and told herself to stay calm and find the strength to face her fears. Like when you were playing tennis against a tough opponent—it was no good holding back and being defensive and allowing them to dominate and control. You had to take your courage in your hands and rush the net. Face them head-on. She met his cold, black eyes.

'Is this your way of telling me that you're firing me?'

He gave a soft laugh. 'Oh, believe me, Jess—if I was planning on firing you, you would have known about it by now. For a start, we wouldn't be having this conversation, because it would be a waste of my time and my time is very precious. Do you understand what I'm saying?'

Yes, she understood. She thought how *forbidding* he seemed. From the way he was behaving, nobody would ever have guessed they'd once been lovers. She had seen his ruthless streak before—it had been essential in his role as bodyguard to one of Russia's richest men. But around her he had always been playful—the way she'd sometimes imagined a lion might be if it ever allowed you to get close enough to pet it. Until their affair had finished, and then he had acted as if she was dead to him.

Was that why he was doing this—to pay her back for having turned down his proposal of marriage, even though at the time she had known it was the only thing she *could* do?

She must not let him intimidate her, nor allow him to see how terrified she was of losing her livelihood. Because Loukas was the ultimate predator…he saw a weakness and then moved in for the kill. That was what he had been trained to do. She clasped her hands together and looked at him. 'So why are we having this conversation?'

'Because I have a reputation for turning around failing companies, which is what I intend to do with this one.'

'How?'

He was looking at her calculatingly, like a butcher weighing a piece of meat on a set of scales. 'You are no longer a teenager, Jess,' he said softly. 'And neither are the girls who first bought the watch. You are no longer a tennis star, either—you are what's known in the business as a has-been. And there's no point glowering at me like that. I am simply stating a fact. You were taken on because of who you were—a shining talent whose dreams were shattered. You were the tragic heroine. The sporty blonde who kept on smiling through the pain. Young girls wanted to be you.'

'But not any more?' she said slowly.

'I'm afraid not. You're trading on something which has gone. The world has moved on, but you've stayed exactly the same. Same old shots of you with the ponytail and the pearls and the Capri pants and the neat blouses.' His eyes glittered. 'I get bored just thinking about them.'

She nodded, her heart beating very hard, because it hurt to have him talk to her this way. To have her life condensed into a sad little story which left him feeling 'bored'. She met his black eyes and tried to keep the pain from her face. 'So what are you planning to do about it?'

'I am giving you the opportunity to breathe some life back into your career—and to boost Lulu's flagging sales.'

She wished she'd taken her raincoat off, because her body was beginning to grow hot beneath that scorching stare. She tried to keep her voice calm. To forget that this was Loukas. To try to imagine that it was the previous CEO sitting there, a man with a cut-glass accent who used to ask her for tennis tips for his young daughter. 'How?'

He leaned back in his chair, his outward air of relaxation mocking the churned-up way she was feeling inside.

'By giving you a new look—one which reflects the woman you are now and not the girl you used to be.

We make you over. New hairstyle. New clothes. We do the whole Cinderella thing and then reveal you to the public. The nation's sweetheart all grown up. Just imagine the resulting publicity that would generate.' His eyes glittered. 'Priceless.'

She shifted uncomfortably in her chair. 'You make me sound like a commodity, Loukas,' she said, in a low voice.

He laughed. 'But that's exactly what you are. Why would you think any differently? You sell images of yourself to promote a product—of course you're a commodity. You just happen to be one which has reached its sell-by date, I'm afraid—unless you're prepared to mix it up a bit.'

She met the hard gleam of his eyes and a real sense of sadness washed over her. Because despite the way their affair had ended, there had still been a portion of her heart which made her think of him with...

With what?

Affection?

No. Affection was too mild a description for the feelings she'd had for Loukas Sarantos. She had *loved* him despite knowing that they were completely wrong for each other. She had loved him more than he'd ever known because she'd been trained to keep her feelings locked away, and she had taken all her training seriously. The way they'd parted had filled her with regret and she'd be lying if she tried to deny that sometimes she thought about him with a deep ache in her heart and a very different kind of ache in her body. Who didn't lie in bed at night sometimes, wondering how different life might have been if you'd taken a different path?

But now? Now he was making her feel angry, frustrated and stretched to breaking point. He made her want to pummel her fists against him, but most of all he made her want to kiss him. That was the most shameful thing of all—that she was still in some kind of physical thrall to him. She wanted him to cover her mouth with one of his hot kisses. To make her melt. To feel that first sharp and piercing wave of pleasure as he entered her and have it blot out the rest of the world.

She stared into his mocking eyes, telling herself that her desire was irrelevant. More than that, it was dangerous, because it unsettled her and made her want things she knew were wrong. No good was ever going to come of their continued association. He wanted to change her. To make her into someone she wasn't. And all the while making her aware of her own failures, while he showcased his own spectacular success.

Was that what *she* wanted?

'Why are you doing this, Loukas?'

'Because I can.' He smiled. 'Why else?'

And suddenly she saw the Loukas of old. The man who could become as still as a piece of dark and forbidding rock. Foreboding whispered over her skin as she rose to her feet. 'This isn't going to work,' she said. 'I just can't imagine having any kind of working association with you. I'm sorry.'

'You should be.' His voice was silky. 'I've had my lawyers take a good look at your contract. Refuse this job and you aren't in line for any compensation. You leave here empty-handed. Have you thought about that?'

Briefly, Jessica imagined Hannah, happily backpacking in Thailand. Hannah who had defied all expectations to land herself a place at Cambridge University. Her teenage half-sister on the other side of the world, blissfully oblivious to what was going on back home. What would she say if she knew that her future security was about to be cut from under her, by a black-eyed man with a heart of stone?

But as she bent to pick up her handbag she told herself that she would think of something. There were opportunities for employment in her native Cornwall—admittedly not many, but she would look at whatever was going. She could turn her hand to plenty of other things. She could cook and clean or even work in a shop. Her embroidery was selling locally and craftwork was becoming more popular, so couldn't she do more of that? Better that than to stay for a second longer in a room where the air seemed to be suffocating her. Where the man she had once loved seemed to be taking real pleasure from watching her squirm.

Her fingers curled around the strap of her handbag. 'You might want to think about changing your own image rather than concentrating on mine,' she said quietly. 'That macho attitude of yours is so passé.'

'You think so?' he drawled, leaning back in his chair and surveying her from between narrowed eyes. 'I've always found it particularly effective. Especially with women. Most of them seem to get turned on by the caveman approach. You certainly did.'

With his middle finger, he began to draw a tiny circle on the contract and Jessica found herself remembering when he used to touch her skin that way. The way he used to drift his fingertip over her body with such light and exquisite precision. She'd been unable to resist him and she wondered whether any woman would be capable of resistance if Loukas Sarantos had them in his sights.

And suddenly he looked up and smiled—a cruel, cold smile—as if he knew exactly what was running through her mind.

'Yes,' he said softly. 'I still want you, Jessica. I didn't realise quite how much until I saw you today. And you'd better understand that these days I get everything I want. So I'll give you time to reconsider your decision, but I'm warning you that my patience is not infinite. And I won't wait long.'

'Don't hold your breath,' she said, meeting his eyes with a defiant look which lasted only as long as it took her to walk out of his office, her heart pounding as she headed for the elevator.

He didn't follow her. Had she really thought he would? Had there been a trace of the old Jessica who thought he might rise to his feet and cover the distance between them with a few purposeful strides, just like in the old days? *Yes, there had.* And wasn't part of her still craving that kind of masterful behaviour? Of course it was. What woman could remain immune to all that brooding power, coupled with the steely new patina which his wealth had given him?

She shook her head as she left the building, realising that Suzy had been right. He *was* dangerous and the way he made her feel was more dangerous still. Far better that she walked away now and left him in the past, where he belonged.

Hurrying through the emerging rush hour, she caught the train to Cornwall with seconds to spare, but the usually breathtaking journey was shrouded in darkness. The January evening was cold and rain lashed against the carriage windows, seeming to echo her gloomy mood.

She leant her head back against the seat, wondering if she was crazy to have turned her back on a job which had been her security for so long. Yet surely she'd be crazier still to put herself in a situation where Loukas held all the power.

Her love for him might have been replaced by a mixture of anger and frustration—but she was far from immune to him. She couldn't deny the sharp kick of desire when she looked at him, or her squirming sense of frustration. And if that frustration had been unexpectedly powerful, was that really so surprising? Because there had been nobody else since Loukas. No other lover in eight long years. He had been her first man and the only man. Wasn't that ridiculous? And unfashionable? He'd accused her of being stuck in a rut, but he didn't know the half of it.

Because nobody had come close to making her feel the way Loukas had done. She'd *tried* to have relationships with other men but they had left her feeling cold. She stared out of the window as the train pulled into the darkness of a rain-lashed Bodmin station. Other men had made her feel nothing, while her Greek lover had made her feel everything.

Just under an hour later and she was home. But the sight of the little Atlantic-facing house which usually filled her with feelings of sanctuary tonight did no such thing. Rods of rain hit her like icy arrows as she got out of the taxi. The crash of the ocean was deafening but for once she took no pleasure from it. Tonight the sound seemed lonely and haunting and full of foreboding.

And of course, the house was empty. She seemed to rattle around in it without the noisy presence of her half-sister. Jessica listened to the unusual sound of silence as the front door slammed closed behind her. She missed Hannah. Missed her a lot. Yet who would have thought it? It certainly hadn't been sunshine and laughter when Jessica's father had split from her mother, to marry his long-term mistress who was already pregnant with his daughter, Hannah.

Jessica had been badly hurt by her parents' bitter divorce and the news that she was going to have a stepmother and a brand-new baby sister had filled her with jealousy and dread. There had been plenty of tensions in their 'blended' family, but somehow they had survived—even when Jessica's mum had died soon after and the villagers had whispered that she'd never got over her broken heart. Jessica had tried to form a good relationship with her stepmother and to improve the one she had with her perfectionist father. Until that terrible day when an avalanche had left both girls orphaned and alone.

After that, it had been a case of sink, or swim. They'd *had* to get along, because there had been no alternative. Jessica had been eighteen and Hannah just ten when the policeman had knocked on the door with that terrible expression on his face. The authorities had wanted to take Hannah into care but Jessica had fought hard to adopt her. But worse was to come when Jessica realised that her father had been living a lie—spending money on the back of her future earnings, which were never going to materialise. The lawyers had sat her down and told her that their affluent lifestyle had been nothing but an illusion, funded by money they didn't have.

She'd been at her wits' end, wondering how she could support herself and Hannah, because there was precious little left after the big house had been sold. That was why the Lulu job had been such a lifesaver. It had given her money to pay the bills, yes, but, more preciously, it had given her the time to try to mother her heartbroken half-sister in a way that a regular job could never have done.

She had learnt to cook and had planted vegetables. And even though the plants hadn't done very well in the salty and wind-lashed Cornish garden, just the act of nurturing something had brought the two sisters closer together. She had attended every single school open evening and had always been there for Hannah, no matter what. She'd tried not to freak out when the young teenager was discovered smoking dope at a party, telling her that everyone was allowed one mistake. She'd stayed calm the year Hannah had flunked all her exams because of some school bad-boy who'd been giving her the runaround. Instead, she had quietly emphasised the importance of learning and told her how much she regretted her own patchy education—all sacrificed in the name of tennis. And somehow love had grown out of a relationship which had begun so badly.

Jessica had cried when she'd seen Hannah off at Heathrow Airport just before Christmas, with that ridiculously bulky rucksack dwarfing her slender frame, but she had waited until the plane had taken off before she had allowed the tears to fall. Not just because she kept her emotions hidden as a matter of habit, but because she knew this was how it was supposed to be. She knew that saying goodbye was part of life.

And today she'd said goodbye to a part-time modelling career which had never been intended to last. She'd had a good run for her money but now it was time to try something new.

Jessica bit her lip as the rain beat down against the window and tried to block out the memories of Loukas's mocking face. She would think of something.

She had to.

## CHAPTER THREE

BUT FATE HAD a habit of screwing things up when you least expected it and three things happened in rapid succession which made Jessica regret her decision to walk away from Loukas Sarantos and his job offer. Her washing machine packed up, her car died, and then Hannah had her wallet stolen while swimming off a beach in Thailand.

Jessica's first thought had been sheer panic when she'd heard the teenager's choking tears on the other end of the line, until she started thinking how much worse it could have been. And once her fears had calmed down to a manageable level, she felt nothing but frustration. But it was a wake-up call and the series of unexpected expenses forced her to take a cold, hard look at her finances and to face up to them with a sinking feeling of inevitability. Was she really deluded enough to think she could manage to live by selling a few framed pieces of *embroidery*? Why, that would barely cover the electricity bill.

She stood at the window, watching the white plume of the waves crashing down over the rocky beach. There *were* alternatives, she knew that. She could sell this house and move somewhere without a lusted-after sea view, which added so much money to the property's value. But this was her security. Her rock. When they'd had to sell their childhood home, this had become a place of safety to retreat to when chaos threatened and she hadn't planned on leaving it any time soon. Especially now. She'd read somewhere that young people were left feeling rootless and insecure if the family home was sold when they went off to college. How could she possibly do that to Hannah, who had already lost so much in her short life?

She thought about what Loukas had said to her, his words both a threat and a promise.

*I won't wait long.*

She picked up the phone and dialled the number before she had a chance to change her mind and asked to speak him. He's probably no longer interested, she thought, her heart pounding loudly. I've probably offended his macho pride by making him wait.

'Jess.' His deep voice fired into her thoughts and sent them scattering.

'Loukas?' she questioned stupidly, because who else could make her shiver with erotic recall, just by saying her name?

'I'd like to say that this is a surprise,' he said softly. 'But it isn't. I've been waiting for your call, although it hasn't come as quickly as I would have expected.' There was a pause. 'What do you want?'

Jessica closed her eyes. He knew exactly what she wanted—was he going to make her crawl in order to get it? She opened them again and saw another wave crash down onto the rocks. Maybe she *was* going to have to swallow her pride—but that didn't mean she needed to fall to the ground and lick his boots.

'I've been thinking about what you said and on reflection...' She drew in a deep breath. 'On reflection, it does seem too good an opportunity to turn down. So I've decided to accept the offer—if it's still on the table.'

At the other end of the line Loukas clenched and unclenched his free hand, because her cool response frustrated him far more than her opposition had done. He liked her when she was fighting and fiery, because fire he could easily extinguish. Making ice melt was different—that took much longer—and he had neither the time nor the inclination to make his seduction of Jessica Cartwright into a long-term project. She was just another tick on the list he was working his way down. His heart clenched with bitterness even while his body clenched with lust. She was something unfinished he needed to file away in the box marked 'over'. He wanted her body. To sate himself until he'd had his fill. And then he wanted to walk away and forget her.

'Loukas,' she was saying, her voice reminding him of all the erotic little things she used to whisper. She had been an incredibly quick learner, he remembered, his groin hardening uncomfortably. His innocent virgin had quickly become the most sensual lover he'd ever known.

'Loukas, are you still there?'

'Yes, I'm still here,' he said unevenly. 'And we need to talk.'

'We're talking now.'

'Not like this. Face to face.'

'But I thought...'

Her voice tailed off and Loukas realised that he *liked* the heady kick of power which her uncertainty gave him. Suddenly he wanted her submissive. He wanted to be the one calling all the shots, as once she had called them. 'What did you think, Jess?' he questioned softly. 'That you wouldn't need to see me again?'

He could hear her clearing her throat.

'Well, yes,' she said. 'I always deal with the advertising agency and the stylist—and the photographer, of course. That's what usually happens.'

'Well, you're wrong. None of this is *usual*, because I am in charge now. I like a hands-on approach—and if the previous CEO had possessed any sense, he would have done the same. You need to meet with our new advertising agency and for that you need to be in London. I'll have someone at Lulu book you into a hotel.'

'Okay.' She cleared her throat again. 'When did you have in mind?'

'As soon as possible. A car will be sent to pick you up this afternoon.'

'That soon?' Her voice sounded breathless. 'You're expecting me to be ready in a couple of hours?'

'Are you saying you can't? That you have other commitments?'

'I might have,' she stalled and something made her say it, though she wasn't quite sure what. 'I might have a date.'

There was a pause. 'Then cancel it, *koukla mou*.'

As his words filtered down the line, Jessica froze, because even though it had been a long time since she'd heard it, the Greek term sounded thrillingly familiar. My doll. That was what it meant. Jessica bit her lip. He used to say it to her a lot, but never with quite such contempt. Once she had trembled with pleasure when he had whispered it into her ear but now the words seemed to mean different things. They seemed tinged with foreboding rather than affection.

'And if I don't?' she questioned defiantly.

'Why not take a little advice, mmm? Let's not get this relationship off on a bad footing,' he said. 'Your initial refusal to cooperate irritated me but your game-playing is starting to irritate me even more. Don't make the mistake of overestimating your own appeal, Jess—and don't push me too far.'

'And is that…' she drew in a deep breath '…supposed to intimidate me?'

'It's supposed to make you aware of where we both stand.'

There was a pause and his voice suddenly changed gear. It became sultry and velvety. It sounded *irresistible*.

'Do you really have a date tonight, Jess?'

She wanted to say yes—to tell him that some gorgeous man was coming round to take her out. A man who was carrying a big bunch of flowers and wearing a soppy grin on his face. And that after champagne and oysters, he would bring her back here and make mad, passionate love to her.

But the vision disintegrated before her eyes, because the thought of any man other than Loukas touching her left her cold. And how sad was that?

'No,' she said flatly. 'I don't.'

'*Thavmassios.*' His voice dipped with satisfaction. 'Then I will see you later. Oh, and make sure you bring your passport.'

'What for?'

'What do you think? The new team want to use an

exotic location for the shoot,' he said impatiently. 'Just *do* it, will you, Jess? I don't intend to run everything past you for your approval—that's not how it works. It's certainly not how *I* work.'

He terminated the connection and Jessica found herself listening frustratedly to a hollow silence. But there was nothing she could do about it. She was going to have to change her image, if that was what it took. She would accept the makeover and smile for the camera and do her best to hold onto her contract for as long as she could. But that was all she would do. She knew what else he wanted and that certainly wasn't written into the deal.

She didn't have to sleep with him.

She closed all the windows, turned off the heating and emptied the fridge and two hours later a sleek black limousine arrived to collect her, slowly negotiating its way along the narrow, unmade road which led to her house.

It felt disorientating to hand her bags to the uniformed driver and slide onto the back seat as the powerful vehicle pulled away. During the journey she tried to read but it was impossible to concentrate. Her mind kept taking her back to places she didn't want to go— and the past was her biggest no-go destination. She stared out of the window and watched as the Cornish countryside gave way to Devon and found herself thinking about Loukas and the way he used to come and watch her practising, way before they'd got to know each other.

The public footpath used to cross right by their tennis court when she had lived at the big house, and she would look up with a fast-beating heart to find a dark and brooding figure standing there. It used to drive her father potty, but it was a public space and he could hardly order the Greek bodyguard away. Not that he would have dared try. Loukas Sarantos wasn't the kind of man you would order to do anything. She'd been a bit scared of him herself. He had been so dark and effortlessly powerful, and the way she'd caught him looking at her legs had made her feel... It was difficult to put into words the way he'd made her feel. She had tried very hard to steer her thoughts away from him and to concentrate on the fact that she double-faulted every time he watched her.

'He will destroy your career!' her father had roared and Jessica had promised that she wouldn't see him— though at that point he hadn't even asked her out.

And then she'd run into him in the village when her father had taken his wife and Hannah up to London and Jessica had been given a rare day to herself. She hadn't gone near a tennis ball all day and that had felt like a liberation in itself. She'd been feeling restless and rebellious and had wandered to the nearby shop to buy herself chocolate. Her hand had been hovering over the purple-wrapped bar when a deeply accented voice had said,

'Do you really think you should?'

She had looked up into a pair of mocking black eyes and something had happened. It had felt like being touched by magic. As if her heart had caught fire. She didn't remember what they'd said, only that he'd flirted with her and she'd flirted back in a way which had seemed to come as easily as breathing—because how could you not flirt with a man like Loukas? He had been exotic, different, edgy and enigmatic, but that hadn't mattered. Nothing had mattered other than the urgent need to be near him.

She'd offered to show him the famous borehole which was set in the surrounding cliffs like the imprint of a giant cannonball. His stride had been longer than hers and she remembered the wind whipping her ponytail as they'd stared down into the dark hollow. He'd told her that it reminded him of the diamond mine owned by his Russian boss, but she hadn't been particularly interested in hearing about diamonds. All she'd wanted was for him to kiss her, and he must have known that, because mid-sentence he'd stopped and and said, 'Oh, so *that's* what you want, is it, little Miss Tennis?' And he had caught her in his arms and his dark head had moved slowly towards hers and she had been lost.

The kiss had sealed a deal she hadn't realised they were making. Jessica had wanted to have sex with him instantly, but something had made her pull back. Because even though she'd wanted him very badly, instinct had told her that he was a man used to women falling at his feet and she should take it slowly. And somehow she had.

Two weeks had felt like an eternity before she'd let him take her virginity, and if part of her had wondered if all that sensual promise could possibly be met, she'd discovered that it could. Oh, it had. For someone who'd spent her life relying on her body to help her win, who had worked through all the pain and injuries, she had now discovered a completely different use for it. An intense pleasure which had made the rest of the world fade away. He had made her gasp. He had made her heart want to burst with joy. She had been hooked on sex and hooked on him.

They had snatched what moments they could and maybe the subterfuge had only added to the excitement. He'd told her his boss wouldn't approve of their relationship and Jessica had known her father would have hit the roof if he'd known. But that hadn't stopped her falling in love with Loukas, even though she would sooner have flown to the moon than showed it. Until the night when she'd blurted it out to him. She could remember even now the slow way he had smiled at her...

And then her father had found her contraceptive pills. Even now she cringed at the humiliating scene which had followed. She should have told him it was none of his business, but she had been barely eighteen and had spent her life being told what to do by someone for whom ambition had been everything. He had confronted Loukas. Told him he had *taken advantage* of his daughter, and had threatened to go to his boss. And what had Loukas done? She bit her lip, because even now it hurt to remember him squaring up his shoulders, as if he'd been just about to step into the fray. In a gruff and unfamiliar voice he had offered to marry her.

And her response? She had said no, because what else could she have said? She'd known he had only been asking her because he'd felt it was the right thing to do and she couldn't bear to trap this proud man in a relationship he'd never intended. Had she been able to see the two of them together—even ten years down the line? No, she hadn't. And if she was being honest, her career had been too important for her to want to risk it on the random throw of an emotional dice. She'd been working towards being a champion since she'd been four years old. Had she really been prepared to throw all that away because Loukas had been offering something out of a misplaced sense of duty?

But her heart had been breaking as she'd ended their affair, even though she'd known it was the right thing to do. She remembered the way he had looked at her, an expression of slowly dawning comprehension hardening his black eyes, before he had laughed. A low, bitter laugh—as if she had just confirmed something he'd already known.

She remembered the way she'd felt as he had turned his back on her and walked away—a clear bright pain which had seemed to consume her. That was the last time she'd seen him, until the moment she'd walked into the penthouse office at Lulu's—a bodyguard no longer but an international tycoon. Jessica shook her head in slight disbelief. How on earth had he managed that?

The slowing pace of the traffic made her realise that they'd hit central London and that the limousine was drawing up outside the Vinoly Hotel, a place she'd never stayed in before. The company usually put her up in the infinitely larger Granchester whenever she was in London and she wondered why they'd sent her here.

The driver opened the door. 'Mr Sarantos says to inform you that a suite has been booked in your name and that you are to order anything you need.'

Jessica nodded and walked into the interior of the plush hotel, whose foyer was dominated by a red velvet sofa in the shape of a giant pair of lips. A Perspex chair on a gilt chain was suspended from the ceiling and impossibly cool-looking young people in jeans and expensive jackets were sprawled around, drinking coffee and tapping away furiously on their laptops.

The receptionist smiled as she handed her a key card and an envelope. 'This was delivered for you earlier,' she said. 'We hope you have a pleasant stay with us, Miss Cartwright. The valet will show you to your suite.'

Jessica didn't have to look at the envelope to know who it was from. Her heart was racing as she recognised Loukas's handwriting—bold and flowing and unlike any other she'd ever seen. She knew his education had been patchy. He'd taught himself to read and write, but had ended up at the age of seventeen without a single qualification, other than a driving licence. But that was pretty much all she knew because he had been notoriously tight-lipped about his childhood. A sombre look used to darken his face whenever she dared ask, so that in the end she gave up trying—because wasn't it easier to grab at rainbows rather than chase after storms?

She waited until she was in her suite before opening the envelope, so intent on reading it that she barely noticed the stark decor of the room. Loukas's message was fairly stark, too.

> *I trust you had a good journey. Meet me in the dining room downstairs at eight. In the wardrobe you will find a black dress. Wear it.*

Jessica's mouth dried. It was an explicit request which sounded almost sexual. Had that been his intention? Did he plan to make her skin prickle with excitement the moment she read it, or to make her feel the molten pull of desire? Walking over to the line of wardrobe doors, she pulled open the first to find a dress hanging there—noting without any sense of surprise that it was made by a renowned designer. It was deceptively simple—a masterpiece fashioned from heavy silk and Jessica could instantly see how exquisitely it was cut. She thought how beautifully it would hang, and wasn't there a tiny part of her which longed to wear it? Because it was a sexy dress. A woman's dress. The kind of garment which would be worn in the knowledge that later a man would remove it.

Heart pounding, she turned away from the temptation it presented and everything else it symbolised and stared defiantly at her own belongings. She resented his peremptory tone and much else besides. He had no right to order her what to wear. The job hadn't even started and already he was acting as if he owned her. Being summoned here within the space of a few hours was one thing, but no way was Loukas going to decide on her wardrobe.

By eight she had showered and changed and was heading down towards the restaurant. Outwardly composed, she announced her arrival to the maître d' but her fingers were trembling as she was shown across the candlelit room to where Loukas was already seated.

This time she was prepared for his impact, but it made little difference to her reaction. Illuminated by the soft glow of candlelight, he was occupying the best table in the room and looking completely at home— as if he owned the space and all that surrounded him. She saw the unmistakable darkening of his eyes as she approached, but the flicker of a nerve at his temple indicated a flash of anger, rather than lust.

And suddenly she began to regret the determination with which she had pulled on a cream-coloured dress which fell demurely to just below the knee. She knew she must appear faintly colourless among the exotically clothed women in the room, but surely maintaining her independence was more important than blending in with the slick, city crowd. More importantly, it would send out a subliminal message to her former lover, telling him that she was still very much her own woman, no matter how much she needed the job.

He said nothing until she had been seated and presented with a menu, but he waved the waiter away with an impatient hand, and when he spoke his voice felt like the brushing of dark velvet all the way down her spine.

'I thought I told you to wear the black dress?'

She met his gaze with the imperturbable stare which had once served her so well on the tennis court. 'No woman likes to be told what dress to put on, Loukas.'

'I beg to differ.' His voice was soft. Dangerously soft. 'Why would you object to wearing a costly gown which would make you look amazing?'

'Because I don't want or need your costly gowns.'

'I see.' Reflectively, his finger moved across his lips. 'And presumably you chose that bland-looking outfit to ensure I wouldn't be attracted to you?'

Jessica felt her cheeks grow hot. She might not have dressed to impress but she knew she looked neat and smart, and it hurt to hear him say something unnecessarily cruel like that. Was that the reason she started defending herself—why she was foolish enough to try? 'You didn't used to complain about the colour of my clothes.'

'That's because I was young and I didn't care what you wore. Actually, I was more concerned about getting you naked.' He paused to slant her a flinty smile. 'Something which was never a problem after your initial reluctance.'

'Well, at least that side of things need no longer concern you.'

'*"That side of things"?*' he mimicked in amusement. 'Don't be coy, Jess. If you're talking about sex, why not just come out and say it?'

'Okay, I will.' Jessica waved her menu in front of him, pleased that the candlelight camouflaged her sudden blush. 'And sex isn't on the menu, I'm afraid.'

He leaned back in his chair and smiled. 'Your defiance excites me,' he said. 'Mainly because I wasn't expecting it.'

'No?'

'No.' He shook his head. 'I thought you might be happy to put on a dress which your average female would lust after.'

'Maybe I'm not your average female.'

'No, maybe you're not.' His lashes came down to half shield the ebony gleam of his eyes. 'I was also wondering whether or not you would be *compliant* and it gives me a perverse kind of pleasure that you weren't.'

'Really?' She raised her eyebrows. 'And why's that?'

He smiled. 'Because if you present a man with a woman who is disobedient, then he is conditioned to want to *tame* her. To sublimate her unruly temperament. And that is something which fills me with anticipation and excitement.'

His words washed over her—edged with an eroticism she couldn't ignore. And suddenly Jessica felt out of her depth. As if she'd underestimated him. As if she'd unwittingly signed up for something more than a change of image and a brand-new advertising campaign. He looked so powerful as he sat there. As if he was playing a game, only she didn't know what that game was. Because although this man looked like Loukas—a very polished Loukas—she realised that he was a stranger to her.

*He had always been a stranger to her, she realised with a sinking heart. Hadn't he always kept a side of himself locked away?*

But her face betrayed nothing, her smile as polite as if they were discussing nothing more controversial than the January weather. 'Do you really think it's acceptable to invite a woman for dinner and then to talk about taming her?'

This time his smile was edged with definite danger. 'Doesn't that turn you on—a masterful man taking control of a stubborn woman? I must say, it has always been one of my enduring fantasies, my little Ice Queen.'

*Ice Queen.* Jessica didn't react to that either. It was a long time since she'd heard the term which had dogged her junior years as a player and followed her onto the senior circuit. She had hated it, although her father had approved. He'd said it meant she'd achieved what she'd set out to achieve—a cold unflappability. Or rather, what *he* had set out to achieve. All Jessica knew was that being cold didn't make you popular with the other players, even if the ability to keep your feelings hidden made you a formidable opponent. Not showing when you were angry, or sad, or rattled had distinct advantages when you were playing tennis—just not in real life. It made people think you had no real feelings. It made them call you Ice Queen. And it made men like Loukas Sarantos interested in you because they thought you presented the ultimate challenge.

'I'm not interested in your sexual fantasies,' she said quietly.

'Honestly?'

'No. What I'm interested in,' she said, dragging her thoughts away with an effort, 'is how you've become so incredibly rich.'

'Not right now,' he said, with silky resignation—as if he'd been expecting the question a whole lot sooner. 'Here comes the waiter. Let's deal with him first. Do you know what you want to eat? Perhaps you would like me to order for you?'

Jessica bristled. He was doing it again, just as he'd tried to do with the dress. That whole command *thing* which was teetering on the brink of domination. She was perfectly capable of ordering her own food and she ought to tell him that, but, faced with the prospect of deciphering a long menu beneath a gaze which was making her feel so *conflicted*, Jessica shrugged her acceptance.

She listened while he quizzed the sommelier and the waiter with a knowledge he clearly hadn't acquired overnight. It was strange seeing him like this in public—giving orders where in the past he had taken them. As strange as seeing him in his expensive suit. She was left feeling dazed when they were alone once more and two glasses of white wine had been poured for them. All she knew was that she mustn't let him dominate her. That she needed to start asserting herself, just as she had done so often on the tennis court.

'So are you going to tell me?' she persisted, with a determination which seemed to well up from somewhere deep inside her. From the far end of the room a jazz pianist began playing something haunting and sultry and the music seemed to invade her senses as Jessica stared at him. 'What has happened to you to make you the man you are today, Loukas?'

# CHAPTER FOUR

LOUKAS STARED INTO Jessica's aquamarine eyes—as cool as any swimming pool he'd ever dived into—and wondered how to answer her question. His instinct was to tell her that his past and his career trajectory were none of her business. Was her sudden interest sparked because she was turned on by his obvious wealth like most of her sex?

Yet in a way she had been partly responsible for the dramatic turnaround in his fortunes, though not in a way which either of them could have predicted. Her rejection of him had cut deep. Deeper than he could ever have anticipated. Her cool dismissal of his proposal had kicked like a horse at his pride and his heart, leaving him angry and empty. And bewildered. Because hadn't he once vowed to himself that never again would he give a woman the opportunity to hurt him?

'I stopped working for Dimitri Makarov,' he said.

She frowned. 'You mean, you got tired of being a bodyguard?'

Loukas gave a hard smile in response to her question. Yes, he had grown tired of living life through someone else. Of standing on the sidelines. Of always having to abide by someone else's rules and someone else's timetable. And waiting—always waiting.

'It was time for a change,' he said, watching the way her hair gleamed in the candlelight. 'I didn't want to carry on indefinitely and at that stage Dimitri's personal life was so out of control that the two of us were living like vampires. He never went to bed before dawn and, as a consequence, neither did I. We spent our life in casinos and then we'd take a plane to another country and another casino, grabbing sleep where we could.'

His Russian boss had been out of control—and so had he. Each of them running from their particular demons and seeking refuge in the bottom of a whisky glass. On the rebound from Jessica, Loukas had gone from woman to woman, despising them all no matter how much they professed to love him, because hadn't he proved once and for all that you could never believe a woman when she said she loved you?

And then one morning he had woken up and looked in the mirror, barely able to recognise the ravaged face staring back, and had known that something needed to change. Or rather, that *he* needed to change. 'It was time for something new,' he finished flatly. 'A new direction.'

He watched while she took a sip of her wine—a wine as cool and as pale as she was.

'So what did you do?' she questioned. 'Go to college?'

Loukas couldn't hold back the bitterness of his answering laugh, but he waited while their food was placed before them—fish and vegetables stacked into intricate towers standing in puddles of shiny orange sauce. Why the hell could you never get simple food these days? he wondered fleetingly. 'No, Jess—I didn't go to *college*,' he said sarcastically. 'Those kinds of opportunities aren't really a good fit with someone like me. I started working as a bouncer at a big nightclub in New York.'

She narrowed her eyes. He thought she looked disappointed. Was that still too *thuggish* an occupation for someone of her delicate sensibilities to accept?

'And what was that like?' she asked politely, like someone making small talk at a cocktail party.

'It was like every man's fantasy,' he said softly and now he could see the surprise in her eyes, and yes, the hurt—and suddenly he found that he was enjoying himself and that he wanted to hurt her some more. To hurt her as she had hurt him. 'It's a power trip to be in a position like that,' he drawled softly. 'It gives you a kick to turn away people with overstuffed wallets who ask if you know who they are. Not a particularly admirable admission—but true. And women love bouncers. *Really* love them,' he finished deliberately. 'It's one of the perks of the job.'

She had been sawing at a piece of pumpkin on her plate, but suddenly she put her fork down and he noticed that her hand was trembling. And that was unusual, he thought with satisfaction, because Jess had always had the steadiest hands of anyone he'd ever known. Hands that could throw a tennis ball up to a certain height with pinpoint accuracy. Hands that could smash a ball into kingdom come. He could see the faint uncertainty in her eyes as she asked the inevitable question.

'And I suppose there must have been, well...*lots* of women?'

He shrugged, because if a female asked you a question as dumb as that, then they deserved to hear the answer. He thought about the pieces of paper slipped into his hand or stuffed into the pockets of his jacket. About waking up in vast bedrooms on the Upper East Side with some sinewy heiress riding him until he cried out. The tiny thong he'd found stuffed in his jacket pocket when he'd been going through airport security and the knowing wink of the uniformed official when he'd seen it. He smiled. 'Enough,' he said succinctly.

'But bouncers don't get to be big bosses,' she said, her words sounding forced and rushed, as if she suddenly wanted to change the subject. 'They don't get to own companies the size of Lulu.'

'No, they don't.' He picked up his wine and swirled it round in the glass, thinking that at one time he could have lived for a month on the money this bottle had cost.

'So, how...' she waved her hand through the air, as if he owned the expensive restaurant too '...did you get all this?'

He drank some wine. 'I started to hear rumours that Dimitri's new protection was not to be trusted. And then one day his secretary contacted me and begged me to help. I'd left months before and didn't want to get involved, but she was worried sick—crying down the phone and telling me she thought he was in danger. So I travelled to Paris to talk to him but by that time he had become so big that he thought he was invincible. He agreed to see me, but he wouldn't believe any of the things I'd discovered about the people he was associating with.' His mouth hardened into a grim line. 'Dimitri only ever listened when it was something he wanted to hear. So I gave up trying and planned to take a flight out of the city that same night.'

'But something…stopped you?' she said, breaking into the sudden silence as his words tailed away. And suddenly her eyes were very wide, as if she'd seen something in his face which she wasn't supposed to see.

'Yes, something stopped me,' he agreed grimly. 'It transpired that his new bodyguard was connected to a gang who were on the brink of stealing from my ex Russian boss, and my presence in the city was seen as a bonus, because I knew more about Dimitri's affairs than anyone else. And that pretty much sealed my fate. They captured me on the way to Charles de Gaulle airport.'

'They *captured* you?' she said, only now her voice had a break in it, as if she didn't quite believe the words she was saying. 'What…what happened?'

For a moment the only sound was the tinkly little flourish which came at the end of the jazz player's song and the smattering of applause which followed.

He shrugged. 'They beat me and threatened me. Said I would die unless I told them what they wanted to know.'

'They said you would *die*?' Her face had gone completely pale.

'It's the underworld's way of suggesting you hand over the information they want,' he said sardonically.

And…did you?'

'Are you crazy?' He picked up his glass but this time he didn't drink from it. 'I was expecting to die anyway, so I was damned if I was going to tell them anything first.'

She was blinking at him as if she'd never really seen him before. 'You thought you were going to *die*?'

He heard the frightened squeak of her voice and thought how protected she'd always been. But then, most people had been protected from the kind of worlds he had inhabited. 'Yeah,' he agreed with soft sarcasm. 'Just like something out of a film isn't it, Jess?'

She shook her head, as if his flippancy was inappropriate. 'So what saved you?'

He shrugged. Tonight the wine tasted good, just as everything had tasted good when he'd first been released. He remembered falling to his knees on the dank concrete of that underground car park with drops of blood dripping darkly from his nose, telling himself that never again would he take anything for granted. But he had, of course. He'd discovered that gratitude didn't last very long.

'Dimitri started to believe that maybe I had been speaking the truth and some hunch made him have me followed to the airport. They got to me in the nick of time, and when I was brought back to his place and he saw the state I was in, I think it made him realise he couldn't carry on the way he was—something his secretary had been telling him for a long time. And he gave me diamonds as a reward for what I'd done.'

'Diamonds?' she questioned blankly.

'He owns one of Russia's biggest mines. He gave me jewels which were priceless and he told me to learn to love them.' He saw her flinch at the word, as if he had just sworn. And maybe he had. Maybe it was easier to think of love as a profanity than as something which was real. He remembered Dimitri's words as he had run his fingers through the glittering cascade. *Learn to love these cold stones, my friend, for they are easier to love than women.*

'And did you?' Jess's cool voice broke into his thoughts. 'Learn to love them?'

He smiled. 'I did. It's easy to love something which is so valuable, but I developed a genuine interest in them. They began to fascinate me. I liked their beauty and perfection and the way all that value could be hidden in the pocket of a man's jacket. I liked the fact that they only ever increase in value and I cannot deny that it gave me pleasure to realise their power over people. Women will do pretty much anything for diamonds,' he said deliberately.

'Will they?' came her light answer, as if she didn't care.

'Some I sold and others I kept,' he continued. 'I'm planning to use some of them as the centrepiece of the new launch. No more wristwatches for you from now on, my blue-eyed doll. You will wear my diamonds, Jess.'

She moved the palm of her hand so that it lay on her breastbone, like someone who had grown suddenly short of breath, but the movement only drew attention to the little pulse which was hammering at the base of her throat.

'So was...' she seemed to pick her words carefully '...was the fact that you bought Lulu just a coincidence?'

'In what way?'

She opened her lips slowly, like someone afraid of setting off a verbal landmine.

'You didn't just buy Lulu because I was working there?'

He gave a soft laugh. 'What do you think?'

'I'm not...I'm not sure.'

But Loukas knew she was lying. Would the Lulu takeover have been *quite* so enticing if she hadn't been involved? Of course not. Plenty of business opportunities came his way and his emotions were never involved. But this was different and it was because of Jess. He felt the sudden hardening of his groin. Because didn't her involvement guarantee the kind of satisfaction which went way beyond mere profit and loss?

'I heard the company was struggling because the management had become lazy, and I realised that I could turn it around. Take a famous brand and bring it bang up to date and you can't fail.' He smiled. 'And you know what they say...buy weak, sell strong.'

She was looking at him in faint surprise, as if she hadn't expected the slick soundbites of the professional negotiator to come from his lips. He felt the flicker of anger. *Because deep down she still thinks of you as a thug. A wall of muscle, without a life of your own or a brain you might be capable of using.*

'But of course your connection to the company made the prospect irresistible,' he said softly. 'Because I wanted to see you again.'

To see whether his desire for her had diminished. Whether the sight of her cool face would leave him cold. He glanced at her untouched plate and his gaze moved upwards. He saw the way the candlelight flickered over her neat breasts and suddenly he was overcome by a wave of lust so powerful that if he had been standing up, it might have knocked him off his feet. Because surprise, surprise, he thought bitterly, it hadn't left him—his desire hadn't left him at all. If anything, it had only increased—as if the years in between had only sharpened his sensual hunger. Right now it was consuming him like a newly lit fire and when he looked at those cool, parted lips he wanted to lean across the table and crush them beneath his. To slide his hand beneath her dull little dress. To move his fingers against her heated flesh. To bring her to a disbelieving orgasm and then have her suck him sweetly to his own.

His mouth hardened.

So what was he planning to do about it?

'You're not eating, Jess,' he said and he could hear how husky his voice sounded. He wondered if she was aware how heavy his groin felt, hidden by the snowy drapery of the tablecloth.

'Neither are you.' She pushed her plate away and nodded her head, as if she'd come to some kind of decision. 'And I'm not surprised. This meal was a bad idea. Just because we're going to work together doesn't mean we have to eat together. I'm going back to my room. I'll order something from Room Service.'

'I'll get the check and come with you.'

'No, honestly. You don't have to.' She licked her lips and gave a forced kind of smile. 'In fact, I'd much rather you didn't.'

'I insist.'

His silky determination silenced her and Jessica watched as he summoned the waiter and signed the check. She wondered if he cared how their behaviour must look to other people. Did the waiter consider it odd? Two people barely touching the amazing food or spectacular wine which had been placed before them. Two people sitting opposite one another, their bodies stiff and tense, looking as if they were engaged in some silent battle when in reality they were trying to ignore the sexual hunger still burning between them. She was aware of people watching as they weaved their way through the tables. The velvet-lined doors swung softly closed behind them, blotting out the faint chatter and low strains of music—and Jessica psyched herself up to say a dignified goodnight.

'Thanks, Loukas.'

'There's nothing to thank me for. I'll see you to your room.'

'But—'

He cut across her objection before she'd had a chance to voice it. 'Again, I insist.'

What else would he try to insist on? she wondered desperately as the elevator doors slid together, shutting out the rest of the world.

She tried to drag her gaze away from the chiselled perfection of his face. The elevator felt claustrophobic. Worse than that—it felt dangerous. There was no giant desk or restaurant table between them now, only a limited space so that he felt much too close, yet much too far. She could practically feel the heat radiating from his powerful body and the air seemed full of the scent which was so uniquely Loukas. She closed her eyes and breathed it in. A hint of citrus cut with spice, and underpinned with a raw and potent masculinity which took her straight back to the past. It filled her lungs, reminding her of all the pleasure he'd brought her. Reminding her of his hard kisses and soft kisses and all the in-between kisses. Of how he used to thrust so deep inside her. The first time, when it had hurt. And the second time, when it had felt as if she'd gone to heaven.

Could he hear the increased breathing, no matter how hard she tried to control it? Probably. His sense of hearing was acute—just like all his other senses. It was one of the things which had made him such a good bodyguard, as well as being such an amazing lover.

And suddenly Jessica found herself resenting the fact that he hadn't so much as touched her. He hadn't even done what anyone else in his position would have done—given her a cool kiss on either cheek when she'd walked into his office. No matter what he was feeling inside, that would have been the civilised thing to do.

But Loukas wasn't civilised, was he? Beneath the exquisite suit and unmistakable veneer of wealth, he was still the same man he'd always been. Basic and primeval and oozing testosterone. But he wasn't acting on it. He wasn't acting out her vivid fantasy of playing the primitive male and pinning her up against the wall and just *taking* her, as he'd done so often in the past.

Did he guess what she was feeling—or wanting? Was that why he was looking at her with that infuriating half-smile on his lips, which was completely at odds with the hunger which had begun to spark like dark fire in the depths of that burning gaze?

She found herself praying they would reach her floor soon, yet part of her never wanted to get there. She wanted to stay here, trapped in this small moving box with him—just the two of them—until one of them cracked.

Did she give herself away?

Was there some small movement which indicated

the struggle she was having with herself? She wondered if she'd wriggled slightly or whether something about her posture had indicated that her breath felt as if it were trapped in the upper part of her throat.

'Oh,' he said slowly, his words suddenly shattering the fraught silence, as if she had just said something which required an answer. 'It's like that, is it?'

And he reached out to cup her chin with his hand, drawing his thumb almost lazily over lips which had begun to tremble uncontrollably. The mere touch of him was electrifying, the effect of it so profound that her head jerked, like a puppet on a string. Jessica's heart began to pound as he slipped the thumb inside her mouth and she couldn't seem to stop him from doing it, even if she'd wanted to. Pavlov's dog, she thought helplessly, aware that he was watching her, still with that infuriating half-smile on his face.

Her eyes had fluttered to a close as her lips closed round the thumb, and she wondered if that was to avoid the mockery in his eyes or because it meant she could pretend. Pretend that this was a normal interaction between a man and a woman, instead of one tainted with bitterness and regret. She felt him move the thumb very slightly—in and out, in and out—demonstrating a provocative mimicry of sex. *Kiss me,* she prayed silently as she sucked. Take some of this aching away and *just kiss me.*

'Open your eyes, Jess.'

Reluctantly, her lashes fluttered open and she found herself meeting the hardness of his piercing black gaze.

'Do you want me to kiss you?' he questioned softly as he withdrew the thumb so slowly that she almost groaned.

Had he read her mind, or had she said the words out loud without realising? Reluctantly, she nodded her head in silent acquiescence.

'Then ask me. Ask me nicely and I'll consider it.'

The corresponding rush of resentment gave her a last-minute reprieve and she glared at him. You don't have to do this, she told herself. You don't have to do what he says. 'Don't play games with me, Loukas.'

'I thought games were your speciality.'

'Go to hell.'

And then he *did* kiss her, laughing a little as he pulled her against him—his hard body driving every objection clean from her mind. All she could think about was how strong he was, and how good it felt to be back in his arms. Within the circle of his powerful embrace she felt warm, like an ice cube which had started to melt. She felt *safe*. But that didn't last long... And maybe that was the wrong description, because how could she possibly feel safe when his hands were sliding down over her breasts like that and making her moan with pleasure? It felt the opposite of safe when her nipples were thrusting against her dress and aching for him to bare them.

The lift pinged to a halt and Jessica felt the punch of frustration as Loukas dragged his mouth away from hers. His gaze was smoky, his expression suggesting he'd been as blown away by that kiss as she had. But his look of sensual surrender quickly cleared and was replaced by a cold-eyed assessment. For a minute she thought he was about to hit the button to send them back down the way they'd come—as if their evening would be spent riding an elevator which represented a private and no-threat world where none of the normal rules applied.

But she was wrong. He kept his finger firmly on the *doors open* button as his black gaze sizzled over her.

'So,' he said.

'So,' she repeated, more to gain time than anything else.

'Aren't you going to invite me inside?' he questioned.

Every fibre of her being was screaming at her to say yes. To open the door and do what she wanted to do more than she could remember wanting anything. She knew exactly what would happen. The look on his face told her that it would be quick. He would rip at her clothing. Push aside the damp panel of her panties with impatient fingers. She could almost *hear* the rasp of his zip as she pictured him freeing himself. Her fingers were itching to reacquaint themselves with that silken, steely shaft—to rub it up and down until he began to groan…

Blood rushed through her veins as she thought of that first intimate touch just before he entered her—the moist tip of him pressing against her—and she could have wept with longing and frustration. Would he be able to tell that there had been no lover since him? That he had been the one and only man she'd ever been intimate with? Would he laugh in disbelief if he knew, or would it simply make him gloat with insufferable pride? That he was still able to make her—the cool and contained Jessica Cartwright—into someone she barely recognised.

He had offered her the job and was now making it very clear that he wanted her. For a man with Loukas's reasoning, one would automatically follow the other. Payback time. And would that be such a terrible thing? If she had sex with him again it might make her look at things more rationally. Reassure herself that she'd built him up in her mind because she'd been young and impressionable. And this was a modern world, wasn't it? She should be able to sleep with whom she pleased.

She opened her mouth to say yes, but something stopped her—and that something was the look in his eyes. Was that *triumph* she could read there?

Some of the heat left her blood. She thought about how she'd feel in the morning if she woke up and found him beside her. Would she be able to deal with the aftermath of such a rash act? She doubted it. Because intimacy terrified her. It brought with it hurt, and pain. And surely only a fool would do something in the knowledge that it was going to bring them pain.

She shook her head. 'No, Loukas,' she said. 'I'm not.'

He bent his head forward, as if he didn't believe her, as if he could change her mind by shortening the physical distance between them. His breath was warm against her face.

'Are you sure?' he whispered.

It took every bit of will power she possessed to step back and shake her head, but will power was something she was good at. It was will power which had made her stand outside in all weathers, smashing ball after ball over the net while her father shouted at her. Will power which had dragged her out of bed on those cold winter mornings while the rest of her schoolfriends had snuggled beneath the duvet while their mothers made toast.

'Quite sure,' she answered. 'I'm going to bed. Alone. Goodnight.'

The faint flare of surprise she saw in his eyes gave her no real pleasure. It didn't cancel out the ache in her body or the yearning in her heart. Stepping inside her suite, she shut the door on his hard and beautiful face and resisted the desire to smash her fist against the wall.

## CHAPTER FIVE

Frustration was never a good feeling to wake up to, but Jessica supposed it was preferable to regret.

Standing beneath the pounding jets of the shower, she scrubbed furiously at her skin, as if doing that would wash the Greek from her memory, but nothing could shift the annoying thoughts going round and round inside her head. Had she been crazy not to invite Loukas into her suite, to kill the fantasy of her ex-lover once and for all? To make her realise that she'd been building him up into some kind of god for all these years, when in reality he was a mere mortal?

She reminded herself of the evening they'd shared. He had shown her no real affection, had he? He had taken her to dinner, then made a cold-blooded move on her afterwards. He had made her feel more like a potential conquest than an object of desire. Was she so desperate for sex that she was regretting not having settled for *that*? No, she was not. She needed to keep her wits about her and she needed to stay in control.

Pulling on a pair of linen trousers, she buttoned up her shirt and twisted her hair into a bun and was just clipping pearl studs into her ears when the phone beside the bed shattered the silence. She hesitated for a moment before picking up the handset. 'Yes?'

'Sleep well?'

The deep voice washed over her like dark honey. It made staying in control seem like the hardest thing in the world.

'Like a log,' she lied. 'Did you?'

'No, not really.' His voice dipped. 'I kept being woken up by the most erotic dreams imaginable and they all seemed to involve you. I blame you for my disturbed night, Jess.'

'Because you didn't get what you wanted?'

Loukas didn't answer. If only it were as simple as that. If only his frustration could be put down to the fact that she'd stopped him making love to her—but it wasn't that simple. It was starting to feel *complicated* and he didn't do complicated. Why had it become so important to possess her again, and why was she so determined to fight him?

He knew she wanted him—she'd made that very clear—and yet she had resisted. He wondered if she revelled in the power it gave her—to tap into that icy self-control which she pulled out just when you were least expecting it. She had fallen apart in his arms the moment he'd touched her, and yet still she had said no.

His mouth hardened. He was aware that he had the double standards of many men to whom sex had always come easily, but his attitudes had been reinforced by the unhappiness of his childhood and the things he had witnessed. Those things had soured him towards the opposite sex and the women he had met subsequently had done little to help modify his prejudices.

But Jess was different. She had always been different. Not just because she was streamlined and blonde, when his taste had always tended towards fleshy brunettes. She was the one woman who had walked away from him. The one he had never been able to work out. She had that indefinable something called *class*, which no amount of money could ever buy. It had been her aloofness which had first drawn him to her—something he'd never come into contact with before. That sense of physical and emotional distance had fascinated him and so had she. She was the first woman he'd ever had to woo. The first—and only—woman he'd ever bought flowers for. Had she secretly laughed at his cheap little offering—when sophisticated bouquets had awaited her when she walked off the tennis court? He'd often wondered whether it had been her secret fantasy to take someone like him as her first lover. Someone as unlike her as possible. Someone who knew what it was all about, but who could safely be discarded afterwards. Her *piece of rough*. Had he served his purpose by deflowering her and introducing her to pleasure?

He considered the options which lay open to him. He could walk away now. Leave the new advertising campaign in the hands of the experts, and keep his own input to the bare minimum. Or he could pay her off with an overinflated sum, since money was the reason she was here. He could find a fresher, newer model, with none of the baggage which Jessica Cartwright carried. And he could easily find himself another lover. One who would not cold-bloodedly shut the door in his face, but who would welcome him with open arms and open legs.

But he had not finished with her. Not yet. His list

was not yet completed. He had met his brother. He had dealt with his mother's betrayal and uncovered all the dark secrets she had left behind. He had built up a fortune beyond his wildest dreams. He had made some of his peace with the world, so that only Jessica remained—and he needed her. He needed to take his fill of her, because only then would he be free of her and able to walk away.

'Maybe I didn't get what I wanted last night, *koukla mou*,' he said softly, 'but I always get there in the end.'

He heard her suck in a deep breath.

'What happened between us last night. You must realise that it changes everything.'

He affected innocence. 'How?'

There was a moment of silence. He could hear her searching for words. He wondered if she would try to hide behind those polite little platitudes which didn't mean a thing.

'I can't possibly work alongside you now!'

'Don't make such a big deal out of it, Jess,' he said. 'Our bodies are programmed to react towards each other that way. You want me and I want you. We've always had chemistry. Big deal. We're both grown-ups and neither of us are in relationships—at least, I'm not and I'm assuming you aren't either.'

'Isn't that something you should have asked me before you leapt on me in the elevator?'

'I don't know if I would describe it as *leaping*,' he commented drily. 'And I was assuming you might have put up some kind of objection had that been the case.'

'How do you manage to twist everything I say?'

'Is that what I am doing, *koukla mou*?' he questioned innocently.

'You know you are.'

'So why don't we put down what happened to curiosity and leave it at that? The advertising team want to meet you at their offices,' he added. 'My car will be outside your hotel at eleven.'

Jessica was left staring at the phone as he did that frustrating thing of ringing off before she felt the conversation was finished. Though really, what was there left to say? She ordered breakfast from Room Service, nibbling half-heartedly on a piece of wholemeal toast, and drank two cups of coffee strong enough to revive her. But when she went down to the front of the hotel just after eleven, it was to find Loukas sitting in the back of a car parked directly outside, reading through a large sheaf of documents.

'Oh, it's you,' she said as he glanced up, and was caught in his ebony gaze. Her heart gave a punch of excitement she didn't *want* to feel, but was it really so surprising that she was reacting to him? Last time she'd seen him he'd had his tongue down her throat and she had been in danger of dissolving beneath his touch. Was he remembering that, too? Was that why his eyes were gleaming with inky provocation and his lips had curved into a mocking smile?

'Yes, Jess. It's me.'

She swallowed as the driver shut the door behind her. 'I wasn't expecting to find you here.'

'But hoping you might?'

'You're…'

'I'm what, Jess?'

She shook her head. 'It doesn't matter.'

'Oh, come on,' he taunted softly. 'Why hide behind that frozen expression you're so fond of—why not come out and say just what you're thinking for once?'

She stared at him, her heart beating very fast, and suddenly she thought, What the heck? Why *shouldn't* he know how she felt about him? She wasn't on a tennis court now and he wasn't her opponent. Well, he *was*, but not in the traditional sense. What did it matter if she was honest with him—the world wouldn't stop turning if she told him the truth, would it? But it wasn't easy to voice her emotions, when she'd been drilled to keep them hidden away ever since she could remember. Wasn't that why sex with him had been so wonderful—and so scary—because it had knocked all those barriers down, and for a little while had made her feel free? 'Actually, you're the last person I wanted to see.'

'Liar,' he said softly. 'Stop pretending—most of all to yourself. Your body language gave you away the moment you saw me again. Even you can't disguise the darkening of your eyes or the unmistakable tightening of those delicious breasts.'

'How come you're even *here*?' she said crossly as the car pulled away from the kerb.

He laughed. 'I live here.'

'You live in a hotel?'

'Why not?'

'Because…because a hotel is somewhere you stay. It's not a real home.'

'For some people it is.'

Loukas stared out of the window as the streets of London passed them by. Would it shock her to discover that he'd never really had a home of his own, just a series of places in which to stay? He remembered the too-thin curtain at one end of the room, and the saving grace of the cotton-wool plugs which he'd crammed into his ears and which had blotted out most of the sounds. 'Actually, it's ideal for all my needs,' he said. 'It's big, it's central and there are several award-winning restaurants just minutes away from my suite. I send out for what I want. My car gets valet parked and there is effective security on the door. What's not to like?'

'But don't you like having all your own things around you?'

He turned back to look at her. 'What things?'

She shrugged. 'Oh, you know. Pictures. Ornaments. Photos.'

'The clutter of the past?' He smiled. 'No. I'm not a big fan of possessions. I try to live by the maxim that you should always be able to walk away, with a single suitcase and your passport.'

She frowned. 'But what about the future? Do you plan to live in a hotel for ever—is that what you want?'

'There is no future,' he said softly. 'There is only what we have right now and right now all I want to do is kiss you, but unfortunately there isn't time.' He reached for his jacket. 'We're here.'

Heart pounding, Jessica stared out of the car window. 'Here?'

'Zeitgeist. The best advertising agency in London.'

She looked up at the cathedral-high dimensions as they entered the modern building, forcing herself to concentrate on her surroundings instead of focusing on how much she had *wanted* him to kiss her back then. 'Tell me why we're here?'

'Gabe and his team would like to show you a mock-up for the new campaign. They've been in pre-production for weeks and want to present you with your brief.'

They were ushered into a huge room filled with a confusing amount of people. She was introduced to Patti, the stylist—a spiky-haired blonde in a bright green mini-dress and a pair of chunky boots who was swishing through a rail of clothes. The long-haired art director was peering at photos of a woman standing on a gondola—a gondola!—who looked suspiciously like her. And when she looked a bit closer she could see that it was indeed her—with her head superimposed onto the body of some sleek model wearing a series of revealing evening dresses, set off with dazzling displays of diamonds.

There was a dynamism in the air which was almost palpable and nothing like the rather slow pace of the advertising agency Lulu had employed before. In fact, it was all a bit of a whirlwind experience, made all the more intense by Loukas at her side—warm and vibrant, and impossible to ignore. He took her over to the far side of the studio to meet Gabe Steel, the agency's owner—a striking man with dark golden hair and steely grey eyes.

'When Loukas explained that he wanted a complete change of image for the Lulu brand,' Gabe was saying, 'I could see it was a change which was long overdue. So we're ditching the Grace Kelly look and going for something more modern. We've had a lot of fun putting these new ideas together, Jessica—and I think you're going to like them. I showed them to my wife last night and she certainly did.' He smiled. 'So why don't you sit down and you can see what we have in mind?'

Jessica sat down on a chair which had clearly been chosen more for style than comfort and watched as the art director and Patti whipped through a series of photos, showcasing different pieces of jewellery.

'We're taking out a two-page spread in one of the broadsheets just in time for Valentine's Day,' explained Gabe, 'which only gives us a few weeks to play with.'

'Valentine's Day?' repeated Jessica, thinking that no other date could have rubbed in her single status quite so effectively.

'Sure. It's one of the jewellery business's most profitable times of the year—and Lulu needs to capitalise on that in a way it has failed to do before. The young girls who used to buy the wristwatch are all grown up now, and we want to show the world that you've grown up, too. We want to show that the new Jessica is definitely not a girl any more. And she won't be wearing a waterproof wristwatch, she'll be wearing jewels—preferably some which have been bought for her by a man.'

'My jewels,' interjected Loukas softly.

Jessica thought how weird it was to hear herself being spoken about in the third person. She stared nervously at the photos. Surely they weren't expecting her to wear clothes like *those*—with half her breasts on show, or a long dress slashed all the way up the way up her thigh?

'The shoot is booked to take place in Venice, as you can see from the mock-ups,' Gabe continued. 'It's the most romantic city in the world and a perfect setting for the kind of look we're aiming for. In winter it's moody and atmospheric, which is why we'll be shooting in black and white with the iconic Lulu pink as the only colour.' He smiled at her. 'The team are going out first to set up the locations and I gather you and Loukas are flying out separately.'

Every face in the room turned to look at her, but all Jessica could see was the gleam of Loukas's black eyes and the faint curve of his mocking smile. Since when had they been travelling out *separately* and why hadn't anyone bothered to tell her about it? She didn't think she'd ever shouted at anyone in her life but right then Jessica wanted to stand up and yell that she didn't want to go *anywhere* with the arrogant Greek—least of all to a city famed for romance, to advertise a campaign which was *all* about romance.

She wanted to be back in Cornwall, far away from him and the uncomfortable way he was making her feel. She had been fine before he'd come back into her life. Things might have been predictable, but at least they had felt *safe*. She hadn't been racked with longing, or regret. She hadn't started thinking about the fact that they'd never even spent a whole night together.

Did she *really* have to take this job—with all the complications which accompanied it? Again, she thought about selling up and buying a cheaper apartment away from the sea.

But then her half-sister's face drifted into her mind and she felt the sharp stab of her conscience. She thought of Hannah sobbing in her arms following the terrible avalanche which had killed her parents. Things had been bad enough when they'd been forced to sell the big house, but they had chosen the new one *together*, and Hannah loved her current home. It was her home, too, and what right did Jessica have to deprive her of that security, just because being around Loukas bothered her more than it should have done?

She didn't have to sleep with him, no matter how much she wanted him. And there was nothing to stop her making it clear to him that it wasn't going to happen. A new sense of determination filled her, because hadn't she come through far worse than having to resist a man like him?

So she gave Gabe a smile—the same smile she always used when people asked if she missed playing tennis. A very useful smile to have in her repertoire. It was bright and convincing.

And it didn't mean a thing.

'I can't wait,' she said.

# CHAPTER SIX

LOUKAS WATCHED AS Jessica stood in the gondola, her new, shorter hair being ruffled by the wind. Her face was pale, her eyes looked huge, and the tension surrounding her was almost palpable. Not for the first time that day, he clenched his fists with frustration, because this had been his idea and on paper it had seemed like an outstanding one. All the boxes had been ticked. She wore a tight-fitting, corseted black ballgown which hugged her slender body and emphasised her neat little breasts. Long black satin gloves came up to her elbow and a waterfall of diamonds glittered against her breasts.

It should have been perfect. Jessica Cartwright looking exactly as the team at Zeitgeist had wanted her to look. Sleek and grown-up and very, very sexy.

Yet she stood there like a waxwork. Her eyes seemed empty and her expression blank. Even her smile looked as if it had been plastered on.

He shook his head in disbelief as he thought back to the way she'd been in his arms the other night, when he'd kissed her in the elevator. She had been fire that night, not ice—but where was all that fire now?

His eyes bored into hers.

There was nothing left but embers.

From her precarious position in the Grand Canal, Jessica met Loukas's stony black gaze, which was boring into her from the side of the water. None of the crew were happy—she could tell. Not one of them, but especially not Loukas, who seemed to have been glaring at her since the shoot had got underway. The chill Venetian wind whipped around her as she tried to keep her balance, which wasn't easy when she was standing on a bobbing gondola.

She felt cold—inside and out. Around her neck hung a priceless dazzle of blue-white diamonds which shone like a beacon in the gloom of the winter day. Her newly bare neck—shorn back in London of its protective curtain of long hair—was now completely exposed to the wintry Venetian elements. Strands of the sleek new style fluttered around her chin and were starting to stick to her lip-gloss. And even though Patti the stylist stood next to her—poised with a hairbrush and a big cashmere wrap—that didn't stop Jessica from feeling ridiculously underdressed. These photos were light years away from the demure and sporty shots she usually did for the store and she felt *stupid*. No. She felt exposed.

And vulnerable.

Her eyelashes were laden down with more mascara than she'd ever worn before and consequently the smoky make-up they'd been aiming for looked as if someone had given her two black eyes. The glossy, cyclamen-pink lipstick, intended to echo the colour of the brand's iconic packaging, gave her an almost clown-like appearance. And the dress. Oh, the dress. She didn't even want to get started on the dress. It was everything she wasn't—vampy and revealing. Ebony satin fitted so closely on the bodice that she could barely breathe and cut so low that her cleavage was now an unflattering sea of goosebumps. Beneath the swish of the full skirt her knees were knocking together with a mixture of nerves and embarrassment. Because even though the city was relatively quiet in February, the odd tourist had stopped to take her photo and she hated it.

She hated trying to look *sexy and sophisticated*, which was the look the art director had told her he wanted—since she felt neither. She felt like a fraud—and wouldn't they all laugh themselves silly if they discovered that she hadn't made love to a man in eight long years?

Of course, having Loukas standing watching her wasn't helping. In fact, it was making everything a whole lot worse. Against the misty grey and white of the Venetian backdrop, the Greek stood out like a dark spectre on the bank of the canal. The light from the water caught him in its silvery gleam and the city's sense of the hidden and the deep seemed to reflect back his own unknowable personality. Two burly security guards flanked him, their eyes fixed on the fortune in gems which shimmered against her skin.

The art director looked at his watch and frowned. 'Okay, we're losing the light. Let's call it a day, shall we? Same time tomorrow, people.'

As some of the crew sprang forward to help her from the gondola, Jessica could see the art director muttering something to Loukas, who was nodding his head in thoughtful agreement. His black gaze held hers for a moment and she felt the skitter of unwanted desire whispering over her skin. Why was he even here? Why didn't he go back to London and leave her alone? Surely she might be able to come up with what they wanted if he weren't standing there, like a fire-breathing dragon, making her feel inadequate in all kinds of ways. Holding the voluminous folds of the black satin skirt of her dress, she stepped onto the bank and was handed the cashmere shawl.

'We're going to St Mark's Square for coffee, though maybe you deserve a brandy after all that,' said Patti, rubbing her hands together before putting them over her mouth and blowing on them. 'Fancy coming along once you've taken your necklace off and changed?'

'Not right now. I'm going to take Jess back to the hotel,' came a dark and silky voice from behind her.

Jessica glanced round to see Loukas walking towards her, like a character who had just stepped from an oil painting. His dark cashmere overcoat matched the dark gleam of his hair and today he seemed devoid of all colour. Today, he was all black. The hard-edged smile he glimmered at her set off faint warning bells, though she wasn't sure why.

'Because she looks frozen,' he added deliberately.

Yes, she was frozen, but, although her skin felt like ice, her blood grew heated when his fingers brushed against her neck as he unclipped the heavy diamonds and handed them over to the waiting security guard. She felt lighter once the jewels had been removed and she wrapped the shawl tightly around herself, trying to hide herself from Loukas's searching gaze. But nothing could protect her from the way he was making her feel, as self-conscious beneath that piercing stare as she had been during their journey out here.

They had taken a scheduled flight from London, which had been just about tolerable, because at least Loukas had been working while Jessica attempted to read a book. But when they had arrived and their waiting water taxi had taken them towards the city, she'd felt herself unwillingly caught up in the romance of the moment, no matter how hard she tried to fight it.

She had felt as if she were in a film as the sleek craft sped through the choppy grey waters, leaving a trail of white plume behind them, and the iconic skyline of cities, churches and domes loomed up ahead of them. She had failed to conceal her gasp of pleasure as they'd entered the Grand Canal and Loukas had turned to her and smiled. A complicit smile edged with danger and, yes, with promise.

And Jessica had shivered just as she was shivering now.

'Let's walk back to the hotel,' he said as the crew began to disperse.

Picking up the heavy skirt to prevent it from dragging on the damp bank, she looked at him. 'You really think I can walk back to the hotel wearing this?'

'You don't imagine that women in ages past had to struggle with dresses similar to that?' he mused. 'Think of the famous masked ball they hold here every February. And you'll be warmer if we walk. Come on. It isn't far.'

'Okay,' she said, and pulled the cashmere closer.

She stuck close to his side as they began to weave their way through the narrow streets, past shop windows filled with leather books and exquisite glassware and over tiny, echoing bridges. It was like being in the centre of an ancient maze and it wasn't long before Jessica had completely lost her bearings. 'You seem to know exactly where you're going,' she said.

'Unless you think I'm planning to get you lost in Venice, never to be seen again?'

She looked up at him and her heart gave a funny kind of thud. 'Are you?'

He laughed. 'Tempting, but no. Look. We're here.'

It was with something almost like disappointment that Jessica glanced up to see their hotel ahead of them, with light spilling out from the elegant porticoed entrance. Heads turned as they walked into the palm-filled foyer and she guessed that they must make a bizarre couple with her in the flowing ballgown and Loukas in his black cashmere coat. She could feel the swish of her dress brushing over the marble floor and felt her cheeks grow pink when the pianist broke into a version of 'Isn't She Lovely?' and a group of businessmen started clapping and cheering as she passed them by. She wanted to dive into the elevator but her suite was on the first floor and the sweeping staircase seemed the most sensible option for getting there. But the voluminous skirt of her dress took some manoeuvring and she was out of breath by the time she got to the top.

'Not quite as fit as you used to be?' Loukas said, his black eyes glinting.

'Obviously not, since I'm not playing competitive tennis any more, but I'm fit enough. I'm just not used to dragging this amount of material around with me.'

There was a pause as they reached her door and she fumbled with her key card to open it.

'So, are you going to have dinner with me tonight?' he asked.

She shook her head. 'Thanks for the offer, but I'm going to have a bath and try to get warm again. My hands feel like ice.' She hesitated as she looked up into his face and then swallowed. 'They didn't like what I did today, did they? I could tell.'

He shrugged. 'It was all new to you. You're used to being brisk and breezy, to wearing casual clothes and looking sporty—and suddenly you're expected to start behaving like a vamp. You're operating outside your comfort zone, Jess, but don't worry. You'll get it right tomorrow.'

'And if I don't?'

His eyes glinted again. 'We'll just have to make sure you do.' He brushed a reflective finger down over her spine. 'Have you thought how you're planning to get out of this dress? Unless you're something of a contortionist you might have something of a problem, since it has about a hundred hooks.'

Jessica was trying not to react to the brush of his finger and she cursed the restrictive fastenings intended to give her an hourglass shape. She knew what he was suggesting but the thought of him helping her undress seemed all wrong. Yet what else was she going to do? Patti and the crew were in some unknown bar in an unknown city, and, short of waiting for them to return, she certainly couldn't undo it herself.

'Would you mind?' she said casually, as if it didn't bother her one way or the other.

'No, I don't mind,' he said, just as casually, as he followed her into the suite.

It was the most beautiful place she had ever stayed in, but Jessica barely noticed the carved furniture or the beautifully restored antique piano which stood beneath a huge chandelier. Even the stunning view over the Grand Canal and the magnificent dome of the Salute church couldn't distract her from the thought that Loukas was here, in her hotel room.

'Aren't you going to turn around and look at me, Jess?' he questioned softly.

She cleared her throat, wondering if he could hear her nervousness. 'You're supposed to be undoing my dress,' she said. 'And you can't do that unless I have my back to you.'

There was a split second of a pause. She thought she heard him give a soft laugh as he unclipped the first hook, and then the second. She wanted to tell him to hurry up and yet she wanted him to take all the time in the world. She could feel the rush of air to her back as he loosened the gown and she closed her eyes as another hook was liberated. Was this how women used to feel in the days before they were free to wear short dresses and trousers, or go without a bra? A sense of being completely within a man's power as he slowly undressed her?

Her breath caught in her throat because now there was a contrast between the air which had initially cooled her skin being replaced by the unmistakable warmth of a breath. Her eyelashes fluttered. Was he… was he breathing against her bare back?

*Yes, he was.*

It felt like the most intimate thing imaginable. She swallowed, because now his lips were pressing against the skin and he was actually *kissing* her there.

Her eyes closed. She knew she ought to say something but every nerve in her body was telling her not to break the spell. Because this was anonymous, wasn't it? It was pleasurable and anonymous, and she didn't have to think. She didn't have to remember that this was Loukas and that there was bad history between them. She didn't have to look into those gleaming black eyes or see triumph curving his lips into a mocking smile. All she was conscious of was the feel of his lips brushing against her and the hot prickling of her breasts in response.

The dress had slid down to her hips and his hands were moving to skim their curves as if he was rediscovering them. Luxuriantly, he spread his fingers over the flesh and she thought she heard him give a sigh of pleasure. She swallowed, but still she didn't say anything, because it was easier to play dumb. To want it to continue yet not be seen to be encouraging it. Her heart began to beat even faster because now he had started brushing his fingers over her lacy thong and with that came a wave of lust so strong that it washed away the residual grains of her conscience.

'Mmm,' he said as the dress fell to the ground, pooling around her ankles and leaving her legs completely bare. He was kissing her neck and his fingers were hooking into her panties and she felt a molten rush of heat.

She knew she should stop him. But she couldn't. She just *couldn't*. It had been so long since she had done this and she was cold. So cold. And Loukas was making her feel warm. Warmer than she'd felt in a long time.

His fingers had moved from her hip and were now inside her panties, alighting on her heated flesh with a familiarity which seemed as poignant as it was exciting.

'It's been a long time,' he said almost reflectively, drifting a fingertip across the engorged bud.

Jessica's body jerked with pleasure. She wanted to say something—anything—as if to reassure herself that she was still there and that it was all real. But the words simply wouldn't come. His touch had robbed her of the power to speak. Her breath had dried in her throat and all she could think about was the hunger building up inside her and dominating her whole world. Her thighs seemed to be parting of their own accord and she felt the warmth of his breath as he smiled against her neck.

'You are very wet, *koukla mou*,' he murmured.

She swallowed as her eyes closed. 'Yes.'

'Wet for me?'

'Y-yes.'

'Have you been imagining me touching you here?'

'Yes!'

'And...*here*?'

'God, yes.' Jessica gasped, even though his words seemed to contradict his actions. Because what he was saying was provocative, but strangely cold. He was objectifying her, she realised with a brief rush of horror and she tried to pull away. To end it while she still could. But by then it was too late because she was starting to come and he was giving a low laugh of triumph as he swivelled her round to cover her mouth with his, his hand still cupping her flesh while his kiss drowned out her broken cry of surrender.

His tongue was in her mouth as she pulsated helplessly around his finger and the combination of that double invasion only increased her pleasure, until she thought she might have slid to the ground, if he hadn't been holding onto her so tightly. Time passed in a slow, throbbing haze before her eyelids fluttered open to find Loukas watching her, still with that faintly triumphant smile on his face. Slowly, he withdrew his finger and she noted that it wasn't quite steady.

'Jess,' he said and picked her up and carried her into the bedroom to lie her down on the bed.

'Loukas,' she whispered, and the tip of her tongue came out to slide over her parted lips.

Loukas felt the savage beat of his heart as he looked at her glistening mouth and his erection was so hard that it took him a moment or two before he was able to move. He wanted to tear off his clothes and just *take* her. But not yet. Not until he was in control of his feelings. Until he was certain that he was in no danger of being trapped by the powerful spell she had always been able to weave around him.

He tried to study her objectively as he shrugged off his overcoat and hung it over the back of a chair, then went back towards the bed on which she lay. Strange that she should have been so cold and uptight in front of the camera today and yet had fallen apart the moment he'd touched her. But hadn't that always been her way? He gave a bitter smile. The only time he'd ever been able to penetrate her haughty exterior—in more ways than one—was when she was naked and writhing beneath him. Because outside the bedroom, or the sitting room, or the car—or wherever else they happened to have been doing it—she had always been the very definition of cool.

But not now.

Her eyes were smoky, her face flushed with satisfaction and her thighs parted in such open invitation that he was almost tempted to bury his head between them and lick her. He thought how at home she looked, lying back against the brocade covering the ornate four-poster bed. But of course, she was. This place was classy and luxurious; it was the environment to which she was most suited. *The one in which he had never quite fitted.*

He reached out his hand and laid it over her left breast. He could feel her heart pounding beneath the lace of her provocative bra as he circled a thumb over the nipple which was peaking through the scarlet and black lace. 'You never used to wear such frivolous underwear when I was with you, *koukla mou*,' he observed silkily. 'So what happened? Did the men who followed me demand that you dress to please—or have your tastes simply changed and evolved with time?'

Jessica opened her mouth to tell him that Patti had taken her shopping after they'd been to the hairdresser, explaining that the revealing gowns wouldn't tolerate anything except the briefest of bras, and that her panties should preferably match *to get her in the mood* for the shoot. Except that it hadn't worked out that way, had it? She had stood posing like a female ice cube in the dramatic and sexy dress and had only really come to life when Loukas had touched her.

She bit her lip. And how he had touched her. She had forgotten how exquisite an orgasm could feel when it was administered by the only man she had ever really cared about. She had forgotten how weak and powerless it could make you feel. As if all your strength had been sapped. It could make you vulnerable if you weren't careful, and she needed to be careful.

She shouldn't have allowed it to happen, but now

that she had she wanted it continue. She had acted foolishly but maybe understandably—or at least, understandable to her. She was like someone who'd broken her diet by opening a packet of cookies. But why stop at one, when four would be much more satisfactory and make the sin worthwhile? She didn't want her enduring memory of sex with Loukas to be a one-sided, rather emotionless pleasuring. She wanted to make love to him properly. Hadn't she wanted that for years? She wanted to feel him inside her. Deep inside her. Filling her and heating her as nothing else could.

She reached up her hand and began to unbutton his shirt, determined to approach this as if they were equals. Because she wasn't some little virgin who'd just been seduced, and though she might lack his undoubted sexual experience, there was no reason for him to know that.

'Do you really want to talk about other men at a moment like this?' she questioned coolly, slipping free another button and rubbing her hand against his hair-roughened chest.

His mouth tightened as he leaned forward and began to tug at the belt of his trousers. 'No,' he said. 'I don't. And soon you won't be able to, because I'm going to make you forget every other man you've had sex with. You won't be able to remember a single damned thing about them, because all you'll be able to think about is *me*.'

The arrogant boast shocked her but it thrilled her, too. Nearly as much as it thrilled her to see him peel off his clothes to reveal his body in all its honed olive splendour. It was as magnificent as it had ever been but suddenly Jessica gasped because there—zigzagging over the side of his torso like a fleshy fork of lightning—was a livid scarlet scar. Her fingers flew to her lips before reaching out to touch it, as tentatively as if it might still hurt. As if it might open up and begin to bleed all over the bed.

'What happened to you?' she whispered.

'Not now, Jess,' he growled.

'But—'

'I said, not now.' His hand slid between her thighs and began to move, effectively silencing all further questioning. 'Does that kind of detail please you?' he rasped. 'Does it turn you on to think that your rough, tough bodyguard has the mark of violence on his body?'

There was something in his tone she didn't understand—some dark note which lay just beneath the mockery—and Jessica was confused. But by then he was stroking her again and his mouth was on her breast, and she was growing so hot for him that she could barely wait for him to slide on the condom and position himself over her.

She was trembling as he made that first thrust and the sensation surpassed every fantasy she'd ever had about him. But to her surprise, he was trembling, too, and for several moments his big body stayed completely still, as if he didn't trust himself to move.

She wanted to whisper things to him. Soft, stupid things. She wanted to tell him that she wished she'd married him when he'd asked her. That she'd thrown away the best chance of happiness she'd ever had. But nobody could rewrite history—and didn't they say everything happened for a reason? Even if right now it was difficult to see what that reason could possibly be.

And then all the nagging thoughts were driven from her mind because her orgasm was happening again. It built up into a crescendo and sent her into total meltdown—and the shuddered moan which echoed around the room told her that so, too, had his.

# CHAPTER SEVEN

THE ROOM WAS very quiet for what seemed like a long time and, when she spoke, Jessica's words seemed to splinter the peace. She turned onto her side and stared into the face of the man beside her.

'How did you get that scar?'

Loukas stirred and stretched. Completely comfortable in his nakedness, he raised his arms and extended his powerful legs in a movement which should have distracted her, but nothing could have distracted her right then. All Jessica could see was the livid mark zigzagging over his flesh.

'How?' she whispered again, when still he didn't answer.

His face became shuttered as he drifted a fingertip over her nipple and watched it wrinkle and harden. 'As a topic for pillow talk,' he drawled, 'it's not exactly up there with telling me how much you enjoyed your orgasm.'

Jessica didn't react. He made what had happened sound so *clinical*. But maybe for him it was. Did legions of women purr the morning afterwards and tell the dark and charismatic Greek how much they had enjoyed their orgasm? She scooped back her hair and peered at him. 'Was it in Paris?' she persisted.

'Was what in Paris?' He stopped stroking.

'You told me that you were...captured there.' She hesitated. His face was still shuttered, but she persisted. 'Was it back then?'

Loukas lay back, pillowing his ruffled head on his folded arms as the chandelier glittered fractured light on their bare skin. He sensed she wouldn't give up until she had an answer and something told him he was going to find it harder to silence Jess than he would the average lover. 'No, it wasn't then,' he said dismissively.

'So...when?'

He turned his head to look at her and frowned. 'Does it matter?'

'Of course it matters.' She gave a barely perceptible sigh. 'What is it with you, Loukas? You never talk about your past, and you never did. I was with you for months and ended up knowing almost nothing about you.'

He gave the flicker of a smile. 'You knew plenty.'

'I'm not talking about the way your body works.'

He gave a short laugh. She had grown up in a land of milk and honey, in a world light years away from his. He thought about the big house with the tennis court and the bright green lawns which swept down to the sea. About privilege and belonging and all the things he'd never had. 'What difference does it make to know about my past?'

'It might make me feel as if I wasn't in bed with a stranger,' she said quietly.

It wasn't the first time the accusation had been

levelled at him, but, when Jess said it, it felt different. Come to think of it—everything about Jess felt different. 'I thought the anonymity aspect appealed to you,' he drawled. 'You certainly seemed turned on when you had your back to me earlier. For a minute I thought you might be pretending I was someone else.'

'Don't try to change the subject.'

'I'll do anything I please. Just because I've made love to you doesn't give you the right to censor my speech, or to demand answers.'

She bit her lip. 'Is it such an awful story, then?'

'Yes.' He said the word without planning and it was like an overfilled balloon being popped by the prick of a needle. Like a bruise beneath your fingernail which only a white-hot lance would relieve. 'Yes,' he repeated. 'Awful gets pretty close to it.'

'Won't you tell me?'

His instinct was to distract her—either by making love to her again, or by heading off to take a shower. Because she wanted to talk about the old Loukas, and he had spent a long time forging a new Loukas, a man as hard as the diamonds which were at the core of his fortune and a success beyond his wildest dreams.

He had uncovered secrets he would have preferred to have left alone, and had hidden them away deep inside himself. But secrets left their mark, he was discovering—a dirty mark which left a stain if you didn't expose it to the sunshine and the air. He looked into Jess's cool features, but for once her face was showing the emotions she usually kept contained. He could see the concern shadowing her eyes. He could hear an anxious softness in her voice, and something made him start talking. 'How much do you know?'

She shrugged. 'Not a lot. That you were an only child and your mother brought you up in Athens, and that you never knew who your father was.'

Loukas twisted his mouth into a grim smile. How easily a whole life could be condensed into a single sentence—black and white, without a single shade of grey in between. 'Did I tell you that we were poor?'

'Not in so many words, but I...' Her words tailed off.

'You what, Jess?' he said silkily. 'You guessed?'

She nodded.

'How?'

'It doesn't matter.'

'Oh, but it does. I'm interested.'

Reluctantly, she shrugged. 'You just always seemed so...oh, I don't know...restless, I guess. Like a shark moving through the water. Like you were always looking for something.'

It startled him how accurate her words were and Loukas nodded. Because she was right. He *had* been looking for something—he just hadn't known what it was. And then, when he'd found it...

'We were dirt poor, my mother and I,' he said, wanting to ram home the fundamental differences between them. To shock her. To convince her—and him—that all they shared was a rare electricity in between the sheets. 'Sometimes I used to hang around at the backs of restaurants to see what food they were throwing away at the end of a day's trade, and I'd take it home...' Take it home and hang around outside until his mother had finished with whoever she was currently *entertaining*. He remembered the different men who had stumbled out, some of them trying to cuff him on the mouth, while others had pressed a few coins into his hand. But Loukas had never kept those coins. He'd put them in the poor box at the nearby church... unwilling to accept money which was *tainted*, no matter how hungry he'd been. 'Although I took what jobs I could, just as soon as I was old enough—running errands, sweeping restaurants, polishing cars—anything, really.'

'And your mother?' she questioned hesitantly. 'Did she work?'

'She didn't have time to work,' he said bitterly. 'She was too busy devoting herself to whoever her current love interest was. She always had to have a man around and a child like me was only ever going to get in the way. So for the most part, I was left to my own devices.'

'Oh, Loukas,' she breathed.

'I lived from hand to mouth,' he continued grimly. 'I worked at the ferry port in Piraeus as soon as I was old enough, until I'd saved up enough money to take myself off to a new life. I didn't go back to Greece for a long, long time. I did my own tour of Europe, only it was nothing like the ones you see advertised in the glossy brochures. I lived in the shadows of Paris. I learnt to box in the Ukraine, and for a while I won amateur fights all over the continent, until Dimitri Makarov asked me to be his bodyguard.'

'And that was when you met me,' she said slowly.

Loukas nodded slowly. Yes. That was when he'd met his fairy-tale princess, with her white skin and her blue eyes and the cutest little bottom he'd ever seen. Her coolness had fascinated him; she'd been restrained and cautious—nothing like his mother or all the women he'd subsequently been intimate with. She hadn't been predatory or coquettish. In fact she'd fought against an attraction which had been almost palpable. And hadn't the fact that his princess had presented him with her virginity been like a master stroke in capturing his heart as well as his body, culminating in that proud proposal of marriage which had been thrown back in his face? He gave a bitter laugh. What a fool he had been.

'Yes,' he said, with a note of finality. 'That was when I met you.'

'And did you ever…?' She drew in a deep breath and he saw the rise of her tiny breasts. 'Did you ever see your mother again?'

Loukas flinched, because it didn't matter what hurt and what pain she had caused him—she was still his mother.

'Only once,' he said flatly. 'I'd been sending her money for years, but I couldn't face returning. And then, when she was dying I went back to find her living in a…hovel.' His voice tailed off, before taking on a bitter note. 'In thrall to her latest boyfriend—a vulture who was systematically bleeding her dry of her dignity, as well as all the money I'd sent her. I remember how weak she was when she took my hand and told me that she *loved* this particular loser. And even though she'd been a notoriously bad picker of men all her life—this one was in a class of his own. He had neglected to give her any pain relief—he'd been too busy spending her money at the casino.'

'Was that when you got the scar?' she said slowly.

Loukas nodded, realising how alien this must all sound to someone like her. *'Neh,'* he drawled, the flicker of anger not far from the surface. He remembered being young and fit and prepared to fight fairly, but his mother's lover had not. He hadn't seen the glint of steel as the knife had come flashing down out of nowhere, and at first he hadn't even registered the strange, digging sensation in his flesh, which had heralded the eruption of blood. Loukas's voice shook with rage. 'The only good thing that came out of it was that he was arrested and jailed and no longer able to steal money from my mother. But by then it was too late anyway.'

'What do you mean?' she whispered.

'She died later that week, just as I was being discharged from hospital,' he said, his face twisted with pain. 'I found all her paperwork and I understood at last why she had never wanted to talk about my father.' He met the question in her eyes. 'Like I said, she was a bad picker of men and that my father was abusive to her came as no real surprise. But the most interesting thing was that I discovered I had a twin brother.'

She tipped her head back, her eyes huge. *'A twin brother?'*

He nodded. 'Alek had been brought up by my father—a very different kind of upbringing from mine. I had him tracked down and I met him in Paris.' It had been that meeting which had made Loukas decide to lay *all* of his ghosts to rest. To make him want to move on and live his life in a different way. And hadn't Jess been the most persistent ghost of them all—the one who had hovered on the periphery of his mind like some pale and interesting beauty?

'How…' her voice trembled '…how can you possibly have discovered that you have a twin? Why didn't your mother ever tell you?'

'Because my father was powerful,' he said. 'And she was running away from him. She couldn't physically—or financially—take two tiny babies, so she chose to leave Alek.'

'How? How did she choose?'

He shook his head. 'Doesn't matter how. She knew she could never go back and so she decided to cut out that part of her life completely. To pretend it had never happened.' He gave a short laugh. 'And if I'm being objective, I think I can almost understand why. Far better to cut her losses and run, than to face up to the fact that she'd left her other son with a cruel tyrant.'

'Oh, Loukas.'

She reached her hand towards his face as if to stroke his cheek but he caught her wrist in an iron-hard grip of his own. Turning her palm upwards, he ran his tongue slowly over the salty flesh, his eyes never leaving her face.

'I don't want your pity, Jess,' he said softly. 'That's not the reason I told you.'

She trembled beneath the lick of his tongue. 'Why *did* you tell me?'

He thought about it. It was more a question of why he had kept it hidden before but now he could see that he had been ashamed. Ashamed of the circumstances which had forged him. So hungry for his cool and classy Englishwoman that he had cultured a deliberate elusiveness, so that she would accept him for his present, and not his past.

But she had not accepted him at all. He had still not

been good enough and maybe for someone like her, he never would be.

He didn't answer her question, but fixed her with a steady gaze. He remembered the way she'd breathlessly whispered that she loved him and how, for a short while, he had believed her. But words were easy, weren't they? His mother used to profess love, then leave him alone and frightened while she went out with her latest man. 'Why did you turn down my proposal?' he said suddenly.

She bit her lip and looked down at the rumpled sheets. 'Because...because I thought you were doing it to be chivalrous. To save me from my father's anger.'

'First time in my life I've ever been called chivalrous,' he said sardonically. 'But I don't think you're being entirely honest, are you, Jess? Maybe you did it to protect your fortune from a man who had nothing—who might want to marry you for all the wrong reasons?' he said, and the faint flush of colour to her cheeks told him everything he wanted to know.

'Well, there was that too,' she admitted haltingly, lifting her eyes to his as if she should be applauded for her honesty.

Loukas gave a bitter laugh. She had looked on him as someone with an eye for the main chance—able to provide her with sex, but best kept at arm's length when it came to permanency, or commitment.

And wasn't it crazy that *even now* it still hurt to realise that?

He didn't handle pain well. Physical pain was no problem, but emotional pain he found unendurable and he'd learnt that there was only one way to guarantee immunity. Don't get involved. Don't let anyone close enough to inflict it. It was a simple but effective rule as long as you stuck to it. And with Jess he'd been stupid enough to take his eye off the ball for a while.

'But you know something?' he questioned. 'You did me a kind of favour, in a way. I realised that marriage was completely wrong for someone like me.'

'Is that why you've never settled down with anyone else? Why you still live in luxury hotels, instead of having a real home?'

*'Neh.'* He gave a soft, cynical laugh. 'I've grown used to my life. I wouldn't have it any other way.'

'And children? What about them?'

'What about them? Why the hell would I want to bring children in the world, just to screw them up? I know what that's like and so does my twin brother.'

'Right,' she said uncertainly.

He thought he could see a flicker of darkness in her eyes—as if his words were hurting *her*. As if she wanted to reach out and stroke his pain away. And he didn't need that. He didn't need her sympathy, or understanding. He didn't want her looking at him as if he were a puzzle she could solve, because he was fine just the way he was. He didn't want her making him *feel* stuff, because life was so much easier when you didn't. There were a million things he didn't want from her and only one thing he did.

He pulled her closer, so that he could feel the warm softness of her skin. Her face was turned up to his and her lips were eagerly parted, and for a while he just teased her. He brushed his mouth over hers—back and forth—until she made a sound halfway between frustration and desire. Sliding her hand around the back of his neck, she pulled him down towards her and he felt a heady rush of sexual power as she clung to him.

*This*, he thought, just before he kissed her—this was all he wanted from Jessica Cartwright.

# CHAPTER EIGHT

What a difference a day could make. Or a night. A night when Loukas had seemed determined to show Jessica everything she'd been missing.

Sex.

Her throat dried.

A devastating masterclass in desire and satisfaction.

She had hardly slept a wink and by rights she should have felt terrible when she met the crew to resume shooting the following morning. But terrible was the last thing she felt. She felt *alive*. As if all her senses had suddenly exploded. The diamonds, which yesterday had hung like a millstone around her neck, today made her feel pampered and decadent as they glittered against her skin—and the close-fitting silk of her bodice no longer felt constricting. She was conscious of the way it clung to her breasts—thrusting them upwards and giving her a bit of a cleavage and reminding her of the way Loukas had licked his way over every inch of them during the sensual night they'd shared.

*'Wow,'* said the photographer softly as she stood in the gondola—only today she had no trouble keeping her balance, despite the rocking motion of the distinctive craft. And when she was told to pout and look

dreamy, she had no problem with that, either. In fact, it was difficult to look anything *but* dreamy when all she could think about was the man whose black eyes had grown opaque and smoky as he had lowered his head to kiss her.

But kisses could blind you to the reality and she had to keep reminding herself that it had only been about sex—*because how could it ever be anything else*? He'd made it clear that experience had hardened him. That he had changed and now there was no room in his life for marriage. She thought about the way his voice had grown cold when she'd asked about children, and—bearing in mind the things he'd told her—could she honestly blame him for not wanting any? All the things he'd told her about his childhood made her aware of just how grim his early life must have been. No wonder he'd been so reluctant to speak about it in the past. And then to discover out of the blue that he had a twin brother—a discovery like that must have rocked his world.

So she was going to have to be very mature. To accept the person he was, and if last night was the only night they would ever share, then she would accept that, too. No tears. No regrets. And definitely no recriminations. She'd had her chance a long time ago and she had blown it. She had no one to blame but herself.

This time Loukas didn't watch over the photo shoot, telling her he needed to work, before slipping away from her room in the early hours. She supposed he hadn't wanted anyone to see him leaving, knowing that it might muddy the waters if the crew discovered that the CEO was sleeping with the model.

She spent the entire day being photographed, but

that ice-cube feeling was a distant memory. The ballgown was followed by a slinky white silk trouser suit, with nipped-in jacket and wide palazzo pants. The diamond necklace had been replaced with neat diamond studs and, with a nod to her previous career, she wore a tennis bracelet—a narrow row of diamonds, which glittered discreetly at her wrist. The last shot of the day was of Jessica wearing a monochrome minidress, teamed with waterproof boots as she stood in the centre of a flooded St Mark's Square, and even though her arms were covered with goosebumps she didn't feel particularly cold. Patti fed her sips of hot coffee and torn-off little pieces of croissant. Tourists gathered to watch, only today she didn't mind, and when the art director called it a day and came over to congratulate her, she experienced a feeling of real achievement. She'd done what she had set out to do. She had pulled it out of the bag and given them what they wanted. She'd shown them—and herself—that she was capable of change, and wasn't that a very empowering feeling?

They all trooped back to the hotel through the echoing streets of the darkening afternoon and Loukas was just coming down the sweeping staircase, leaving Jessica wondering whether someone had rung ahead to tell him they were on their way. Her heart pounded as she watched him move, so dark and so vital, capturing the attention of every person in the place. He walked over to talk to the art director and she tugged the cashmere wrap closer, feeling her nipples tightening beneath the soft material, afraid someone might notice and work out why. They chatted intently for a moment and then he looked round, his black gaze sweeping around until it had found her, and her heart began to race even faster as he walked across the foyer towards her.

A faint smile lifted the edges of his mouth. 'I gather you excelled yourself today,' he said.

She smiled, trying to ignore the sudden yearning deep inside her. Trying to convince herself that she only felt this way because he was a powerful, alpha male she'd spent the night with and that was how nature had conditioned her to react. 'Thanks,' she said.

'I'm tempted to ask what has changed since yesterday,' he murmured. 'But I think we both know the answer to that, wouldn't you say, *koukla mou*?'

She tilted her chin. 'Are you looking for praise?'

'Why would I need to do that when you gave me all the praise I could possibly want last night?' His lashes shuttered down to half conceal the ebony glint of his eyes. 'Would you like to repeat some of it, in case you've forgotten?'

'That won't be necessary,' she said hastily. She could see Patti and the others moving towards the elevator—presumably to pack—and her heart grew heavy as she realised that it had all come to an end. *And she didn't want it to come to an end.* 'I guess I'd better go and pack as well.'

'Well, you could. Or you and I could stay on for an extra day and give ourselves a chance to see the city properly?'

She stared at him.

His eyes glittered. 'What's the matter, Jess—doesn't the idea appeal?'

'It's not that. Surely you have…' She tried to keep

the tremor of excitement from her voice. She shrugged. 'Oh, I don't know. Work to do.'

'I'm the boss. Work can wait—while I, on the other hand…'

His words trailed off, smoky, suggestive and edged with a raw hunger which left her in no doubt what he was thinking. But it had been a long time since Jessica had engaged in sexual banter and she'd forgotten the first rule about keeping it light.

'What?' she whispered.

'I don't want to wait,' he said softly. 'And I don't intend to. I still want you. I want you so badly that I'm hard now, just standing this close to you. So hard that I want to rip those trousers from your delicious legs and put my hands where that silk has been.'

He had lowered his voice so that only she could hear, but even so Jessica found herself looking around, terrified that a passing guest would overhear, or that someone discerning would correctly interpret their body language.

'Loukas,' she said, only the word didn't come out as it was supposed to do. It came out all throatily, like a husky invitation instead of a protest.

He shook his head, as if pre-empting her objections. 'One night wasn't enough. Not nearly enough to cancel out eight long years of a slow-burning fever in my blood. A fever which has never quite gone away, no matter how many other women have graced my bed. Has it been like that for you too, Jess?' His voice dipped. 'I'm guessing so. Because you were wild for me last night. Wild,' he finished silkily.

Her instinct was to play it down. To clamp down on the feeling before it had started to grow and take hold. It was a survival mechanism which had served her well in the past. It meant she'd been able to accept a promising tennis career which had ended before it had even begun. It had enabled her to turn down his offer of marriage because she'd known that had been the right thing to do. And this time round she knew it would be best if they kept last night as a one-off. A single, amazing night they'd shared, which was never going to happen again. Because one night was easy to be objective about; any more than that and she was running straight into trouble.

She opened her mouth to say no, but something in his face was making the words die on her lips. Was it a sudden softness about the eyes which reminded her of the man he'd once been, before life had taken him and roughed him up even more?

Because something about the way he was looking at her touched a part of herself she'd thought had died a long time ago, and she was surprised he hadn't worked out for himself the reason why she'd been so *wild* for him last night. Not just because she'd been living in a sexual desert since he'd walked out of her life, but because he made her feel *stuff.* Stuff like joy and intense pleasure. Stuff like love.

She chewed on her lip. In the past she wouldn't have been able to spontaneously extend a trip abroad, because Hannah would have been at home and Jessica had always prided herself on being there for her. But Hannah was thousands of miles away and nobody else knew or cared where she was. She could think of that as isolation, or she could think of it as being free. A negative or a positive—the choice was hers.

'Okay,' she said. 'It seems a pity to come all this way and not see something of the city.'

He slanted her a conspiratorial smile. 'That's what I thought.'

Her hands were trembling as she went to her room to change into jeans, sweater and a waterproof jacket—almost glad that the day was grey and misty and she could put on normal clothes. The kind of clothes she wore at home, which made her feel more like herself and not some manufactured glamour puss.

She met Loukas back downstairs and they left the hotel, but soon after the narrow streets had begun to swallow them up, he steered her into a darkened bar.

'You need a drink,' he said firmly. 'And you missed out on lunch, didn't you?'

'It's nearly four o'clock, Loukas. We won't get lunch at this time.'

'I know that. But Venice is a city which is prepared for all eventualities.' He sat her gently down on a bar stool and nodded at the proprietor, who was polishing a glass. 'You drink a glass of local wine, which the locals call an *ombra*, and you eat some of these delicious little snacks, which are known as *cicchetti*. See? Tiny little plates of seafood, vegetables and polenta. Come on, Jess. Relax. Stop looking so uptight.' He lowered his voice. 'Pretend it's last night and I'm kissing you.'

Loukas wondered what she was thinking as she turned her remarkable eyes to his. He sensed a struggle within her, as if she was still fighting him off, and maybe it was that which drew him towards her. Was it her slight air of resistance—of *restraint*—which reinforced his growing realisation that this *thing* between them was still not settled?

Why not?

His jaw tightened. She should have been smitten with him by now—and that wasn't arrogance, it was fact. One night of sex was usually enough to guarantee adoration from whomever had shared his bed, and their history gave Jess more reason than most to have fallen under his spell. But that was the thing with her. The closer you got, the more she seemed to pull away, and all it did was to fire up his dominant hunter instincts. He sipped at his wine. Was that the reason he wanted her so much—because she kept him at arm's length unless he happened to be buried deep inside her body?

She sipped her wine, glancing round at the shadowy interior of the small bar as if soaking up the atmosphere.

'You seem to know your way around Venice pretty well,' she observed.

'I do. It was another part of my *grand tour*, even though I had nothing very much in my pockets when I first arrived.'

'So how did you survive?'

He shrugged. 'There is always work if you are prepared to do anything—and I was. I went to all the great European cities and set myself a goal. Six months in each, by which time I wanted to feel as comfortable as if I was a native of that city.'

'And was there any particular shortcut?'

'Not one that you'd probably want to hear.'

Her cheeks went pink. 'You mean—through women?'

He shrugged. 'I told you that you wouldn't like it.'

'It doesn't bother me at all.'

'Liar,' he said softly and leaned forward to brush

his lips overs hers, tasting the wine and the warmth in that brief kiss. 'Want to see some more of Venice?'

She nodded and he found himself linking her fingers through his as they started walking along the canal. Her hands were cold and despite their tennis-honed strength they felt fragile and small within his. He found himself thinking that he didn't usually do this kind of thing. He didn't wander hand in hand with a woman, pointing out the secret churches and hidden squares and feeling high with the sheer beauty of the city, almost as if he'd never really seen it before.

The afternoon became devoid of all natural light and as the streetlights began to glow, the deserted streets took on the atmospheric feel so beloved of film-makers. Loukas saw someone snap on a light in one of the great flats along the Grand Canal and a golden glow spilled down, turning Jess's hair into molten gold. They wandered off down one of the narrow streets and he was thinking about taking her to that little bar near the Rialto, when he felt her tugging at his sleeve.

'Did you hear that?' she asked.

Frowning, he shook his head.

'Listen,' she said, putting her finger over her lips.

He frowned, but all he could hear was the lap of the water and the echoing sound of music coming from a long way off. 'I don't hear anything.'

'Shh! There it is again.'

And then he heard it—would have recognised it instantly if it hadn't held such poignant memories for him. The terrified sound of a child's cry. He stiffened, every sense on full alert as he began to move purposefully in the direction of the sound. He could hear

Jess's rapid breathing beside him, just before he saw the huddled shape of a child ahead of them—a boy—his face streaked with tears, his brown eyes wide and frightened.

Jess began to run towards him, but Loukas caught her arm, speaking to her in English, in a low voice. 'Wait. Be careful,' he said.

'Be *careful*?' She turned on him. 'What are you talking about, Loukas? He's just a *child*.'

'And this could be a scam. It's a well-known method for fleecing tourists. Children used as decoys to lure unsuspecting foreigners. There are pickpockets in this city, just like everywhere else.'

Angrily, she shook his arm away. 'I don't care,' she said fiercely. 'I'm willing to take the risk of losing a few euros. I want to help him. Let me *go*!'

But he shadowed her as she ran forward and the boy turned his face upwards and choked out his frightened words.

*'Aiutami,'* he said. *'Aiuto.'*

Remorse flooded through Loukas as immediately he crouched and looked into the tear-filled eyes. 'I will help you,' he said gruffly, in the same language. 'Where are your parents?'

'I don't know!' cried the boy and Jess put her arms around him as if it was the easiest thing in the world, and Loukas felt his heart clench as he watched her soothing him, listening carefully to what the child said in a breathless dialect he thought might be Sicilian.

'He says he lost sight of his parents and when he heard them calling for him, he began to run,' he translated. 'Only he took the wrong turning and began to panic. He ran even faster, and that's when he realised he could no longer hear them. He couldn't hear anything. He isn't hurt, but he's frightened.'

'I'm not surprised,' she said fervently as she stroked the boy's curly hair. 'Venice is a beautiful city by day, but it must be scary if you're a child and you're lost. All that water.' She shivered. 'Tell him that we're going to help find his parents.'

Loukas nodded as he lifted the boy to his feet and began to speak in a calm, low voice before turning to her and meeting the question in her blue eyes.

'I've explained that we'll take him to the *questura*—the police,' he said. 'And that we'll probably find his parents there, waiting for him. Come on, Jess. He wants you to take his hand. Oh, and his name is Marco.'

'Marco,' she said softly as the little boy clung to her hip and wept.

# CHAPTER NINE

'THAT POOR CHILD,' said Jessica as she switched on one of the lamps and the room was flooded with a soft golden light. 'He was absolutely terrified.'

'I'm not surprised,' said Loukas, shutting the door softly behind him. 'Getting lost in Venice age seven isn't something to be recommended.'

'Do you think he'll be okay?'

'He'll be fine.' He frowned. 'Are *you* okay?'

Jessica nodded, hoping her smile would convey a sense of serenity she was far from feeling. They were back in her hotel room where they'd discovered champagne sitting in an ice bucket, delivered by the grateful parents of Marco Pasolini. She and Loukas had bumped into the fraught and terrified couple outside the entrance to the police station, where they had taken the little boy, who had still been tightly holding her hand. A voluble reunion had followed, with Marco's mother alternately sobbing and scolding her young son, before scooping him into her arms and covering his face with endless kisses. His father, meanwhile—according to the translation which Loukas had provided afterwards—proceeded to offer them the use of his Sicilian villa, his ocean-going yacht or any other part of his extensive estates, any time they cared to use them.

But now that the worry and the drama had died away, Jessica was left feeling exhausted. The experience had shaken her up more than she'd realised and had only increased her growing sense of disassociation. She felt as if she shouldn't really be here, in this room, with Loukas. As if their passion of the night before had been something unplanned and probably regrettable and now, in the harsh light of day, she wasn't sure what they were supposed to do next. Would he start peeling off her clothes and expecting another acrobatic performance, like last night? She hoped not. She felt shy and inexperienced, as if she couldn't possibly live up to his expectations.

She thought about his instinctive reaction when they'd stumbled across the lost child. He had thought it was a scam.

'I'm fine,' she said, taking off her jacket and realising that her legs felt a little shaky. She sat down on a chair very suddenly and looked at him. 'Why did you jump to the conclusion that Marco was a pickpocket? That was a pretty harsh and cynical thing to do, in the circumstances.'

He gave a short and bitter laugh. 'Because I spent too many years as a bodyguard, and suspicion is something which was drummed into me. Something I learnt to live with. If you work for one of the world's wealthiest men, threats come from the most unlikely directions—something I learnt to my own cost. You learn never to trust what you see, or to believe what you hear. That nothing is ever as it seems.'

'That seems a pretty grim way to live your life.'

He raised his eyebrows. 'A cup half empty, rather than half full?'

She nodded. 'Something like that.'

'Or you could say that way you stand less chance of disappointment. If you don't have raised expectations, then they can't be smashed,' he said, his ebony gaze locking with hers. 'You were brilliant with him, by the way,' he added slowly. 'A natural.'

She heard a note of surprise in his voice, which he couldn't quite disguise. 'Something you weren't expecting?'

He shrugged. 'I never had you down as the maternal type.'

Maybe, she thought, because he must find it hard to recognise the 'maternal type', if such a thing existed. His own mother had always put the men in her life first, so could she really blame him if his perception of others was warped—if he had no real experience on which to base his judgements? Or maybe because he remembered her as single-minded and focused, letting her tennis dominate her whole life.

'I don't know if I was born that way, but it's something I learnt,' she said slowly. 'I had to. I became something of a substitute mother for my half-sister.'

'The little girl who was always hiding your hairbrush?' He frowned. 'Hannah?'

Jessica smiled. Funny he should remember that. 'That's the one. When my dad...*our* dad...and her mum were killed, I stepped in to look after her. Well, I had to really.'

'No, you didn't,' he said suddenly, another frown darkening his face. 'Presumably you had a choice and you chose to look after her. How old was she?'

'Ten.'

'And you were, what—eighteen?'

She nodded, thinking how beautiful he looked, silhouetted against the Venetian skyline. The shutters were still open and the spotlighted dome of the magnificent Salute church, which stood behind the wide band of gleaming water, could be seen in all its splendour.

'Yes,' she said. 'I was eighteen. The authorities wanted to foster her out to a proper family, but I fought very hard to keep her. I didn't...' Her words tailed off.

'Didn't what?'

She hesitated. She kept things locked inside her because that was what she'd been trained to do, just as she'd been trained to use a double-handed backhand. And when you did something for long enough it became a habit. A bit like Loukas, when he saw only danger around him. If you built a wall around your emotions you were safer—at least, that was the theory. But the rush of emotions she'd experienced today, following the incredible sex of last night, had left her feeling...

She wasn't sure. She didn't feel like Jessica Cartwright, that was for sure.

'I didn't want to let her go. Not because I loved her.' She cleared her throat. 'But probably because I didn't—at least, not at first. We'd never had an easy relationship. She was the adored child of two people who were very much in love, while I was the cuckoo in the nest—the offspring of the first marriage, a bad marriage, a marriage which should never have happened. At least, that's what I once heard my dad telling my stepmum. Hannah was always on the inside, in the warmth, while I always seemed to be out in the cold, literally, on the practice courts. And I think Hannah was a bit jealous of my tennis career. She used to hide my hairbrush, and sometimes my tennis racquet. She even threw away this stupid little mascot I carried around, until my father told me that champions didn't need mascots—they needed technique and determination.'

'So why did you fight so hard to keep her?'

'Because she was on her own and hurting,' she said simply. 'How could I not reach out to her?' But it hadn't been easy, because Jessica had been lost and hurting, too. She had missed her father. She had missed her career. And she'd missed Loukas. She'd missed him more than she could ever have imagined.

She realised she was cold. She was hugging her arms tightly around herself and wishing she hadn't taken off her jacket, especially now that Loukas's hard black gaze was sweeping over her.

'Why don't you go and take a bath?' he suggested roughly.

Awkwardly, she got to her feet. 'Good idea,' she said and went off into the bathroom, suddenly feeling self-conscious and realising that he hadn't touched her since they'd got back. Maybe he felt as cautious as she did, she thought as she upended lime and orange oil into the water and slowly lowered her aching body into the tub. Perhaps he'd realised that there was too much history for them to be able to enjoy a casual affair. Or maybe she wasn't capable of operating on that level.

Because already her feelings for him were changing. Minute by minute, she could feel it happening. She'd started to care what he thought of her. She'd started searching for emotions in his dark eyes. And it was a waste of time. He'd been completely honest about his reasons for wanting to have sex with her again—so why try to make it into something it wasn't? Embarking on a quest to make it into something it could never be was only ever going to bring her heartbreak.

She lay in the water for a long time—long enough for the skin at the ends of her fingers to become white and wrinkled. Long enough for Loukas to have grown bored with waiting, and to have made his escape, perhaps leaving behind a note scribbled on a piece of hotel notepaper. Because he certainly wasn't knocking at the bathroom door, asking her how long she was going to be.

Was he aware that a strange kind of shyness had crept over her as they'd stared at one another over the head of little Marco? That in that moment, she had glimpsed the little boy he'd once been and all the sadness he had known. She'd found herself thinking of the children she might have had with him. But Loukas doesn't want children, she reminded herself. He had been very clear about that.

Dragging a brush through her damp hair, she put on the massive bathrobe which was hanging on the back of the door and padded barefoot into her room, to find Loukas stretched out in one of the chairs, seemingly fast asleep. His eyes were closed and his face looked curiously relaxed as classical music drifted out from an unseen sound system.

She stood there, uncertain of whether or not she should wake him, when his lashes flickered apart and she was caught in the gleam of his ebony eyes.

'Hi,' he said softly. 'Good bath?'

She nodded, the lump in her throat making it impossible for her to speak because as he'd asked the innocent question it had sounded so heartbreakingly... *domestic*. It mocked her and taunted her with its implied intimacy. A real intimacy, which they'd never really shared.

There was a sudden knock on the door and she looked at him.

'Room Service,' he said, in answer to the question in her eyes

'I didn't order anything from Room Service.'

'No, but I did. Why don't you just get into bed, Jess? You look shattered. And don't look at me as if I'm the big, bad wolf, *koukla mou*.' His voice dipped. 'I am perfectly capable of being in the same room without leaping on you.'

She nodded, feeling the see-sawing of her own emotions in response to the things he was saying. She hadn't wanted sex, but suddenly she was finding that maybe she did. Only he seemed more concerned with getting his dinner!

But at least his back was turned as he answered the door, so that he wouldn't see her nakedness as she let the bathrobe slide to the floor before getting quickly into bed. It felt blissful as she sank into the mattress, the sheet cool and smooth beneath her clean skin, the duvet falling on top of her like a big, soft cloud.

She told herself she wasn't hungry but she must have been, because when he brought the food over to her—some sort of vegetable broth, followed by a toasted cheese sandwich—she began to devour it with an appetite which felt heightened. Comfort food, that was what they called food like this, and never had a description seemed more apt. After she'd finished she lay back against the feathery bank of pillows as the sound of violins filtered softly through the air.

'Better?' he questioned.

'Much.' She yawned. 'I didn't know you liked classical music.'

'Too brutish a sound for a rough, tough ex-bodyguard?' His eyes glittered. 'You thought I'd be more into heavy metal?'

Too comfortable to object, Jessica smiled lazily. 'Something like that.'

'Why don't you close your eyes, Jess? Stop fighting it. You look exhausted.'

His deep accent was lulling her. It felt like velvet pressing against her skin. She wanted to ask him what he was planning, but her eyelids were heavy and she thought about his words and wondered what she was trying to fight. She drifted into a sleep which was light enough to feel the mattress dip when he got in beside her. He pulled her against him and the pleasant shock of honed muscle and warm skin told her that he, too, was naked. Did that mean he *did* want sex?

'Loukas,' she mumbled.

'Shh,' he said, his arms tightening around her waist as he pulled her even closer and the room fell into darkness as he clicked off the lamp.

She must have slept because when she drifted back into consciousness, it was to find her head pillowed comfortably against his shoulder, her lips right next to the burr of his unshaven jaw. She kissed it. She couldn't help it; her lips seemed programmed to brush over that proud curve. He mumbled something as his hand slid down to cup her bottom while the other reached behind her head and guided her lips towards his.

That first kiss was lazy. It seemed to happen in slow motion, as if they had all the time in the world. As if she'd never really kissed him properly before. And maybe she hadn't. Beneath the protective cloak of darkness it seemed that there were a million ways to explore a man's mouth, and Jessica was about to discover every one of them. She could feel him smile as, slowly, she traced the tip of her tongue over the cushioned surface. He gave a murmur of satisfaction as she pressed kiss after little kiss against him. His body felt warm and comfortable against hers and soon she began to trickle her fingertip over his chest, allowing it to continue its path inexorably downwards. But he stopped her when she reached the dark whorls of hair which lay at the base of his belly, wreathing the sudden hard jerk of his erection.

'No. Not yet,' he said urgently. 'I'm so turned on, I hardly dare risk putting on a condom.'

She swallowed, because something about his words had sent crazy thoughts splintering into her mind. 'But you will?'

'Yes, I will. Even though I long to feel myself naked inside you. My skin bare against your skin. My seed in your body.'

His words excited her, but presumably that had been his intention. They reminded her that for Loukas this was all about technique—a bit like tennis, really. It might feel deep and emotional and highly intimate, but that was her stuff. Her stupid desires. And she mustn't give into them. She mustn't.

But it was hard not to be swept away when he was kissing each of her breasts with a thoroughness which felt almost like tenderness. Or when he lifted her up effortlessly to slide her down on top of him, murmuring silky words in Greek which sounded almost *loving*. Suspecting that he would want to watch her moving up and down on him, she waited for him to reach over and put the light on—but he didn't. And the lack of a spotlight on her face meant that she could give into what she really wanted to do, and what she wanted to do more than anything was not hold back. So she tangled her fingers in this thick hair and she told him he was beautiful. And if his big body stiffened for a moment and she sensed his sudden suspicion, that was quickly forgotten when she rode him with a determination which suddenly seemed outside her own control.

'*Jess,*' he gasped, and she'd never heard him say her name like that before.

But then her thoughts were blotted out and her body tensed around him.

And the most stupid thing of all was that she found herself wishing that he *hadn't* worn a condom.

# CHAPTER TEN

'THESE ARE AMAZING,' said Gabe Steel slowly. 'Probably the most amazing transformation I've seen all year. Cinderella doesn't come close to it.'

Loukas stared at the mocked-up advert which covered most of the advertising chief's large desk and drank in the images staring back at him. Jessica Cartwright looking like he'd never imagined she could look. Who would have thought it? He shook his head slightly. He'd stayed away on the second day of the shoot and knew the crew had been pleased with the results, but even so. Hard to believe this was the same Jess who wore classy clothes in shades of cream and taupe while her sensible ponytail bobbed behind her. The same Jess who had stood wobbling awkwardly in the gondola during the first shoot, looking like a little girl dressed up in her mother's clothes.

His throat tightened.

The black and white photos were broken only by the magenta gleam of her lips and the Lulu ribbon which lay in a gleaming swirl by her feet. Against the imposing backdrop of the iconic city, she tipped her head at an angle and looked straight into the lens. Her breasts were highlighted by the low-cut bodice, showcasing the diamonds which blazed like ice fire next to her pale skin. A gentle breeze had lifted the blonde hair so that the blunt-cut strands whipped around her chin, and her smoky eyes were emphasised by the heavy fringe.

But it was more than her beauty or the air of fragility she seemed to project, or even the way her eyes seemed full of a strange, clear light. She personified sex…that was the thing. It radiated from every pore of her body. It was there in every gesture she made. The pout of her lips was defiant and the hand slung carelessly against her jutting hip made her look like every man's fantasy come true. The teenage sweetheart was all grown up.

'What the hell happened to her?' Gabe was asking, his eyes narrowing as he looked at Loukas.

Loukas didn't answer. How could he possibly answer, when he knew it would sound like some kind of chest-thumping macho boast if he told the truth? *She looks like a woman who has just been thoroughly ravished and I should know because I was the one doing the ravishing.*

And that was another shock to the system. He hadn't expected the sex to be so good. He'd thought that once the novelty of having her in his arms again had worn off, he would realise that there were plenty of lovers more exciting than Jessica Cartwright. He'd tried to convince himself that he had built up the memory of their lovemaking in his mind to be something it wasn't. Only it hadn't turned out that way. It had been mind-blowing. Every time. He'd felt as if he were touching the stars. He'd spent his entire time in the city in a dazed and permanent state of arousal.

Was that why he had persuaded her to stay on?

Why one night had turned into two and then three? He'd intended them to fly back to England the day after they'd returned Marco to his parents, but something had stopped him and he told himself it must have been sex. But there had been something else which had made him want to prolong it, and that had been the nagging certainty that this relationship would not survive the cold light of reality. A love affair in Venice was one thing, when you could get swept away by the history and the atmosphere and the sheer beauty of the city. But life back in the UK, with their normal lives threatening to collide? No way.

He realised that Gabe was still staring at him, waiting for a reply to his question.

'I guess she grew up,' said Loukas simply.

'You know we have to capitalise on this?' said Gabe. 'Give the campaign a kick-start. Show the world that this is going to be big...'

Almost absently Loukas nodded as he studied the shot of her in the black and white dress and a pair of rubber boots, standing ankle-deep in water in a flooded St Mark's Square. They'd caught her looking up at something overhead—a bird?—and she was *giggling* and, despite being all grown up, suddenly she looked about eighteen again. Something clenched at his heart. 'How?' he questioned huskily.

'We throw a cocktail party for the press at the Granchester on Monday night, with the new look Jessica as the guest of honour.'

Loukas frowned. 'Isn't that a little short notice?'

'Not on a Monday—and not with your name attached to the invitation,' said Gabe drily. 'It's amazing the space people can find in their diaries if the person holding the party is influential enough. I'll get Patti to sort out Jessica's wardrobe and make sure she has something suitable to wear.' He frowned. 'Another dress, I think, and some of the best gems in your collection. But not diamonds this time. Let's go for something different.'

'Sapphires,' said Loukas slowly, and the thought of the darker hue contrasting with the aquamarine gleam of her eyes sent a thrill of desire skittering over his skin. 'She will wear my sapphires.'

Jessica stared at herself in the mirror. This time the dress was blue, and her jewellery gleamed as darkly as the midnight sky. She lifted her hand to her hair, watching her reflection mimicking the movement, her fingertips brushing against a small sapphire and diamond clip which glittered like starlight.

The sound of a footfall disturbed her and as she looked up to see Loukas reflected back in the glass, her heart began to pound erratically.

'You look beautiful,' he said.

She closed her eyes and shivered as he lowered his head to plant a kiss on one bare shoulder. 'Do I?'

'You know you do. You don't need me to tell you that, Jess.'

But that was where he was wrong—she *did*. She stared at his dark, bent head. She still felt like someone playing dress-up. She still felt vulnerable—especially since they'd arrived back in England and Loukas had persuaded her to stay in London. He'd told her that it was crazy not to use her luxury suite at the Vinoly Hotel, while they continued to *enjoy* one another. He had said this while trickling one finger over the swell of her naked breast and she hadn't really been in a position to say no. In fact she hadn't been in a position to do anything except make love, which was what he had been doing to her at the time.

But the reality of being in London like this didn't sit comfortably. Loukas went into the office each morning, and although she made sure that she took advantage of all that the city had to offer—including a gorgeous exhibition of Victorian embroidery—she felt like a fish out of water. As if she was waiting all the time. Waiting for him.

And Loukas seemed...well...*different*. She stifled a sigh. It wasn't something she could put her finger on. Was his lovemaking more cold-blooded than it had been in Venice, or was that just her imagination? It wasn't something she could really discuss with him without causing offence—and she didn't want to offend him. She wanted... She stared at his reflection in the mirror as he continued to kiss his way along her shoulder... She didn't know what she wanted, only that it was unlikely to involve roses and moonlight. Not from him. She sensed that for him it was already over, like when you turned an egg timer and the sand started to trickle away—the countdown had begun.

But she wasn't going to let him see her insecurities or her fears. She was going to take it all in her stride, because she was good at doing that. So as he lifted his lips from her shoulder she was able to smile so widely that she almost convinced herself she was happy. She thought about the evening ahead and sent him a slightly anxious look. 'So all I have to do tonight is chat to people and twirl around?'

'You've got it in one. Why don't you practise now?' His voice lowered. 'Twirl around. Go on.'

'Loukas.' Something in his face was turning her stomach to jelly. 'You…mustn't.'

'Mustn't what?'

Her voice sounded breathless. 'You can't kiss me now because my lipstick will—'

'Tough,' he said darkly, blotting out all her objections and kissing her so thoroughly that afterwards she had to apply the magenta-coloured gloss all over again.

But his behaviour during the short journey to the Granchester seemed to reinforce her growing insecurity. Nobody would have ever guessed they were a couple because he made no outward sign that they were anything more than working colleagues. He didn't touch her, or take her hand in his. There was no complicit smile which might indicate to the world that she was sharing his bed. Tonight she was very definitely the employee and he the boss, and she found herself thinking that their relationship had always been defined by secrecy.

A barrage of photographers was waiting outside the hotel and she kept her smile pinned to her lips as she was dazzled by the blinding wall of flash which greeted their arrival. Because she knew they weren't just here to see the jewellery. They were here to gaze in curiosity at her new, glossy image. They were hoping that she had bitten off more than she could chew, because there was nothing the press liked more than to bear witness to failure…

Inside, the Venetian photos had been blown up and mounted on the walls, so that they dominated the smaller of the Granchester's two ballrooms. Everywhere she looked she could see herself and, once Jessica had become acclimatised to the slightly surreal sensation, she found herself glancing round in disbelief. She looked so *different*. But it wasn't just the sharp new haircut or the heavier than usual make-up. It wasn't even the dress or the diamonds which made her look so unrecognisable. It was the shining look in her eyes—as if she were nursing the most beautiful secret in the world.

And Jessica realised with a jolt that she looked like a woman…if not actually *in* love, then certainly bordering on the edges of it.

But the camera lied. She knew that.

Pushing aside her confused thoughts, she tried to work the room as she knew she should. She spoke to a couple of women who worked on glossy magazines and was introduced to a man who wrote the diary section of an upmarket tabloid. But despite her outward air of confidence, she found it impossible to relax, especially as Loukas was on the other side of the room and had barely acknowledged her all evening.

She didn't dare eat anything for fear of smudging her lips and the single sip of cocktail she indulged in felt strong enough to blow her head off. This isn't my world, she thought desperately. It never really was. Everyone else seemed to know their own place in it, but not her. The smile plastered to her lips felt forced and she was terrified her conversation sounded dull to these urban high-flyers. Because they sure as hell weren't interested in talking about embroidery or growing vegetables.

It was with a feeling of relief that she saw Patti and slipped into a corner to talk to the stylist, feeling relaxed for the first time all evening, when suddenly she glanced across the room to see Loukas deep in conversation with a brunette. He'd been talking to other women, of course—she'd clocked that—but this seemed more...*intimate*.

The woman was wearing a sparkly dress so short that it made Jessica's own feel as if it had been borrowed from a museum. He was leaning his head forward to listen intently and as the woman spoke her dark hair swayed like a glossy mahogany curtain. Jessica could feel herself tensing as she saw him laugh and Patti must have noticed the direction of her glance, because she turned her head and smiled.

'Yeah. Stunning, isn't she? *And* she's French. Used to be a human rights lawyer before she started writing for one of the papers and now she's one of the best-paid feature writers in the country. Life is so unfair, isn't it?'

Don't ask it, Jessica urged herself. *Just don't ask it.*

She asked it.

'They seem to know each other very well?'

Patti smiled. 'Yeah. I think they were lovers for a while, in Paris.'

'Really?' Jessica wondered if that squeaking reply was really her voice. Was that sick pounding of her heart due to an unwanted wave of *jealousy* which she had no right to feel?

She tried not to let it spoil the rest of the evening, telling herself she wasn't even going to mention it. Even in the car on the way back to the hotel, she managed to make small talk and to look suitably pleased when Loukas told her how happy everyone was with her performance.

He brushed his hand over her waist as they stopped outside her suite and reached into her bag for her key card.

'Hey,' he said softly. 'Want to come to mine?'

'Not tonight. Would you mind?' She forced a smile. 'I'm very tired.'

'So?' He stroked a reflective fingertip over her ribcage. 'Haven't I proved that I'm capable of letting you sleep, even if having you naked beside me drives me crazy with desire?'

'Who was that woman?'

Her blurted question seemed to come out of nowhere and he raised his eyebrows. 'There were a lot of women there this evening, Jess.'

'The brunette. The one in the mini-dress.'

'Ah, yes. Maya.' He smiled. 'Her name is Maya.'

Heart pounding, she pushed open the door and walked inside and he followed her.

'Why, were you jealous?' he continued, almost conversationally.

*'No.'*

'Liar.' He gave a soft laugh. 'You were. You are. I can read it on your face.'

And that was Jessica's wake-up call. He wasn't *supposed* to be reading *anything* on her face, because one of her great strengths was to hide her feelings behind a cool mask. *Wasn't* it? If he'd started seeing things like jealousy in her eyes, how soon before he started seeing other things, too? Stuff she was trying to deny even to herself because she knew that it was pointless. Stuff like still caring for him when she knew there was no future in it. Stuff like falling in love with him all over again.

And then a thought occurred to her and a terrible wave of suspicion washed over her, so that she had to fight it like crazy. She knew he was ruthless. He'd told her he was ruthless. Had he...had he deliberately gone out of his way to make her fall for him, just so that he could do to her what she'd done to him all those years ago?

'Like I said, I'm very tired.'

His face darkened. 'Is Maya the reason for the icy look and frozen behaviour? Is talking to an ex-lover such a terrible thing to do when I meet her socially? What would you have me do, Jess? Tell her I'm sorry, but I happen to be sleeping with someone who wants to keep me on a leash?'

She shook her head, telling herself that she was being stupid but it didn't seem to help. *Because this was the world he operated in. A world full of sophisticated ex-lovers he bumped into at parties and then made as if it didn't matter. Because it didn't.* Not to him. A man didn't get a reputation as a playboy because he sat at home every night, nursing a cup of cocoa. Playboys had partners. Lots of them. Playboys were known mainly for the fact that they never settled down, and she needed to accept that. You didn't get a second chance in life. Not with someone like Loukas.

'Of course not,' she said. 'It was completely unreasonable and I don't know what came over me.'

He tilted her chin with his fingers so that she had nowhere to look except into the dark gleam of his eyes. 'So what shall we do to make it better?'

It wasn't easy but she gave the smile she knew was expected of her. The one with just the right amount of flirtation. One which managed to convey that she'd just had a temporary blip, but that everything was fine again.

Except that it wasn't. She felt as if she were standing on the edge of a cliff which had started to crumble and any minute now she would lose her footing and fall, if she wasn't sensible enough to take a step back.

*This wasn't going anywhere. She'd known that from the beginning. So get out now, before it's too late.*

Putting her arms around his neck, she drew him close and heard his soft laugh as he slid down the zip of her dress with practised fingers. She closed her eyes as his fingers found her bare skin and, automatically, she began to shiver.

Once more, she told herself.

One more night.

## CHAPTER ELEVEN

SHE WAS GONE when he returned from work next evening and as Loukas looked at the single sheet of paper which was all that was left of her, he realised that it came as no great surprise. Last night in his arms, she had been mind-blowing but he'd sensed something in the way she'd kissed him before he'd left for work that morning…a certain sadness which no amount of sexual chemistry could disguise. Her lips had lingered on his in a way which had seemed wistful rather than provocative. And when he stopped to think about it, hadn't there been a little catch in her voice as she'd said goodbye?

He hadn't needed to read the few words she'd written on hotel notepaper to know that she wasn't planning on coming back.

He stared at it.

*Thanks.*

He frowned. For *what*, exactly? The job or the sex?

*I had a fabulous time in Venice, and I'm glad that the photos were such a success, but I'm missing*

*Cornwall and I have a garden which is missing me.*
*Take good care of yourself, Loukas.*
*Jess.*

She hadn't even put a kiss, she'd just drawn one of those stupid, smiley faces and he screwed up the sheet of paper, crushing it viciously in the palm of his hand. She'd walked out on him. She'd turned her back on him. Again. She was arrogant, she was haughty and he didn't need this.

*He did not need this.*

Stalking over to the drinks cabinet, he poured himself a glass of vodka and tossed it back in one deft mouthful, the way Dimitri had taught him.

Only the liquor didn't do what it was supposed to do. It didn't douse the fury which had started to flame inside him. It didn't stop him from wanting to haul her into his arms and...what?

Have sex with her?

Yes. His mouth twisted. That was what he wanted. All he wanted.

He paced around his suite, wondering why tonight it felt like a cage, despite the unparalleled luxury of the fixtures and fittings. Because he'd grown used to having her just along the corridor—was that it? And how the hell could that happen in such a short time?

Because it hadn't *been* a short time, he realised. This had been bubbling away under the surface for years.

He forced himself to concentrate on work, losing himself in the negotiations to open a branch of Lulu in Singapore's Orchard Road. And there was other good news which should have helped put Jessica Cartwright into the background of his mind. His sales team informed him excitedly that sales of precious stones in the London store alone had shot up by a staggering twenty-five per cent following the Valentine's Day advert—and they were planning to use the same advertisement on a global basis. It really *was* going to be big.

He went to the gym every night for punishing workouts, which left his body exhausted but his mind still racing. He turned down dinner invitations and threw himself into his work, which for once did not provide its all-encompassing distractions.

But life went on and the press was still going crazy. Gabe Steel phoned to say that his agency had been fielding calls from media outlets ever since Jess's piece had gone to press, since everyone was keen to discover how the sporty tennis star had transformed herself into such a vamp. Would she like to give an interview to one of the papers? Would she do a short slot on breakfast TV, or the even more popular mid-morning show? Were they planning to use her in another campaign any time soon?

'And?' bit out Loukas. 'It was supposed to be a one-off.'

'I know, but we'd be crazy not to capitalise on this,' said Gabe. 'The trouble is that nobody can get hold of her. She isn't answering her phone, or her emails. I'm thinking of sending—'

'No. Don't bother doing that. I'll go,' said Loukas, and it wasn't until he'd put the phone down that it occurred to him that Gabe hadn't questioned why the company boss should be chasing down to the other end of the country after some random model.

He set off early in the morning, just as the sun was beginning to rise and the roads were empty, save for the occasional lorry. It was a long time since he'd been to Cornwall and it brought back memories of a different life. He remembered the first time he'd seen it. His Russian boss had owned huge chunks of land there, as well as mooring one of his boats in Padstow—and the summer he'd spent there had been the most glorious of his life. For a boy brought up in the crowded backstreets of Athens, it had felt like a different world to Loukas. The wildness and the beauty. The sense of being remote. The salty air and the crash of the ocean. As the roads began to narrow into lanes and he passed through picture-perfect little villages, he thought how little had really changed.

And wasn't it funny how your feet automatically guided you to a place you hadn't seen in eight long years? The Cartwright mansion could still be seen from a distance, like some shining citadel outlined against the crisp blue of the winter sky, with its mullioned windows and its soaring roofs, and the lavender-edged gardens which swept right down to the cliffs. Across to one side, where the land was flatter, was the footpath which passed the tennis court where once he had watched Jess practise.

But when he rang the doorbell, a woman in her thirties appeared—a small child hiding behind her legs. The woman smiled at him and automatically touched her hair.

'Can I help you?'

He frowned, trying to work out who she could possibly be. 'I'm looking for Jess. Jessica.'

'Cartwright?'

'That's right.'

'She doesn't live here any more. We bought it from the people she sold it to. She's up on Atlantic Terrace now—near the cliff path. The little house right on the end, the one with the crooked chimney—do you know it?'

He didn't know it but he nodded, his mind working overtime as he thanked the woman and parked his car in the village, telling himself it was because he needed the exercise and not because he didn't want to be seen by Jess as he approached.

But that wasn't strictly true. His thoughts were reeling and he was trying to make some sense of them. Had she sold up to simplify her life, or because it was too big for her and her half-sister?

He found what was in fact a cottage and it was small. Very small. He rapped loudly on the door, but there was no reply and suddenly he wondered what he was going to do if she'd gone away. She could be anywhere. He didn't know a single thing about her daily life, he realised. He'd imagined her life staying exactly the same, while his own had moved on. It had been part of his fixed image of Jess—the upper-class blonde in her country mansion. Because wasn't it easier to be angry with a stereotype than with a real person?

He walked to the back of the property and that was where he found her, attacking the bare earth furiously with a spade. She didn't hear him at first and as he found himself looking at the denim tightening over her buttocks, it was difficult not to appreciate the sheer grace of her movements.

She must have heard him, or sensed him, because suddenly she whirled round—her face growing through a whole series of emotions but so rapidly that he couldn't make out a single one except for the one which settled there, and it was one which was distinctly unwelcoming.

She leant heavily on the spade as if she needed it for support. 'What are you doing here, Loukas?'

*'Parakalo,'* he said sardonically. 'Nice to see you, too.'

She seemed to remember herself and forced a cool smile.

'Sorry. It just came as a bit of a shock, you creeping up on me like that.'

'Creeping?' he echoed.

'You know what I mean.' She shrugged, but the movement seemed to take a lot of effort. 'I mean, obviously, you're not just passing.'

'Obviously.'

She looked at him with her eyebrows raised as if she wanted him to help her out, but something stubborn had taken residence inside him and he didn't feel like helping her out.

'So why are you here?'

It was a question he'd been asking himself during the four-and-a-half-hour drive but had given up on it because he couldn't seem to find a satisfactory answer. 'You haven't been answering your phone. Or your emails.'

She held her finger to her lips and began to tap them, as if considering his accusation. 'I don't think that's written into my contract.'

'Maybe it isn't,' he said, feeling a nerve beginning to flicker at his temple. 'But I don't think it's unreasonable of us to want to get hold of you, is it?'

'*Us?*'

'Zeitgeist,' he bit out, wondering what the hell was the matter with her. Why she was being so damned stubborn. And so remote. Hadn't they just spent the best part of a week being about as intimate as a man and woman could be? 'And Lulu,' he added. 'You know. The people who provided you with work.'

'I was told it was a one-off.' She gripped the handle of the spade. 'And you were the one who told me that.'

'With hindsight, I might have spoken a little hastily.'

Her gaze was steady. 'If only we all had the benefit of hindsight, Loukas.'

He frowned. He didn't want this impenetrable *wall* between them. He wanted her onside. 'The campaign has been a huge success.'

'Ah.' She smiled. 'The campaign.'

'We've been inundated with requests for interviews, TV—'

'So have I,' she said sharply. 'My answer machine keeps getting filled up with messages, even though I clear it at the end of every day.'

'But you didn't think to answer them?'

'Actually, I did. And then decided not to.' She wrapped her jacket more tightly around herself and gave an exaggerated shiver. 'I'm getting cold just standing here.'

'Then why don't you take me inside and offer me some of your legendary English hospitality?'

Jessica hesitated when she heard the sarcasm in his voice, but she could hardly say no. And the trouble was that she didn't want to say no. She wanted to know what had brought him here—appearing on her horizon like some dark avenging angel. Most of all she wanted him to kiss her, and that was where the danger lay. She had missed him so much that it had hurt and yet now that she had seen him again her heart had started aching even more. This was a lose-lose situation and his presence here wasn't going to help her in the long term. But you couldn't really turn a man away when he'd driven all this way to see you, could you?

'You'd better come in,' she said.

He followed her into the kitchen and she could sense him looking around as she put the kettle on. What did he think of her dresser, with the eclectic collection of jugs, or the cork board studded with all the postcards which Hannah had sent from her travels? Was he comparing it to his huge but cold suite at the Vinoly and did it all look terribly *parochial* to his sophisticated eye?

The wind had ruffled his black hair and he was dressed in jeans more faded than hers, along with a battered brown leather jacket. His casual clothes started playing tricks with her memory. Like a flashback, they gave her a glimpse of the man he had once been. The big bear of a bodyguard who used to watch her from the side of a tennis court. But flashbacks were notoriously unreliable—they always painted the past in such flattering shades that you wanted to be back there. And that was impossible. The past was the refuge for losers who couldn't cope with the present, and she wasn't going to be one of those losers.

She made tea and took the tray into the small sitting room which overlooked the Atlantic. She thought about lighting a fire but then decided against it, because he wasn't staying long. He definitely wasn't staying long.

'So...' She put a steaming star-decorated mug on a small table beside one of the chairs, but he didn't take the hint to sit down—he just strode over to the window and stood there, staring out at the crashing ocean, his silhouetted body dark and powerful and more than a little intimidating.

He turned back, eyes narrowed. 'Did you move because the house was too big?'

She thought about saying yes. It would be understandable, after all—especially now that it was just her. But Jessica knew that she couldn't keep hiding behind her cool mask, thinking that to do so would offer her some kind of protection. Because she'd realised that it didn't. Masks didn't stop you wishing for things which were never going to come true. And they didn't stop your heart from hurting when you fell for men who were wrong for you.

'No,' she said. 'I moved because I had to. Because my father had built up massive debts which were only revealed after he was killed in the avalanche.'

His eyes narrowed, but there wasn't a flicker of emotion on his own face. And suddenly she was glad that he hadn't come out with the usual platitudes which people always trotted out, platitudes which meant zero and somehow ended up making you feel even worse. Maybe they were more alike than she'd thought. Or maybe now that they had entered the dark worlds of death and debts, he suddenly felt on familiar ground.

He sat down then, lowering his mighty frame into a chair which up until that moment had always looked substantial.

'What happened?'

She watched as he picked up his tea and sipped it. 'Like everyone else, he was banking on me winning a Grand Slam, or three. He was very ambitious.' She shrugged. 'They say that fathers make the best and the worst coaches.'

'You didn't like him very much,' he said slowly.

His words came out of the blue. Few people would have thought it and even fewer would have dared say it. It would be easier to deny it but her chin stayed high and defiant as she met his eyes with a challenge. 'Does that shock you?'

He gave a hard smile in response. 'Very little in life shocks me, *koukla mou.*'

The soft Greek words slid over her skin, touching her at a time when she was feeling vulnerable, but she tried not to be swayed by them. She cleared her throat. 'He did his best. He did what he thought was right. It's just that he never really allowed me to have a normal life.'

'So why didn't you stand up to him?'

Recognising that his question was about more than the unbending routine of her tennis years, Jessica picked up a match and struck it to the crumpled-up paper in the grate, seeing the heated flare as it caught the logs and hoping it would warm the sudden chill of her skin. Because sometimes it was easier to be told what to do than to think for yourself. It meant you could blame someone else if it all went wrong. And it was hard to admit that, even to herself.

'There were lots of reasons why I didn't stand up to him, but I suppose what you really want to know is why I wasn't stronger when it came to you. Why I let him drive a wedge between us.' She sensed that he was holding his breath but she couldn't look at him. She didn't dare. Because if she removed her mask completely—mightn't he be repulsed by the face he saw beneath?

She threw an unnecessary log onto the fire. 'I thought we were too young to settle down and my career was very important to me.'

'But that's not the only reason, is it, Jess?'

There was a pause. 'No.' Her voice sounded quiet against the crackle of the fire. She stared into the forest of flames, losing herself in that flickering orange kingdom. 'I was an unsettled child. My parents split up when I was very young. My dad left my mum for a younger woman who was already pregnant with his child—Hannah—and my mum never really got over that. I lived with her shame and her bitterness, which didn't leave much room for anything else.'

She picked up her tea and cupped her hands around it. 'When she died I went to live with my father and that's when the tennis really kicked off. At last I had something to believe in. Something I could lose myself in. But my stepmother resented the amount of time it took him away from her and I think Hannah was a bit jealous of all the attention I got.' She gave a slightly nervous laugh. 'I mean, I'm probably making it sound worse than it was, but it was—'

'It sounds awful,' he interjected and she found herself having to blink back the sudden threat of tears, because his sympathy was unexpectedly potent.

'I'd already learnt not to show my feelings,' she said. 'And that became a useful tactic on the tennis court. Soon I didn't know how to be any other way. I learnt to block my emotions. Not to let anything or anyone in. Now do you understand?'

He nodded. 'I think so.'

'I didn't want to make you any promises I couldn't keep,' she rushed on. 'And marriage was an institution I didn't trust.'

But it had been more than that. On an instinctive level she had recognised that Loukas was a man who had been in short supply of love, who needed to be loved properly. And hadn't she thought herself incapable of that?

'There's something else,' he said. 'Something you're not telling me.'

It hurt that he could be so perceptive. She didn't want him to be perceptive—she wanted him to be brash and uncaring. She wanted him to reinforce that she'd done the right thing, not leave her wondering how she could have been so stupid.

'Jess?' he prompted.

'I thought you would leave me,' she said slowly.

'Like your father left your mother?'

'I was so young,' she whispered. 'You know I was.'

He looked at her and started speaking slowly, as if he was voicing his thoughts out loud. 'I'd like to tell you that my feelings haven't changed, but that would be strange, as well as a fabrication—because of course I feel differently eight years down the line.'

Her lips had started trembling and no amount of biting would seem to stop them. 'You do?'

He nodded. 'I still care about you, *koukla mou*. You're still the one woman who makes my heart beat faster than anyone else. Still the one who can tie me up in knots so tight I can't escape, and I don't think you even realise you're doing it.'

'So what are you saying?' she whispered.

Loukas opened his lips to speak, but an inbuilt

self-protection forced him to temper his words with caution. Just like when you were negotiating a big takeover—you didn't lay all your cards on the table at once, did you? You always kept something back.

'I'm saying that it still feels...*unfinished*. That maybe we should give it another go. What's stopping us?'

She put her mug down and pulled the scrunchy from her hair, shaking her head so that a tumble of hair fell loosely around her cheeks.

'Loads of things. We live in different worlds, for a start,' she said. 'We always did, but it's even more defined now. I'm a country girl with a simple life. The annual photo shoot in London was just something I did to finance this life. The rest of the time, I forget all about it.'

'I'm not forcing you to become the global face of Lulu if you don't want to be,' he said impatiently. 'That's not what this is all about.'

'You're missing my point, Loukas,' she said, and now she was gesturing to something he hadn't noticed before, which lay on a small table in the corner of the room. A piece of cloth covered with exquisite sewing. He narrowed his eyes. It looked like a cosmic sky, with bright planets and stars sparking across an indigo background.

'Yours?' he questioned.

She nodded. 'Mine.'

'It's beautiful,' he said automatically.

'Thank you. It's something that's become more than a hobby and I've sold several pieces through a shop in Padstow. I'm into embroidery and gardening and now that Hannah's gone away, I was even thinking of getting a cat—that's how sad I am. You, on the other hand, live permanently in a hotel and drive around in a chauffeur-driven car. You occupy a luxury suite in the centre of London and you get other people to run your life for you. We're polar opposites, Loukas. You don't have a real home. You don't seem to want one and I do. That's what I want more than anything.' Her voice trembled, as if it hurt her to say the words. 'A real home.'

## CHAPTER TWELVE

Loukas didn't answer straight away. It was easier to watch the Atlantic crashing on the rocks in the distance and to listen to the crackle of the fire, rather than having to face up to what Jess had just told him. He'd never heard her be so frank and realised it must have taken a lot for her to put her feelings on the line like that. And even though he was determined to hold something back, that didn't mean he couldn't proceed with caution, did it?

'What if I told you that the reason I don't have a home is because I don't know how it works?' he said. 'And that I've never been sufficiently interested in the concept to find out?'

'Well, there you go. You've answered your own question.'

'But you could show me,' he continued, as if she hadn't interrupted.

She stared at him and there was a mutinous look in her eyes as if she didn't believe him. As if she was waiting for him to pull out the punchline and start laughing. But he wasn't laughing, he was deadly serious and maybe she picked up on that. 'Because I don't feel this thing we have between us has run its course,' he said.

'This *thing*?'

'Don't get hung up on words, Jess.' His voice deepened. 'I'm Greek, remember?'

'As if I'm likely to forget.' She tucked a strand of hair behind her ear. 'And I don't really understand what you're suggesting.'

He shrugged. 'That I move in here with you and see whether I'm compatible with home life.'

She laughed. 'But you're an international playboy.'

He gave her a slow smile. 'That could be negotiable.'

'And you have a job.'

'I also have a computer and a phone—and the ability to pull back and delegate.' He looked at her steadily. 'And it's been a very long time since I had a vacation.'

Jessica stared down at her fingernails, her initial disbelief at his suggestion morphing into a feeling of confusion. She suspected he was motivated more by ambition than any real emotion. He'd said himself this *thing* felt *unfinished* and maybe that was bugging him—because he was the kind of man who didn't like to leave things unfinished. Maybe this was all about great sex and the fact that they were still so attracted to one another. Was he banking on that attraction burning itself out, so that he could walk away? Just using the lure of *home* as a legitimate way to get his foot in the door?

Yet if he left now, what then? Would she spend the rest of her life regretting it and wondering *what if*? Too scared to face up to something which had lain beneath the surface of her life for so long, something which subconsciously might have been holding her back. There had been many times she'd wished she had the chance to do it all over again and now the opportunity was presenting itself. By allowing him access to her life, mightn't the pedestal she'd placed him on begin to crumble, freeing her from his power over her?

'If I said yes,' she said slowly, 'it could end at any time.'

'I can't guarantee—'

'No, Loukas.' She cut him off with a shake of her head, embarrassed that he thought she was trying to back him into a corner. 'I'm not asking you to pledge anything or promise anything. I'm trying to be practical because I'm a practical person.' She drew in a deep breath. 'If either of us wants out, at any time—any time at all—then we have to be able to say so. No questions. No post-mortems. Just a shrug and a smile, and a simple goodbye.'

His dark eyes gleamed. 'This is beginning to sound like my dream scenario.'

'I aim to please,' she said lightly.

He stood up and walked across the room and Jessica could almost *feel* the testosterone radiating from his powerful body.

'You certainly do. You please me very much.' His voice dipped. 'But if this is such an equal and such a *practical* arrangement, then surely I get to make a few requests myself, *koukla mou*.'

Something in the darkness of his face made her throat turn to parchment. 'Like what?' she questioned breathlessly.

'We may be playing house, but we aren't going to be constrained by house rules. We don't clock in and clock out. You won't start slamming cupboards if I'm late for dinner.'

'But you might be the one cooking dinner, and I might be the one who's late.'

'I might.' His eyes glittered. 'Just so long as you don't try to change me,' he said as his gaze travelled slowly over her body and seemed to linger there. 'And no rules about sex, either. We don't use it as a weapon or as a negotiating tool.'

'Gosh. You sound as if you've had some pretty bad experiences with women.'

'You think so?' He gave a cynical smile. 'I'd say it was the normal experience of a wealthy and attractive man who happens to be good in bed. And before you start pulling faces like that—I'm trying to be honest.' He paused. 'But again, in the pursuit of fairness—perhaps I should ask you the same thing. Have you had bad experiences with men?'

She hadn't been expecting the question and therefore hadn't prepared an answer, but now was not the time to make the announcement that there hadn't *been* anyone except for him. Apart from making her look hopelessly out of touch, mightn't it also make him wary? He might realise that nobody else had come close to making her feel the way he had done. That she had fallen for him big time. That she was expecting a whole lot more than he could ever give.

So she smiled. 'I thought we were going to have fun,' she said. 'Not rake up stuff about the past. The past has gone, Loukas, and this is what we're left with.'

'So it is.' He pulled her to her feet, tipping her chin upwards so that there was nowhere to look except at him, and when he spoke again his voice had deepened and suddenly it no longer sounded steady. 'I want you, Jess.'

'Let's go upstairs to bed,' she whispered.

He shook his head. 'I don't want to go anywhere. Draw the curtains.'

Her hands were trembling as she did as he asked, turning back to see his face looking shadowed in the suddenly subdued lighting broken only by the dancing flicker of the fire.

'Loukas,' she said uncertainly, and suddenly he was all over her. His hands were fumbling with the zip of her jeans, yanking them down to her ankles before impatiently tugging them off and hurling them to one side. He was peeling her sweater over her head and she was urging him on—silently positioning her body to make access easier. She shrugged the leather jacket from his broad shoulders and heard it slide to the floor. She eased the zip of his jeans down, but he was so aroused—the hard ridge of him so *big* beneath her still-trembling fingers—that he pushed her hand away.

'No. Let me,' he said succinctly, before freeing himself.

She gasped as he did so and it felt so deliciously decadent to be stripping off in the shadowy firelight that she reached down to cradle him in her hands but, again, he pushed her away—rapidly disposing of his own remaining clothes until they were both naked before the golden flicker of the flames.

'Now,' he said, but his voice sounded so tight and urgent that it was almost as if she had never heard him speak before. She was breathless and wet as he eased the condom on himself with an exaggerated amount of care, as if only by doing that could he hang onto a self-control which seemed perilously close to deserting him. And then he positioned himself over her, that first deep thrust making her moan and his subsequent rhythm making her moan ever more. Until he stopped and a mumbled protest fell from her lips.

'L-Loukas—'

'Open your eyes,' he ordered. 'Open your eyes and look at me.'

Reluctantly she let her lashes flutter apart to meet his smoky black gaze, afraid of what he might be able to read when all her defences were down. She tried to tell herself that this was what every woman felt when she was having sex with a man, but on some fundamental level she knew that wasn't true. Because surely it wasn't normal to feel as if your heart were on fire. As if you wanted to burst with joy. Those were the feelings you associated with love.

But Loukas wasn't looking for love. The reason he wanted her to open her eyes was to gauge her level of satisfaction, and there was no hiding *that*.

Her lashes flickered open completely, and he smiled.

'That's better,' he said. 'Tell me what you like, Jess. Tell me what you want me to do to you.'

She wondered what he expected—a verbal map to indicate just which zones she found most erogenous, or an expressed preference for a different position? But in reality, there was only one thing Jessica wanted Loukas to do to her.

'Just kiss me,' she said, because that was the closest she could get to asking him to love her.

## CHAPTER THIRTEEN

*BE CAREFUL WHAT you wish for.*

Jessica stood at her bedroom window, watching Loukas in the garden below as he chopped logs and added them to the growing pile. It made for a compelling image. His strong arms swung in an arc as the blade splintered into the wood—drawing attention to the honed definition of muscles rippling across his shoulders and his broad back.

Her throat dried. How many times had she longed for a scenario like this, in those lonely moments when her fantasies about him wouldn't respond to censorship, no matter how hard she'd tried? She'd dreamed of Loukas being back in her life and in her bed—with the freedom to conduct their relationship openly in a way which had never been possible before. And now she had it. No more moments of passion sandwiched in between the strictures of her career and the demands of his billionaire boss. Now *he* was the billionaire—although she no longer had a career, she thought wryly. Still. It should have been great. It should have been almost perfect.

So why the questions which still whirled around in her mind, which felt as if they had no real answers?

Ever since he'd moved into her Cornish cottage, they'd behaved like a couple. They'd done stuff. The normal stuff which other people did. They'd cooked dinner and shopped for food, and at first it had been disorientating to see Loukas in the local store, standing among all the villagers and the occasional tourist. People stopped what they were doing and turned to look at him and it was easy to see why. With his leather jacket and faded jeans, he looked larger than life—tall and indomitable. A dark, head-turning presence who seemed to come from a very different world.

Because he had. That was exactly what he had done. He'd known violence, rejection, pain and despair and those things had given him an edge which marked him out from other men. No wonder everyone else had always seemed so pale and so tame in comparison. No wonder no other man had ever been able to coax her into his bed.

Very quickly Jessica discovered that she liked having him around. She liked being part of a couple and doing coupley things. It made life more interesting to have a man to watch a scary film with, and play the old-fashioned board games which she taught him and which he was soon winning. She liked the feel of his warm, naked body when she got into bed at night and his arms wrapped around her waist when she woke up in the morning. She liked knowing they could make love whenever and wherever they liked.

But she was also aware of the subtle boundaries which surrounded them. The unspoken, instinctive restrictions. They never talked about the future and they never used the word love. He might have seamlessly slotted into having a home, but it still felt like *her* home, not his. As if he had invested nothing in it, nor was he planning to. Of course he hadn't. Because, when she stopped to think about it for long enough, could she really imagine Loukas Sarantos living the rest of his life in some rural Cornish outlet?

And despite his intention to delegate, his other life soon began to snap around at his heels, like a puppy demanding to be played with. It started with the odd phone call here and there and the beginning of a mounting pile of emails which needed to be dealt with. Soon there were conference calls, which he told her he had to take.

Jessica usually absented herself for those. She would go out into the garden, hearing his deep voice drifting through the open window—often speaking Greek—while she stared down at the bare soil and wondered when the first daffodils would push through and show that spring was nearly here.

She had just straightened up from plucking a weed from the ground after one such call, when she felt the warm caress of Loukas's hand splaying over her denim-covered buttock and she gave a little shiver of pleasure.

She threw the weed onto the compost heap. 'Everything okay?'

'The conference call was fine. And then my brother rang.' There was a pause. 'My twin.'

Jessica turned around, hearing his deliberate emphasis of the word and knowing just why he did that. She guessed it was still weird for him to acknowledge that he actually *had* a twin—the amazingly successful Alek Sarantos. She knew that contact between the two men had been minimal, but maybe that wasn't so surprising, since neither had known about the other's existence until they were grown men.

'How is he?'

He shrugged. 'He's okay. Actually, he's in London.'

'Oh.' Wasn't it stupid that just the mention of the city sounded vaguely *ominous*, as if it posed some kind of threat? She felt as if his other world—the one she wasn't part of—was beginning to inch towards them. Her smile didn't slip. 'That's nice.'

'Mmm. He wants me to have dinner with him. I thought I'd stay up for a few days. Do a little work while I'm there.' He narrowed his black eyes. 'You could always come with me.'

She lifted her hand to his face, her fingertips drifting over the sculptured outline of his unshaven jaw and feeling its rough rasp. Yes, she could. She could accompany him to London, a trip which would require a frantic mental inventory about what to wear. She could gatecrash his meeting with his newfound brother and inhibit their burgeoning relationship. She could hang around the Vinoly while he went into the office, or dutifully kill hours doing cultural things with which to impress him when he got home.

She got a sudden scary glimpse of how the future might look, once the initial wild sexual excitement had started to fade. He would probably start making more trips to London and each time he came back, it would be a little harder for them to reconnect. That was how these things worked, wasn't it? How long before he told her he was moving back permanently to the city, to the rented hotel suite he called home? Deep-down she knew she didn't fit into his life in London and that was his base.

*So shouldn't she start getting used to that—with pride and with dignity?*

'You need some time on your own with Alek,' she said. 'I'll stay here.'

His mouth tightened. 'Right.'

She saw the sudden flinty look in his eyes. Did it matter to him if she accompanied him or not?

So ask him. Just go right ahead and ask him.

But the different ways of phrasing such a question were really only a disguise for the one which could never be asked.

*How do you feel about me, Loukas?*

A more confident woman might have come right out and said it. A more sexually experienced one almost certainly would have done. But Jessica had been protecting herself from pain for so long that she would sooner have walked barefoot across the rough cliff path than risk getting hurt again.

'When will you leave?' she said as they began to walk back towards the house.

'I'll leave immediately. Why hang around? There's just one thing I need to do first.'

She turned her face up to look at him. 'What's that?'

'I'll show you.'

He linked his fingers with hers and led her inside, taking her straight upstairs and stripping off her clothes with speed rather than finesse. His eyes were still flinty and his mouth hardened into an odd kind of smile just before he drove it down on hers in a punishing kind of kiss.

He entered her urgently and as Jessica clung to his thrusting body she was filled with a terrible sense of *sadness*—as if she'd just failed a test she hadn't even known she was taking.

The house was quiet after he'd left. It was the first time she'd been without him for weeks. Long, lazy weeks which now seemed to have passed in a flash. She kept looking up, expecting to see him, telling herself it was crazy how quickly she had become used to having him around.

She kept busy, working hard on her embroidery and selling a small piece privately, before hearing about the possibility of a commission for a much larger piece. She gardened and made bread and went for long clifftop walks. Then she took a call from an excited Hannah, who told her that she'd met a young Australian vet in Bali.

'Oh, Jess,' she sighed. 'He's gorgeous. You'd really like him. He wants me to go to Perth next. That's where his folks live.'

'That sounds lovely,' said Jessica, even though inside she wanted to scream, *Please don't fall in love with a man from the other side of the world, so that I probably won't see you very much.*

Because you shouldn't use your own selfish needs to try to change someone else's behaviour, should you? Wasn't that one of the reasons why she never dared bring up the subject of the future with Loukas—because she sensed there could never be any compromise about their different lifestyles? Or because she wasn't sure if his feelings for her went any deeper than a powerful sexual attraction? She thought about him, miles away in London, and her heart clenched. Did he miss her, she wondered, and did he have any idea how much she missed him?

She spoke to him that evening and the sound of laughter and glasses clinking in the background made her feel very alone. And it was her own stupid fault. She thought that if he'd suggested her joining him, she would have been booking her ticket from Bodmin station quicker than a flash. But he didn't. Just as he didn't know *exactly* when he would be back.

'Soon,' he said.

But *soon* was inconclusive. *Soon* gave her the chance to dwell on all the things which were nagging away inside her. Maybe his brother was lining him up with a nice Greek girl. Maybe the lure of London had enticed him back and the thought of returning to this quiet little hamlet had filled him with horror.

Or just maybe he was missing her as much as she was missing him. What if that was a possibility? And once she allowed herself to consider *that* possibility, it altered everything. It scared her. It excited her. It made her feel as if she were floating three inches about the ground. She thought about some of the things he'd told her. About a mother who had always put other men before her son. Didn't that mean he would be reluctant to trust the love of women—or wary about putting his own feelings on the line? So wasn't it time to start grabbing at a little emotional courage—to dare show Loukas that she wanted him? To stop worrying about the fear of rejection and tell him she cared.

A text arrived from him in the early hours and she stared at it sleepily.

Back tomorrow. ☹ xxx

She woke, still with that walking-on-air feeling. She cleaned the house from top to bottom and swept the path. At the village store, she bought coffee, bread and wine—and when she got home went out into the garden, snipping off bright stems of foliage to cram into a beautiful blue and white vase. When he arrived she would tell him she'd missed him. Or ask him whether he wanted her to return to London with him. Because home was where you made it, wasn't it? She might not particularly like London, but wouldn't she rather live there with him than live in the countryside without him? Couldn't she show him that she could be adaptable?

She'd just washed the mud from her hands when the phone started ringing and eagerly she snatched it up, surprised but pleased to hear Patti, the spiky-haired stylist from Zeitgeist, on the end of the line and remembering the conversation they'd had at the launch party.

'If you're ringing about meeting for coffee, then it'll have to wait,' said Jessica. 'I'm in Cornwall.'

'Oh, okay.' There was a pause. 'Jessica...this might sound like a crazy question but I don't suppose Loukas is with you, is he?'

Afterwards, Jessica would think how strange the human brain was—that it could sift out a single word from a sentence and focus on that alone.

'Why would it be crazy?' she asked, because maybe it was time to stop pretending this wasn't happening. To start acknowledging that she and Loukas were in some sort of *relationship*.

'Oh, just that someone at Lulu said they thought you two were dating.'

'I don't know that I'd exactly describe it as dating. But, well, yes. He's been staying here.'

'So it worked,' said Patti, in a flat kind of voice.

'What worked?'

'It doesn't matter.'

'Oh, come on, Patti—you can't do that. You can't half say something and then leave me wondering the worst.'

There was a pause. 'I like you, Jessica. I like you very much.'

'And I like you, too. Mutual admiration society established. So what aren't you telling me?'

Another pause. 'Remember when the photos weren't working that first time in Venice? You know—when you were all wooden in front of the camera.'

'Yes, I remember. What about it?'

Patti's voice sounded hesitant. 'It's just that the art director said that what they really needed was for you to look like a woman who had just had sex. And the next day you did. The photos were absolute dynamite and everyone thought…'

'Everyone thought, what—that Loukas had taken the suggestion literally?'

'Something like that,' said Patti uncomfortably. 'And I wouldn't say anything, but… Well, it's just that he has such a reputation, and I'd hate to see you getting hurt. I'm sorry. Maybe I shouldn't have said anything.'

'No,' said Jessica, with soft urgency. 'You should. Don't worry about it, Patti. You did exactly the right thing. You told me something I needed to know.'

She couldn't settle to anything after that. Loukas rang to say he was on his way back and she slumped down into the chair, her embroidery untouched and nothing really registering until she saw the low flash of winter sun glinting from his windscreen.

Her heart had started pounding and her palms were

clammy. Wiping them down over her jeans, she prepared to greet him. And even while her heart was feeling the pain, she was running the whole scene like a film through her mind. This is the last time I'll see him drive up here like this, she thought. The last time he'll walk up this little path with the sun glinting off his black hair. The last, dying moments of being a couple were almost upon her and Jessica could barely summon up a smile with which to greet him.

But she didn't want this to turn into some kind of awful screaming match. She'd witnessed enough of those before her parents' divorce to put her off displays of high emotion for ever. She would be very calm and very dignified. It might even come as something of a relief to Loukas. For all she knew, he might have been trying to work out a diplomatic way of ending it himself. She wasn't going to do accusations, or regret. She would do it neatly and without a scene, just as she'd promised right at the beginning.

His sleek car came to a halt and he got out. She saw those impossibly long legs unfolding themselves and the expression on that dark and rugged face making her feel…

She gave herself a mental shake. She wasn't going to *feel* anything. It was safer that way.

The crunch of the gravel was replaced by the sound of a door being opened and closed and then suddenly he was standing in front of her, framed in the doorway, like some dark and golden statue come to life.

'Hello, Loukas,' she said.

'Hello, Jess.'

Loukas waited for her to jump out of the chair and fling her arms around him. But she didn't. She just sat there in her jeans and sweater staring up at him, with those extraordinary aquamarine eyes narrowed and giving nothing away.

She never gave anything away, did she?

'Did you have a good trip?'

'Good in parts,' he said, just about to tell her that he'd missed her when something stopped him, only he wasn't sure what. He stared into her tense face. Perhaps he was starting to get a good idea.

He looked around the room, noticing the spray of berried branches in a blue and white vase and he narrowed his eyes in surprise, because that wasn't usually the kind of detail he noticed.

'So how was your brother?'

'Is my brother the reason you're sitting there looking so uptight?' he questioned. 'Is my brother the reason you haven't kissed me, or looked as if you're pleased to see me?'

'I'm very pleased to see you.'

'Liar,' he said softly. 'Or maybe you're just not as good at hiding your feelings as you used to be. Are you going to tell me what's bugging you, Jess—or are we going to play a game of elimination?'

She shook her head as if she was having some kind of silent tussle with herself and when she spoke, it was as if she was picking her words with care.

'Let me ask *you* a question, Loukas. How important was it to turn the company around, when you bought Lulu?'

He shrugged. 'Very important—naturally. I'm a businessman and success is part of the deal—the biggest and most measurable part there is.'

She nodded as if his answer had just reinforced

something she already knew, and suddenly her hands were clenching into fists so tight he could see the whitening of her knuckles.

'Did you have sex with me just to get me to relax for the photo shoot?' she hissed.

*'What?'*

'You heard me perfectly well. Don't try to think up a clever answer—just tell me the truth.'

'You seem to have already decided for yourself what the truth is, without bothering to reference me first,' he snapped. 'Where the hell has all this come from?'

'It doesn't matter where it came from. Just that I heard that after the first disastrous shoot in Venice, the art director said I needed to look as if I'd just had sex.' Her cheeks were flushed and her eyes defiant as she stared him full in the face. 'And so...'

Her words tailed off and he felt his heart clench with anger. 'And so you thought that I would make the ultimate sacrifice for the sake of the company? That I'd take you to bed and loosen you up, thus ensuring that we had the requisite sultry photos to headline the new campaign. Is that what you thought, Jess?'

She opened her mouth and then closed it again, before nodding her head so vigorously that her blonde hair shimmered up and down.

'Yes,' she said fervently. 'That's exactly what I thought because it's the truth, isn't it, Loukas?'

He stared at her for a long moment and then he began to laugh.

## CHAPTER FOURTEEN

Feeling wrong-footed, Jessica stared into Loukas's face—wondering how he had the *nerve* to laugh at a moment like this.

'What's so funny?' she demanded.

Only now the smile had gone. It had died on his lips, leaving nothing in its place but a look of withering contempt.

'You are,' he said. 'You're priceless. Do you really think that I would have cold-bloodedly had sex with you, just to make a better photo? I've heard of naked ambition, but really! Just how far do you think my dedication to the company goes, Jess? Do you think I would have done the same if I'd only just met the model, or found her physically repulsive? That I'd be acting like some kind of male whore?'

She glared at him. How dared he try to turn this round? 'You were talking to loads of different women at the party!' she accused. 'You know you were. Just not to me. But then, you've been hiding me away like a dirty secret, haven't you? You acted like you barely knew me at the party. Like we were strangers!'

He frowned. 'Because I didn't think either of us were ready to go public right then. And yes, I was talking to other women there—but it doesn't automatically follow that I was planning on having sex with them.'

Her eyes bored into his. 'Not even Maya?' she accused.

'Maya?' he echoed blankly, until his face cleared. 'Oh, Maya. You mean my ex-lover? Why, would you have had me blank her and be rude to her by ignoring her? That isn't the kind of behaviour I'd expect from a classy lady like you, Jess.'

His sarcasm washed over her and she glared at him. 'You hired me for all kinds of reasons,' she bit out. 'But I got the distinct impression that the main one was because you wanted to get even with me. That you'd never quite forgiven me for everything that happened before. And please don't try and make out I'm a fool, Loukas—or that I imagined it. You did. You know you did.'

There was a pause before he answered and then he sucked in a breath and nodded his head slowly. 'At the beginning, maybe I did,' he said. 'But things change, Jess—only you seem to be blind to them. You only ever see the shallow stuff—you never dare scratch beneath the surface, do you? When we reconnected again after all those years I agree that initially I felt a mixture of anger and lust. And if you really want the truth, I thought that getting you out of my system was going to be simple.'

'By sleeping with me?' she demanded.

'*Neh*. By sleeping with you.' He gave a cynical laugh. 'Actually, sleeping had nothing to do with it. I wanted you wide awake and very present. I wanted to do something that I'd been unable to forget and that was to have sex with you again. But you fought me all the way. You didn't just fall into my arms, even though I knew you wanted to. You forced me to get to know you again and to realise—'

'Realise what?'

'It doesn't matter.' He shook his head and his voice had grown cold now—as cold as the icy glint from his eyes. 'None of it does. Doesn't matter that I indulged you—'

*'Indulged me?'*

'*Neh.* I treated you with kid gloves,' he gritted out. 'I was cautious and careful. I put my business on hold and came to live with you here because I know you don't like London, but it still wasn't enough, was it? Because nothing is ever enough for you, Jess. You couldn't wait to think the worst of me—to give you a reason not to trust me. A reason to send me away and lock yourself away again—with all your beauty and your warmth hidden behind the frozen front you present to the world.'

'Loukas—'

'No!' he flared impatiently. 'I don't intend to spend my life tiptoeing around you, while you imagine the worst. Believe what you want to believe, because I'm done with this. And I'm done with you.'

His tone was harsh and Jessica stared at him, wondering what he was doing, then realised he was tugging his car keys from the pocket of his jacket and preparing to leave.

*He was preparing to leave, only this time the look on his face told her he would never come back.*

'Loukas,' she said again, fingertips flying to her mouth in horror. But her gasped word didn't stop him or make his stony face relax. He was opening the front door and the chill March wind was whistling through the door as he walked out, sending the temperature plummeting.

Frozen, he'd called her, and she *felt* frozen. Frozen enough to feel as if she were encased in ice when she heard a door slam and the sound of an engine firing into life. She turned her head to see the car bumping over the grass onto the unmade road, with Loukas's stony profile staring straight ahead.

He was going.

*He was going.*

'Loukas!' She ran outside and the cry was torn from her throat as she screamed it into the wind, but if he heard her, he didn't stop. And if he saw her that made no difference either, because the car continued to move forward. Waving her arms in the air, she started to run after it. To run as she hadn't run in years. It was like running across the court for a ball she knew she would never reach, only…

The last time that had happened she had ruptured her cruciate ligament and ended her career with a sickening snap, but this time she couldn't move as fast as her teenage self and her footsteps slowed to a stumbled halt. This time all that she had ruptured was her heart, yet somehow the pain seemed just as intense.

Sinking to her knees on the damp ground, she buried her face in her hands and began to cry, great sobs welling up from somewhere deep inside her chest until they erupted into a raw howl of pain. She wept at her own stupidity and timidity—at her lack of courage at going after something she realised now was irreplaceable. She could have had him—the only man she had ever cared about—but she'd been too proud and too stupid and too scared to give it a go. Too afraid of being hurt to take a risk, when everyone knew that love never came without some element of risk.

Hot tears dripped through her frozen fingers, drying instantly in the chill wind, and as she began to shiver she knew she couldn't stay there for ever. Her teeth chattering, she rose slowly to her feet, blinking away tears as she stared into the distance and saw the dark shape of a distinctive car parked on the clifftop and her heart missed a beat.

Loukas's car.

She blinked again as she realised that her eyes weren't playing tricks on her, but that it was definitely *his* car and he hadn't gone.

*He hadn't gone.*

With stumbling steps she began to run—expecting at any moment to see it disappear into the distance in a swift acceleration of power. But it didn't and her stride became longer—her panting breath making clouds of vapour in the chill air as she began to make silent pleas in her head. *Please don't go. Please just give me one more chance and I'll never let you down again.*

Out of breath, she reached the car at last. He was sitting perfectly still, staring straight ahead until she began to rap on the window and then he turned his head to look at her. His black eyes were flinty and his dark features were unreadable, but these days such a look was rare. She remembered the night when she'd been exhausted and wrung out in Venice. When he'd put her to bed and fed her melted cheese. When he'd made her feel safe and cherished as well as desired, and her heart swelled with an immense feeling of love and longing.

'Don't go,' she mouthed, through the glass. 'Please.'

He didn't say a word as he took the key from the ignition and climbed out of the car. He stared down at her for a long moment and then the flicker of a smile appeared on his lips.

'I wasn't,' he said, 'planning on going anywhere. I just needed time to cool down, before I said something I might afterwards regret.'

'Oh, Loukas,' she said, her words still muffled from all the crying she'd done.

But as Loukas looked at her he knew it had been more than that. He'd wanted to see if she would come after him, and she had. He'd wanted to show her that he had staying power. He needed her to know that she could trust him, because without that there could be no real love. And he knew he really couldn't hold back any longer.

'Because what I really want to say is that I love you, Jess,' he said simply. 'I love you. Completely, absolutely and enduringly.'

'Oh, Loukas,' she said as she flung her arms around his neck and pressed her cold face to his. 'I feel exactly the same about you. I love you so much, and I've made such a mess of showing you.'

'Then show me,' he said fiercely. 'Show me now.' And when she lifted her face to his, her eyes were very bright as he brushed his lips over hers.

The kiss deepened. He kissed her until they were both breathless and when he pulled away they were smiling—as if they'd just allowed themselves to see something which had been there all the time. He put her into the car and snapped her seat belt closed and when he'd parked outside her cottage, he took her hand

and led her inside. He made coffee and smoothed the hair from her eyes and it was only when she was sitting snuggled up against him on the sofa that he looked down at her gravely.

'But there are a few things we need to get cleared up before we go any further.'

'Mmm?' she said dreamily, her head resting against his shoulder.

'Just for the record—I know you aren't a city girl,' he said. 'And you don't have to be, because all I want to do is to marry you and make a home with you. Where that home will be is entirely up to you.'

'Loukas—'

'No, Jess,' he said. 'Hear me out. I need you to know that I'm not saying any of this in reaction to what has just happened. I need you to know that I've been thinking about this and have wanted it for a long while.'

She opened her eyes wide. 'You have?'

'I have. When I was in London I talked to my brother about it, in a way I've never talked to anyone.' He smiled. 'Except maybe you. I told him that I was in love with you but that I thought you were scared because you kept pushing me away every time I tried to get closer.'

She sniffed again. 'And what did he say?'

'He said that deep down most people are scared of love, because they recognise it has the power to hurt them like nothing else can. And that there are no guarantees in life.'

'You mean that nothing is certain?'

'Absolutely nothing,' he agreed, and now she could see the pain in his own eyes. 'But we both know how important it is to succeed at this. We've both had things happen which make it hard for us to believe it ever can, but I know it can. I think we both want this relationship to work more than we've ever wanted trophies, or money in the bank, or houses and cars.' His voice deepened. 'I know I do.'

'So do I,' she said in a squeaky voice which sounded perilously close to more tears.

'Because at the end of the day, love is the only thing which matters, and it is important that we mark that love.' He reached into his pocket and pulled out a familiarly coloured magenta box, tied with the distinctive Lulu ribbon. 'Which is why I want to ask you to be my wife.'

She swallowed. 'You've already bought me a ring?'

His face was grave. 'Well, I had the choice of some of the world's finest jewels.'

He flipped open the box and Jessica blinked. She had been expecting to be dazzled by diamonds, but all that lay on the indigo velvet was a small, metal ring-pull—the type you found on a can of cola.

She looked at him in surprise, with the first flicker of amusement tugging at her lips. 'And this is my engagement ring?'

He shrugged. 'Everything seemed such a cliché. Aquamarine to match your eyes, or diamonds for their cold and glittering beauty? With a whole empire at my disposal I was spoilt for choice—and I gather that, these days, the trend is to let women choose what they really, really want.'

'Put it on,' she said fiercely, and as he slid the worthless piece of metal onto her finger she saw that it was trembling. And she thought that being with Loukas Sarantos made a mockery of the steady hands which had once been her trademark. But she was smiling as she cupped his face in her hands and pressed her own very close.

'I don't want your diamonds,' she whispered. 'You're the only thing I really, really want. Your love and your commitment. They are more precious to me than all the jewels in the world, and I will treasure them and keep them close to my heart. Because I want you to know that I love you, Loukas Sarantos. I always have and I always will. A diamond isn't for ever. Love is.'

# EPILOGUE

'Happy?' Loukas nuzzled his mouth over Jess's bare shoulder and felt her wriggle luxuriously.

Turning her head towards his, she smiled.

'Totally,' she sighed.

'Sure?'

'How could I not be?' She traced his mouth with a tender finger. 'You're my husband and I'm your wife. Your pregnant wife.'

He saw the way that her eyes flashed with joy and that pleased him. It pleased him that he could read her so well—and that these days she was happy to let him. And he recognised you couldn't change the past overnight. You had to work at things. No pain—no gain.

And yet the gain.

Ah, the gain.

He sighed with contentment as he stared out of the window, where the massive Greek sun was beginning its scarlet and vibrant ascendancy. The most dazzling sunrises he'd ever seen had been here, on the island where he'd been born and then taken away from as a wriggling baby, too young to remember its powdery white sands or the crystal seas after which it had been named.

Until now.

Kristalothos was one of the most beautiful places he'd ever seen, although he'd been reluctant to return at first, because it symbolised a dark time of his life. But Jess had gently persuaded him that it would be healthy to lay this particular ghost to rest.

His first trip back had been with his twin, Alek—just the two of them, when they'd stood and stared at the luxury hotel which had replaced the fortress in which Alek had grown up. It had been razed to the ground and now, as a luxury hotel, it was a place of light, not shade. And the two brothers had swum and fished, and listened to the night herons as they'd gathered around the lapping bay. And they'd talked. They'd talked long into the night, having conversations which had been over thirty years in the making.

Loukas had gone home to Jess and told her that the island was a paradise and when she'd suggested spending part of their honeymoon there during their tour of the Greek islands, he had readily agreed. He wanted to show her the place of his birth and to share it with her. He wanted to share pretty much everything with her.

He looked at the platinum and diamond wedding band which gleamed on her finger. It had been the most amazing wedding—especially for a man who didn't like weddings. But he had liked his own. He had liked making those solemn vows and declaring to the world that Jessica Cartwright was his. She had always been his, and she would remain so for as long as he drew breath.

Hannah had been their bridesmaid—resplendent in

a blue silk dress which had contrasted with her gap year tan—overjoyed to have the big brother she'd always longed for.

Alek had been his best man and his wife, Ellie, Jess's matron of honour. And their young son, named Loukas after his uncle, had been the cute hit of the day as he had toddled down the aisle as pageboy behind the bride.

One of the first things Loukas had done was to terminate the contract on his suite at the Vinoly. He had told Jess he was prepared to work as much as possible from the west of the country, if she really wanted to stay there. But Jess had changed, just as much as he had. She hadn't wanted to be apart from him for a second longer than she needed to be, and she'd agreed to live in London, just so long as they had a garden.

So now they were in Hampstead, with not only their own garden, but a huge heath nearby, on which they would soon be able to take their son or daughter in a big, old-fashioned pram.

'Are you?'

Her soft voice broke into his thoughts and he stirred lazily as he met her questioning look. 'Am I what?'

'Happy.'

He smiled as he placed a hand over her still-flat belly and looked up into her shining eyes. 'I love you, Jess Sarantos,' he said. 'I love you more than I ever thought I could love anyone and you're now my wife. Does that answer your question?'

'It does,' she murmured and gave a contented little wriggle as he continued to stroke her belly with that same seductive, circular movement. She closed her eyes. 'Mmm. That's nice. Any ideas about what you'd like to do today?'

'More of the same,' he said, his husky words made indistinct by the lazy pressure of his kiss. 'Just more of the same.'

* * * * *

# A CONTRACT FOR HIS RUNAWAY BRIDE

**MELANIE MILBURNE**

To Denise Florence Monks. You were not just
our help in the house – and in the garden and with
house-sitting – but our help and support during
some very difficult times. I will always treasure my
memories of you. Your love and compassion for our
family, our pets and even our friends was amazing.
Even right to the end, you were thinking of others.
Rest in peace.

# CHAPTER ONE

Elodie Campbell glanced at her designer watch and muttered a colourful curse. The one time in her life when she was bang on time for an appointment and she was kept waiting. Who was this guy who thought it was okay to leave her out here with her nerves ripping her stomach to shreds?

This meeting was her last chance for financial backing.

It had to go ahead.

To fill the time—and to settle her anxiety—she'd glanced through the artfully splayed glossy magazines five times. One of which featured a spread of her on a photo shoot in Dubai. Then she'd consumed two expertly brewed black coffees. Maybe the second coffee hadn't been such a good idea. Restless at the best of times, now she was so fidgety she wanted to pace the floor...or punch something.

She crossed one leg over the other and kicked her top foot up and down in time with the tick-tock of the second hand on the clock above the receptionist's desk.

The clock went around another eight and a half minutes and Elodie was close to screaming. Not just a scream of frustration but one that was so loud it would shatter the windows of the swish-looking office tower. Normally people had to wait for her. Her identical twin, Elspeth, had inherited the punctuality gene. Elodie had got the chronically late one.

The longer she waited, the worse her anxiety spiked. What if this meeting turned out like the last? Her options were running out—especially since the recent scandal attached to her name. Her previous financial backer had pulled out once he'd heard about her role in sabotaging a society wedding. Urgh. What was it with her and scandals? If she couldn't secure financial backing, how could she leave her lingerie modelling career behind? She was tired of playing on her looks. She wanted to prove she had more than a good body. She wanted to design her own label of evening wear, but she needed an investor in her business to get it off the ground.

Another five minutes crawled past like a snail on crutches.

Elodie blew out a breath and sprang up from the sofa in the plush reception area on the top level of the London office tower. She strode over to the smartly dressed receptionist with a smile so forced it made her face ache. 'Could you give me an update on when Mr Smith will be available?'

The receptionist's answering smile was polite but formal. 'I apologise for the delay. He'll be with you shortly.'

'Look, my appointment was—'

'I understand, Ms Campbell. But he's a very busy man. He's made a special gap in his diary for you. He's not usually so accommodating. You must've made a big impression on him.'

'I haven't even met him. All I know is, I was instructed to be here close to thirty minutes ago for a meeting with a Mr Smith to discuss finance. I've been given no other details.'

The receptionist glanced at the intercom console where a small green light was flashing. She looked up again at Elodie with the same polite smile. 'Thank you for being so patient. Mr…erm… Smith will see you now. Please go through. It's the third door on the right. The corner office.'

The corner office boded well—that meant he was the head honcho. The big bucks began and stopped with him. Elodie went to the door and took a deep calming breath, but it did nothing to settle the frenzy of flick knives in her stomach. She gave the door a quick rap with her knuckles.

*Please, please, please let me be successful this time.*

'Come.'

Her hand paused on the doorknob, her mind whirling in ice-cold panic. Something about the deep timbre of that voice sent a shiver scuttling over her scalp like a small claw-footed creature. Elodie ran the tip of her tongue over her suddenly carpet-dry lips, her throat so tight she couldn't swallow. Surely her nerves were getting the better of her? The man she was meeting was a Mr Smith. But how could this Mr Smith sound so like her ex-fiancé? Scarily like him.

She turned the doorknob and pushed the door open, her gaze immediately fixing on the tall dark-haired man behind the large desk.

*'You?'* Elodie gasped, heat flooding into her cheeks and other places in her body she didn't want to think about right now.

Lincoln Lancaster rose from his chair with leonine grace, his expression set in its customary cynical lines—the arch of one ink-black brow over his intelligent bluey-green gaze, the tilt of his sensual mouth that was not quite a smile. His black hair was brushed back from his high forehead in loose waves that looked as if they had last been combed by his fingers. He was dressed in a three-piece suit that hugged his athletic frame, emphasising the broadness of his shoulders, the taut trimness of his chest, flat abdomen and lean hips. He was the epitome of a successful a man in his prime. Potent, powerful, persuasive. He got what he wanted, when he wanted, how he wanted.

'You're looking good, Elodie.'

His voice rolled over her as smoothly and lazily as his gaze, the deep, sexy rumble so familiar it triggered a host of memories she had fought for seven years to erase. Memories in her flesh that were triggered by being in his presence. Erotic memories that made her hyper-aware of his every breath, his every glance, his every movement.

Elodie shut the door behind her with a definitive click. She clenched her right hand around her slim-line purse and her other hand into a tight fist and stalked towards his desk. 'How dare you lie to me to get me here? You know I'd never willingly be in the same room as you.'

His eyes shone with amusement, which only fuelled her anger like a naked flame on tinder. 'You answered your own question. I wanted to meet with you and this seemed the only way to do it.'

*'Mr Smith?'* She made a scoffing noise. 'Couldn't you be a little more original than that? And why not meet me at your Kensington office?'

'In another life, Smith could well have been my name.'

There was a cryptic quality to his tone and a flicker of something in his expression that piqued her interest.

'I'm using this office for a few weeks while my other premises are being renovated.' He waved a hand at the plush chair in front of his desk. 'Take a seat. We have things to discuss.'

Elodie remained standing, her fists so tightly balled she could feel her fingernails cutting half-moons into the skin of her palm and the soft leather of her purse. 'I have nothing to discuss with you. You've no right to waste my valuable time by luring me here under false pretences.'

'Sit.' His one-word command was as sharp and implacable as the steely *don't-mess-with-me* glint in his eyes.

Elodie raised her chin, a frisson skittering over her flesh at the combative energy firing between them like high-voltage electricity. Fighting with Lincoln had formed a large part of their previous relationship. Their strong wills had often clashed and their passionate fights had nearly always been resolved in bed. The thought of *this* fight ending that way made her heart race and her pulse skyrocket.

'Just try and make me.'

She injected her tone with ice-cold disdain to counter the fiery heat pooling between her legs. Only Lincoln Lancaster could have this effect on her, and it made her furious to think he still had the power to make her feel things she didn't want to feel. Dangerous feelings. Overwhelming feelings. Feelings she couldn't control.

One side of his mouth came up in a half-smile, and the slow burn of his gaze sent tingles cascading down the length of her spine to pool in a ball of molten heat in her core.

'Tempting as that is, right now, I want to discuss a proposal with you.'

'A proposal?' She unclenched her fists and gave a bark of scathing laughter. 'There's nothing you could ever propose to me that I would find irresistible.'

There was a long beat of silence. A silence so weighted, so intense, it sent goosebumps popping up along the skin of her arms.

His unreadable eyes held hers in a lock that made her blood tick with excitement. It was an excitement she wished she could quell, but it seemed her body had a mind of its own when it came to Lincoln.

And somehow, she suspected he knew it.

Lincoln came around to perch on the corner of his desk, close enough to her for her to catch a tantalising whiff of his aftershave. The citrus notes were fresh and clean, the base notes a little more complex, reminding her of the rich, earthy scent of a densely wooded forest after rain. His eyes were an unusual mix of green and blue—a bottomless ocean with flashes of kelp and green sea glass swirling in their unreachable depths. She couldn't drag her eyes away from the dark shadow of regrowth peppering his jaw. How many times had she run her fingers over that prickly stubble? How many times had she felt its sexy rasp on the sensitive skin of her inner thighs?

Her gaze drifted to his mouth and her stomach bottomed out. Suddenly she found it hard to breathe. Those sensually curved lips had explored every inch of her body, stirred her into cataclysmic pleasure time and time again. She had never had a more exciting lover than Lincoln Lancaster. His touch had set fire to her body, making it erupt into roaring flames of need only he could assuage. Every lover since—not that there had been many—had been a bitter disappointment. It was as if Lincoln had ruined her for anyone else. No one could ignite her flesh like he had. No one could make her feel the things he made her feel. It seemed her body was programmed to respond to him and him alone.

'How about we start again?' His voice had a disarmingly gentle note, but his gaze was still unwavering on hers. 'You're looking good, Elodie.'

The pitch of his voice went down half a semitone

to a deep burr that put her resolve to resist him in Critical Care. He was impossible to resist when he laid on the charm.

Elodie swallowed the choking lump of her pride, intrigued by his change of tactic. Intrigued by why he had set up this meeting under a false name and in a high-rise office tower that was on the other side of town from his London base. Intrigued to find out exactly what he was proposing. Office renovations aside, surely he could have contacted her without the need for pretence?

'Thank you.' She glanced behind her to locate the chair and sat—not because she wanted to do as he had commanded earlier, but because right then her legs were feeling decidedly unsteady. She positioned her leather purse on her lap, her fingers absently fidgeting with the silver clasp. 'You said you had something to discuss with me? A proposal?'

Lincoln rose from his perch on the edge of the desk and went back to sit in his office chair. He rolled the chair forward and then rested one of his forearms on the desk. His other hand reached for a sheaf of papers.

'A business proposal.' His gleaming eyes met hers and he added, 'You weren't expecting any other type of proposal, were you?'

Elodie schooled her features into cool impassivity. 'I can't imagine you'd be interested in repeating past mistakes.'

An inscrutable smile tilted one side of his mouth. 'I hear you're interested in some financial backing for your own evening wear label.' He drummed his fingers on the paperwork beneath his hand. 'Are you interested in hearing my terms?'

Elodie ran the tip of her tongue over her lips, aware of another moth-like flicker of excitement in her blood. Could this be her chance to fulfil her dream at last? She had never aspired to be a lingerie model, but she had played the role with aplomb. *Smart, successful, sassy, sophisticated* and *sexy* were the five words to describe her brand. A brand she had never intended adopting in the first place but had somehow drifted into. Lincoln was offering her an escape route—but he'd mentioned terms. What would they be? Dared she even ask? He was one of the most successful self-made businessmen in the country. He turned around ailing businesses within a year or two for a sizeable profit. Did he see her venture as a sure bet?

'You want to finance me? But…but why?'

He shrugged one broad shoulder, his expression as unreadable as a mask. 'I never allow emotions to get in the way of a good business deal.'

Did that mean he was confident she could succeed? How strange that he of all people believed in her potential. 'You think I can be successful?'

His gaze was suddenly laser-pointer-direct. 'Do you?'

'I…' Elodie chewed at the inside of her mouth and lowered her gaze from the penetrating heat of his. 'I think so.'

'Not good enough. You have to believe in yourself or no one else will.'

The chiding edge to his tone made her straighten her back in her chair. She brought her gaze back to his. 'I do believe in myself. I've wanted to get out of modelling for a while now. I want to prove I have more to offer the world than my looks.'

'A wishbone and a backbone are two different things. How much do you want it?'

She disguised a tiny swallow. 'More than anything.'

One dark eyebrow lifted over his mercurial gaze. 'Are you sure about that?'

Elodie lifted her chin, locking her gaze on his. 'Positive.'

Lincoln pushed the paperwork across the desk to her. 'Good. Because in here are my terms. You can read them at your leisure, but I can summarise them for you here and now if you like.'

Elodie laid her purse on the floor and took the sheaf of documents, but she knew it would take her ages to read through it carefully due to her dyslexia. And so did he. Not that he had ever made an issue of her learning problems in the past—if anything he had been surprisingly accommodating and understanding. It was another way he had charmed her into thinking he cared about her for more than her looks—more fool her.

'Please do.'

He leaned back in his chair, one forearm still resting on his desk. His posture was casual—almost too casual, given the searing intensity of his gaze. 'I'll put forward the necessary finance for you to launch your label.'

He named a sum that made her perfectly groomed eyebrows almost fly off her face. She knew he was wealthy, but surely that was a ridiculous amount of money to be offering her—especially given the way their relationship had ended.

Elodie rapid-blinked, her heart thumping like a hard fist against her ribcage. *Ba-boom. Ba-boom. Ba-boom.* 'But why would you want to do that?'

He held up a hand like a stop sign, his expression difficult to read. 'Allow me to state my terms without interruption.' He lowered his hand to the desk and continued. 'The money is yours if you'll agree to be my wife for six months.'

Elodie stared at him with her mind reeling, her pulse racing, her stomach freefalling. *His wife?* Was he joking? Was this some sort of candid camera prank? And why only six months? Wasn't a marriage meant to be for ever?

The money was more than enough to launch her label. Along with her own savings, the money would mean she would be able employ the necessary staff to help her achieve her dream. But to become his wife? To live with him, sleep with him, spend every day with him…? *Risk the chance of falling in love with him?*

She had come perilously close to losing herself in their relationship in the past.

Could she risk the same happening again?

Elodie narrowed her eyes and leaned forward to

place the papers back on his desk. 'Is this some kind of joke?'

Lincoln picked up a gold cartridge pen and rocked it back and forth between two of his long, tanned fingers. 'It's no joke.'

His gaze remained marksman-steady and it sent a shiver of reaction through her body. Could he see how much his presence unsettled her? Could he sense the magnetic power he still had over her? A power she fought to resist with every cell of her body...

She swallowed and tried not to stare at his fingers—tried not to recall how those fingers felt when they touched her, excited her, pleasured her. She forced her gaze back to his, her heart thumping so loudly she was surprised he couldn't hear it. 'You know I can't do that.'

He tossed the pen to one side and it rolled up against a glass paperweight with a soft tinkle that seemed overly loud in the silence. 'Your call. But I should warn you this offer is only open for twenty-four hours. After that, it's off the table and won't be repeated.'

Elodie rose from her chair in one agitated movement, her arms going around her middle. She wanted to slap him for being so arrogant as to think she would accept. She wanted to grab him by the front of his shirt and...and...press her mouth to... *No.* She slammed the brakes on her wayward thoughts. She did *not* want to go anywhere near his sensual mouth.

'I can't believe you're doing this. What can you possibly hope to achieve?'

'I need a wife for the period of six months. It's as simple as that.'

She curled her top lip. 'I'm sure you have plenty of willing candidates to choose from.'

'Ah, but I want you.'

The silky smoothness of his tone threatened to put her willpower on life support, but Elodie raised her chin at a defiant angle, determined to hold her ground for as long as she could.

'What about the woman I saw you with last time we ran in to each other? She looked like she was madly in love with you. I was surprised you could still breathe with her arms clasped around your neck like that.'

His smile was indolent, his eyes glinting. 'She was in love with me. And that's why she's not suitable for this position.'

Elodie frowned so hard even a hefty shot of Botox wouldn't have prevented her wrinkling her brow. 'I don't understand… Are you saying you don't want—?'

'I can hardly want someone to be in love with me if I only want them to be my wife for six months.'

Elodie stood behind the chair and grasped the back with both hands. Something low and deep in her belly was doing somersaults. Rapid somersaults that made her intimate muscles twitch in memory of his rock-hard presence.

'Why only six months?'

He rose from the desk and slipped off his jacket, hanging it on the back of his chair. His movements were methodical, precise, as if he were mentally preparing a speech. His expression was cast in lines of gravitas she was not used to seeing on his face.

'My mother is terminally ill. She wants to see me settled before she dies.'

Elodie's frown deepened to one of confusion. 'Your mother? But you told me your mother died a couple of months before we met.'

His lips moved in a grim smile—a stiff movement of his lips that had nothing to do with what a smile was meant to be. 'That was my adoptive mother. I only met my biological mother a couple of years ago.'

Her eyes widened and she became aware of a sharp pain underneath her heart. A burrowing pain that almost took her breath away. He was adopted? Why had he never mentioned it? She knew every inch of his body, knew how he took his coffee, what brand of suit he preferred, knew his taste in literature and film, knew how he looked when he came... But he had never told her one of the most important things about himself.

'You never told me you were adopted. Did you know when we were—?'

'I always knew I was adopted.'

'But you chose not to tell me, the woman you asked to be your wife?'

Anger laced her tone and the pain in her chest burrowed a little deeper, a little harder, as if working its way towards her backbone like a silent drill. Why hadn't he told her something as important as that? It only confirmed the suspicions she'd had all along—he hadn't been in love with her. He'd been attracted to her, but love hadn't come into it at all. He had chosen her for her looks, not for *her*.

And wasn't that the miserable story of her life?

# CHAPTER TWO

'But you chose *not* to be my wife, remember?' Lincoln said, with an edge of bitterness that even after all these years he couldn't quite quell. Nor did he want to. His bitterness had fuelled the phenomenal success he'd achieved in the seven years since Elodie Campbell had left him standing at the altar.

He would never admit it to her, but she had actually done him a favour by jilting him. It had galvanised him, motivated him to build an empire that rivalled some of the largest in England, if not the world. He had quadrupled his income, built his assets into an enviable portfolio that gave him the sort of security most people only dreamed about. Aiming for success had always been his passion, a driving force in his personality, but her rejection had amped up his drive to a whole new level. Everything he touched turned to gleaming gold. He *made* it do so. Nothing stood in his way when he was on a mission to achieve a goal.

Nothing and no one.

But seeing her again stirred other feelings in him that were equally difficult to ignore. Feelings he had squashed, buried, disposed of with ruthless determination.

Her beauty had always been captivating. Her long wavy red-gold hair hung halfway down her back like a mermaid's. Her heart-shaped face with its aristocratic cheekbones, retroussé nose and uptilted bee-stung mouth gave her a haughty, untouchable air that had drawn him from the first moment he'd met her. Her body was slender, and yet her feminine curves made him ache to skim his hands over them as he'd used to do.

She was strong-willed and feisty, passionate and impulsive, and no one had ever excited him or stood up to him as much as her. He had never forgotten the thrill of arguing with her. A fight with her had not been just a fight—it had been a full-on war that always ended explosively in bed. He got hard just thinking about it.

No one had ever pushed back against him the way Elodie did.

And no one had ever humiliated him the way she had.

The business proposal he was offering now was his way of ruling a line underneath their relationship. If she accepted his terms he would be the one to end their relationship this time. He had loved her and lost her, and he would never give her, or indeed anyone, the power to make a fool of him again.

Elodie moved away from the chair she was holding on to and wrapped her arms around her middle. 'It seems my decision to jilt you was the right one.'

She threw him a glance so frosty he wished he hadn't taken off his jacket. 'How could you have withheld something so important from me?'

Lincoln shrugged one shoulder. 'It wasn't something I talked about to anyone.'

'But why? Were you ashamed of it? Were you upset at being relinquished as a baby?'

'I was neither ashamed nor upset.'

Lincoln had known since he was old enough to understand the concept that he had been adopted. His adoptive parents had been loving and supportive parents and his childhood mostly happy. He had also known his younger brother and sister were his parents' biological children. But instead of feeling pushed aside and less important, he had been reassured by his parents that he was the reason they had been able to have their own biological children. That their love and nurturing of him had unlocked their unexplained infertility.

'But while we're on the subject of withholding information—why did you choose to run away on our wedding day instead of talking to me about your concerns? You've never adequately explained your actions, and nor have you apologised to me face to face.'

Twin circles of colour bloomed in her cheeks and her gaze slipped out of reach of his. 'I'm sorry if you were embarrassed. I—I just couldn't go through with it.'

Lincoln let out a stiff curse. 'The least you could have done is told me to my face. It would have saved a lot of unnecessary expense.'

'Oh, so it was the money angle that upset you the most?' Her voice had a cutting edge, her blue gaze flashing fire. 'You were the one who wanted a big wedding and insisted on paying for everything.'

'Only because I didn't want to put that sort of load on your mother. I knew your father wouldn't help out.'

Elodie bent down to pick up her purse off the floor near her chair, her long glossy hair momentarily hiding her expression. She straightened and shook her hair back over her shoulders. 'I have to go.'

He ached to run those silken strands through his fingers, to lift handfuls of her fragrant hair to his nose and breathe in her exotic scent. It had taken him months to get rid of the smell of her perfume in his house, even though he had instructed his housekeeper to remove every trace of Elodie. Every room had seemed to hold a hint of her distinctive scent, lingering there to silently mock him.

*Look what happens when you fall in love. You are left with nothing but memories to taunt you.*

'I want your answer by five p.m. tomorrow.'

Her defiant gaze met his and a lightning bolt of lust slammed into his groin. 'I gave you my answer. It's an emphatic, don't-embarrass-yourself-by-asking-me-again *no*.'

Lincoln leaned his hip against the corner of his desk and folded his arms across his chest. He hadn't expected her to say yes at the first meeting. It wasn't in her nature to do anything without a fight and, frankly, he admired that about her. But seeing her again had proved to him she wasn't immune to him, and that gave him the assurance that she would eventually agree to his terms.

That he wasn't immune to her was an issue he would have to address at some point. He would not allow her the same sensual power she'd had over him in the past. The sensual power that had made him propose marriage within a couple of months of meeting her. The stunning physicality of their relationship had blindsided him to the reality of her using him, rather than loving him. She had said the words but she had still bolted. That was not love—that was betrayal of the highest order. And he would not allow it to happen again.

'Don't let your emotions get in the way. I can help you achieve your dream. It can be a win-win for both of us.'

'Why are you doing this?'

'I told you—I need a temporary wife.'

'But marrying someone you don't love and who doesn't love you is hardly honouring your biological mother in the final weeks or months of her life. Won't she be able to tell it's not a love match?'

'Nina Smith knows you jilted me seven years ago. She's a hopeless romantic who believes I'll never be happy until we get back together. She disapproves of my playboy lifestyle and wants to see me settled before she passes on.' His mouth stretched into a cynical smile and he added, 'You were good at pretending to love me in the past. I'm sure you'll do an excellent job this time around—especially given the amount of money I'd be paying you.'

Her lips were tightly compressed. 'If—and it's a big if—if I accept your offer, I won't sleep with you.'

Lincoln pushed himself away from his desk and picked up the sheaf of papers, held them out to her. 'You won't be required to. It's written in the contract. You'll find it on page three.'

She took the papers from him as if he was handing her a dangerous animal. She laid them on the desk and began to read painstakingly through the pages. Then her eyes rounded and she lifted her gaze back to his. 'A paper marriage?'

Lincoln smiled a victor's smile. 'Won't that be fun?'

Later, Elodie would barely recall leaving Lincoln's office. She'd only vaguely remember stalking past the smartly dressed receptionist and getting into the lift. Her mind was numb all the way down to the ground floor. It was still barely functioning by the time she met her twin, Elspeth, for coffee in Notting Hill half an hour later.

'I was about to give up on you,' Elspeth said as soon as Elodie dropped into the chair opposite with a thump. 'Hey, are you okay? You look a little flustered. What's wrong?'

'Sorry I'm so late.' Elodie placed her purse on the table. 'My meeting ran over time.'

'How did it go?'

Elodie was reluctant to share every detail of the meeting with her twin, even though they were close. It was still too raw.

Lincoln didn't want to sleep with her. It was to be a paper marriage.

The one thing they had got right about their relationship was sex. They'd been dynamite together. No one could ever say there had been something wrong with their sex life. They'd been more than compatible. Why, then, did he want a hands-off arrangement? Did it mean he would have someone else on the side? That she would be humiliated by him conducting numerous affairs under her nose?

'It was…interesting.'

Elspeth leaned forward, her eyes bright. 'So, what was this Mr Smith like? Was he keen to back your label?'

'He was very keen.'

'So why are you frowning?'

Elodie let out a sigh and poured herself a glass of water from the bottle on the table. 'Mr Smith is an alias.' She glanced at her twin's intrigued expression and added, 'It was Lincoln.'

Elspeth's eyebrows shot up. 'Lincoln?'

'Yup. He wants to back my label.'

'Wow.' Elspeth sat back in her chair, her expression puzzled. 'Why would he want to do that?'

Elodie gave her a look. 'Because he wants something in exchange.'

She couldn't keep this to herself any longer. Raw as it still was, she had to talk it through with someone, and who better than her twin?

'Me.'

Elspeth's eyes rounded to the size of the saucer

under her coffee cup. 'He wants you back? Oh, how romantic. I always thought he still had feelings for you, and—'

Elodie pursed her lips and shifted them from side to side. 'Not exactly. He wants me to marry him for six months. A paper marriage.'

Elspeth's mouth dropped open. 'A paper marriage? You mean no sleeping together? Seriously? What did you say?'

'I said no.'

'No?'

Elodie frowned. 'Why are you looking at me like that? Do you think I should agree to such a preposterous proposal?'

'I guess if you said yes it would give you both time to sort out your differences. There's clearly unfinished business between you. And if he's going to finance your label—well, surely that's a bonus?'

Elodie leaned her elbows on the table and, bending forward, rested her forehead on her splayed fingertips. 'Argh! I hate that man *so* much. I thought I knew him so well, and yet he kept one of the most important things about himself from me.'

She lifted her head out of her hands and filled her twin in on the circumstances behind Lincoln's proposal.

'I knew I was right to jilt him. This proves it. He didn't allow me to know him. The *real* him.'

Elspeth stroked a gentle hand over Elodie's wrist. 'If you can't bear the thought of accepting the money from him, then let Mack help you. He's happy to finance your label and—'

Elodie raised her face from her hands and sat up straighter in her chair. The thought had crossed her mind before, but she knew she could never ask her twin's fiancé for financial help. She wanted to keep her financial affairs separate and under her control.

'No. I can't accept money from Mack. I have twenty-four hours before I have to give my final answer to Lincoln.' She drummed her fingers on the table for a moment, her thoughts going around on a hamster's wheel. 'You know, there could be a positive spin on this... Imagine the press exposure I'd get if I went back to Lincoln. Who doesn't love a romantic reunion story? The news of us getting back together would go viral. It would boost my profile enormously. Lincoln said it could be a win-win, but I didn't see how until just now.' She beamed at her twin. 'He thinks he has me under his control, but he's in for a big surprise.'

Elspeth chewed at her lower lip, her face etched in lines of concern. 'I hope you know what you're doing.'

Elodie tossed her hair back over her shoulders. 'I know exactly what I'm doing. And, what's more, I can't wait to do it.'

Elodie dressed carefully for her follow-up meeting with Lincoln. She wasn't vain, but she knew the good-looks fairy had been especially generous to her and her twin. And years of being in hair and make-up sessions had given her skills that rivalled some of the top professionals.

Her make-up highlighted the blue of her eyes and the updo of her hair showcased the slim length of her neck. She put on diamond droplet earrings—a gift from one of the lingerie designers. She slipped on an emerald-green designer dress gifted to her after a photo shoot. It came to just above her knee and had a deep cleavage.

She smoothed the close-fitting dress over her slim hips and turned from side to side in front of her full-length mirror. Lincoln might think he could keep her at arm's length, but she had a point to prove. A point to win. A score to settle. He might not have ever loved her, but he'd desired her with a ferocity she knew she could trigger in him again. She'd seen the way he'd looked at her, his scorching gaze running over her body, the way he'd kept glancing at her mouth.

She smiled at her reflection. 'Let's see how long you can keep your hands off me now, Lincoln Lancaster.'

Lincoln was reading through some paperwork in his home office when he caught sight of Elodie on the security camera screen on his desk. He dropped the pen he was holding and stared at her for a long moment, drinking in her feminine form like a badly dehydrated man might stare at a long, cool glass of water, hardly daring to believe it was real.

She was dressed in a stunning green dress that left little to the imagination—and he didn't need much imagination, because he remembered every sexy curve of her body. He had explored and tasted every inch of it, and spent many a night since their breakup aching to do so again. No one had ever worked him up as much as Elodie Campbell. And that irritated the hell out of him.

The desire to settle down had come upon him the moment he'd met her. At twenty-one, she'd been bright and funny and wildly entertaining. He'd been twenty-eight years old, and still reeling from the sudden death of his adoptive mother. Falling fast and hard for Elodie had made him long to recreate the secure family unit he had grown up with. And watching his father slide into a deep depression had only reinforced Lincoln's desire to settle down. He'd figured it would offer his dad some hope for the future—a beautiful daughter-in-law, grandkids at some point…

Elodie's energy and vitality had lifted him out of his own funk of grief and within a couple of months he'd found himself on bended knee with an expensive diamond ring in his hand. He had never been the impulsive, spur-of-the-moment type, but something about her bewitching personality had unlocked the armour around his heart.

It was a decision he had come to regret, and bitterly, but now he had the power to end their relationship—this time around on his terms.

The only thing he was grateful for was he had never actually told her he loved her out loud. He had shown it in a thousand ways, but saying the words had been difficult for him. Elodie, on the other hand, had professed to love him many times—which just showed how empty those three little words could be. They were cheap, and overused, and he had been fooled by them, but he would not allow himself to be taken in by them again.

Elodie used people to get where she wanted to go, and she had used him callously and deceptively. She had been a virtual unknown before her fling with him, but her career had taken off after she'd jilted him. She had ruthlessly used him to get the social exposure she'd craved. That was the thing that niggled at him the most—she had used *his* public humiliation to launch her career.

Now she needed him in her quest for a career-change and he was happy to help. More than happy to help. Because this time around he would call the shots. Each and every one of them. Or die trying.

Elodie shifted her weight from foot to foot, annoyed that Lincoln was keeping her waiting again. She knew he was home, for his top-model sports car was parked in the driveway and there were lights on in his Victorian mansion.

She pressed her finger on the bell once more and looked directly into the security camera positioned above the entrance. She considered waving, but then the stained-glass and glossy black arched double front doors suddenly opened automatically, and she stepped inside.

The doors whispered shut behind her with a barely audible click, somehow giving her a vague sense of being imprisoned. She shook off the sensation and straightened her shoulders. She wasn't one to be intimidated by anyone or anything—even if this house did hold some memories she wished she could forget. Disturbingly sexy memories that made her body feel hot all over.

'Hello?' Elodie's voice echoed eerily in the spacious foyer.

The floor was light-coloured Italian marble with grey flecks and the walls a chalk-white. From the high ceiling hung a large crystal chandelier, and a grand sweeping staircase with black balustrading wound its way to the upper floors. A walnut and brass inlaid drum table with curved pedestal legs was positioned in front of the staircase, and a cymbidium orchid in luscious full bloom was situated on top, with a selection of hardback wildlife and wilderness books.

On the other side of the foyer there was a large brass inlaid dresser with twin crystal lamps either side of a gold-framed mirror that made the area seem even more spacious. Another orchid was positioned between the lamps, and either side of the dresser were two dark grey velvet wing chairs, which gave a welcoming and balanced feel to the formal entrance.

The sound of a footfall on the staircase brought her gaze up and she watched as Lincoln came towards her. She was glad it was him and not his crotchety old housekeeper, who had never made her feel welcome in the past. Hopefully Mean Morag had long gone.

Lincoln was wearing casual latte-coloured chinos with a light blue open-necked casual shirt that made the blue in his eyes dominate the green. The shirt was rolled halfway up his strong tanned forearms, the rich dusting of masculine hair spreading from his arms to the backs of his hands and along each of his fingers reminding her of the potent male hormones surging through his body.

'I've been expecting you.'

His voice held a trace of amusement, and she wondered how long he had been watching her via the security camera.

'It took you long enough to open the door.' Elodie threw him a churlish look. 'I was freezing my butt off out there.'

His eyes ran over her outfit from head to toe, lingering a moment on the deep valley of her cleavage. 'Then maybe you should have worn a coat.'

And spoil the knock-his-socks-off effect? No way.

Elodie sent her gaze around the foyer once more. 'You've redecorated since I was here last.'

No doubt he'd gone to great expense to rid his house of every trace of her. She seemed to recall he'd had a fling with an interior designer a few years ago. One of many glamourous women he'd been seen out and about with in the seven years since their cancelled wedding. Lincoln could barely change his brand of toothpaste without the press commenting on it, which was why her decision to accept his proposal would be so lucrative and important for launching her label.

'What do you think?' he asked.

She gave an indifferent shrug. 'It's nice enough.'

Lincoln's smile was sardonic, making her wonder if he could read her mind. 'Would you like a drink?'

'Sure.'

He led the way to a grand sitting room off the foyer, which had three large windows on one side overlooking the formal garden. A large sofa and matching armchairs were positioned in the middle of the room on a luxurious rug that left a wide boundary of the parquet floor on show. The grand fireplace had a large mirror above the mantelpiece and another crystal chandelier hung from the ceiling. Lamps were tastefully situated between each of the three large windows, on antique tables, and there were fresh flowers on the round coffee table in front of the sofa and chairs.

Elodie plonked herself down on one of the chairs and crossed her legs, watching as Lincoln went to a cleverly hidden drinks cabinet complete with fridge on the wall further along from the fireplace. 'Have you still got the same housekeeper?'

'I have, actually.' Lincoln took out a bottle of champagne and set it on the top of the cabinet with two tall crystal flutes. 'Will that be a problem for you?'

Elodie inspected her nails rather than meet his gaze. 'Why should it be?'

He popped the cork on the champagne. 'I seem to recall you and Morag never quite hit it off.' He proceeded to pour dancing bubbles into the two glasses.

'That's because she didn't respect me. I was your partner…your fiancée. But behind your back she treated me like I was gold-digging trailer trash. It was one of the first things she said to me when I met her. "You're only after his money and fame".'

That she had benefited from that fame after their breakup was neither here nor there, in her mind. Elodie had not agreed to marry him for any other reason than she wanted to be with him. Because... Because she'd been a silly little fool back then, who'd thought lust equalled love.

A taut line formed around Lincoln's mouth, as if he recalled every heated argument they'd used to have over his housekeeper. 'Perhaps you didn't treat her with the respect she deserved.'

He came over with the two glasses of champagne, handing one to her. Elodie did everything she could to avoid touching his fingers as she took the glass, but in spite of her efforts a tingle shot up her arm when his fingers brushed hers.

'Or perhaps she always knew you weren't going to stick around.'

Elodie made a snorting noise and took a generous sip of her champagne. 'She was just plain rude to me. She should have retired years ago.'

'Elodie.' The was a heavy note of censure in his tone and a frown was carved deep into his forehead.

She gave a nonchalant shrug and took another sip of champagne. 'So, aren't you going to ask me what I've decided about your proposal?'

Lincoln sat opposite her on the large sofa and stretched one of his strongly muscled arms along the back. 'I already know what you've decided. You wouldn't be here if your answer was still a flat-out no.'

Elodie circled one of her ankles round and round, not sure she was comfortable with him being able to read her so well. 'I've thought it through and I agree with you. It can be win-win for both of us—especially with the on-paper-only clause.' She raised her glass in a mock toast, painting a sugar-sweet smile on her lips. 'I would never have accepted without that.'

Lincoln rose from the sofa and placed his champagne glass on the coffee table between them with a thud. He straightened and nailed her with his gaze. 'There are some ground rules we need to establish from the get-go. Just because we don't sleep with each other doesn't mean we sleep with anyone else during the duration of our marriage. Is that clear?'

Elodie raised her eyebrows and whistled through her teeth. 'My, oh, my... That's going to be harder for you than me, isn't it? Celibacy isn't quite your thing, as I recall. You had someone else in your bed within a week of our cancelled wedding.'

His jaw became granite-hard. 'And that rankled, did it?'

'Nope.' She injected her tone with insouciance. 'I didn't want you, so why would I be upset someone else did?'

His eyes bored into hers with the intensity of an industrial strength drill, but Elodie was determined not to look away first. The tension in the air was palpable. A vibrating, pulsating tension that travelled along the invisible waves of silence like an electric current.

'But you want me now.' A cynical smile slanted his mouth and his eyes glinted challengingly.

Elodie laughed and tipped back her head. She drained her champagne glass, then leaned forward to set it on the coffee table next to his. 'Actually, I think you've got that the wrong way around. It's you who wants me.'

'And you know this because…?'

Elodie rose from the sofa and sashayed over to where he was standing, driven by an irresistible and recklessly rebellious urge to make him eat his words. She stood right in front of him and, locking her gaze on his, slid her hands up his muscular chest to rest on the tops of his impossibly broad shoulders. She breathed in the intoxicating scent of him—the wood and citrus and salty male scent that sent her senses into a tailspin. His eyes were hooded, his expression inscrutable, but she could sense a palpable tension in him.

'I know this because of the way you look at me.' She ran her index finger down the straight blade of his nose. 'It's the way you've always looked at me. Like you want to lick every inch of my body.' She kept her voice husky and whisper-soft, her gaze sultry.

He drew in a breath and let it out in a jagged stream. 'I told you the rules.'

Elodie moved a little closer, so her breasts brushed against his chest. A wave of incendiary heat swept through her at the contact, making her inner core contract with longing. She lifted her finger to his lips, tracing the sensual shape with deliberate slowness. 'You know all about me and rules.'

Lincoln grasped her by the upper arms in a hold that hinted at the coiled tension in his body. His eyes were diamond-hard, his expression grimly determined. 'We're not doing this.' The words were bitten out through tight lips.

Elodie stood on tiptoe, which pressed her breasts even more firmly against his chest. Her mouth was so close to his she could feel the warm waft of his breath mingling intimately with hers. 'But we both want to, don't we?'

She brushed her lips against his firm ones but he didn't respond. Goaded by his intractability, she pressed her lips on his and then slowly stroked her tongue along the seam of his mouth. He smothered a groan-cum-curse deep in his throat and crushed his mouth to hers.

It was a kiss that contained so many things—unruly and fiery passion, frustration, and even a little anger. Elodie didn't care. All she wanted was his mouth on hers, working its old magic on her senses. His tongue entered her mouth with a commanding thrust so like the way he'd used to enter her body she almost came on the spot. The taste of him was so familiar it triggered a firestorm of lust in her flesh. She groaned against his lips, winding her arms around his neck, needing, wanting, aching to be closer to the hard ridge of his erection.

No one could turn her on like Lincoln. No one. His touch was so electric, his kiss so explosively passionate, she had no hope of resisting even if she'd wanted to.

But just as quickly as the kiss started it ended, as if a cord had suddenly been tugged out of an electric appliance.

Lincoln pulled away from her with a cynical smile. 'Not going to happen this time, baby.'

Elodie disguised her disappointment behind a cool smile. 'Let me guess—there's someone else? I hope you're not going to humiliate me by seeing her while you're married to me.'

'You're a fine one to accuse *me* of humiliation.' There was no mistaking the bitterness in his tone, or the rigid set of his jaw. 'I think you deserve the prize for that.'

Elodie wasn't proud of the way she had ended their relationship, but at the time it had seemed her only escape route. She had let things go too far without talking to Lincoln about her career plans and her worries over how their relationship would cope. How she would juggle being a wife with being a lingerie model.

He had said he wanted children at some point. Even his father had mentioned how much he was looking forward to grandchildren. But what would have happened to her career if she'd got pregnant sooner rather than later? At the age of twenty-one, having children wasn't even on her radar. And even now, at twenty-eight, she still hadn't heard a single peep from her biological clock. Her career was her focus. Her drive and ambition left no room for anything else.

'I understand how embarrassing it must have been for—'

'But it achieved what you wanted it to achieve, didn't it? You were a nobody until you got involved with me. Jilting me got you the press attention you always wanted, and you built your career off the back of it.'

Elodie stared at him speechlessly for a long moment, her mind whirling like clothes in a tumble dryer. He thought she had *used* him? That nothing about her involvement with him had been more than a tactical move to gain fame? That might be her plan now, but back then she *had* loved him. Truly loved him. Had told him so many times. Her feelings for him had been overwhelming—so much so they had contributed to her rash decision to jilt him.

She had sensed that if she married him, her career would never be a priority. Her priority would be him. His priority would never be her. To Lincoln, all she would have been was a trophy wife. He had never told her he loved her, and until the last moment she had been too star-struck by him to see that was a problem—an alarm bell she should have paid far more attention to. She had fooled herself into believing he was one of those men who wasn't comfortable with expressing his emotions. She had fooled herself into thinking he actually *felt* the emotions just because their lovemaking was so incredible.

But complete strangers could have incredible sex—love had nothing to do with it.

Elodie walked over to the drinks cabinet, where Lincoln had left the champagne bottle, and brought it over to refill her glass. She placed the bottle down on the coffee table and sent him a sideways glance. 'I find it highly amusing that you're accusing me of using you when all you wanted was for me to be a trophy wife, a bit of arm candy to show off to all your friends and business associates. You didn't love me.'

Lincoln compressed his mouth into a flat line. 'At least we're equal on that score. Love was never a part of our relationship.'

There—he had admitted it. He had never loved her. Elodie did everything in her power to disguise the pain his words evoked. But then she had always been good at masking her emotions, and if she couldn't mask them she ran away from them.

Growing up with a twin with a life-threatening nut allergy had taught her how to play down her panic, to keep cool under pressure, never to show the turmoil she was actually feeling at the thought of losing her sister. In a perverse kind of way, she had adopted a devil-may-care approach to life. And her rebellious streak had strengthened as her mother's overzealous attention had focussed more and more on her twin. Negative attention was better than no attention, and it was a pattern that had followed her through life.

'I'd like to know more about what you expect of me during our six months marriage,' she said, with no trace of the turmoil she was feeling. 'What are our living arrangements, for instance?'

Lincoln picked up his glass of barely touched champagne but didn't drink from it. 'We'll live together but have separate rooms.'

Elodie raised her brows. 'And what's your housekeeper going to think about that?'

Would she have to endure more rejection? More stinging little asides from the housekeeper about how she wasn't good enough for Lincoln and never would be? Words that had been reinforced by the rejection of her father and everyone else who had never believed in her and only seen value in her looks, not in her as a person.

'She'll think what I pay her to think.'

'You're not worried she might leak the truth about our relationship to the press?'

'No.'

Elodie twirled the contents of her champagne glass, her eyes still trained on his masklike expression. 'What about when either of us needs to travel for work? Are you going to come with me and expect me to come with you?'

'We'll be together as much as possible, when work and other commitments allow.'

Elodie wondered what his 'other commitments' might be. For a man with such a healthy and robust sexual appetite, she couldn't imagine him taking on celibacy for six days, let alone six months. And how would she cope with living with him in close proximity? Especially given their passionate history? The sexual chemistry between them was ever-present. It was like a current in the air...a humming, buzzing frequency that sent tingles all over her flesh.

She took a sip of her champagne and then asked, 'Are we having a big wedding? I mean, it would look more romantic and convincing if we—'

'No.' The word was delivered bluntly. 'We'll be married in a register office with only two witnesses.'

'No press?'

His gaze was steely. Impenetrable. 'I'll make an announcement once we are officially married.'

'And when will that be?'

'Tomorrow.'

Elodie widened her eyes, felt her heart slipping sideways in her chest. 'That soon? Don't you have to get a license and stuff?'

'Already done.'

How had he been so confident of her agreeing to his proposal? Did he think she still had feelings for him? Feelings he could take advantage of to suit his own ends? But her feelings for him were in deep freeze. She had locked her heart in a block of ice that was resistant to his charm. She could not afford to fall for him again.

'You were so sure I'd say yes?'

'I've learned that nothing is ever a certainty with you, but let's say I was quietly confident.'

'You do know I'm only doing it for the money, don't you?'

His half-smile was cynical. 'But of course.'

Elodie put her glass down and tucked a loose

strand of hair behind her ear. 'And when do I get to meet your mother?'

'The following day. We'll fly to Spain and spend a couple of days there.'

'She lives in Spain? Is she Spanish, or—?'

'English. But she enjoys the warmer climate there. It's where she wants to spend the rest of her days.'

'What if it doesn't suit me to fly to Spain?' Elodie asked, not sure she wanted to agree to his plans without some token resistance, even though Spain was one of her favourite destinations and she was increasingly intrigued to meet the woman who had given Lincoln up as a baby.

What had been her reasons? Her circumstances? What had made her feel she had no choice but to hand her baby over to others to rear?

'People will expect us to have a short honeymoon. And I'd prefer you to meet Nina as soon as possible. Her health is unreliable. Her doctors can't seem to agree on how long she's got.'

Elodie could only imagine how sad it must have been for him to have finally found his birth mother, only to face the prospect of losing her all over again. He obviously cared about her, otherwise why go to the trouble and inconvenience of marrying his ex-fiancée, the woman who had publicly humiliated him seven years ago?

Elodie wanted to make a good impression on Nina—not for Lincoln's sake but for the woman herself. But how could she, given the train wreck of their history? How much had he told his birth mother about her? And what if Nina had already done her own research? The internet was full of the scandals that clung to her name, with the latest one naming her as the 'other woman' in a misnamed 'love triangle' that had seen a society wedding cancelled—eerily, like hers had been—at the altar.

Her twin, Elspeth, had been there, in a twin-switch, because Elodie had had a financial meeting that meant she hadn't been able to get there for the rehearsal in time. Then the meeting had been extended, which had given her the perfect excuse not to go to the wedding at all. She had dreaded the fallout if the bride had ever found out she'd had a one-night stand with the groom...

The only good to come out of it had been Elspeth meeting the groom's older brother, Mack MacDiarmid, and now they were happily in love and getting married in a month's time.

'But what if Nina doesn't like me?'

'She'll love you, because she believes you to be the love of my life.'

Elodie couldn't hold back another frown. 'Is that what you told her?'

His expression was unreadable. 'It's what she wants to believe.' He lifted his glass to his lips and drained the contents. He lowered the glass to the coffee table with a definitive thud and added, 'And you will do everything in your power to make sure she continues to believe it. Understood?'

Elodie gave him a mocking salute. 'Loud and clear.'

Lincoln held her defiant gaze for a beat or two. 'I'll pick you up at ten in the morning. Pack what you need for the time being, and anything else can be picked up later. I'll cover the rent on your flat for six months. The ceremony isn't until twelve, but we have some legal paperwork to see to first. And I'd appreciate it if you'd keep up appearances with all your friends and family and associates. We'll have a dinner celebration here with my family—and yours, if they can make it. I know it's short notice, but I don't want anyone to suspect our relationship isn't the real deal in case it gets back to Nina.'

'You mean lie to them?'

'I'm sure it won't impinge on your conscience too badly.' He flicked an invisible piece of lint off his rolled-up sleeve and continued, 'I heard about your deception at Fraser MacDiarmid's wedding. It created quite a scandal. How did Elspeth cope with pretending to be you for the weekend?'

'She got herself engaged to Mack MacDiarmid, so I'd say very well indeed. But that raises another issue. Their wedding's in a month's time, and since you and I'll be married you'll be expected to be there with me. It's likely to be a big affair. Will you be able to act like a devoted husband who's madly in love with his wife?'

'I'll do my best.'

'And we'll have to share a room if everyone thinks we're in love and sleeping together.'

The thought of it sent a tremor of unease through her body. Not because she was worried he would take advantage of such a situation, but because she wasn't sure she could resist him if he did. There was a particular intimacy about sharing a room, even if not sharing a bed. Taking turns to use the bathroom, dressing and undressing and moving about the space they shared... It would stir a host of memories she had spent the last seven years doing her level best to forget.

Lincoln's smile didn't reach his eyes. 'We will have to give the appearance of being in an intimate relationship at all times and in all places. And, judging from your kiss a few minutes ago, that's not going to be too hard for you to achieve.'

'That kiss was hardly one-sided. I thought you were going to make—'

'I wasn't.' His tone was adamant and it cut her like a knife. 'I meant what I said about the rules. A paper marriage is a lot easier to dissolve than a consummated one. Once the six months is up we'll get a simple annulment and move on with our lives.'

He made it sound so simple, so clinical, when her feelings about him and their arrangement were anything but. Six months as his wife on paper. Six months acting the role of devoted intimate partner. But another way of looking at it was to think of it as six months building her career, making the most of the time to launch her own label. Being Lincoln's wife would lift her profile like nothing else could.

*His wife...* How those words made her insides tighten with unruly desire.

Elodie leaned down to pick up her purse. 'I'd better get going. I'll need my beauty sleep for the big day tomorrow.'

Lincoln placed a hand on her wrist as she straightened. 'I won't be made a fool of twice.'

She held his determined gaze, her skin tingling where his fingers curled around the slender bones of her wrist. 'Nor will I.' She brushed off his hand with a stiff smile. 'Let's leave the intimate touching for when there's an audience, shall we? Or have you already changed your mind?'

A devilish glint appeared in his eyes. 'If I do, you'll be the first to know.'

# CHAPTER THREE

ELODIE TOOK OVER an hour to decide what to wear for her wedding day. *Her wedding day.* What a mockery those words were in the context in which she was becoming Lincoln Lancaster's wife.

Her wedding day seven years ago had involved a team of hair and make-up experts, a designer gown and a hand-embroidered veil that had had a train two metres long. Her bridesmaids, including her twin, Elspeth, had attended her, along with a cute flower girl and a cheeky little boy who had been ring bearer. The church, complete with an angelic-sounding choir, had been packed with guests and flowers.

A fairy tale setting without the happy ending.

She didn't like to think too deeply about her regrets over how she'd ended her relationship with Lincoln. She knew she had hurt her mother and her twin—especially Elspeth, who'd had received a lot of undeserved criticism when everyone had assumed she must have known something.

But even Elodie hadn't truly known what she was going to do until she'd done it. It had been an impulsive decision that, at the time, had felt like her only option. She suspected the only hurt she had inflicted on Lincoln was to his pride. He hadn't been in love with her, so it wasn't as if his heart had been shattered by her jilting him. But even so, she did feel a twinge of guilt that she had bolted without talking to him face to face.

And now she was facing another wedding day with Lincoln. But what had changed in seven years? He still didn't love her, and he was only marrying her to give his birth mother her dying wish to see him settled. Elodie couldn't help feeling compromised about lying to someone who had so little time left. What if his mother saw through their act? What if his mother was like his housekeeper and disliked her on sight?

The streak of rebelliousness in Elodie's nature had her reaching for a black dress for their wedding. But then she thought of Lincoln's mother and changed her mind, and chose a cream one instead. There would be photos of the event, and no doubt they would go online. She couldn't afford for anything to look amiss—especially when she hoped to use her marriage to Lincoln as a platform to build her own success.

She made sure her hair and make-up were perfect, and she put on pearl earrings and a pearl necklace that teamed nicely with the classic cut of her calf-length dress.

The doorbell sounded and Elodie took a deep calming breath and addressed herself in the mirror. 'You can do this.'

\* \* \*

The door opened and Lincoln's breath stalled in his throat. Elodie didn't have to try too hard to look stunning at the best of times, but right now she could have stopped traffic. Air traffic. Her cream dress had a swirly skirt with a chiffon overlay that fell to her shapely calves, and the upper part of the outfit clung to her curves in all the right places. Places he had touched, kissed and caressed in the past and wanted desperately to do so again.

His continued desire for her was a problem, given the terms of their marriage. He wanted no complications, and sleeping with Elodie Campbell would be one hell of a complication. Not because it wouldn't be exciting, thrilling and deeply satisfying—because it would be all that and more. But sleeping with her in the past had made him fall in love with her, and he couldn't allow his feelings to be triggered again. Besides, he was only allowing six months for their marriage. His mother's doctors hadn't been precise on her expected lifespan, but they had all agreed it would be a matter of three or four months, tops.

'You look stunning,' he managed to say once he could get his voice to work.

'I dragged this old thing out of the back of the wardrobe,' Elodie said. 'I figured you wouldn't want me to wear my old wedding dress.'

Lincoln frowned. 'Do you still have it?'

A fleeting sheepish look came over her face. 'It was custom-made and cost a fortune.'

'You could have sold it.'

'Nah, too much trouble.' She turned to collect her purse and keys and her phone off the small hall table. 'I keep it as a reminder not to do stupid things.'

'Do you still have your engagement ring?'

She turned to look at him with a frown pulling at her brow. 'I took it back to your house. Didn't you find it?'

'When did you bring it?'

'I dropped it off after I left the church when I… left. No one was home, so I used my key and left that as well, with a note.'

Lincoln wasn't sure he should believe her. The ring had been ridiculously expensive, and would have fetched a decent sum if she had sold it. He hadn't specifically asked for it back. He hadn't been interested in any contact with her after that humiliating day. But it had niggled at him all these years that she hadn't done the decent thing and at least offered to return it. And if she had returned it, why hadn't his housekeeper mentioned it? Surely Morag would have found it in her spring-cleaning efforts the following day? Trusting Elodie was not something he was prepared to do.

He slipped his hand inside his jacket pocket and took out a ring box and handed it to her. 'Just as well I have a backup.'

Elodie took the ring box from him, her forehead still cast in a small frown. She prised open the lid and stared at the classic halo diamond ring he had chosen. It was far simpler than the one he had purchased for her seven years ago, but no less expensive.

Money wasn't an issue for him when he had a goal to achieve. And making Elodie his wife for six months was his primary goal.

'Aren't you going to try it on?'

'Sure.' Elodie took the ring out and handed him back the box. She slipped the ring over her finger and held her hand up to the light to inspect the quality of the diamond. 'It's lovely. But I'll definitely give it back to you in person once we end our marriage.'

Lincoln held her gaze for a beat. 'No. You can keep it as a souvenir—like the wedding dress.'

She gave him a defiant look. 'I'm not the sentimental type.'

He gave a crooked smile and leaned down to pick up the two large suitcases near the door. She had never been one to travel light. 'Come on. We have some paperwork to sign before we get married.'

'You mean a pre-nuptial agreement? That sort of thing?' Elodie said on her way with him to his car.

'We both have assets to protect. As I said before—it will make an annulment a lot less complicated.'

'You didn't get me to sign one seven years ago.' There was an accusatory note in her voice.

'I didn't have as many assets back then, and nor did we actually get married, so it's a moot point.'

'But what if we had got married and subsequently divorced? Weren't you taking a risk by not insisting on a pre-nup?'

Lincoln shrugged one shoulder and opened the passenger door for her. 'Maybe I trusted you back then.'

'But you don't now?'

A wounded look came into her blue eyes. He held her gaze for a pulsing moment. 'Trust has to be earned once it's been broken.'

'I was never unfaithful to you. And I did bring back your damn engagement ring.'

She got into the passenger seat and swished the skirt of her dress out of the way, her expression stormy.

Lincoln closed the door of the car and walked around to the driver's side. He slipped in beside her and pulled down his seatbelt, clipped it into place. He turned to look at her, but she had turned her head to look the other way.

'Elodie, look at me.'

'No.'

He reached out his hand and captured her small, neat chin, gently turned her to face him. He frowned at the shimmer of tears in her eyes. He blotted an escaping one with the pad of his thumb.

'Tears?'

He couldn't keep the surprise out of his voice. He had never seen her cry—not even when they'd had furious arguments with each other in the past. She'd always given as good as she got and never resorted to floods of tears.

Elodie batted his hand away, her expression churlish. 'I'm not crying. It's just a reaction to my new eyeshadow. I—I think I must be allergic to it or something.'

Lincoln brushed his bent knuckles across the

creamy curve of her cheek. He couldn't stop his gaze from drifting to the plump contours of her mouth.

'Hey…'

His voice came out low and deep and husky, and her shimmering eyes crept up to meet his. Something in his chest came loose, like a tight knot unravelling. He brushed the pad of his thumb over the cushion of her lower lip, back and forth, watching as her pupils dilated and her lips softly parted. He leaned closer and lowered his mouth to hers in a feather-light kiss. It was a mere brush of his lips across her soft ones, but it sent a shockwave of ferocious lust through his body.

He eased back to gaze into her eyes before he was tempted to take the kiss deeper. 'Let's see if we can get through the rest of today without fighting, hmm?'

She brushed at her eyes with an impatient flick of her hand. 'Good luck with that.'

Their meeting with his lawyer was held in a smart office a few blocks from where they were to be married. There were documents to read and papers to sign, but Elodie found it almost impossible to concentrate. Her lips were still tingling from Lincoln's brief kiss in the car, and her emotions were see-sawing.

She couldn't remember the last time she had shed tears. She didn't do emotional displays—she had taught herself not to—but for some reason Lincoln's lack of trust in her had stung far more bitterly than it should. So what if he didn't believe her about the stupid engagement ring? She knew the truth, even if he didn't believe it.

How could two people be so unsuited to marry? They were enemies, not lovers. There was so much residual angst between them and yet they were about to become man and wife. Lincoln had called a truce, but how long would that last?

A short time later they arrived at the register office. Lincoln had organised two employees from his office to act as witnesses.

The ceremony was conducted with brisk efficiency and zero sentimentality. Had that been Lincoln's plan? To make this ceremony as different as it could possibly be from their wedding day seven years ago? There were no flowers, no angelic-sounding choir, no bridesmaids, no flower girl and impish little ring bearer. Just two people she had never met before, witnessing what was supposed to be the happiest day of one's life.

'You may now kiss the bride.'

Elodie was jolted out of her reverie when Lincoln drew her closer. His hands framed her face and his mouth came down to hers in a kiss that totally ambushed her senses.

His kiss was gentle, and yet passionate, tender and yet determined, and she was swept away on a rushing tide of longing. She forgot where they were...was not conscious of anything but the exquisite sensation of his lips moving sensually on hers. Her lips remembered every contour of his mouth, every movement of his lips as they stirred her senses into rapture.

She opened her mouth under the delicious pressure of his, and while he didn't deepen the kiss, it was no less thrilling. In fact, it intensified the experience, heightening all her senses to every subtle movement and sensation. The soft press of his lips on hers, the intake of his breath, the audible gasp of hers, the tilt of his head as he changed position, the slight rasp of his masculine skin against her soft feminine skin, the splay of his fingers as he cradled her face in his hands.

It was a kiss that stirred sleeping feelings into wakefulness—feelings Elodie had thought would never come back to life. Feelings she didn't want to come back to life because they threatened to take over her life and her dreams and aspirations.

That could *not* happen.

It *would* not happen.

She would not *let* it happen.

The repeated clicking of a camera shutter was the cue Elodie needed to pull away. She kept her features in a mask of pretend happiness for the photographer, knowing that every photo would be crucially important to achieving her goal.

Lincoln put his arm around her waist and led her outside, where some paparazzi were waiting. 'This shouldn't take too long,' he said in an undertone. 'Leave the talking to me.'

Elodie glanced up at him with a frown. 'Why? I can speak for myself. I handle the media all the time. Besides, I want to make the most of the attention on us. It will put a spotlight on my new label like nothing else could.'

His lips tightened momentarily, as if he was going

to argue the point with her, but then he gave a sigh. 'Fine, but don't overplay it.'

One of the journalists pressed forward with a recording device. 'Congratulations to you both. Can you tell us how you got back together?'

Elodie beamed at the journalist and leaned her head lovingly on Lincoln's broad shoulder. 'We realised we'd never fallen out of love and decided to get married as soon as we could.'

'We're happy to be together again,' Lincoln said, his arm around her waist tightening. He led her down a series of steps to the footpath, with the group of journalists moving backwards in order to keep snapping pictures.

'Lincoln, congratulations on winning back your runaway bride. Does this mean we'll be hearing the patter of tiny feet any time soon?'

'We haven't made any plans in that regard,' Lincoln said with a cool smile. 'Now, if you'll excuse us, we're looking forward to some time alone to celebrate our marriage.'

Lincoln led Elodie to his car, half a block away, with the paparazzi following all the way, taking numerous shots of them together. Elodie kept her blissful bride face on, but inside she was ruminating on his comment about children.

Did he still want children some time in the future? Obviously not with her, as their marriage was not going to be long-term. But did he one day want to settle down and raise a family, similar to the one he was raised in?

Even though she didn't feel any particularly strong maternal urges, she couldn't help feeling a twinge of jealousy that another woman, one day in the future, would be the mother of Lincoln's children. But what place did her jealousy have in a six-month marriage agreement? None. She had signed the paperwork and she had accepted the terms. Their marriage was not the happy-ever-after type. It was an agreement so that she could receive the necessary finance for her label and Lincoln could assure his mother, before she died, that he was finally settled with the 'love of his life'.

Lincoln helped Elodie into his car and was soon behind the driver's seat and pulling away from the kerb. 'Nice work back there. You almost had me convinced you'd fallen madly in love with me.'

'Ha-ha.' Elodie gave him the side-eye and then turned to smile sweetly for the lingering journalists. Once they had driven clear of the paparazzi, she twisted in her seat to look at him. 'That comment you made about kids back there to the paps… *Are* you planning on having a family one day? I mean, after we end this arrangement?'

There was no change in his expression, but his fingers tightened ever so slightly on the steering wheel. 'No.'

Elodie frowned. 'But when we were together seven years ago you talked about having a family.'

'That was then—this is now.'

'I understand that you don't want any kids with me, especially since we'll only be married a matter of months, but I thought you'd still want to—'

'I don't.' His tone was curt.

'But why?'

His gaze was fixed on the road ahead, his jaw set as hard as granite. 'Meeting my biological mother changed my mind.'

'But I thought you liked her? She's obviously someone you care about, otherwise why would you be marrying me to make her happy in her final months of life?'

He sent her a grim look. 'I care deeply about her.'

'Have you met your biological father?'

'He died before I was born.' There was no trace of emotion in his voice, and yet she sensed a deep sadness behind his dispassionate answer.

'How?'

'Car crash.'

'How sad for your mother. Did that have something to do with why she gave you up?'

'We haven't discussed it much. She seems reluctant to talk about it, so I don't push it.'

Elodie studied his inscrutable features. What was the story behind his conception?

Thankfully, the forced adoptions of several generations ago were no longer common. Most women who relinquished a baby these days did so because they wanted their child to have better opportunities than they could provide. It was still a difficult decision, and no doubt there were still elements of pressure on some women from their family of origin. But these days there were safety measures in place to give the relinquishing mother a chance to change her mind during the process of adoption. There was even open adoption now, where children maintained their contact with the birth mother while being raised by adoptive parents.

'How are your brother and sister?' she asked.

'Aiden and Sylvia are both doing well.'

Elodie nibbled at her lower lip for a moment. 'Are they adopted as well?'

'No, my parents naturally conceived Aiden a year after adopting me, then Sylvia came eighteen months after him.'

'Wow, that's amazing. But did it make you feel on the outside at all?'

'Not really. My parents were devoted to us all, and my mother in particular insisted that she wouldn't have been able to have her own children if I hadn't come along. She said it so often I eventually believed it.'

'She sounds like she was an amazing person.'

'She was.'

Elodie had seen photos in the past of his family, and never once questioned Lincoln's place in it. She had even met them in person at their engagement party, and they had seemed like a normal family. He even looked a little like his adoptive father, Clive. It still hurt that he hadn't told her he was adopted. It made her feel shut out and insignificant—feelings which had added to the reasons she had run away from their wedding day.

'How did Aiden and Sylvia take the news of our reunion? Are they coming tonight to celebrate?'

'They're looking forward to seeing you again.'

She glanced at him in surprise. 'So they've forgiven me for jilting you?'

'You'll have to ask them yourself.'

She rolled her eyes and gushed out a theatrical sigh. '*Really* looking forward to that.'

He gave a wry sound of amusement. 'Did you manage to convince any of your family to come tonight?'

'Actually, Elspeth and Mack happen to be in London at the moment, so they'll come. Which reminds me—Elspeth has a serious nut allergy, remember? I'll have to talk to Morag about making sure her food is not contaminated.'

'I've already spoken to her.'

'Thanks, but I'm not afraid of her, you know.'

Elodie was touched he'd remembered her twin's allergy, but wouldn't have minded a showdown with Morag to establish some boundaries. *Start as you mean to go on*, was her credo now. She was not going to allow the housekeeper to walk all over her feelings this time around.

'I know, but I want things to go as smoothly as possible.'

Elodie shrugged and continued. 'Mum can't come, but not because she didn't want to—she's in Ireland with her new partner, visiting his family.'

She decided against telling him she had told her twin the truth about their marriage. She could trust Elspeth to keep quiet and play along with the charade.

'Were your mother and Elspeth surprised by your announcement?'

'Mum is impossible to surprise these days. I think it's because of all the impulsive things I've done in the past.'

He gave a wry *been-there-experienced-that-first-hand* grunt. 'What about Elspeth? Was she surprised when you told her?'

She swivelled in her seat to look at him. 'No, because she thinks you've always been in love with me.'

Lincoln's mouth tightened just a fraction. 'Then let's hope she keeps that fantasy going for the next six months.' He changed gear and added, 'Is your father coming tonight?'

Elodie gave a mirthless laugh. 'No way. I know better than to ask him. He's always got something more important to do.'

She felt rather than saw the weight of Lincoln's glance on her, and mentally kicked herself for revealing her father issues. Showing vulnerability was a no-no in a relationship such as theirs. A transactional relationship that had no place for sharing emotional baggage. Not that she had ever shared much of her baggage in the past… She hated showing any sign of emotional neediness, especially to someone like Lincoln, who was so in control of his emotions—if he had any, that was.

'What about your father? Has he forgiven me too?'

'You won't have any problems on that score. He forgave you long ago.'

*But have you?* Elodie wanted to ask, but she stayed silent.

If the roles had been reversed, she would have

found it near impossible to forgive him if he had jilted her. Rejection was her worst nightmare.

Her fear of being abandoned came from her childhood. Her father had proudly paraded his cute twin girls around until they'd stopped being cute. As a young child Elodie had gravitated towards her father, because her mother had been so obsessed with keeping Elspeth safe from her nut allergy.

Elodie had thought she was her father's favourite, like Elspeth was her mother's. But how wrong she had been. She'd lost her first tooth and her father in the same week. He'd moved on to build a new life and a family with another woman. He hadn't even made the time to come to her ill-fated wedding.

But then, why would he have needed to? He had given her away years ago.

# CHAPTER FOUR

THE CELEBRATORY DINNER was not something Lincoln was particularly looking forward to, but he was immensely glad of the distraction. Acting the devoted husband was going to be a stretch, but he preferred it to the alternative. Going home to be alone with Elodie until they flew to Spain the following day was too tempting to think about.

Their kiss at the wedding ceremony had stirred up a host of erotic memories he had tried for years to suppress. The hands-off paper marriage he was insisting on was not going to last long if he didn't pull himself into line. He needed to prove to himself that he could resist her this time around. But resisting her would be so much easier if he could ignore the way she lit up a room as soon as she entered it.

It wasn't just her natural beauty—it was her vibrant energy that spoke to him on a cellular level. He had never met a more exciting lover, and the thought of revisiting their passion was a persistent background hum in his body. A hum he was finding it increasingly difficult to ignore.

Lincoln led the way inside his house and then shrugged off his jacket and hung it over one of the velvet wing chairs in the foyer. 'We have a couple of hours before our guests arrive. I have some emails to deal with in my office. I'll leave you to re-familiarise yourself with the house. Morag has put you in the guest room next to mine.'

Elodie raised her neat eyebrows, her eyes alight with mischief. 'The one with the connecting door?'

Lincoln flattened his mouth into a firm line. 'The door will remain locked.'

She raised her chin, her eyes still glinting. 'Which side is the key on?'

He had to force himself not to stare at the perfect curve of her mouth. That pillow-soft mouth he could still taste on his lips. 'My side.'

She made a moue with her lips. 'Shouldn't there be one on my side too? I mean, fair's fair and all that.'

'I can't imagine any circumstances in which you would need to enter my room.'

Elodie's eyes danced as they held his in a challenging look. 'Oh, can't you?'

A hot shiver ran down his spine and set spot fires in his groin. He reached up to his neck to loosen his tie, which right then was all but strangling him. 'I'll see you later.'

He began to walk away, but one of her slim hands landed on his forearm in a light but electrifying hold. Another shiver shimmied down his spine and hot, hard heat filled his pelvis.

'Don't you think we should rehearse how we're going to behave in front of our guests tonight?'

'Rehearse?'

She moved closer, sliding her hand down his arm, her fingers ever so lightly brushing over the back of his hand. His skin tingled and his pulse quickened. He could smell the exotic notes of her signature scent—a mix of musk, tuberose and something that was unique to her.

'We'll need to look comfortable touching each other like lovers do.'

Her smile had a sultry tilt that made the heat in his groin smoulder to boiling point.

'Right now, you look tense and uncomfortable.'

Tense was right. He had never felt so hard in his life. He placed his hands on her wrists, intending to put her away from him, but somehow, he found himself doing the opposite. The magnetic pull of her body called out to the humming need in his. He brought her flush against him, not caring that she could feel every throbbing beat of his blood against her lower body.

'Is this the sort of thing you mean? Getting up close and personal?' He kept his tone cynical, but his mind was whirling with the possibility of tweaking the rules.

Elodie moved against him, her yielding softness against his hardness sending a torrent of lust through him. She eased her wrists out of his hold and wound her arms around his neck, her cinnamon-scented breath teasing his senses into overdrive.

'You want me so bad…'

Her voice had a throaty quality to it that only did more lethal damage to his self-control. Lincoln put his hands on her slim hips, holding her to the jutting ridge of his arousal. The feel of her against him sent his senses spinning. She was impossible to resist in this playfully seductive mood. But resist he must.

'We'll embarrass our guests if we don't show some restraint.' His gaze lowered to her mouth and his heart rate spiked. 'Kissing is fine, holding hands, hugging...but that's all.'

Elodie stepped on tiptoe and planted a soft-as-air kiss to his lips. She pulled away so slowly her lips clung to his like silk catching on something rough.

She sent the tip of her tongue over her lips and smiled at him, her eyes still twinkling. 'Is that chaste enough for you, baby?'

Her purring tone was almost his undoing. *Almost.* He knew she was toying with him and he wasn't going to be so easily manipulated—even though every male hormone in his body was begging him to give in to the temptation she was dangling before him. No one could turn him on like Elodie Campbell. Smart, sassy, sophisticated, sexy—all the things her brand defined her as were catnip to him. But he had to resist her for as long as he could. To prove to himself she no longer had the power over him she'd once had.

Lincoln took her by the upper arms and put her from him, keeping his expression impassive. 'You're playing a dangerous game, sweetheart. And you won't win it.'

Elodie gave a carefree laugh and reached up and

pulled her long hair out of its updo, letting the silken tresses fall about her shoulders in fragrant bouncing waves. 'Don't bet on it.'

She blew him a kiss and turned on her sky-high heels and walked away, leaving him burning, burning, burning with rabid lust.

Elodie entered the bedroom next to Lincoln's and closed the door and leaned back against it with a whooshing sigh. She knew it was dangerous, tempting Lincoln into changing his mind about the terms of their marriage. But knowing he wanted her gave her a sense of power—an addictive sense of power she couldn't resist exercising.

Lincoln was a man who held strong opinions. Once he made up his mind he found it difficult to change it. It was one of the reasons they'd locked horns so much in the past. They were both strong-willed and opinionated and neither of them wanted to back down.

If by some miracle she managed to change his mind, she would be flirting with even more danger. The danger of allowing her feelings into the passion they shared. That had been her mistake in the past—falling for him because he was such a fabulous lover. She had confused physical chemistry with emotional attachment. How had she been so foolish to not recognise it? Just because a man knew how to make your blood sing, it didn't mean he was in love with you.

Seven years ago, Lincoln might have been in lust with her—just as he was now—but love had never been part of his commitment to her. He had been willing to marry her, to live with her and have a family with her, but he hadn't been willing to offer her his heart. What sort of star-struck, lovesick idiot had she been to accept him on those terms back then?

Since their breakup Elodie had never felt anything for any of her lovers—not that there had been many. She had actively encouraged a party girl image to go with her smart, successful, sassy, sophisticated and sexy brand. Those five *S*-words sold the lingerie and swimwear she modelled. But no one had come close to exciting her the way Lincoln had.

Sex for her had been a purely mechanical thing before she'd met him. She had never orgasmed with a lover before him and she hadn't since. It was as if he had cursed her to be unable to fully function sexually without him. Which was part of her reason for wanting to revisit their passion. She needed to know if he still had the same sensual power over her. Judging from the kisses they had shared, it was looking highly likely.

Why was he so insistent on keeping their marriage on paper? It didn't make sense. They both stood to gain from their arrangement—why not exploit it to the fullest extent?

Elodie came downstairs a few minutes before their guests were due to arrive. She wandered into the kitchen to get a glass of water and came face to face with Morag, the housekeeper. A shiver of apprehension scuttled over her flesh, her heart-rate increased and a sense of dread as heavy as stone filled her stomach. She mentally prepared herself for attack, knowing it would be a miracle for the housekeeper to welcome her with open arms, especially after the way she had left Lincoln standing at the altar seven years ago.

She hid her unease behind a breezy smile. 'Hi, Morag. Nice to see you again.'

The older woman's lips pursed. 'So, you're back.'

Elodie waved a hand in front of her body. 'As you see. And blissfully happy. Aren't you going to congratulate me?'

'Congratulations.'

Never had someone sounded less sincere.

'Thanks. It's nice to be back.'

Morag wiped her hands on a tea towel and tossed it to one side, her expression set in disapproving lines. 'How long are you staying this time?'

Elodie gave a tinkling laugh. 'For ever, of course.'

The lie slipped off her tongue with such ease it was almost scary.

Morag harrumphed and picked up a paring knife. She began slicing into an avocado, her brow heavily furrowed. 'If I thought you truly loved him I'd be happy for you.'

Her voice had the stern quality of a buttoned-up schoolmistress dealing with a rebellious child.

Elodie shrugged off the housekeeper's comment with a nonchalant up-and-down movement of one shoulder. 'You're entitled to your opinion, I guess.'

Morag glanced at her with a narrow-eyed look. 'He deserves better than the likes of you.'

Elodie tried to suppress the bubble of anger that

rose in her chest, but it was like trying to hold back a flood. And along with the toxic tide of anger there was a deep twinge of hurt because the housekeeper saw her as a taker, not a giver.

She wasn't by nature a people-pleaser. She went her own way and didn't give a damn what people thought about her—or at least she pretended she didn't give a damn. What was it about her that Lincoln's housekeeper disliked so much? It had irritated her in the past, but now, for some strange reason, it hurt as well. Was there something about her that both Morag and her father saw? A flaw that made her unacceptable? Unlikeable? Unlovable?

She moved to the other side of the kitchen to find a glass, but because the kitchen had been remodelled she couldn't find one. 'Where do you keep the glasses?'

'Third cupboard on the right.'

'Thank you.' Elodie found a glass and took it over to the sink and filled it with water. She drank the water and then placed the glass upside down on the draining board. Then she turned and leaned back against the sink to look at the housekeeper. 'Did you know Lincoln was adopted when we were together seven years ago?'

Morag continued artfully arranging the sliced avocado on the seafood starters she was making for dinner. 'I knew.'

Elodie couldn't hold back a frown. He'd told his housekeeper and not her? How was that supposed to make her feel? How could she not feel upset and unimportant? Someone under his employ knew the intimate details of his life, and yet the woman he had asked to marry him did not. He had chosen *not* to tell her.

'Did he ask you not to mention it to me?'

Morag lifted her gaze from her food preparation to meet hers. 'I only knew because his mother Rosemary mentioned it to me in passing one day. Lincoln never told me himself and I didn't see it as my business to tell anyone else.'

'Not even his fiancée? The woman he'd chosen to be his wife?'

The housekeeper gave her an unwavering look. 'I think you already know the answer to that question. It's why you didn't go ahead with the wedding. You didn't love him the way he deserves to be loved.'

Elodie pushed herself away from the sink in agitation. Her feelings about Lincoln had always been the issue. The depth, the intensity, the overwhelming need of him she knew could put her in a vulnerable situation from which she might never escape.

'I wasn't ready for marriage back then. I was young—only twenty-one.'

'And you're ready now?' Scepticism was ripe in the housekeeper's tone.

Elodie straightened her shoulders, her chin at a defiant height. 'You bet I am.'

The first guests to arrive were Elspeth and Mack. Seeing her twin hand in hand with her gorgeous Scottish fiancé made Elodie feel faintly jealous. Not that she wasn't happy for her twin—she was. It was so nice to see her shy and reserved sister enjoying all the things she had missed out on before. But it was obvious Mack adored Elspeth—he could barely take his eyes off her and Elspeth glowed like never before. She was practically incandescent with love.

Elodie had once fooled herself that Lincoln looked at her the same way Mack did her twin. But she had mistaken lust for love and she wasn't going to be so stupid as to do so again. But the lust was real. It still throbbed between them and she was determined to bring him to his knees with it.

She smiled a secret smile. She knew how to seduce Lincoln. She had done it so many times before. He was holding out on her to prove a point. He wanted control this time around. But so did she. And she would damn well get it.

While Lincoln was chatting to Mack, Elodie quickly lured her twin aside to speak to her in private. She led Elspeth to a small room a few doors down from the formal dining room and closed the door once they were inside. 'Els, you're not supposed to know my marriage to Lincoln isn't the real deal, so please keep it under wraps. And, whatever you do, don't tell Mum.'

Elspeth frowned. 'But what about Mack? I've already told him and—'

Elodie let out a stiff curse. 'Will he say something to Lincoln, do you think?'

'I don't think so. He's the soul of discretion at the best of times.'

'Better have a word to him, just to make sure.'

Elspeth took one of Elodie's hands in hers. 'You probably should tell Lincoln that I know. It's not good to keep secrets in a marriage.'

Elodie gave a cynical cough of a laugh. 'Try telling Lincoln that. He's the one who didn't tell me anything about himself when we were together before.'

'Maybe you didn't spend enough time getting to know him. You did have rather a whirlwind relationship.'

'Look who's talking!'

Elspeth blushed a delightful shade of pink, her blue eyes shining with happiness. 'I know, right? It was crazily fast, and I still can't believe Mack and I are getting married next month. He's everything I ever dreamed of in a partner. I only wish you and Lincoln could sort things out and be—'

'Not much chance of that,' Elodie said, and opened the door to return to the dining room. 'Come on. Mean Morag, the crotchety old dragon of a housekeeper, will blame me if dinner is spoilt.'

Lincoln watched Elodie and her twin walk together into the dining room, where the other guests were assembled. The twins were eerily alike, but while he had only seen them together a handful of times, he could always tell them apart. Elspeth was a more introverted and reserved version of Elodie. But that was what had drawn him to Elodie in the first place—her vibrant zest for life and her devil-may-care attitude. She didn't just dare to step where angels feared to tread—she stomped in with her sky-high heels and laughed while she did it.

She was smiling now, her beautiful white teeth framed by a vivid red lipstick, her make-up perfect, her hair a voluminous cloud around her slim shoulders. She had changed into a tight-fighting black dress that clung to her feminine curves in a way that made him fantasise about peeling it off her later.

But the rules were the rules and he needed them in place. He had rushed into a fling with her in the past and it had blown up in his face. This time he wanted control. And falling madly in love and lust all over again was not going to help him maintain it.

Elodie came over to him and nestled against his side, gazing up at him adoringly. He had never said she wasn't a good actor. No one would ever think she wasn't thrilled about being married to him. But then, she was getting a heap of publicity out of their reunion. The photos of their wedding had already gone viral, and he was fielding dozens of requests for an exclusive interview. No doubt so was she.

Lincoln slipped his arm around her waist, the feel of her against his side sending shivers down his spine. 'Come and say hello to Dad, and to Aiden and Sylvia and their partners.'

He led her to where his family were gathered, enjoying the drinks and nibbles provided by Morag.

'Welcome home, Elodie, my dear,' Clive Lancaster said with a warm smile. 'This is my partner, Jan.'

Elodie smiled and greeted everyone in turn. 'It's

so nice to see you all again. And so good of you to be here to celebrate with us tonight at such short notice.'

Clive clapped a hand on Lincoln's shoulder, his eyes shining with warmth and fatherly affection. 'I wouldn't have missed it for anything. I've waited a long time for Lincoln to settle down with the only woman he has ever loved. And maybe I'll get those grandbabies now, eh?'

'Ri-i-i-ght...' Lincoln smiled and ignored the twinge of guilt in his gut about the truth of his marriage to Elodie.

He didn't like lying to his family, but needs must in this case. He had to provide his biological mother with the peace she longed for before she passed away. Nina still agonised over her decision to relinquish him as a baby. She longed to see him happily settled, to have the assurance that her decision hadn't permanently damaged his ability to love and be loved.

But love wasn't part of his arrangement with Elodie and nor had it ever been, in spite of her regular and gushing declarations of it in the past. If she'd loved him she wouldn't have jilted him. In his mind it was a simple as that. If she had truly had deep feelings for him she would have expressed her concerns about their relationship—not left him standing in front of a congregation of guests looking like a fool.

There was a part of him that would never forgive her for that. The humiliation had stung then and it still stung now—which was why he was keeping firm control of the way things would play out between them going forward.

\*\*\*

Elodie sipped glass after glass of champagne and nibbled at the delicious food the housekeeper had placed in front of her and the other guests. Lincoln was seated at the head of the long dining table, his father at the other end. Elodie was on his left and felt acutely conscious of everyone—particularly the members of his family, who were watching her every movement, gesture or expression.

Her face was aching from smiling, and her brain was fried from trying to make convivial conversation with everyone. Normally she loved a good party. She could work any room like a pro without a moment's worry about putting a foot wrong or, indeed, about what anyone thought of her.

But for some reason it felt wrong to be pretending to Lincoln's family that their relationship was genuine. The only thing that was genuine was the lust simmering between them. She was aware of the pulse of it every time Lincoln took her hand, his fingers warm and strong around hers. Every time he locked gazes with her, every time he brought her hand up to his mouth and kissed her bent knuckles, or the ends of her fingers, a lightning-fast current of erotic energy passed from his body to hers, leaving her wanting, wanting, wanting…

Clive rose towards the end of the meal, glass in hand. 'Let's toast the happy couple. To Lincoln and Elodie. May your future be bright and happy and fulfilling and blessed with children.'

Elodie reached for her glass but, anxious, somehow managed to knock it over instead. 'Oops.'

Lincoln righted the glass and refilled it within seconds. He held his glass against hers. 'To us.'

She clinked her glass against his, her expression as radiant as her twin's. 'To us.'

But then, she was good at masking her true feelings. No one would ever guess at the turmoil inside her at the thought of having Lincoln's baby. He didn't love her. How could she raise a family with someone who didn't love her? It was asking for heartbreak. The sort of heartbreak she had run away from seven years ago. The sort of heartbreak her mother had suffered.

Where was the 'for ever love' Elodie's father had once claimed to feel for his wife and his cute twin daughters? It had gone away like a wisp of smoke as soon as someone more interesting came along.

'Now for the first dance,' said Sylvia, Lincoln's young sister. 'Go on, you two. Show us your moves.'

Elodie wasn't the type of person to blush, but as soon as Lincoln gathered her in his arms a rush of heat flowed from her cheeks to her core. He held her close, hip to hip, thigh to thigh, cheek to cheek, as they danced to the music Aiden had jumped up to put on the sophisticated sound system.

It was a romantic ballad that was poignant and bittersweet—which perfectly described her situation. It wouldn't matter if she were married to Lincoln for six months or six decades. She would never be able to guarantee he would love her the way she longed to be loved. He could *act* as if he did. No one looking at him now would think he wasn't madly in love with her. But she was too much of cynic to think he would ever open his heart to her. She was still a trophy wife—a beautiful bit of arm candy to show off to his dying mother and convince her she hadn't done the wrong thing in relinquishing him as a baby.

Lincoln tipped up her chin and looked into her eyes. 'Did I tell you how beautiful you look tonight?'

Elodie smiled, even though his words kind of proved her point. He loved the way she *looked*. He didn't love *her*.

'You look pretty damn awesome yourself.' She linked her arms around his neck and swayed against him with the music. 'You feel pretty damn awesome too.'

His hands grasped her hips but he didn't separate their bodies. He brought her harder against him, in spite of their watchful audience. His blue-green gaze blazed with lust...the same lust she could feel pounding in her own body.

He lowered his mouth to just below her ear, his lips sending shivers coursing down her spine as he spoke in an undertone. 'You're enjoying yourself a little too much, aren't you?'

Elodie gave a breathy laugh and rolled her head further to one side, to give him better access to the sensitive skin of her neck. 'You're making it hard not to enjoy myself. No one would ever think you weren't desperate to get me alone right now.'

His hands tightened on her hips and his lips moved

across her skin as lightly as a feather, stirring her nerves into a frenzy.

'I am desperate to get you alone…but not for the reason you think.'

His voice was a low, rough burr of sound that made her spine tingle from top to bottom. She framed his face in her hands, staring into his eyes with brazen defiance. 'You mean you're *not* going to make mad, passionate love to me on our wedding night?'

'You know the rules.'

His eyes glinted with determination and she could feel the war going on in his body. He was fighting their mutual attraction, but she was confident she would bring him down.

She smiled a sultry smile. 'I just love it when you draw a line in the sand.'

'Why?'

'Because I get such a kick out of stepping over it.'

And then she planted her lips on his.

## CHAPTER FIVE

FOR A MOMENT Lincoln forgot they weren't alone. As soon as her lips met his a fire erupted in his body. An inferno of lust that left no part of him unaffected. His groin tightened, the backs of his legs tingled and his self-control scrambled to get back on duty.

But it was always this way with Elodie. Her passionate and rebellious nature spoke to him in a raw, primal way that was nothing short of overwhelming. Need pummelled through his flesh, making him hot and tight within seconds.

He had existed for seven years without this heady rush of excitement. How had he done it? It seemed impossible that he had lived in a wasteland of substandard sensuality when he could have had this fiery intensity of lust. Her mouth was soft and yet insistent, and he answered it with the thrust of his tongue, mating with hers in a playful duel that sent another rush of blood to his groin.

'Get a honeymoon suite, you guys!' called out his brother Aiden with a laugh.

Lincoln lifted his mouth off Elodie's with a cynical smile only she could see. 'We'll finish this later.'

One way or the other, he *had* to get control of his desire for her. She was exploiting it and he was in danger of caving in like a horny teenager lusting over his first crush.

'Ooh, I can hardly wait.' Her eyes danced with mischief and she eased out of his arms to go and sit next to her twin.

Lincoln went back to the table and pretended to listen to a conversation between Mack and his father. He picked up his wine glass and took a token sip, but no amount of alcohol could make him as drunk as Elodie's sexy mouth. That soft and supple mouth had in the past been all over his body, sending him to the stratosphere multiple times.

He suppressed a shudder and picked up his water glass instead and took a long draught. He put the glass back on the table and caught Elodie's eye. She smiled and gave him a fingertip wave, and another rush of heat flowed through his flesh.

It was probably only a few minutes later that everyone began to leave, but to Lincoln it was like hours. Finally, the door closed on the last of their guests and Lincoln and Elodie returned to the dining room, where Morag was busy clearing everything away.

'Let me help you with that,' Elodie said, stepping forward to help stack some plates.

'Leave it,' Morag said, without even turning from the table to look at Elodie. 'You'll only end up breaking something.'

Lincoln frowned at his housekeeper's clipped tone. He had never heard her be so brusque with Elodie—or indeed with anyone before. But then, Morag hadn't seen him enter the room with Elodie, as her back was to the door. He'd always thought Elodie had exaggerated the housekeeper's behaviour towards her in the past. Elodie was a bit of a drama queen and liked being the centre of attention. Morag's no-nonsense, stay-in-the-background personality was the total opposite. But now he wondered if he would have done better to keep an open mind. He had known his housekeeper a lot longer than Elodie and sided with her. Had that been a mistake?

Elodie continued stacking the plates, her lips in a tight line, her handling of the top-shelf crockery not exactly gentle. The clatter and clang of cutlery and china was obviously her way of showing how upset she was.

'It may surprise you, Morag, but I'm quite domesticated these days. I can stack a dishwasher, do my own laundry and cook a decent meal.'

'You'll need more skills than that to keep your husband happy,' Morag shot back.

Elodie placed the plates on the trolley that would ferry them back to the kitchen. 'I have plenty of *those* skills too.'

Her tone was pure sass, and her *don't-mess-with-me* expression a warning even he took note of. He knew all about those skills of hers. The sensual skills that gave him thrills like no other person ever had before or since. The sensual skills he was trying not to be tempted by. But he realised he had vastly underestimated the explosive chemistry that still existed between them. Would it lessen if he indulged it or would it get out of control?

'Morag, why don't you leave this for us to clear away?' Lincoln said. 'You've worked long enough today. Go home and we'll see you when we get back from Spain.'

Morag turned from the table and wiped her hands on her apron, her expression unrepentant. 'She'll only bring you trouble. She doesn't love you.'

'It's none of your damn business *what* I feel about him,' Elodie flashed back, blue eyes blazing.

'Elodie—' Lincoln began in a calming tone, but she was having none of it.

'You always side with her,' Elodie said, turning to him. 'I'm your *wife*, for God's sake. You're supposed to... Oh, never mind.' She tossed the cutlery she was holding with a loud clatter on top of the plates on the trolley. 'I'm going to bed.'

She stalked out, slamming the door behind her.

Lincoln sighed and raked a hand through his hair. Drama and Elodie were never far away from each other, but he would have to get used to it—and so would his housekeeper. Otherwise the following six months would be unbearable.

Sacking Morag wasn't an option. She had been a stalwart support for more years than he could count—first to his mother, as a long-term friend, and since his mother's death Morag had been his link to her—one he wasn't ready to sever. She often gave him little vignettes of the two of them growing up as close friends, stories of their escapades and adventures and childhood games that kept his mother alive for him in his mind.

'Morag, go easy on her, yeah? I want things to work this time.'

The housekeeper's mouth tightened. 'She'll break your heart again. You mark my words.'

He wanted to tell his housekeeper that he hadn't had his heart broken, just his pride, but Morag had witnessed first-hand the fallout from Elodie jilting him.

'I'm not going to allow anything like that to happen,' he said, with the utmost confidence.

He was in control now. Emotions were not part of their relationship this time around and he was going to keep it that way.

Elodie was in her en suite bathroom, taking off her make-up, when there was a knock at the door. 'Go away.'

'Come on, sweetheart, open up,' Lincoln said, rapping his knuckles on the door again.

She slammed the toner bottle down on the counter and tossed the cotton pad in the bin. She opened the door and glared at him. 'If you've come to give me a lecture about being nicer to your housekeeper, then you're wasting my time and yours.'

'I've come to apologise.'

Elodie knew she shouldn't be mollified so easily, but something about his tone made her anger melt away. Her shoulders went down on a sigh and she came out of the bathroom, tightening the ties of her wrap around her waist a little more firmly.

'You're seven years too late with your apology.' She threw him a petulant look from beneath her lowered lashes. 'She's always been unnecessarily rude to me.'

Lincoln came over to her and raised her chin with his index finger, locking his gaze on hers. 'I'm sorry I didn't listen to you about that in the past. I can see there's tension between you.'

Elodie made a scoffing noise. 'Tension? You don't know the half of it.'

He placed his hands on her shoulders and gave them a gentle squeeze. 'I thought you didn't care what people thought of you?'

She lowered her gaze from his to stare at the collar of his shirt. 'I don't. But I don't think someone you employ to take care of your house should treat your… your…wife like she's gold-digging trailer trash. I earn my own money—heaps of it, actually. Not enough to launch my own label, but still…'

Lincoln raised her chin again, to mesh his gaze with hers. 'I've spoken to Morag and you shouldn't have any trouble in future.'

'And if I do?'

He drew in a breath and released it in a long exhalation. 'Then I'll deal with it.'

'How? By firing her?'

He released her, stepped back and rubbed a hand over his face. 'I don't know. She's worked for me a long time. She was a friend of my mother's—they went to primary school together. She had a rough time growing up, then she married a brute of a man who physically abused her every chance he got. They had a couple of kids who both ran off the rails and barely speak to her now. She finally got the courage to leave him and has worked for me ever since. Plus, she developed Type Two diabetes recently. She would probably find it hard to get another job that pays as well and with such flexible hours.'

Elodie sat on the edge of the bed with her hands resting either side of her thighs. She was secretly impressed by his commitment to his housekeeper. Morag was clearly a vulnerable person who had been taken advantage of in the past. Her heart ached for her and what she had been through. It was no wonder she didn't find it easy to let people into her life. It reminded her a little bit of herself.

'My God. I'm sorry to hear Morag has been through all that. She doesn't deserve to be treated that way. No one does. But hurt people don't heal themselves by hurting others. You have to work through your own pain rather than project it on to someone else.'

Lincoln twisted his mouth into a grimace. 'I guess that's how it plays out sometimes. She's a little set in her ways.'

Elodie flopped backwards on the bed, flinging her arms above her head. 'Oh, God, I'm so tired of how the world can hurt people. It's one of the reasons I want to work for myself. You would not believe the rubbish I've had to put up with for years.'

Lincoln came and sat beside her on the bed, but he didn't touch her. Even knowing he was within touching distance made every cell in her body throb with awareness.

'What sort of stuff? Sexual harassment?' His frown was heavy, his expression gravely serious.

She rolled her eyes like marbles in a jar. 'Nothing I couldn't handle on my own.'

He reached out and brushed a strand of hair back from her forehead. 'You shouldn't have to handle that stuff on your own. That stuff shouldn't happen in the first place.'

'Yeah, well, it still does.' She rolled over so she was facing him on her side, even more conscious of how close his body was to hers. 'Thanks for listening. I don't talk to anyone about this stuff except Elspeth, and half the time I don't tell her the full extent of it. It would shock her too much.'

'You try to be strong for her, don't you?'

Elodie let out a puff of air. 'Yes, well... I'm not the one with the life-threatening allergy, am I? When our father left...' She frowned and then continued, 'I didn't see it coming, you know? I thought he would always be there for us, and for me in particular, because he always called me his favourite girl. It was all lies. He didn't love anyone but himself.'

'I'm sorry you had such a jerk of a father. I can only imagine how that has impacted on you.'

Elodie met Lincoln's gaze, finding in it a warmth

and an emotional connection that was completely disarming. 'I think I've spent a lot of my life pretending to be someone I'm not. The cutesy outgoing twin, the cheeky extroverted kid who caused drama wherever she went. The blissfully happy bride-to-be...until I got cold feet, when the reality of being your wife—anyone's wife, for that matter—hit me.' She twisted her mouth and continued, 'I've had to be tough all my life. And I can see now why Morag is the way she is. It's emotional armour to keep from getting hurt.'

His eyes held hers, his pupils dark as black holes in outer space. 'It was never my intention to hurt you or block you from your dreams.' He took one of her hands in his and gave it a gentle squeeze. 'I wish you'd talked to me about this stuff way back then.'

'Yes, well... We didn't do a lot of talking, as I remember. Apart from arguing. And then having make-up sex.' She gave a rueful smile and continued, 'It was nice being with your family tonight, although I couldn't help feeling guilty about all the pretence.' She frowned and added, 'I can't help worrying that they'll be terribly hurt when we end this. I mean, your father seemed so convinced I'm the love of your life.' She gave an incredulous laugh and added, 'I can't imagine being the love of *anyone*'s life. I'm too much hard work.'

Lincoln stroked his fingers through her hair in a slow, mesmerising fashion, sending shivers over her scalp and down her spine.

'Sometimes hard work brings its own rewards.'

His eyes became hooded and drifted to her mouth,

and a wave of longing coursed through her. He leaned on one elbow, his other hand stroking up and down the length of her satin-covered thigh.

'I like your sister's fiancé, Mack. They seem a good match.'

'Yes, she's very happy and I'm happy for her.' Elodie toyed with one of the buttons on his shirt and added, 'I consider myself a bit of a matchmaker, actually. If I hadn't got her to go in my place to the wedding she might never have met Mack.'

There was a beat or two of silence.

'Why did you have a one-night stand with Mack's brother Fraser that night?' Lincoln asked. 'The night we ran into each other at that bar in Soho?'

Elodie shuffled away and sat upright and hugged her knees. 'I hope you're not going to go all double standards on me about having a one-night stand. You've had plenty.'

'I'm not denying it, but it seemed out of character for you.'

She gave him the side-eye. 'Were you jealous?'

'No.' His expression was masklike, except for a knot of tension in the lower quadrant of his jaw.

Elodie got off the bed and smoothed her hands over her satin wrap. 'It was awful, if you want to know...'

She wasn't sure why she was telling him about a night she would rather wipe from her memory for good. Running into Lincoln with his latest squeeze had rocked her far more than it should. The stunning young woman had been draped all over him, her adoration for him obvious for all to see. It shouldn't have upset Elodie one iota, but for some reason it had thrown her into a tailspin. His partner had looked *so* in love with him. The same way Elodie had once looked up at him—as if he was the only man in the world who could make her happy.

Her mind back then had run through a reel of thoughts—would he announce their engagement soon? Would they settle down and have the family he had once wanted with her?

To distract herself, she'd flirted outrageously with Fraser MacDiarmid, determined to show Lincoln she was completely and utterly over him, but it had backfired spectacularly a few months later.

Lincoln rose from the bed in a single movement and came over to her. 'Did he…hurt you?' A thread of anger underpinned his voice and his expression was a landscape of concern.

Elodie hugged her arms around her middle and gave him a stiff, no-teeth-showing smile. 'It was consensual but crappy sex.'

His eyes held hers. 'You didn't enjoy it?'

'If you're asking did I come, then, no, I didn't.'

*Why are you telling him that?*

But it seemed now she'd opened her mouth, she couldn't stop confessing the rest. She gave him a pointed look. 'It's your fault, you know. You've spoilt me for anyone else.'

A frown formed on his forehead. 'What do you mean?'

She blew out a long breath. 'I haven't enjoyed sex since we broke up.'

There was a weighted pause.

'Have there been many lovers?' Lincoln's tone was mild—casual, almost—and yet she sensed an undercurrent of avid interest he was trying his best to hide.

Elodie unwound her arms from around her middle. 'Not as many as I've led people to believe.' She speared a hand through the loose tresses of her hair and continued, 'I suppose that gives your male ego a massive boost? That I can't come with anyone else?'

His expression didn't register surprise, for hardly a muscle moved on his face, and yet she still suspected he was shocked. Deeply shocked. And why wouldn't he be? The press had documented her every move over the last seven years, linking her with various high-profile men. She had played to the cameras, using every opportunity to lift her profile. Some of the men she had had flings with—many she had not.

'Casual sex isn't for everybody.' His tone was as hard to read as his expression.

Elodie gave a mirthless laugh. 'You seem to do all right. As I recall, you didn't even wait a week before finding someone else after our breakup.'

Seeing him in a gossip magazine with an attractive partner within a week of their aborted wedding had struck at her heart like a closed-fist punch. If he had cared for her even a little, wouldn't he have waited just a while in case she changed her mind? But, no. He'd moved on so rapidly it had confirmed she had done the right thing in calling off their wedding. For if he had loved her wouldn't he have at least tried to change her mind rather than replace her?

Lincoln rolled his bottom lip over his top one in a contemplative gesture, his eyes still holding hers. After a long moment, he released a long-winded sigh. 'I didn't sleep with anyone for months after we split up.' His voice was low and rough around the edges.

Elodie stared at him, her heart skipping out of its normal rhythm. 'But...but I thought... *Really?*' She leaned on the word, suddenly desperate to know the truth. 'Why not? And why did you give everyone the impression you'd moved on so quickly?'

Lincoln looked down at the floor, where he was idly using the toe of his shoe to straighten the fringe of the Persian rug. When he raised his gaze back to hers his expression was still unreadable.

'I'd better let you get some sleep. We fly first thing in the morning.' He moved across to the door with long, purposeful strides.

'But wait,' Elodie said, following him, placing a hand on his arm before he could open the door to leave. She looked up into his enigmatic features, her mind whirling from what he'd told her. 'Was it because you were hoping I'd come back to you? You thought I might change my mind?'

He held her gaze in an unwavering lock for endless seconds, but there was no clue to what he was thinking. It was like trying to read the expression on a marble statue.

'Do you really think I would've taken you back?' he said at last, in a cynical tone that stung far more than it should.

Elodie kept her expression as masklike as his. She removed her hand from his arm and stepped back. 'No.'

The door closed behind him and she let out a rattling sigh.

Why would he if he hadn't loved her in the first place?

The journey to Valencia in Spain the following day took just over six hours door-to-door. Elodie spent most of it with her head buried in a collection of fashion magazines, determined to keep her distance, knowing that as soon as they were in Nina Smith's presence the charade of being a happily reunited loved-up couple would begin.

Lincoln seemed just as disinclined to talk—he had business papers in his briefcase and wore a preoccupied frown for most of the journey.

A car was waiting for them at the airport, with a young uniformed driver called Elonzo. *'Buenas tardes, Señor Lancaster.'* He smiled shyly at Elodie and added, *'Señora, mucho gusto.'*

'It's nice to meet you too,' Elodie said, with an answering smile that made the young man blush in spite of his olive complexion.

Lincoln helped Elodie into the car and they were soon on their way to the villa at Sagunto, about twenty minutes' drive from the airport. The sunshine was blindingly bright, the air warm in comparison to the chilly autumn weather back home.

'Have you been to Sagunto before?' Lincoln asked.

'No, but I've been to a few other places in Spain.

It's one of my favourite destinations. The people are so friendly, the food is great—and don't even get me started about the weather.'

Lincoln gave a lazy smile and laid his arm along the back of her seat. 'You've already won over one heart.' He nodded towards the young driver, who was shut off from them by a panel of glass for privacy. 'Let's hope Nina is as easy to win over.'

Elodie angled her head to look at him. 'You don't call her "Mum" now that your adoptive mother has passed away?'

He absently toyed with the loose strands of her hair, sending electrifying tingles down her back.

'I don't think it's appropriate. My adoptive mother will always be my mother, so too my father. They earned the titles by the love and care they gave me all those years.'

'Given you had such a nice childhood, I find it intriguing as to why you no longer want children yourself.'

His hand stopped playing with her hair and went back to resting along the back of her seat. A line of tension formed around his mouth. 'When my mother died I was thrown off course, as were my father and siblings. Pancreatic cancer took her so quickly. One minute she was well, the next she was critically ill, and she died within a few weeks. Dad went into a slump. I'd never seen him so low…' He released a long sigh and continued, 'Then I met you and I suddenly saw a future. A bright and happy future that would include kids and family life—the sort of family life my parents had given me.'

Elodie frowned, not sure she liked his reasons for wanting to marry her back then. They didn't seem to have anything to do with *her*. She could have been any suitable woman to fill the role as his wife and future mother of his children. He had liked what she represented—a beautiful wife to grace his home—but he hadn't loved *her*.

'But you don't hanker after that family life now?'

'Aiden and Sylvia are planning on having kids with their partners,' Lincoln said. 'My father will be thrilled to have a bunch of grandkids to dote on. I can concentrate on my work and on living life the way I prefer.'

'Footloose and fancy-free.' She didn't state it as a question but as a statement of fact. 'Once a playboy, always a playboy.'

Lincoln gave a mercurial smile. 'My inner playboy is on pause for the next six months.'

Elodie gave him a pointed look. 'Can I trust you on that?'

His eyes drifted to her mouth and then back to her gaze. 'The discipline will be good for me.'

# CHAPTER SIX

Nina was waiting for them in the salon, where bright shafts of sunlight were coming in from the large windows, casting her in a golden, almost ethereal glow. She rose from the sofa and came towards them with both hands outstretched, her expression warm and welcoming.

'It is so lovely to meet you at last, my dear. Lincoln has told me so much about you.'

Elodie took the older woman's soft hands in hers and gave them a gentle squeeze. 'It's wonderful to meet you too. And lovely of you to have us stay with you for a couple of days.'

Nina kissed Elodie on both cheeks and then, releasing her hands, turned to Lincoln. Her eyes watered, as if she could barely believe he was really standing there in front of her. It touched Elodie to see the love in Nina's eyes.

'Lincoln, darling, thank you for bringing your beautiful wife to meet me. I know you're terribly busy, and I really do appreciate it.'

Lincoln enveloped his biological mother in a gentle

hug. It was as if he was worried he might break her. She was indeed a little thin, and had a frail air about her, but her eyes were sparking and clear.

'It's always good to see you. How have you been?'

Nina eased out of his hold with a crooked smile. 'So-so. Some days are better than others. But today is a good day.' She beamed at Elodie. 'Shall we have a drink to celebrate your marriage? Alita has made some sangria. We can go out to the terrace and enjoy the view.'

A short time later they were sitting under a large umbrella on the terrace with tall glasses of delicious and refreshing sangria in front of them. Elodie couldn't take her eyes off the stunning vista in front of her: ancient Roman ruins, including an outdoor theatre, interspersed with lush green hills and the port of Sagunto in the distance.

'Wow, it's so lovely…' She put her glass down before she was tempted to drain it. The last thing she wanted to do was get tipsy in front of Nina. But then, being here with Lincoln, especially with him sitting so close and holding one of her hands, was enough to make her feel drunk.

'It's my happy place,' Nina said, with a smile that encompassed Lincoln as well.

'Have you lived here long?' Elodie asked, reaching for one of the marinated olives on the tapas plate on the table.

'Two years,' Nina said and, glancing lovingly at Lincoln, added, 'Lincoln bought the villa for me as a birthday gift soon after we met. So very generous of him.'

Elodie put the pit of her olive on the little dish set on the table for such a purpose. She knew all about his generosity. He had bought her expensive gifts in the past—the missing engagement ring being a case in point. It still irked her that he didn't believe she had taken it back to his house. But if he hadn't found it, surely his housekeeper had? It couldn't have disappeared unless someone had stolen it—someone else who'd come into the house that day. Her new engagement ring was even more expensive, but she realised with a jolt that it was his trust she valued the most. That, to her, was priceless. Would he ever give it to her?

'I guess he missed a lot of your birthdays, so it was his way of making up for it.'

Nina's smile faded and she sighed and looked away into the distance. 'Yes, a lot of birthdays…'

Lincoln released Elodie's hand and stood, bending down to drop a light kiss to the top of her head. 'If you will excuse me? I'm going to have a chat to Elonzo about some maintenance that needs doing. I'll see you at dinner.'

Elodie waited until he had walked down the stairs from the terrace that led into the expansive gardens below before she turned back to look at Nina. 'It must have been very difficult to give him up all those years ago.'

Nina's eyes shimmered and her chin gave a distinct wobble. She reached for her glass of sangria but didn't drink from it. Her fingers moved up and down the frosted glass in a reflective manner.

'I wanted to keep him so much. It tore my heart out to give him up. But I was young and left reeling after the death of Lincoln's father. He was killed in a motorcycle accident on his way to see me when I was four months pregnant. I didn't have my family's support. They were deeply religious, and I knew bringing a born-out-of-wedlock child into the family would have a negative impact on the child in the long run.'

She glanced at Elodie, her expression pained.

'I decided to give Lincoln away to give him the best chance in life. I always thought I did the right thing, but when I met him a couple of years ago...' She gave a long sigh and continued, 'I could see he wasn't happy. Oh, he was successful, and wealthy beyond belief, and he'd had a good childhood thanks to his wonderful adoptive parents... But in himself... No. Not happy.'

She looked into Elodie's eyes.

'I blamed myself for that. I tortured myself with it. But now he is back with you he will be content at last. I know it in my heart of hearts.'

Elodie painted a smile on her face, feeling her own heart cramping in her chest at the deception she was complicit in. She was surprised Nina couldn't see through it—but then, didn't people who wanted something so badly see it even when it wasn't there? Nina wanted Lincoln's happiness more than anything else in the world. She believed that happiness and fulfilment could be achieved through being reunited with his runaway bride—*her*.

'I'm surprised you're not angry with me for walking out on our wedding day seven years ago.'

Nina put her glass down and took one of Elodie's hands, holding her gaze once more. 'I didn't know you or Lincoln back then. But I can see you love him now. That's all that matters, yes?'

Elodie looked down at their joined hands, her emotions in turmoil. How could she blatantly lie to a dying woman? It seemed morally wrong to continue the pretence. She sensed a bond with Nina…a connection that was beyond explanation. Or was it because they both loved Lincoln?

'The thing is… I'm not sure he loves me the way I love him.'

There was a silence broken only by the rustling of leaves as a breeze passed by and the tweeting of birds in the shrubbery. In the distance, a motor scooter revved and whined as it went up one of the winding hills leading to the ruins of a castle.

Nina gently stroked the back of Elodie's hand. 'You've always loved him, yes? Even when you called off the wedding seven years ago?'

Elodie met the older woman's gaze, deciding to be honest not just to Lincoln's mother but also to herself. 'I was frightened I was going to lose myself in our relationship back then. Lincoln is so driven and focussed—success is everything to him. And I knew it would be hard to make my own mark on the world while living in his shadow.'

She pulled her hand away and laid it on her lap, curling up her fingers so her engagement and wedding rings caught the light.

'I saw it happen to my mother when my sister developed a nut allergy. She gave up everything to be at home with Elspeth. My dad walked out when we were six, leaving her with the burden of taking care of two little kids, one of whom could die at any moment from anaphylactic shock.' She let out a sigh and continued, 'Mum didn't just lose her career, she lost her potential to be the person she wanted to be. The person she thought she *would* be. I didn't want that to happen to me.'

'We all make choices we have to live with.' Nina gave a wistful smile. 'I've revisited my choice about giving up Lincoln so many times. I wasn't lucky enough to have any other children. I thought I was being punished for not keeping him. Not a day went past that I didn't think of him, wondering what he looked like, what he sounded like, what he was good at and so on. I'd walk past young men in the street and wonder if one of them could be him. I positively ached to find him, but I couldn't summon up the courage until two years ago—I was too terrified that he wouldn't want anything to do with me. I was blessed that he did. And then I realised he wasn't truly happy. I wondered if it was my fault he found it hard to express love because of being relinquished as a baby. You know…what if the bonding issue was ruined for him way back then?'

'But you did what you thought was the best for

him at the time. And he had a happy childhood. His parents loved him as their own.'

'I know, and I'll be forever grateful for that. But, like me, you now have to get to a point where you forgive and accept yourself and your choices. You did what you thought was right at the time by calling off the wedding. And now, like me, you've been lucky enough to get a second chance. Not everyone gets that.'

Elodie gave an answering smile touched by melancholy. 'I guess you're right.'

She might be able to forgive herself, but would Lincoln ever do so? That was the question she had no idea how to answer.

Elodie left Nina soon after, so the older woman could have a rest before dinner. The youngish housekeeper-cum-cook, Alita, escorted Elodie to the suite she had prepared with obvious pride. She opened the door of the bedroom on the first floor with a wide smile, her eyes sparkling as if she had binge-watched romantic movies and television shows for most of her life.

'Welcome to the honeymoon suite, Señora Lancaster. Elonzo brought up your luggage earlier. I hope you will be comfortable.'

'Thank you.'

Elodie stepped into the graciously decorated suite, trying not to notice the king-sized bed made up with snowy-white linen and the array of blood-red rose petals artfully scattered on top. The bed might be big enough to accommodate two people, but when those two people were her and Lincoln what would happen? His hands-off rule was going to be tested to the limit, that was what. And her self-control—never good around him at the best of times—was going to be challenged like never before.

Elodie heard the door close behind her as Alita left and let out a long, ragged breath. She moved across the wide expanse of floor to the bed, picturing Lincoln's dark head on the pillow next to hers.

Something in her belly turned over and her heart skipped a beat. She had fought for years to rid her mind of the erotic memories of being in his arms. The pleasure he'd evoked, the intense feelings he'd stirred in her like no one else. But she only had to close her eyes to recall the sensual glide of his hands along her naked flesh. His touch had sent fireworks through her blood each and every time. How could she share a bed with him and not want him?

The door opened again and she turned to see Lincoln standing there with an inscrutable expression. He shut the door with a definitive click that seemed overly loud in the silence. 'Everything all right?'

Elodie folded her arms and pursed her lips. 'The honeymoon suite has been lovingly prepared for us by Nina's delightful young housekeeper.'

He came further into the room and tossed his phone on the end of the bed. 'I'm sure we'll manage to keep our hands off each other.'

She angled her head at him. 'You think?'

He gave an indolent smile and walked over to where she was standing, stopping just in front of her. Close enough for her to see the green and blue flecks in his eyes and the dark bottomless circles of his pupils.

'What? Are you worried you won't be able to keep your hands off me?'

Elodie unfolded her arms and placed them on his chest. 'I have a feeling you *want* me to put my hands on you. You want it very much.'

Her voice came out as a throaty whisper and she felt her pulse kicking up its pace at his nearness. The salt and citrus smell of him teased her senses, and the hard muscles of his chest beneath her hands reminded her of the potent power of his male body. She could almost feel it rising in the small space between their bodies—the arousal he couldn't hide or deny.

She pressed herself against the swollen heat of his body, relishing the potent length of him responding to her in spite of his rules. There were no rules strong enough to contain the lust they felt for each other. She could feel it in the air like a third presence in the room. A throbbing invisible energy that drew them together as powerfully as a magnet to metal.

Lincoln's eyes darkened and he drew in a sharp-sounding breath, his hands going to her upper arms in a hold that was on the wrong side of gentle. But she didn't care if he left fingerprints on her flesh. She wanted him. All of him.

'You're playing a dangerous game.'

His tone was rough and deep, his fingers momentarily tightening on her arms.

'What's so dangerous about doing what we do so

well, hmm? Or have you forgotten how good we were together?'

His hooded gaze went to her mouth, lingered there for a pulsing moment. 'No, damn you, I haven't forgotten.'

He brought his mouth down on hers in an explosive kiss that sent a rush of heat through her body. His hands left her upper arms to move around her, crushing her closer to him, so close she could feel the hardened ridge of his erection. A frisson passed through her—a delicious frisson that made the hairs on her head stand on end and a pool of molten heat form in her core.

He backed her up against the nearest wall, his mouth still clamped to hers. She arched her spine in a desperate quest for more intimate friction, and gasped when one of his hands lifted her dress to her hips. His hand gliding along her bare thigh sent another wave of intense heat through her core. Damp heat that smouldered and steamed and simmered in secret.

Lincoln's mouth moved from hers to kiss the ultrasensitive skin below her ear, the movement of his lips sending shivers cascading down her spine. He moved lower to the skin of her neck, and then her décolletage, the caresses light but no less tantalising. His hand slid further up her thigh to the edge of her knickers. Fervid excitement sent her pulse-rate soaring and her stomach swooped.

'Oh, God, *yes*...' she gasped against his mouth.

He traced the seam of her body through the lace

of her knickers, his intimate touch making her grind against his hand, desperate to assuage the burning ache of her flesh. He pushed her knickers to one side and his mouth came back down hard on hers, his tongue mimicking the flickering action of his fingers. The tension built in her to snapping point, a rush of sensation barrelling through her until she was swept off into the abyss on a tumultuous tide of pleasure.

Elodie clung to his tall frame, not sure her trembling legs would hold her upright as the aftershocks rumbled through her body. But, as intensely pleasurable as her orgasm had been, she knew she couldn't afford to let him think there was anything more than animal lust between them.

There wasn't and never could be.

She had loved him once, with a consuming, overwhelming love that had almost caused her to give up everything she had planned for her life. But she had come to her senses just in time.

If she had married him when she was twenty-one she would have been little more than a trophy wife. A beautiful woman who would grace his home and bear his children and then be pushed aside when she lost her looks or he got bored with her. She wouldn't have built her career to what it was today. She wouldn't have built her profile to the point where she could use it to fulfil her dream of producing her own designs.

Lincoln had never told her he loved her. She had pressed him a few times, but he had never said those three little magical words. And what was the point of hoping he might say them in the future? He had been blatantly honest about his reasons for marrying her. She was only back in his life because he wanted to give his dying mother end-of-life peace.

There was no other reason.

Elodie straightened her clothes with a sultry smile. 'You certainly haven't lost your touch.' She tiptoed her fingers down to the waistband of his chinos. 'Let's see if I've lost mine, shall we?'

Lincoln's hand captured hers in a firm hold, his expression unreadable. 'No.'

She arched her brows in a cynical manner, determined not so show how much his rejection hurt her. She pulled her hand out of his and opened and closed her fingers, her skin tingling from the heat of his touch. 'You really are serious about those rules of yours, aren't you?'

'I am.'

Elodie shifted her mouth from side to side in a musing way. 'May I ask why?'

'I told you—it will make it a lot easier to dissolve our marriage when the six months is up.'

He moved to the other side of the room, taking his jacket from where it was lying over the back of a chair and moving towards the built-in wardrobe. He slid one of the mirrored doors back and took a coat hanger from the rack. He hung his jacket on it, then placed it in the wardrobe and closed the door again. His actions were precise, methodical, as though the task helped him process his thoughts.

He turned and faced her again, with a light of determination in his gaze that struck a chord of unease in her. 'I don't want any lasting mistakes from our temporary union.'

Elodie frowned, in spite of her determination to act cool and unmoved by his stern composure and stance. 'What do you mean by "lasting mistakes"?'

His eyes bored into hers. 'Are you currently using contraception?'

'Of course.'

A low-dose pill was her only option at the moment, because she had struggled to find one that didn't affect her mood. Not that she was good at remembering to take it regularly. But she'd figured that since she hadn't exactly been putting herself 'out there' since her ill-fated hook-up with Fraser MacDiarmid, it was the best alternative. And since Lincoln was so adamant their marriage was to be on paper only—well, what did it matter if it didn't have the same reliability as other methods?

Lincoln held her gaze for a pulsing moment, then his eyes drifted to her mouth and he sucked in an audible breath. 'We'll have to share the bed or Alita and Nina will suspect something is up.'

Elodie gave him a playful smile, sensing he was struggling to keep to his own rules. It gave her a sense of feminine power that sent a thrill through her flesh. He wanted her, but his fight was not with her but with himself.

'Do you want to toss for which side to sleep on? I seem to remember you like being on the right—or have you changed since we last—?'

'The right is still my preference.'

She made a little snorting noise. 'That figures.'

'Why?'

'Because you always like to be right.'

A crooked smile formed on his lips. 'So do you.'

Elodie shrugged in a nonchalant manner, and went to the dressing table where she had left her cosmetics. She picked up her cleanser and then sat on the velvet-covered chair. She caught his eye in the mirror. 'What?'

Lincoln came over and laid his hands on the tops of her shoulders, still holding her gaze in the mirror. 'I haven't really thanked you properly for agreeing to all this.'

There was a different quality to his tone—a softer, warmer note that made her heart suddenly contract.

'All this?'

'Pretending to be in love and happily married. It means the world to Nina to see us reunited.'

Elodie placed one of her hands over his, where it was resting on her shoulder. 'I really like her. It's so sad that she has so little time left with you…especially as you only found each other a couple of years ago.'

One of his hands began playing with the long tresses of her hair in an absent fashion. His touch sent shivers dancing over her scalp and down her spine.

'Life isn't always fair, but we have to deal with it.' His hand fell away from her hair, the other from her shoulder.

Elodie spun around on the chair and craned her neck to look up at him. 'How will you deal with it? Her death, I mean?'

Lincoln let out a long breath and rubbed a hand over his face. 'The same way I coped with losing my adoptive mother.'

She raised her eyebrows. 'By trying to rush into marrying a woman you barely knew and didn't even love?'

There was a beat or two of silence.

Lincoln continued to hold her gaze, but his was screened—like a blacked-out window in an abandoned building. There was a muscle near the corner of his mouth that twitched once or twice, as if he couldn't decide whether to give a rueful smile or grind his teeth, and then he released a long sigh.

'I wish I'd searched for her earlier. I lost her as a baby and now I'm going to lose her again. When we're only just getting to know one another. She's filled the hole my adoptive mother left behind, but I'm conscious of the time ticking away. Every day that goes by is a day closer to losing her. It's... torturous, to be honest.'

'Oh, Lincoln, I'm so sorry. It must be hard for both of you.'

He gave a stiff movement of his lips that passed for a dismissive smile. 'We'd better dress for dinner. Nina likes to dine early as she gets tired. I'll leave you to get ready in private.'

Elodie watched him stride away to the door of their suite. 'Lincoln?'

His hand had almost reached the doorknob, but he lowered it to his side and turned to face her, his expression guarded. 'Yes?'

His tone was clipped, with an edge of impatience, which only made her all the more determined to get close to him. He had lowered his guard enough to tell her about his sadness over the prospect of losing Nina. What else might he reveal if she encouraged him to be vulnerable with her? Would getting close to him physically unlock more of his emotional armour? What if the Lincoln she'd been engaged to in the past was not the *real* Lincoln? What if, like her, he had kept back a part of himself he allowed few people, if any, to see?

'You don't have to leave while I get ready. We've dressed and undressed in front of each other before—heaps of times. And we can take turns using the bathroom.' A smile played at the corners of her mouth and she added, 'I promise I won't peek.'

The line of his mouth remained tight, but his eyes darkened. 'I'm going for a walk. I'll be back in half an hour.'

He walked out and closed the door with a firm click that sounded as definitive as a punctuation mark.

Lincoln went for a brisk walk through the gardens to get himself back in line. The more time he spent with Elodie alone, the harder it was to resist her. She was flirting outrageously with him, and he would be lying if he said he didn't enjoy every moment of her playful behaviour.

He did. Too much. Way too much.

But it wasn't just the playful flirting that got to him. She had revealed more about herself than she ever had in the past, and so had he. This new emotional connection between them was strange...foreign to him...because he always kept people at a distance. And keeping Elodie at a distance was supposed to be his top priority.

But she was making it near impossible to keep his hands off her—especially as he remembered all too well how clever those little hands of hers could be. How hot and tempting her soft mouth. Kissing her had almost blown the top of his head off. And the passion that flared between them was getting harder and harder to control.

Her cheeky bend-the-rules personality had always appealed to him—mostly because his nature tended to lean towards the colour-between-the-lines conservative. She evoked in his staider personality a recklessness that was exciting to indulge. She made his flesh sing when she touched him. Her lips had set his alight and he could still taste the fresh sweetness of her. It was like a drug he had forgotten how much he craved. One taste and he was addicted all over again.

But their marriage had a short timeline, and he was adamant there would be no casualties in the aftermath. As far as he was concerned this was a business deal like any other. Emotions were not required, and in fact only blurred the boundaries. And he needed boundaries when it came to Elodie.

Firm, impenetrable boundaries.

Lincoln stood for a moment, looking at the view of the ruins of Sagunto Castle. The fortress-style castle had a history going back two thousand years. His history with Elodie was much shorter. And while the fortress he had built around himself was not quite in crumbling ruins, he would still have to be careful to keep it secure.

*But... But...*

A persistent voice kept niggling at him. What if he indulged himself with a little tweak of the rules? After all, he had always kept his emotions out of his sex life. Sex was a physical experience he enjoyed on a regular basis, with like-minded women who played by the same rules. No strings, no promises, no commitment other than for a brief interlude of mutual pleasure.

The pleasure he and Elodie had experienced together in the past was something he couldn't eradicate from his mind or indeed from his body. The memory of possessing her, the slick, wet tightness of her body and her passionate response to him, was something he had never been able to recreate to quite the same degree with anyone else. In fact, for years he'd had trouble having sex without his mind drifting to her.

Maybe these six months would be the antidote to his obsession with her. He could finally move on with his life once he had ruled a thick black line under them as a couple.

End of story.
No sequel.
No reruns.
Finished.

Elodie was doing the final touches to her make-up when Lincoln came back to their suite. She squinted one eye to apply her volume-enhancing mascara. 'The bathroom's free.' She blinked a couple of times and then dabbed the wand back into the container. 'I hope what I'm wearing is okay. Not too OTT?'

Lincoln would have preferred to see her naked, but decided to keep that to himself. The hot pink dress she was wearing should have clashed with her red-gold hair and creamy complexion, but somehow she made everything look stunning on her.

'You look great.'

He moved further into the room, resisting the temptation to touch her. He could smell her perfume—a rich, exotic blend of flowers and spice that teased his nostrils and tantalised his senses. Her hair was piled up in a makeshift bun that somehow managed to looked casual and elegant at the same time. But then, that was Elodie to a tee. She would look glamorous without a scrap of make-up on and dressed in a rubbish bin liner.

She reached for her lip-gloss and leaned closer to the mirror to apply it. He couldn't tear his eyes off her plump lips as she painted the glistening colour on her mouth. She pressed her lips softly together and then glanced at him in the mirror, a mercurial smile forming, her blue eyes sparkling like the diamond droplet earrings dangling from her ears.

'Nice walk?'

'Nice enough.'

She picked up a soft brush and dusted some highlighter down the slope of her nose. 'Still hot outside?'

'Yes.'

*But not as hot as in here*, Lincoln wanted to say, but didn't.

Heat was pooling in his groin—a fiery heat that bloomed and flared like wildfire. If ever there was a time for a cold shower, this was it. He went into the en suite bathroom and closed the door, but even in there he was surrounded by the alluring, bewitching scent of her.

There were wet towels hanging haphazardly over the rail and he suppressed a wry smile. It was certainly an improvement from her leaving them on the floor, as she had so often in the past. He had argued about it with her numerous times, but he had never managed to housetrain her. He wondered now why he'd bothered. Of course, these days Elodie had a team of people picking up after her. She had personal assistants and make-up artists and hair stylists who were at her beck and call, catering to her every whim.

Lincoln had to make sure he didn't become one of them.

# CHAPTER SEVEN

ELODIE WALKED DOWN to the dining room with Lincoln a short time later. He was dressed in a casual suit with an open-necked white shirt that brought out the olive tan of his skin. She had briefly left their suite while he showered and changed, not sure she could trust herself not to melt at his feet if he came out dressed in only a towel slung around his lean hips.

Lincoln's arm slipped around her waist as they entered the dining room.

Nina looked up from her seat with a warm smile. 'You both look so good together—like movie stars or something. I love those earrings, Elodie. Did Lincoln give them to you?'

Elodie flicked one of her earrings with her finger. 'No, I was given them by a lingerie designer a couple of years ago.'

'It must be an exciting life…travelling the world and modelling lovely things,' Nina said.

'Yes, well…it's kind of lost its appeal, to be honest,' Elodie said, as Lincoln pulled out her chair for her. She flashed a smile of thanks to him and returned her gaze to Nina. 'I'm pursuing a new career now.'

'Lincoln told me you're an aspiring dress designer. How wonderfully creative. Maybe you could design something for me...' A flicker of something passed over her face and she continued in a subdued tone, 'Not that I could give you much time to do so, given my diagnosis.'

Elodie reached for the older woman's hand and gave it a gentle squeeze, her own eyes watering. So much for never showing her emotions, but something about Lincoln's biological mum's situation tore at her heartstrings.

'I'm sorry to hear you're so ill. Life can be unfair. Is there nothing that can be done? Nothing at all?'

Nina patted Elodie's hand in a resigned manner. 'There have been so many treatments and experiments and drugs, but I'm something of a mystery to my doctors. I get the feeling they don't know what to do with me now. They've run out of options. I've come to terms with it, more or less. But it will be sad not living long enough to meet my grandchildren... I would have loved that more than anything...' She gave a deep sigh and stretched her lips into a smile. 'But let's not be maudlin. I have much to be grateful for and I count each day as a bonus—especially now you two are back together.'

Elodie wasn't game to look in Lincoln's direction and kept her gaze focussed on Nina's. 'I'd love to design you a dress—in fact, a complete wardrobe of outfits. You might as well make the most of the time you have left. And there are such things as miracles. It's good to have some hope, I guess. That's better than giving up, right?'

Nina's smile was so motherly and affectionate it made Elodie's heart all but explode with emotion.

'Sweet child. I can see why my son fell so hard for you. Design away, my dear. I will be proud to wear every item.'

Elodie was so inspired to get to work on some outfits for Nina that she barely touched the delicious food placed before her during the meal. Her mind was buzzing, and colours and fabric designs were swirling about in her head as she planned a bright and colourful collection.

Finally, the meal came to an end and Nina bade them goodnight and retired to her quarters.

Lincoln picked up his still half-full wine glass and gestured to Elodie to do the same. 'Come out to the terrace for a while. It's a little early to go to bed.'

Elodie raised her eyebrows. Was he prolonging the time before the moment they'd have to go upstairs to share the suite? Surely he wasn't...*nervous*?

She curved her lips into a teasing smile. 'Since when is it too early for us to go to bed? I seem to remember us having quite a number of early nights in the past.'

A glinting light appeared in his gaze. 'That was never the problem between us, was it? The sex?'

She glanced over her shoulder to see Alita, the young housekeeper, hovering in the doorway, waiting to clear the room. 'Thanks for a lovely meal, Alita.'

'You're most welcome, *señora*.'

Elodie turned back to Lincoln. 'The terrace sounds like a good idea.'

And, picking up her own glass, she followed him out through the French doors to where a full moon was shining.

The shift of location gave her a moment to reflect on their past relationship. Making love with Lincoln had always been phenomenal. From their very first time it had showed her a world of sensuality and pleasure she hadn't experienced with anyone else before. But while it had been wonderful in every way, it had also covered up the tiny cracks in their relationship that had been there right from the start. Fine cracks that had developed into the deep fissures she had ignored until the day of their wedding, when she hadn't been able to ignore them any longer.

They hadn't communicated other than through sex. And making love was not a good substitute for effective communication. Perfect strangers could have good sex. She had never been able to share her doubts and fears and insecurities with him and he had never shared his—if he'd had any, that was.

'Actually, I think it was a big part of the problem.'

Lincoln leaned against the stone balustrade with his glass in one hand. 'What do you mean?' There was an edge of guardedness in his tone.

Elodie moved across the terrace to stand within half a metre of him and placed her glass of wine on the balustrade. The last thing she needed was more alcohol to loosen her tongue. 'I think we used the chemistry we had together as a distraction from… other things.'

'What other things?'

She half turned to look up at him, but the moonlight coming from behind him had cast his features into an unreadable shadow. 'When we argued over something, we used sex to clear the air rather than sitting down and talking through stuff. Talking about why we had argued in the first place.' She licked her lips and continued, 'It was a pattern we drifted into from the start. Fight and have make-up sex. We never resolved the underlying issue.'

'Which was?'

'We knew each other physically, but not emotionally.'

Lincoln moved so that he was looking out at the moonlit view, his forehead creased in a frown. 'I'm not saying you were totally to blame for our breakup,' he said. 'I didn't like how you went about it, that's all.'

His grip on his wine glass was so tight, she was worried it might break.

'You should've told me you weren't happy,' he added.

'But that's my point. We never *talked* about things. We never got that far. You were always busy chasing your next big deal, becoming more and more successful, as if that was the only thing that really mattered to you. I was nothing more than an ornament to you. A plaything you enjoyed having at your disposal. I was never your equal.'

He put his glass on the balustrade too, as if he too

was worried it might shatter under his grip. He turned to look at her, his expression still in shadow. 'Why did you feel you couldn't talk to me?'

The quality of his tone had changed—become softer, less defensive, more concerned.

Elodie blew out a soft breath. 'I don't know…' She gave a little shrug and continued, 'Maybe because I didn't think you would understand how important having a career was to me. I got the impression you wanted me to be a homemaker, like your adoptive mother, not a career woman. It scared me because that's what happened to my mum. She gave up everything to take care of Elspeth when she got sick. Then my dad left when we were six and poor Mum was left with nothing. No career, no money and no support other than the pittance he sent only because he was legally required to, not because he wanted to. No wonder she turned into a nervous wreck who never seemed to notice she had two children, not just one. I didn't just lose my dad when he left—I lost my mother too.'

There was a silence.

Lincoln reached out with one of his hands to brush a loose tendril of hair away from her face. 'I'm sorry. I didn't realise how hard that must've been for you. I knew your father was a bit of a lost cause, but I didn't know you felt pushed aside by your mother as well.'

Elodie grimaced. 'It's not really her fault. She did her best, and Elspeth was so sick a couple of times that losing her was a very real possibility. I learned to get attention in other ways—not always sensible ways, mind you…but, hey, it worked until it didn't.'

Lincoln's hand moved to capture one of hers, his fingers warm and gentle as he cradled it as if it was a baby bird. 'I guess none of us get out of childhood without a few issues, but it must have been terrifying to think you might lose your twin. You're still close, yes?'

Elodie smiled a little wistfully. 'Yes, she's amazing—especially now she's in love. She's really blossomed. Mack's been wonderful for her and she for him.' Her smile faded and she added, 'But I guess now Mack will be her go-to person, not me.'

Lincoln began an idle stroking over the back of her hand with his thumb, his gaze still trained on hers. 'I'm sure she'll always have a special place in her life for you.'

'Are you close to your siblings? And your father?'

He looked down at their joined hands for a moment, a slight frown pulling at his brow. 'I'm probably not as attentive a son and big brother as I should be. I'm always busy with work and travelling and so on.' He looked back at her and gave a rueful smile. 'Sylvia is always nagging me to make more time for family gatherings, but it's not the same without Mum.'

There was a thread of sadness in his tone that made her realise how deeply he still missed his adoptive mother. And now he had to face the prospect of losing his biological mother. Was it any wonder he would do anything—including marrying *her*—to make Nina's last days as peaceful and happy as possible?

Elodie found herself moving closer to him, one of her hands going to rest against his chest, the other reaching up to stroke the side of his lean jaw. 'Oh, Lincoln, I'm so sorry you lost her. And now you have to face losing Nina too.'

Lincoln settled his hands on her hips, his expression cast in grave lines. 'The thing that gets me is not knowing for sure when it will be. She looks fine at the moment—you'd hardly think anything was wrong. And yet on another day she can go down quickly and need to be in bed all day.'

'But you said the doctors told you no more than three or four months?'

He let out a serrated sigh. 'That was what they said the last time I spoke to them. It's not a long time, is it?'

'No, but I read this saying once: even the dying are still living. It's important that Nina gets to do all the things she wants to do. I meant what I said about designing a new wardrobe of clothes for her. I was mentally preparing sketches during dinner. I can't wait to get started.'

Lincoln smiled and lifted one of his hands to brush her cheek with his fingers. 'She's quite taken with you. I knew she would be.'

Elodie chewed at her lip for a moment. 'I can't help feeling a bit compromised, though. I mean, pretending we're madly in love when we can barely stand the sight of each other…'

He eased up her chin and locked gazes with her, his expression serious. 'Do you hate me that much?'

The problem was that she didn't hate him at all. She had the opposite problem—she was madly, deeply, crazily in love with him. Had she ever *not* been in love with him? She had tried to deny it, hide it, disguise it, but while it was possible to hide it from him, she couldn't hide it from herself. And hadn't Nina noticed it too? The older woman had intuitively sensed the feelings Elodie was keeping under lock and key for fear of being rejected.

Elodie gazed into the darkness of his eyes and tried to ignore the fluttering of her pulse. Tried to ignore the sensual pull of his body, the magnetic energy that drew her even closer until her hips were flush against his. 'No… I don't hate you…' Her voice came as a whisper, as soft as the night breeze currently playing with the tendrils of her hair.

He framed her face in his hands, his gaze still trained on hers. 'It would be easier if you did, you know…' His voice was as rough as the stone balustrade that held their wine glasses.

'Why?'

'Because then I wouldn't be tempted to do this.'

He lowered his mouth to hers in a long, drugging kiss that sent shivers racing up and down her spine like electrodes. His tongue entered her mouth with erotic intent, the glide and stroke of it against hers sending her senses haywire.

He made a groaning sound and drew her even closer, wrapping his arms around her. He angled his head to deepen the kiss, and a warm rush of longing almost overwhelmed her in its intensity. Kissing him wasn't enough. She wanted to feel his thick, hard presence where she needed it the most.

She moved against him, signalling her need, and he sucked in a harsh breath and kissed her more firmly, as if only just managing to stay in control.

After a few breathless moments, he lifted his mouth off hers, his eyes glazed with lust. 'About those rules…'

Elodie stepped up on tiptoe and planted another playful kiss to his lips. 'Don't tell me you've changed your mind about your silly old rules?'

He gave a lopsided smile and cupped the curves of her bottom in his hands, holding her against the pounding heat of his aroused body. 'Then I won't tell you. I'll show you instead.'

He scooped her up in his arms, and even though she gave a token squeak of protest continued carrying her through the French doors and all the way up the stairs to their suite.

Once they were inside their bedroom, he let her slide down the length of his body to the floor. Every deliciously sexy ridge of his toned body teased hers into a frenzy of want. Need clawed through her tingling flesh, making her wonder how she had gone seven years without feeling anywhere near this height of sensual awareness.

Lincoln crushed her mouth beneath his, the passionate pressure of his lips and the gliding thrust of his tongue into her mouth only ramping up her desire.

He raised his mouth barely a millimetre above

hers, his breath mingling intimately with hers. 'No one turns me on quite like you do.'

Elodie combed her fingers through his hair, barely able to take her eyes off his mouth. How could a man's mouth—this man's mouth—create such a firestorm of need in her body?

'I hate to boost your ego too much, but it's the same for me. I want you even though my head tells me it's a mistake to get involved again.'

He stroked his thumb over her bottom lip, his touch sending tingles straight from her mouth to her core. 'It's only for six months. It's not like we're making any promises beyond that.'

And there was the kicker for her. The time frame. The temporary nature of their marriage. So different from what he had proposed seven years ago. He had once offered her for ever. This time he had only offered for now.

And yet... And yet how could she not accept the new terms? She had not truly moved on from him, in spite of all her efforts. Maybe six months of living and sleeping together as man and wife would help her reframe their relationship. Help her to see it for what it was and always had been—nothing more than a stunning physical chemistry that would eventually burn itself out.

Elodie painted a smile on her lips—a fake smile that pulled at her mouth like too-tight stitches. 'You mean we're not going to fall in love with each other? That's still against the rules, right?'

A flicker of something passed through his hooded

gaze, like a blink-and-you'd-miss-it movement in a deeply shadowed forest. 'Do you think it's likely?' he asked.

'You mean for me or for you?'

'For you.'

Elodie kept her eyes focussed on the sculptured perfection of his mouth rather than meet the probing intensity of his gaze. Of course he wouldn't consider himself in any danger of falling in love with her. He hadn't before, so why would he now? He loved how she looked. He was in lust with her. Was he even capable of romantic love?

'Anything's a possibility, I guess.' She brought her gaze back to his with a carefree smile. 'But what has love got to do with red-hot lust, hey? Not much.'

Lincoln brought his mouth down to within a millimetre or two of hers. 'Speaking of lust...' He brushed her lips with a kiss that made her hungry for more. 'Do you have any idea of how much I want you right now?'

She nestled closer, delighting in the proud bulge of his erection. Her inner core tightened in anticipation. The walls of her womanhood were already slick with moisture. 'I think I've got a fair idea.'

She nibbled at the edge of his mouth with teasing little nibbles that she followed up with a sweep of her tongue. He groaned deep in his throat and grasped her by the hips, bringing her even closer.

'I want to go slowly,' he said in a husky tone.

'Don't you freaking dare...' Elodie pulled his head down so his mouth came back to set fire to hers.

# CHAPTER EIGHT

ELODIE WOKE FROM a deep, blissful sleep to find Lincoln had left the bed. She glanced at the bedside clock and frowned. It was three in the morning. She pushed back the covers and slipped on her wrap, tying the ties around her waist. There was no light on in the bathroom, but the doors leading out to the balcony were open, for she could see the billowing of the silk curtains as the night breeze stirred them. She pushed the curtains aside to find Lincoln standing against the balustrade with his back to her. He was wearing his underwear but the rest of him was naked.

'Lincoln?'

He turned and smiled at her. 'Sorry. Did I wake you?'

'Not really.' She went over to where he was standing and touched him on the arm. 'Can't you sleep?'

He picked up her hand from where it was resting on his arm and brought it up to his mouth, his eyes still holding hers. He kissed the ends of her fingers, one by one, his touch sending tremors of pleasure through her body.

'I guess I've got used to spending the night alone.'

Elodie frowned. 'Alone? I don't understand... You mean you don't spend the night with any of your... your lovers?'

Lincoln released her hand and turned back to look at the moonlit view. His hands gripped the balustrade and even in the low light she could see the straining of the tendons in the backs of his hands. 'I prefer not to.'

Elodie stared at him for a long moment, trying to get her head around this latest revelation. *He no longer spent the whole night with a lover.* Then she recalled that he had said he hadn't been with anyone for months after their breakup, in spite of the photo she had seen in the press the week after she'd jilted him. The photo that had cut at her like a flick knife, making her hate him for moving on so quickly.

She hadn't realised until she saw the photo how much she had wanted him to come after her, to fight for her, to beg her to come back to him. To reassure her that he cared about her, that he wanted to be with her, that even, by some miracle, he loved her.

But he had done none of that.

And because of that damn photo she hadn't made any effort to contact him other than the brief note of apology she had left on the hall table with the engagement ring—which, of course, he claimed he hadn't got.

'Lincoln...you said the other day you didn't sleep with anyone for months after we broke up. Why was that?'

His expression was as screened as the moon was

just then by a passing cloud. 'Don't go reading too much into it.'

'But why did you actively encourage me—and the rest of the world when it comes to that—to believe you'd moved on to someone else the very next week?'

'Why would that upset you? You were the one who jilted me. You made it clear we were over. More than clear.'

Elodie shifted her gaze from his and rolled her top lip over her bottom one, a frown still pulling at her forehead. 'I know I had no right to be upset. I guess I thought you might...try and talk me round.'

He gave a short bark of incredulous laughter. 'Really? You mean come crawling on my hands and knees, begging you to come back to me? Shows how little you knew me back then.'

Her shoulders went down on a heavy sigh. 'Yes, well...that works both ways, doesn't it?'

Lincoln glanced at her, his expression still inscrutable. But then he sighed and raked a hand through his hair, before dropping it back by his side. 'Was there anything I could've said to get you to change your mind back then?'

His tone had lost its sharp, mocking edge and become deeper, almost gentle. Elodie forced a smile, not sure she wanted to reveal any more than she already had. It was funny, but she could parade in the skimpiest lingerie and swimwear on catwalks and billboards all over the world, and yet revealing her vulnerability to Lincoln was the scariest, most terrifying thing of all.

'Probably not.' She wrapped her arms around her body against the chill of the night air.

There was a lengthy silence.

Lincoln stepped closer and lifted her chin with two of his fingers, meshing his gaze with hers. 'It wasn't my best moment, having that photo circulated of me with that young woman.' He gave a rueful twist of his mouth, then lowered his hand from her face and continued, 'You should have heard the dressing-down Sylvia gave me. She thought it was unspeakably crass. But I was angry and bitter. It's not often I get blindsided by someone—especially someone who'd claimed they loved me.'

*But I did love you.*

The words were stuck behind the wall of her pride. The pride she needed to keep from getting hurt all over again.

Elodie moved further away from him, wrapping her arms around her middle to ward off the sudden chill of the night air. 'Look—I was young, and I had stars in my eyes. You showed me a world I'd never had access to before. A world of wealth and privilege and private jets and God knows what else. I fooled myself into thinking you cared about me, but what you cared about was having a beautiful wife. I'd have completed your successful lifestyle. A good-looking wife who you saw as an asset rather than a person in her own right. But you didn't offer me your heart in return.'

'I seem to remember you made the most of our breakup.'

The mocking tone was back, even more biting than before. And the steely look in his eyes was harder than the diamonds on her finger.

Elodie went back into the trench of her pride. 'And why shouldn't I have made the most of it? The sponsors approached me—not me them. I did realise it gave me the perfect opportunity to lift my profile, and I didn't see any reason I shouldn't use it. I was only doing itty-bitty modelling jobs before that, most of which only paid a pittance, and I found them demeaning. I wanted to get more control over the photos and the labels I wore, so shoot me for using our breakup to do it. Besides, you're the one who always says you shouldn't let emotions get in the way of a good business decision. I was simply taking your advice.'

There was a ringing silence.

Then Lincoln's mouth began to twitch with a smile. 'Methinks I've been hoist by my own petard.'

Elodie mock-pouted at him. 'That'll teach you for having one rule for you and another one for everyone else.'

He stepped towards her again and took her by the upper arms. His eyes meshed with hers, and there was a lopsided smile on his lips. He lifted his hand to her face and stroked his finger down the slope of her nose. 'That's another thing I missed about you. You always stood up to me.'

'What? No one else has since?'

He gave a rueful movement of his lips. 'Not quite like you do.' He stroked her bottom lip with his thumb. 'I'm surrounded by sycophants most of the time—people intent on pleasing me. It gets boring after a while.'

Elodie placed her hands against his chest, felt his warmth seeping into her like the rays of the sun. Her lower body brushed against his and a wave of longing swept through her. 'I'm glad you didn't find me boring. But if you were missing a good old ding-dong fight, why didn't you just call me? I'm sure we could have found something to argue about.'

She was only half joking. She had missed their fights too. In fact, she had missed way more than that. She had missed everything about him.

His eyes drifted to her mouth. 'That night we ran in to each other in Soho…' He grimaced, as if the memory pained him. 'When I saw you go off with Fraser MacDiarmid I was shocked at how much I wanted to stop you.'

Elodie arched her eyebrows. 'You said you weren't jealous that night.'

His expression had a hint of sheepishness about it. 'Seeing you again was…difficult. I'd seen you heaps of time on billboards or in magazine spreads and on television, but not in the flesh.' His eyes came back to hers, dark and glittering. 'I was jealous, angry… disappointed that it wasn't me you were going off with instead of him. The thing is, I'd never felt jealous before. It annoyed me that I felt it then.'

Elodie wasn't fool enough to think his jealousy signalled love. He was a proud man who had been publicly humiliated by her jilting him. Seeing her with another man would have triggered him in the same way she had been triggered by seeing him with his beautiful and clearly devoted new partner that night.

She lifted her hands to the tops of his broad shoulders, then slid them down his muscled arms to his strong wrists. His fingers entwined with hers and heat coursed through her body. 'We're going to have to deal with the chance of running into each other in the future—I mean, once we divorce.'

It seemed a good a time as any to remind him of the time frame on their marriage. To remind herself.

Lincoln placed one of his hands in the small of her back, bringing her up against him. 'Let's not mention the *D* word until after Nina passes.'

'But what if she doesn't die within our time frame? I mean, it can happen, you know… People go into remission, or a new drug is released, or—'

'Our agreement is six months and six months only.'

The edge of intractability in his tone was just the reminder she needed to keep her emotions in check.

'Fine.' She pulled out of his hold and sent a careless hand through her hair. 'I'm going back to bed.'

She turned and walked through the French doors, back into the bedroom, aware of Lincoln's footsteps following her. He came up behind her and placed his hands on her hips, pulling her against him. His hands cupped her breasts and a shiver of anticipation coursed over her flesh.

'Want me to join you?'

He spoke against the sensitive skin of her neck, sending another hot shiver racing down her spine like a cartwheeling fiery coal.

'I thought you didn't like spending the whole night with your casual lovers any more?'

Lincoln turned her so she was facing him. His smile was sardonic, his eyes glittering. 'You're not a casual lover—you're my wife.'

'For six months and six months only.' Elodie followed up her statement with a sugar-sweet smile. 'That's still a lot of nights sharing a bed.'

His hands skimmed down the sides of her body, from her shoulders, past her ribcage and waist, to settle on her hips, his gaze smouldering. 'Then let's not waste a single one of them.'

And his mouth came down and sealed hers hotly, explosively, possessively.

It was an urgent kiss that sent a river of fire through her blood and her body. Her inner core turned to molten lava within seconds, her need of him so intense it surged in pulsing and pounding waves through her most intimate flesh.

Lincoln tumbled with her to the bed, only stopping long enough to apply a condom. He rolled her over so she straddled him, his hands caressing her breasts with thrilling expertise. He guided himself into her, his expression a grimace of pleasure at the contact of aroused male flesh against aroused female flesh.

'You feel so damn good...' he groaned.

'You took the words right out of my mouth.'

*Not to mention taking her breath away.*

Elodie moved with him, the rocking motion of their bodies sending her over the edge within moments. She gasped out loud, riding out the powerful orgasm, her hair swishing wildly about her shoulders, her body so rattled and shaken by ripples of pleasure it was like being transported to another world. A world of intense sensuality where no thoughts were necessary.

This was not the time to think of the temporary nature of their relationship. This was not the time to think about the love she had for him that put her at so much risk of heartbreak. This was the time to enjoy a moment of pure ecstatic bliss, of two perfectly in tune bodies.

Elodie came floating back down from the stratosphere to watch Lincoln shuddering through his own release. It looked and sounded as mind-blowing as her own. She scooped her hair back over one of her shoulders and smiled down at him. 'You look like you had a good time.'

He gave a deep sigh. 'The best.'

Elodie lay over him with her head on his chest, their bodies still intimately joined. His hands stroked the curves of her bottom in lazy strokes that sent goosebumps popping up all over her skin.

'If you don't stop doing that, you're going to have to make love to me all over again.'

'Maybe that's exactly what I want to do.'

'So soon?'

'You bet.'

He flipped her so she was lying on her back, then swiftly disposed of the used condom before replacing it with a fresh one. He came back to her, leaning his weight on one elbow, one of his strongly muscled legs flung over one of hers. His other hand caressed her thigh in long slow movements that sent tingles down to her curling toes.

'I could make love to you all night.'

## CHAPTER NINE

The next couple of days passed in a blur of activity. Spending time with Nina was clearly a priority for Lincoln, which only made Elodie love and respect him more, but he also managed to show Elodie some of the tourist spots in the town—including the Roman theatre and the fortress castle.

They walked hand in hand as they explored the sights, and she tried to pretend they were just like any loved-up couple on their honeymoon. There were even times when she caught Lincoln looking at her with an indulgent look on his face, making her wonder if some of his bitterness about their breakup was finally melting away.

Certainly, there was no trace of it in his lovemaking. The passion they shared never ceased to amaze her. It seemed to be getting more intense, and there were moments of tenderness too, that were particularly poignant given their marriage was only temporary.

It was poignant too, to see Lincoln's relationship with his biological mother growing each day.

It touched Elodie to see the care he had for her, the way he made sure she had everything she needed. The villa and its grounds were immaculate, and managed with expertise, and the staff were friendly and supportive.

Elodie couldn't help comparing the lovely Alita with Morag. How could there be two such different housekeepers? One was so helpful, the other so spiteful. One made her feel welcome, the other made her feel like trailer trash, triggering the emotions of the past, when others had done the same. It made the thought of going back to London daunting—not to mention the prospect of leaving Nina, and wondering if it would be the last time they'd see her.

The morning of their departure, Nina wrapped her arms around Elodie in a warm, motherly hug. 'Take care of yourself, my dear. Don't work too hard, will you? And promise to come and see me again soon, yes?'

Elodie blinked back tears, her heart suddenly feeling cramped inside her chest cavity. 'I promise. Thank you for making me feel so welcome.' She eased back to look at the older woman, who was also tearing up. 'I'm so glad you and Lincoln found each other at last.'

Nina's smile was happy-sad. 'I waited a long time to make contact. Too long. But I wasn't sure if he would want to meet me. After all, I gave him up as a week-old baby. Some adoptees find that very hard to understand—why their birth mother gave them away. But I always loved him. I only ever wanted the best for him.'

Elodie stood back as Lincoln hugged Nina and said his own goodbyes. He had better control over his emotions, but she sensed he was also well aware that this could be the last time he saw Nina. She saw it in the set of his jaw, the fixed smile, the shadowed eyes, the aura of sadness that enveloped him.

Once they were in the car, with Elonzo driving, on their way to the airport, Elodie placed her hand on Lincoln's thigh. 'I really like Nina. She's so warm and friendly.'

He took her hand and gave it a gentle squeeze. 'Yeah, she's great.' His voice was sandpaper-rough. 'I'm glad she liked you.'

Elodie glanced at her wedding and engagement rings, glittering on her hand. 'Yes, well…it would've been a disaster if she hadn't, given you've gone to the trouble of marrying me and all.'

His gaze met hers, his expression inscrutable. 'Has it been such a trial so far?'

She leaned closer to plant a kiss on his lips. 'No…' Her voice came out a little husky. 'But I can't say I'm looking forward to living in the same house as Mean Morag. Alita is so lovely and sweet. She falls over herself to help.'

'I hope you don't call Morag that to her face?'

'No, of course not.'

He sighed and ruffled the loose strands of her hair. 'I'll have a word with her about reducing her hours. That way you won't have to run into her so often.'

'I probably won't be home during the day much anyway. I have work to do. I've got to find a studio—

preferably close to the centre of London, which will cost a bomb, but—'

'I know of a place you could use,' Lincoln said. 'It's around the corner from my office—the one that's currently being renovated. It has space for a showroom as well.'

A flicker of excitement coursed through her blood. 'Really? How much will the rent be, do you think?'

'I'll have a word with the landlord. He might do mates' rates or something.'

'Wow, that would be awesome.'

He brought her hand up to his chest, his eyes meshing with hers. 'You might not believe this, but I really want you to succeed.'

Elodie didn't ask for clarification, because she already knew what was behind his motivation for her success. Her career would be all she was left with after their marriage came to an end. It would be her consolation prize.

'I'll do my best,' she said.

Within a few of days of coming back to London, Elodie was setting up her studio with Elspeth's help. Some of the furniture had yet to arrive, and there was a lot more to do in terms of preparing her creative space, but it was like a dream come true to have her own place at last.

'I've got a good feeling about this venture of yours,' Elspeth said, unloading some fabric swatches from a box. 'I can't wait to come in and have some fancy evening wear designed for me by you.'

'Hey, I thought you didn't like dressing up?' Elodie teased. 'What happened to the shy librarian archivist who only wore brown and beige and flat shoes?'

Elspeth pulled the plastic wrapping off one of the velvet showroom chairs and gave a dreamy smile. 'I've decided it's much more fun being a butterfly than a moth.' She bundled the wrapping into a ball and added, 'You haven't told me much about your trip to Spain apart from how nice Nina was. How was it?'

'It was good.'

'Only "good"?'

Elodie took the ball of plastic from her twin and stuffed it in the box she had set aside for recycling. 'We're not having a paper marriage any more.'

Elspeth's eyes twinkled. 'Wow!'

'Wow, indeed.' Elodie picked up one of the sketching sets she'd ordered and placed it on the table. 'This is probably way too much information to share, even for a twin sister, but I've never really enjoyed making love with anyone other than Lincoln.' She glanced at her twin. 'Is that weird, or what?'

'It's not weird at all,' Elspeth said. 'It shows you care about him. You do, don't you?'

Elodie sighed. 'Way more than I should, given we're only staying married for a matter of months.'

'That might change. I mean, Lincoln might change his mind and offer you more.'

'He was pretty blunt about it. Six months and six months only.'

'But he changed his mind about the paper marriage, right?'

Elodie picked up another parcel from the box she was unloading, a small frown tugging at her brow. 'I haven't decided yet if he always intended to tweak the rules or if I managed to convince him. He's so hard to read sometimes.'

Elspeth started to unwrap another velvet chair, a small smile playing about her mouth. 'I can only imagine the lengths you went to in order to change his mind.'

Elodie laughed. 'Now, that *would* be sharing way too much information.'

Elodie got back to Lincoln's London home to find Morag preparing dinner in the kitchen. She hadn't seen much of the housekeeper since she and Lincoln had returned from Spain. She had deliberately stayed away during Morag's working hours. But now that she had no choice but to interact with her, Elodie decided to try a new tactic—to act her way into feeling more positive about the grumpy housekeeper.

It was worth a try. Anything was worth a try.

'Can I do anything to help?'

Morag wiped the back of her hand across her forehead. 'No. I can manage.'

Elodie narrowed her gaze on the older woman's strange-looking pallor. She had a greyish tinge to her skin and beads of perspiration peppered her forehead. 'Are you okay?'

Morag gripped the edge of the kitchen bench with her hands. 'I… I think I might need some insulin…

I might have missed a dose…or eaten the wrong thing…'

Elodie rushed over and took her by the shoulders. 'Let me help you. Come and sit down and I'll get your insulin for you. Where is it?'

Morag sank into the chair with a sigh of relief. 'In my bedroom…' She took a gasping breath and slumped forward with her head bent over her knees. 'In the chest of drawers…top drawer, I think.'

'I'm going to call an ambulance.'

'Don't you dare. I'll be fine once I've had a dose.'

'Maybe you should lie down while I get it?' Elodie suggested. 'I don't want you to fall off that chair.'

Morag lifted her head to glare at her. 'Just bring me the insulin, will you?'

Elodie ground her teeth and ran upstairs to the top floor, where Morag had a small suite of rooms for when she stayed over. She rushed over to the chest of drawers, but the insulin wasn't in the top drawer as Morag had thought. She opened the second and third drawers, rustling through the housekeeper's belongings, but failed to find any medication.

The fourth and bottom drawer was stiff to open, and while she doubted the medication would be stored there, she thought it best to check anyway. She finally managed to get the drawer open and rummaged around the contents. Her eyes suddenly homed in on a velvet ring box, and her heart came to a complete standstill. She stared at the box for countless seconds, her heartbeat restarting with a loud *ba-boom, ba-boom, ba-boom* that made her suspect she was having her own medical crisis.

She reached for the box with a hand that wasn't quite steady, opening it to find her old engagement ring glittering there in all its brilliance. Something dropped like a tombstone in her stomach. Morag had the ring. All this time, the housekeeper had had the ring. But why?

Elodie heard the sound of Lincoln's firm footsteps coming along the corridor and quickly stashed the ring back in the drawer. She tried to shove it closed. The drawer wouldn't close all the way, but there wasn't time to worry about that. She straightened and glanced around the room, and saw an insulin kit sitting on a chair next to the bed. She snatched it up just as Lincoln came through the door.

'You found it? Great.' He took it off her and raced back downstairs, with Elodie in hot pursuit. 'I called an ambulance. It should be here any second now.'

'I offered to, but Morag insisted I didn't.'

'She can be difficult about her illness. She hasn't really accepted it.'

They got back to the kitchen and Lincoln helped administer a dose of insulin as if he had been moonlighting as a physician for years. Morag recovered within a few minutes, but by then the ambulance had arrived and Lincoln insisted she go to hospital to be checked out.

'But what about dinner?' Morag said.

'I'll sort it out,' Elodie said. 'You just concentrate on getting well again.'

Within a short time the paramedics had taken Morag away and Elodie and Lincoln were left alone.

Lincoln took Elodie by the hands, his expression rich with concern. 'Are you okay? You look like you're in shock.'

Elodie *was* in shock. Deep shock. Her heart was still pounding, sweat was trickling down between her shoulder blades, and her stomach was churning along with her brain. Here was her chance to tell him about the ring she had found, but for some reason she couldn't bring herself to do it. What if he thought she herself had planted it there? What if he didn't believe she had found it while looking for the insulin kit?

But if he did believe her, she realised it would poison his relationship with his housekeeper. The breach of trust would be hard to forgive—especially when Morag had worked for him for so long. Besides, she wanted to hear Morag's explanation first.

'I—I'm fine...' She forced a smile that didn't quite work. 'I'm not good in a crisis. Just ask Elspeth. Sick people terrify me.'

Lincoln stroked her hair away from her face, his gaze steady on hers. 'You did a great job of taking care of Morag.'

She gave a dismissive snort, her eyes drifting away from his. 'So, how was your day?'

He reached up to loosen his tie. 'Not bad. How did you go at the studio?'

'It was great. Elspeth came to help me unpack the stuff that's arrived so far. There's still heaps to do, but it feels so good to have my own space. I can't thank you enough for organising it for me.'

He gave her chin a playful brush with his fingers. 'It's my pleasure.'

Elodie plastered another smile on her lips and turned for the kitchen, saying over her shoulder, 'Give me half an hour or so and I'll have dinner ready for you.'

'You're starting to sound very wifey.'

There was a note of amusement in his tone.

She turned around to smile back at him. 'Make the most of it, baby. It's only for six months, remember?'

And then she disappeared into the kitchen.

Lincoln tugged his silk tie the rest of the way out of his collar, threading it through his fingers, a frown pulling at his forehead. Elodie was always reminding him of the temporary nature of their relationship. Was that for her benefit or his? He knew the time frame well enough—he was the one who'd put it in place. And it needed to stay in place, in spite of how well they were getting on.

Settling down to domesticity with Elodie was out of the question. Firstly, because he didn't want to lay himself open to the sort of heartache his father had gone through after losing his mother—loving for a lifetime contained certain devastation, for one partner always outlived the other. It was a fact of life and one he wanted to avoid experiencing first-hand. And secondly, because Elodie was like him—career-focussed.

She had left him before because she had wanted a career more than she wanted to be with him.

Now he was doing all he could to facilitate her career—it was the least he could do to repay her for how warmly she had bonded with Nina. He had hoped they would connect, but he hadn't dared hope they would get on as well as they had. It made him feel a little less compromised about the game of charades he and Elodie were playing.

But there were times when it didn't feel like a charade.

It felt real...scarily real.

Elodie was still mulling over the engagement ring hidden in the drawer upstairs when Lincoln came into the kitchen.

She quickly hung a tea towel over the oven door. 'No peeking. I want to surprise you with dinner.'

'It smells delicious.'

'It needs a few more minutes. Do you want a glass of wine?'

'Sure. You want one?'

'Not tonight.'

The last thing she wanted was to loosen her tongue with wine. The engagement ring incident was still playing on her mind. She couldn't work out why Morag would have done such a thing. Why hadn't she sold the ring? Why had she kept it after all this time? What could the housekeeper hope to achieve by keeping it stashed away? It didn't make any sense.

'I'm having an AFD.'

'Pardon?'

'An alcohol-free day.'

'Right…'

'But you go ahead.'

Lincoln took a bottle of orange juice out of the integrated fridge. 'I'm fine with juice. Would you prefer mineral water?'

'That would be perfect.'

A short time later they were seated in the dining room. Elodie served the chicken chasseur she'd made, along with steamed beans and a potato dish with onions and a dash of cream and fresh herbs.

She picked up her glass of mineral water. *'Bon appetit.'*

Lincoln smiled and picked up his glass, clinked it against hers. 'So, when did you develop an interest in cooking? I seem to recall you could barely scramble an egg when we were together.'

She put her glass down and picked up her cutlery, sending him a glance across the candlelit table. 'Life living out of hotels can be pretty boring. The food starts to taste all the same. I made a point of using my time at home between photo shoots as a chance to experiment. I did a cooking class in Italy, and then another one in France. They were heaps of fun.'

'I'm impressed.'

Elodie shrugged off his compliment. 'It's not that hard. But I freak out a bit when I cook for Elspeth.'

'Because of her allergy?'

'Yeah.' She shuddered and continued, 'Seeing Morag collapse like that was a bit triggering, to be honest. What if neither of us had been home? What if she'd lost consciousness and we'd found her on the floor, and it was too late, and—'

'Elodie, sweetheart.' His voice cut across her panicked speech with calm authority. 'It didn't happen, okay? She's safe and sound in hospital and she will be back to work tomorrow, if I'm any judge.'

Elodie put her cutlery down, her appetite completely deserting her. 'Sorry.' She flashed him an effigy of a smile. 'It's been a long day. I think I'll just clear away and go to bed.'

She put her napkin to one side and began to push her chair back. Lincoln rose from his own chair and came around to help her. He took her in his arms and gathered her close, resting his chin on the top of her head.

'Seven years ago you never really told me much about what it was like for you, growing up with Elspeth and her allergy. You've told me more in the last few days than you did the whole time we were together.'

Elodie laid her cheek against his chest, enjoying the warmth and protectiveness of his embrace and the deep reverberation of his voice beneath her ear. 'I guess we talked about other stuff or didn't talk at all. Or at least not about stuff that was deep and serious.'

He lifted her chin from his chest and meshed his gaze with hers. 'I should have told you about my adoption. I have a habit of compartmentalising my life. I'm not sure it's a healthy or wise thing to do.'

She slipped her arms around his waist. 'At least

you're aware of doing it. That's half the battle, surely? Awareness.'

'It sure is.' He placed his hands on her hips, his expression warm and tender. 'I'll clear this away while you go upstairs and get ready for bed. I'll be up soon.'

'But I'm such a messy cook. There's stuff everywhere in the kitchen.'

'You're not the only one who's become a little more domesticated in the last few years. Now, off you go. I won't take no for an answer.'

Elodie would have put up more of a fight, but she suddenly realised how completely exhausted she was. Her emotions were in a whirlpool and she didn't know how to process them. She was used to blocking out things she didn't want to think about. Used to pushing thoughts to the back of her mind and leaving them there, like stuffing old clothes she didn't want to wear again to the back of the wardrobe.

But the engagement ring sitting in that drawer in Morag's room was playing on her mind so much it made it hard to think about anything else.

Should she tell Lincoln, or leave things until she could talk to Morag? How could she tell Lincoln and be sure he would believe her?

Sure, they were talking and communicating in a way they hadn't done in the past, but it didn't guarantee he would trust her version of events. She had been the one to publicly humiliate him by jilting him. It would be reasonable for him to assume she had sold the ring to finance her career. If she produced it now, it would be her word against his long-term housekeeper's. And he had never trusted her word against Morag's in the past.

It had always been difficult for her to put her trust in someone, to believe they'd have her back no matter what. That they'd *believe* her. She had been portrayed in the press as scatty and fickle—a wild party girl who couldn't care less what people thought of her.

But she did care.

Was it foolish to hope Lincoln might finally trust her now?

Lincoln worked at restoring order to the kitchen for the next forty minutes. Elodie hadn't been wrong when she'd called herself a messy cook—it looked as if she had used every pot and utensil. He was used to good food—his housekeeper was an excellent cook, who always prepared nutritious and interesting meals. But seeing the effort Elodie had gone to over dinner—especially after experiencing the shock of Morag's medical episode—deeply impressed him.

He was learning more and more about her upbringing, and he realised now how little he had understood her in the past. No wonder she had looked done in and gone to bed early. She had been triggered by his housekeeper's sudden collapse—no doubt because of all the times she had witnessed her twin suffering an attack of anaphylaxis.

What could be more terrifying to a small child than to see her twin sister desperately ill? He hadn't realised how pushed aside she had felt by her mother's overprotectiveness of Elspeth. Of course any parent would struggle to balance the needs of their children under such difficult circumstances. But Elodie had hinted at the way she had fought to be noticed—by seeking attention by negative means. Hadn't she done that during their previous relationship? Hadn't her constant bickering over inconsequential things been a continuation of that pattern of behaviour?

Lincoln finally made it upstairs, only to find Elodie soundly asleep. She was curled up in a ball like a sleeping kitten, her hair a red-gold cloud splayed across the pillow. He pulled the covers up a little more and then leaned down to press a light-as-air kiss to the top of her head. She made a soft murmur and burrowed deeper into the mattress, her eyes remaining closed, her dark lashes like miniature fans resting softly against her cheeks.

He stood looking at her for a long moment, and felt something in his chest tightening, straining, like a silk thread pulling against his heart. This subtle shift in their relationship was bringing up other issues he wasn't sure he wanted to face.

But the timeline was set.

He had insisted it was non-negotiable.

Damn it, it *was* non-negotiable.

And yet something about being with Elodie now made it harder for him to imagine going back to his playboy lifestyle. Or was it because he didn't like thinking about her with someone else? He hadn't considered himself the green-eyed monster type, but thinking about her with someone else tied his gut into knots. Strangely, he had found himself confessing to her how eaten with jealousy he had been that night they'd run into each other in Soho—even though he had rigorously denied it before.

Showing any hint of vulnerability was normally anathema to him. He didn't do it in his professional life. He didn't do it in his personal life.

He didn't do it, period.

So why was he even tempted to do it now?

# CHAPTER TEN

ELODIE SIGHED AND rolled over in bed, opening her eyes to find Lincoln lying on his side, watching her in the moonlight. She ran a lazy hand over the dark stubble on his jaw. 'You really are a dreadful insomniac these days, aren't you?'

He gave a crooked smile that made something slip sideways in her stomach.

'I like watching you sleep.'

She wriggled closer, her legs tangling with his beneath the bedcovers. 'I'm not asleep now.'

'So I see.'

Her hand drifted down to the proud rise of his erection. 'What are you thinking about?' she asked.

'Right now?' His tone was so dry it almost crackled, his eyes glittering darkly.

'Right now.'

'I'm a little cognitively impaired right at this very moment, with you touching me like that.'

'Like this?' Elodie ran her hand up and down the length of his shaft, her own arousal intensified by feeling the insistent throb of his.

He groaned and pulled her hand away, moving over her so she was beneath the weight of his body. He caged her in with his arms, his gaze holding hers in an erotic lock that sent tingles to her core. 'I want you.'

The raw urgency in his voice matched the desire pounding through her body. 'I want you too—just in case you hadn't picked up on that vibe.'

'You're not exactly subtle.'

She gave him a twinkling smile. 'Do you want me to be?'

'God, no. I love it when you're so forthright. It turns me on.'

He lowered his mouth to hers in a spine-tingling kiss that lifted each and every hair on her head. His tongue tangled with hers, darting and diving and duelling in a cat-and-mouse caper that thrilled her senses.

He lifted his mouth off hers to work his way down her body, leaving a hot pathway of kisses along her naked skin. He caressed her breasts with his lips and his tongue, sending waves of pleasure through her as strong as electrical pulses. He worked his way down her stomach, circling her belly button with the teasing touch of his tongue. She sucked in a breath as he went lower, his lips exploring her most intimate flesh of all.

She arched her back like a sinuous cat, giving herself up to the sensual attention of his mouth. He knew her body so well, so intimately, there was no question of her not responding. She did—powerfully, passionately, volubly. Her panting cries were almost primal, the thrashing of her body equally so. Her orgasm went on and on, carrying her along on a rushing tide that was almost frightening in its intensity.

She finally collapsed back against the pillows. 'Oh, God, I can't believe you did that. I thought it was never going to end.'

Lincoln gave her a smouldering look and leaned across her to access a condom. He slipped it on and came back to her, one of his hands brushing her wildly disordered hair off her face. 'I love watching you come.'

Elodie scrunched up her face self-consciously. 'Eek! I can only imagine how ugly I look.'

'You couldn't look ugly if you tried.'

She traced the strong line of his collarbone with her finger, her gaze lowered from his. 'Beauty isn't everything…and it fades eventually.' She raised her eyes back to his. 'Millions of people have seen me in sexy lingerie and swimwear, but I don't think they actually see *me*…the real me…mostly because I haven't wanted them to.'

'But now?'

She chewed one side of her mouth. 'I've played on my looks for as long as I can remember. I've used them to get where I wanted to go. Unlike Elspeth, who tried not to be noticed at all. But I want more now. I want to be noticed for my skills as a designer—not because I rock a skimpy bikini.'

'I'm going to miss seeing you in those skimpy bikinis.'

She angled her head at him. 'So you've been checking out some billboards and magazine spreads, have you? I noticed one in your office. Did you know I was in it or was that just a lucky purchase?'

'Lucky purchase.' His eyes shone like wet paint. 'Although coming across you on a billboard almost caused me to run off the road a couple of times.'

'No doubt because you were furious with me for having the audacity to use our breakup as a platform for my success.'

There was a small silence.

'I was angry…livid, actually…' His voice trailed away as if something had changed in his attitude towards her since then.

'But not now?'

He brushed another strand of hair off her face, tucking it gently behind her ear. 'It's hard to be angry with you when you're lying naked in my bed.'

Elodie stroked her hand down his flat abdomen, her smile teasing. 'Do you want me to get dressed?'

His gaze glinted and he lowered his mouth to just above hers. 'Not yet.'

Elodie linked her arms around his neck, the thrill of his lips and tongue against hers sending her pulse racing off the charts all over again. He entered her body with a deep thrust that sent shockwave after shockwave of pleasure through her. His movements were slow at first, but he gradually increased his pace, driving her closer and closer to the point of no return.

The tension built in her body—the delicious tension that incorporated each and every piece of intricate tissue and muscle in her feminine flesh. She arched her pelvis to seek more friction, wanting more, needing more, aching for more. He slipped his hand between their bodies and caressed her swollen flesh, sending her over the edge within seconds. The orgasm rippled through her in smashing, crashing, tumbling waves, sending her senses into a whirlpool of earth-shattering ecstasy.

Lincoln followed her with his own release, the vigorous pumping action of his body sending another wave of tumultuous pleasure through her slick and swollen flesh. He gave a guttural groan and pitched forward over her, giving a whole-body shudder as he spilled his essence.

It was not often Elodie was rendered speechless, but her body was so acutely aware of every part of his where it touched her. The aftershocks were still rumbling through every inch of her flesh, and her heart was hammering against his chest where it was pressed against hers. The physical bliss was unlike any she had experienced with anyone else. And she knew without a doubt that even if she went on to have dozens of subsequent partners no one would ever be able to draw from her such a mind-blowing response.

The realisation of what lay ahead of her once their six months were up—the aching loneliness, the emptiness of shallow going-nowhere relationships—almost made her cry. Almost.

She bit down on her lower lip and squeezed her eyes closed over the sting of tears. She had no right to be upset. She had agreed to the terms and was already enjoying the benefit of them. Her bank account was full of money. More money than she had ever dreamed to see there. Luxury fabrics were on order, due to arrive this week. The studio was just about up and running. She had dozens of sketches in her workbooks and on her laptop. She had staff interviews set up in the coming days. Promotional work to see to… interviews and planning meetings. She even had clients waiting for her to design for them—not just Elspeth and Nina, but other friends and acquaintances.

Her dream was finally coming to fruition and she wanted to cry? She had to get a grip on herself. Emotions and business didn't mix, right? That was Lincoln's mantra and it had to be hers.

It *had* to be. Otherwise she would get her heart smashed to pieces.

Lincoln rolled her over so she was lying face to face with him on her side. He propped himself up on one elbow and stroked his other hand down the slope of her cheek, his frowning eyes searching hers. 'What's wrong?'

She forced her lips into a tight smile and rolled away, sitting upright and tossing her hair back over one shoulder. 'Don't mind me. I'm just trying to recover from having multiple orgasms for the first time in seven years.'

He sat up and shuffled over so he was sitting beside her on the bed. One of his hands stroked down the length of her spine—a warm, soothing stroke that loosened each and every vertebra.

'If it's any comfort, I'm a little shell-shocked too.'

He bent his head and planted a soft kiss to the

top of her shoulder, the touch of his lips making her skin tingle.

'More than a little, actually.'

Elodie turned her head to meet his blue-green gaze. She lifted her hand to his face and traced the prominent line of each of his eyebrows. 'That's good. I'd hate to be the only one feeling dazzled.'

He slid his hand under the curtain of her hair and brought his mouth down to just above hers. 'That's what you do best, sweetheart. Dazzle.'

And he closed the distance between their mouths with a blistering kiss.

It was almost two weeks later when Morag returned to work. Elodie was due home first, as Lincoln was flying back from a meeting in Dublin later that night. He'd asked her to go with him and stay a couple of extra days, but she'd declined, citing another staff interview as well as working on her designs for Nina and helping Elspeth prepare for her wedding.

She was determined to keep her career her main focus. Dropping everything to follow Lincoln around the globe was not going to build her career to the level she desired. If he'd been disappointed with her declining his invitation, he hadn't shown it. But then, why would he? He wasn't in love with her. The arrangement he had with her was temporary. Once their marriage was over he would move on with his playboy lifestyle as if nothing had changed.

Morag was already ensconced in the kitchen, an apron tied around her waist and a wooden spoon in her hand. 'Lincoln told me to take a few more days off but I wanted to get back to work.' She stirred the mixture in the bowl in front of her and added gruffly, 'Thanks for helping me the other night.'

'I was worried about you. Are you feeling better now?'

'I'm fine. I just have to adjust my diet a bit.' Morag gave her a sheepish glance and added, 'No more cookies and chocolate.'

Elodie pulled out one of the bar stools next to the kitchen island and perched on it, wrapping her ankles around the legs. 'Gosh, I can't remember the last time I had a cookie or chocolate.'

Morag frowned. 'Is that because you're always dieting…because of modelling and all?'

'No, not really. It's because I never had them growing up. It was too risky having them in the house because of my twin's nut allergy.'

Morag met her gaze across the width of the bench. 'There's something I want to talk to you about…'

The hesitancy in the older woman's tone was unusual, not to mention her expression. Normally so brisk and forthright, and always wearing a frown, this time she had a worried look on her face.

'When you were looking for my insulin…' She swallowed convulsively and continued, 'I noticed the bottom drawer wasn't closed properly…that things were shifted around in there…'

'Why did you keep it?' Elodie decided to get straight to the point.

The older woman's cheeks developed a dull flush

along her cheekbones. 'I tried to tell Lincoln I'd found it on the hall table, but he was so hungover after the wedding day and so angry...he wouldn't have your name mentioned. I was shocked when I saw it there. I didn't think you'd return it.'

'Because you had me pegged as a gold-digger?'

Morag's blush deepened. 'I know I should have tried to tell him a bit later, but I thought it best not to.'

'Why?'

'I thought if I told him you'd returned it he might consider asking you to come back to him.'

'But you didn't want him to do that, did you?'

Morag pressed her lips together and let go of the handle of the wooden spoon. 'I didn't think you loved him the way he deserved to be loved.' She swallowed again and met Elodie's gaze with an imploring one. 'Please don't tell him what I did. I can't lose this job. It's the only thing I have that brings me pleasure, a sense of purpose, a sense of being needed... I can't tell you how much *he* means to me. My own children don't speak to me now, because their father poisoned them against me. Lincoln is like a son to me. I know that sounds ridiculous, and sentimental, but I watched him grow up. Me and Rosemary, his adoptive mother, were at school together. He's the only connection I have with her now. I don't know his brother and sister the way I know him. I've known him all his life and I can't bear for him to think badly of me.'

Elodie jumped down from the stool and raked a hand through her hair. 'I'm sorry you've had such awful stuff happen to you. No woman deserves to be treated like that. And to lose contact with your children…well, that's heart-wrenching. But you're asking a lot of me to say nothing to Lincoln about this.'

'I know, and I won't really blame you if you choose to tell him. I haven't exactly been very welcoming to you.'

Elodie gave a long-winded sigh. 'I'm not going to tell him. Besides, he probably wouldn't believe me if I did.'

There was a pulsing silence.

'You do love him, don't you?' Morag's expression was tortured with lines of guilt. 'You've always loved him…' Her words trailed off in an agony of realisation.

Elodie stretched her lips into a humourless smile. 'More fool me. He doesn't love me back.'

'I know how that feels…loving someone who doesn't love you the way you love them. You live in hope, wasting years of your life, and for what? To be rejected, cast aside. But you have a second chance with Lincoln. He's married you, after all, and—'

'Our marriage is a sham. We're only together to please his dying biological mother—Nina. But I think you already suspected that.'

'But you're sleeping together?'

Elodie gave her a worldly look. 'It's what you might call a marriage of convenience with benefits.'

Morag opened and closed her mouth, seemingly speechless for a moment. 'I wish I could undo the past. If I had my time over I would tell Lincoln about the ring whether he wanted to listen or not.' Tears shone in her eyes and she continued in a harrowed tone, 'I know it's too much to ask you to forgive me...'

Elodie walked around to Morag's side of the bench and wrapped her arms around her in a hug. 'It's in the past...let's leave it there.'

How could she insist on the older woman revealing her role in the disappearing engagement ring? As much as she wanted Lincoln to know the truth, another part of her understood the motivation behind Morag's seven-year silence. After all, Elodie had her own secret—she loved Lincoln and always had.

And there was no point revealing it now.

Lincoln came home a couple of days later and immediately noticed a different atmosphere in the house. His housekeeper and Elodie seemed to have resolved their differences, for he found them cooking together in the kitchen. Elodie had a streak of flour on one cheek and her hands were busily kneading what looked like pizza dough. Morag was tearing leaves of fresh basil off a plant near the sink, and chatting to Elodie about a trip to Italy she had taken some years ago.

'Oh, hi, Lincoln.'

Elodie looked up with a smile that was so welcoming and bright something in his chest pinged.

'How was your Dublin trip?'

'Fine.' He stepped further into the room. 'Looks like you two are busy.'

'Elodie's teaching me how to make pizza from

scratch,' Morag said. 'I've only ever used shop-bought bases. This is so much better.'

'Smells good so far.' Lincoln dropped a kiss to Elodie's lips, then dusted the flour off her face. 'How's the studio going?'

'Great,' Elodie said. 'I've employed two assistants and they're helping me organise things for my first show. It'll take a few months to get ready, but I'm hoping to have a collection together for spring next year.'

'I'll take over now, if you like,' Morag said. 'You two go and have a pre-dinner drink in the sitting room and I'll let you know when dinner's ready.'

'Thanks, Morag, you're a gem,' Lincoln said.

A minute or two later, Lincoln handed Elodie a glass of champagne in the sitting room. 'Here you go.'

'Lovely, thanks.' She smiled and took a sip, and then screwed up her nose and frowned.

'Is something wrong?'

She put the glass down on a nearby side table. 'I can't believe I'm saying this, but I seem to have lost my taste for champagne. I might just have a juice or mineral water instead.'

Lincoln got the juice for her and then sat beside on her the sofa, his body angled so he could look at her. She was dressed in casual clothes—a pair of black leggings and a grey sweater that had slid off one of her slim shoulders. Her hair was tied in a makeshift bun on top of her head and her face was free of make-up. He could have sat staring at her for hours.

'You seem to have affected a truce with Morag,' he said, to break the silence.

Elodie's gaze drifted away from his to look at her glass of juice. 'Yes, well…we've come to an understanding.'

'You looked very chummy out there. What brought about the change?'

She tucked one of her legs under her and brushed away a stray hair from her face. 'She thanked me for helping her the other night—not that I did much apart from panic.' She shrugged and briefly met his gaze, and added with a smile that didn't reach her eyes, 'I figure I only have to be nice for her for another few months, then I'll probably never see her again.'

Lincoln held her gaze for a beat or two. 'You do like reminding me of the time frame on our marriage.'

And for some reason he didn't like being reminded—even though he was the one who'd put the timeframe there in the first place. Almost three weeks had already passed…soon it would be a month, then two, then three, and before he knew it he would be facing not only the death of his biological mother but the end of his relationship with Elodie.

He didn't know which he was dreading the most.

Elodie gave one of her sugar-sweet smiles. 'I wouldn't want either of us to get carried away because of all the fun we're having.'

He scooted closer to her on the sofa, reaching a hand to her face to stroke a lazy fingertip down the length of her cheek. 'I missed you.' His voice came out as rusty as a hinge on a centuries-old gate.

Something flickered in her gaze and the tip of her tongue slipped out to deposit a light sheen of moisture on her lips. 'I missed you too...' Her eyes lowered to his mouth and she snatched in a tiny breath.

Lincoln brought his mouth to hers, drawn to her with an almost unstoppable force. The softness of her lips beneath his sent a riot of sensations through his body. Heat, fire, throbbing lust. His kiss deepened, his blood thickened, his pulse quickened. His tongue met hers in a dance as old as time, a sexy salsa stirring his senses into manic overdrive.

He slid one of his hands along the side of her face, splaying his fingers against her scalp. Her lips responded to the pressure of his with equal passion and fervour, her soft moans of pleasure sending flames of heat through his body.

He lifted his mouth off hers, holding her face in his hands. 'How long have we got before dinner?'

Elodie stroked his jaw, her eyes shining with arousal, her lips curved in a sultry smile. 'How long do you need?'

'Not long.' Lincoln rose from the sofa and pulled her to her feet, settling his hands about her hips. 'We can save time by going to my study. I seem to remember you liked having fun in there...'

Her pupils flared and she nestled closer, the contact of her lower body sending a wave of powerful need through him that almost knocked him off his feet.

'Sounds like a plan.'

Elodie let Lincoln lead her to his study, a few doors down the long corridor. She went in before him, and once he was inside he closed the door and turned the key in the lock with a sharp click that sent a shiver racing down her spine.

She gave the room a sweeping glance, noting that it had also been redecorated, but stripped down rather than dressed up. It still had strong, masculine lines, with functional furniture—desk, chair and bookshelves and a modern lamp. There was a desktop computer, and a printer and scanner on a cabinet behind the desk. There were no items of sentimentality lying about, no photos or keepsakes. It was a reminder of the cool and clinical components to Lincoln's personality—the inbuilt traits that made it difficult for him to show, let alone feel, sentiment or emotion.

'New office furniture…'

Elodie trailed a hand along the top of his desk. A flood of memories rushed through her mind. Erotic memories of desk sex after one of their legendary arguments. Was he recalling those red-hot episodes? Remembering the explosive passion that had flared between them?

She glanced at him and added, 'I suppose this desk's been used heaps of times?'

Lincoln came towards her, his eyes blazing with incendiary heat. 'Not the way we're about to use it.'

His hands gripped her by the hips again, and he lifted her so she was seated on his desk. Elodie linked her arms around his neck, gazing into the bluey-green kaleidoscope of his eyes. 'You mean you haven't christened it with anyone else?'

'No.'

She didn't like to read too much into his answer, but it surprised her all the same that he hadn't brought any of his lovers into this room. 'Why not?'

His mouth twisted in a rueful grimace. 'Lots of reasons.'

'Give me one.'

His gaze dipped to her mouth and then moved back to her eyes. 'I always associated this room with you. That's why I changed it. I couldn't look at the old desk without thinking of all the times we'd made love on it.'

Elodie brushed her mouth against his. 'I'll let you in on a little secret…' Her voice was little more than a whisper. 'I've only ever had desk sex with you.'

He stepped between her thighs and brought his mouth closer to hers. 'Does it make me sound like an egotist to be pleased about that?'

'Maybe a little.'

He smiled and closed the distance between their mouths in a searing kiss that made the hairs on the back of her neck tingle at the roots. His tongue entered her mouth with a silken thrust that set her blood on fire. Molten heat erupted between her legs, the heart of her womanhood swelling, moistening, aching and pulsing with primal need. His tongue tangled with hers in a dance of lust that made her desire for him escalate to a heart-stopping level.

He left her mouth after a few breathless moments, trailing his lips down the side of her neck to her bare skin, where her sweater had slipped off her shoulder. His hands lifted her sweater and she raised her arms like a child for him to haul it over her head. He tossed it to the floor behind him, then his hands were going to her leggings. She lifted her bottom off the desk to help him remove them from her body, her heart racing, her pulse pounding, her breath catching.

He devoured her with his hungry eyes, his hands running over the globes of her lace-covered breasts with toe-curling expertise. 'I want you naked.' His tone was deep and husky.

'And so you shall have me...once we get things a little more even around here.'

Elodie began to undo the buttons on his business shirt, but she'd only got to the third one when he became impatient. With a grunt, he took over the job, stripping his shirt off and sending it in the same direction as her sweater. She slid her hands over his well-defined pectoral muscles, her blood ticking with excitement. She brought her mouth to his chest, licking with her tongue across each of his flat male nipples, then circling them in turn.

He drew in a ragged breath and placed his hands on the fastener at the back of her bra, deftly unclipping it. He lowered his mouth to her right breast, caressing the tightly budded nipple with his lips and tongue. Need throbbed in every cell of her body, the sensations he was evoking making her breath catch in her throat. He opened his mouth over her nipple and drew on the sensitised flesh, the sucking motion triggering a firestorm in her lower body. Then he moved to her other breast, teasing it into the same sensual raptures, the rasp of his tongue, the gentle graze of his teeth making her pant with longing.

Elodie worked blindly on the waistband of his trousers, desperate to get her hands on him, but he was too intent on pleasuring her. He pushed her back on the desk, pulling her knickers off her with one hand and tossing them to the floor. His mouth came down to her abdomen, his tongue tracing a light teasing circle around her belly button. Shivers coursed up and down her spine and a wave of tingling heat and tension found its way to her core.

His mouth moved down to the heart of her, his lips and tongue separating her folds, all too soon sending her into a freefall of mind-blowing, earth-shattering, dizzying release. She arched her spine, riding out the pulsating waves, unable to control her whimpering cries and panting breaths.

'Wow, oh, wow...' There were no words to describe the bliss still reverberating through her in delicious little aftershocks. But she finally sat upright and reached for him. 'My turn to render you speechless, I think. But we have to get you out of those trousers first.'

'That's easily fixed.'

Lincoln's gaze ran over her flushed features, his eyes smouldering, and he dropped his trousers and his underwear. He moved away briefly, to get a condom from the wallet in his trouser pocket, applying it and coming back to her.

She never got tired of looking at him naked. His lean, athletic build was wonderfully proportioned—

toned muscles, broad shoulders, slim hips, long, strong legs.

Elodie slipped off the desk and pushed him down so his back was against it. She slithered down in front of him, caressing him with her hands first, enjoying the guttural sounds of his pleasure. Then she placed her mouth on him, using her lips and tongue to bring him to the point of no return. He shuddered and groaned and swore under her ministrations, his body finally going slack as the last wave of release flowed through him.

'You really know how to bring me to my knees...' His voice was rough around the edges, his breathing hectic. 'I'm not sure I can stand upright just yet.'

Elodie came up to stroke her hands over his muscular chest. 'My legs are still shaking too.'

He cupped one side of her face in his hand, his eyes holding hers with glittering intensity. 'We'd better not make Morag wait too long to serve dinner, but first I want to do this.'

He brought his mouth down to hers in a long, slow kiss that drugged her senses all over again. It was passionate, and yet surprisingly tender, a kiss that stirred her emotions and fuelled her hopes.

Was it crazy to hope he was becoming as invested in their relationship as she was? Was she a fool for hoping he was moving past the bitterness he had carried against for her the last seven years?

# CHAPTER ELEVEN

A COUPLE OF days before they were due to attend Elspeth and Mack's wedding in the Highlands of Scotland, Lincoln informed Elodie over breakfast that they would have to travel separately, due to an urgent work issue that had cropped up.

Elodie put her cup of tea down and frowned. 'But what if you get held up? We're supposed to be there together. Won't it look odd if we're not?'

'I'll get there—don't worry.' He buttered his toast with a brisk scrape of his knife, the scratching sound loud in the silence. A frown was carved into his forehead, his eyes narrowed in concentration.

'Will you find it…triggering? I mean, being at a traditional wedding?'

He put his knife down with a little clatter against his plate. 'I've been to a few since—so, no, I won't be triggered.' He arched one dark brow and added, 'Will you?'

She bit her lip and picked up her cup again, cradling it in her hands. 'I'm trying not to think about it…'

'How's that working for you?'

'Not well. I feel sick already.'

It was true. She had woken up for the last three days with grumbling nausea, which she'd put down to the anxiety of attending a wedding so similar to her original one.

Lincoln sighed and reached for her hand across the table. 'What's worrying you specifically?'

She shrugged and lowered her cup to the table again. 'I don't want to spoil Elspeth and Mack's special day by drawing any attention to myself. You know what the press are like.'

'Is it because you'll be seeing Fraser MacDiarmid there?'

Elodie grimaced. 'That and other things.'

'What other things?'

She whooshed out a sigh. 'I'm sorry... I'm probably overthinking it all.'

He squeezed her hand, his concerned gaze focussed on hers. 'Sweetheart, talk to me. What is it about attending the wedding that worries you the most?'

Elodie blinked back the sting of sudden tears. Along with the nausea, her emotions were all over the place lately. 'I don't know...it's just the thought of getting ready with Elspeth and the other bridesmaids. It makes me...unsettled. I keep thinking about *our* wedding day—how I suppressed my doubts and fears all the way through the preparations. I sat there with Elspeth and the other girls, pretending to be the blissfully happy bride...'

She gulped and then continued.

'I didn't realise I was going to do a no-show until I was a block away from the church. And then I—I panicked. Like a full-on panic attack. I couldn't breathe, I was shaking, sweating, nauseous. I felt an overwhelming need to get away as quickly as I could. On one level I guess I knew the scandal and hurt it would cause, but right then and there I didn't care. I had to get away.'

Lincoln's hand was stroking hers in a soothing fashion. 'Listen to me.' His tone was as calming and stabilising as his touch. 'I'll be with you at Elspeth and Mack's wedding. I'll reschedule my meeting for next week so we can travel together. I'll help you get through it, every step of the way.'

Elodie met his gaze with her watery one. 'I'm sorry for what I did to you back then. I'm sorry I wasn't mature enough to recognise what I felt until it was too late.'

Lincoln gave a wry smile and squeezed her hand once more. 'It's in the past. We need to move on from it.'

But had he truly moved on? This six-month marriage deal was hardly what anyone could call a moving-on plan. He had once promised her so much more and she had thrown it away. He wasn't offering her a second chance. Their relationship was an interim thing to help comfort his biological mother in her final months of life.

And even though they were only a month into their marriage, Elodie could hear the clock ticking. Loudly.

* * *

'Oh, you look so beautiful,' Elodie said, standing in front of her twin the day of the wedding. 'And I don't think I've ever seen you look so happy. You're positively glowing.'

Elspeth grasped one of Elodie's hands in excitement. 'I'm so happy I could burst.' Then her expression sobered. 'But how are *you*? You don't seem yourself at all. And you haven't touched your glass of champagne.'

Elodie adjusted the right sleeve of her twin's wedding gown. 'I'm fine.' She gave a tight little smile. 'Just a little nervous.'

'Because of seeing Fraser? Don't be. He's done some work on himself and is quite pleasant to be around these days.'

'I'm glad to hear it but, no, it's not about him.'

Elspeth peered at her a little more closely. 'How are things with Lincoln?'

'Fine.'

'Just "fine"?'

Elodie drew in a skittering breath. Even the mention of his name was enough to get her heart racing. He had been so tender and attentive on their journey to Scotland, no one would ever think they were not the real deal, that their marriage was a temporary arrangement.

'He's wonderful.' She sighed and continued, 'So wonderful I keep having to remind myself we're only staying together another few months.'

'You want more?'

Elodie smoothed her hands down her own beautiful dress and sighed. 'Yes, well…haven't I always wanted more? More than he's prepared to give me, that is. Sometimes I think he's developing stronger feelings for me, but what if I'm wrong? It's not exactly something I can ask him. *Hey, honey, do you love me?* I'm not sure that's going to go down well, given the terms he insisted on for our marriage.'

Elspeth grasped both of Elodie's hands. 'I've always thought Lincoln has strong feelings for you. But I don't like to offer you false hope in case I'm wrong. All I can say is be patient with him. Some men take a while to recognise their own feelings.'

Would six months be long enough? Or would she end up bitterly disappointed in the end?

Elodie gave a rueful smile. 'I'd give you a hug, but I don't want to crush your dress.'

Elspeth pulled her into a big squishy hug regardless. 'Love you.'

'Love you back.' Elodie pulled away to look at her twin. 'Are you disappointed Dad isn't here to give you away?'

'Not really. My days of being disappointed by Dad are well and truly over. Besides, I have all I need in terms of love from Mack. And I really like Mum's partner, Jim. He's stable and reliable and so supportive of her.'

Elodie couldn't help thinking she was the only one in her family without the security of knowing her partner truly loved her.

But her twin was convinced Lincoln had done so once.

If so, could he do it again?

Lincoln wasn't part of the bridal party, so he took a seat along with the other guests in the local kirk. It being late autumn, the bridal couple had decided against a garden wedding at Mack's ancestral home, Crannochbrae, but the reception would be held there in the castle. It was also where Lincoln and Elodie were staying, along with other members of the bridal party and close family.

He hadn't seen much of Elodie since they'd arrived, as she was busy helping her twin prepare for her big day. But nothing could have prepared him for seeing her walk down the aisle as the first of the three bridesmaids. He stood along with the other guests, watching her take each step towards the front of the church.

He had said he wouldn't be triggered, but how could he not be? He remembered all too well the air of expectation that day seven years ago. And then the flicker of unease when the time had kept creeping past. He remembered the increasing murmurs of the congregation, the worried glances towards the back of the cathedral. The glances that had then settled on him, standing at the front with his groomsmen. He remembered the slow crawl of humiliation travelling over his skin when he'd considered the possibility that Elodie wasn't coming.

He recalled the moment when someone at the back of the cathedral had been passed a note, and how he'd come towards him, taking so long it had felt like a decade before he'd got to him. He'd taken the note and looked at it blindly, for endless seconds. It had been from the driver who was supposed to have delivered Elodie to the cathedral, informing him that she had bolted.

Lincoln pulled himself out of the past to look at Elodie coming towards him now. Dressed in a close-fitting cobalt blue satin dress that hugged every delicious curve of her body, her face beautifully made up, her hair in a sophisticated updo that highlighted her aristocratic features and swan-like neck, she was carrying a posy of fresh flowers with long flowing ribbons the same colour as her dress.

She glanced at him with a tremulous smile and he smiled back, sending her a wink for good measure. A light blush stained her cheeks and she continued walking up the aisle. He drank in the back view of her before the next bridesmaid came past. And then he watched as the bride came past, so uncannily like Elodie that it triggered him all over again.

The ceremony began and Lincoln listened to the words, watching the rituals and traditions with an uneasy sensation in his gut. Not because he didn't think they were genuine or worthwhile, but because his recent marriage ceremony to Elodie couldn't have been more different.

Was she feeling the same? Were the heartfelt words

and vows and promises and the devoted looks the bridal couple were exchanging making her feel a little short-changed?

But he had been up-front with her about what he expected of their marriage. It was for six months and six months only. One month had already passed. They had five months to go and then it would be over. They would both be free to move on with their lives.

And hopefully, by then, he'd be able to go to any number of weddings and not be triggered at all.

Elodie smiled her way through the official photos, and continued to smile and chat to the others in the bridal party, but all she could think about was how sterile and clinical her wedding to Lincoln had been a month before. Watching Elspeth and Mack gaze into each other's eyes with such devotion had made her ache with envy. If only Lincoln loved her the way she loved him. Had *always* loved him. But her love now was a more mature love—a love that had grown up, letting her recognise her own failings in their previous relationship and how she had to be aware of not falling into old patterns of behaviour.

As she was on the bridal table, she wasn't able to be with Lincoln until the formal part of the reception was over. Then he came over to her with a smile, holding out his hand to her. 'Dance with me?'

Elodie took his hand and joined him on the dance floor in a slow waltz. 'Has it been absolutely dreadful for you on the table with all my rowdy cousins?' she asked.

'Not at all. I had a great vantage point from there to watch you all night.'

'I noticed you looking at me a few times.'

More than a few times. It seemed every time she'd looked his way he'd been looking at her. But then, she'd had trouble keeping her eyes from drifting his way too.

His eyes glinted. 'How could I not notice the most beautiful woman in the room?'

Elodie gave a twisted smile. 'I'm not sure Mack would agree with you on that.' She sighed and, focussing her gaze on the neat knot of his tie, added, 'It was a lovely service. I had trouble controlling the urge to cry.'

Lincoln tipped up her chin with his hand, meshing his gaze with hers. 'Are you disappointed that our wedding last month was the complete opposite?'

She stripped her features of all emotion. 'Why would I be? We agreed on the terms.'

He studied her for a long beat. 'All the same, I could have made it a little less sterile.' There was a note of regret in his tone and a small frown pulled at his brow.

'But we don't have the same kind of relationship as Els and Mack.'

'Perhaps not.' He gave an on-off smile that didn't have time to reach his eyes. 'But then are any two relationships the same? Take us, for instance. Our first relationship was different from what we have now.'

'Do you think so?'

He turned her away from another couple who were getting a little close, his hold warm and protective. 'We talk more now. We don't argue as much. And making love with you is even more exciting and satisfying.'

'Even without the arguments?'

He smiled and brought her right hand up to his mouth. 'I do kind of miss those arguments.'

Elodie gave a sheepish smile. 'Yes, well...we both have strong wills and seem to clash on just about everything.' Her smile faded and she continued with a tiny frown, 'Makes me wonder why we got together in the first place. Our relationship was totally based on lust. I'm not sure it's the best foundation for a lasting union.'

The hand resting on the small of her back pressed her a little closer to the hot, hard heat of his body. 'It's a damn good starting point, though.' He lowered his head so his breath mingled intimately with hers. 'How soon can we go upstairs?'

Desire licked at her with searing tongues of flame. 'Not until the bride and groom leave.'

'How long will that be?' There was an impatient groan in his voice, and he lowered his mouth closer to her.

Elodie smiled against his lips. 'Too long. But I'm sure, knowing you, it will be well and truly worth the wait.'

And it was.

\* \* \*

Elodie woke the following morning with a dizzying wave of nausea. Lincoln was still asleep beside her, one of his arms lying across her body.

She swallowed back the rising bile in her throat and gently eased out of his relaxed hold. She got to her feet and walked carefully to the en suite bathroom, her stomach churning, her mouth dry, her fingertips tingling as if her blood pressure was dropping. She made it to the toilet in time to release the contents of her stomach, but unfortunately there was no way to do so without making a noise.

Lincoln opened the bathroom door and rushed over to her. 'Sweetheart, are you okay?'

Elodie groaned and shook her head. 'Go away. I'll be fine in a minute.'

He pulled her hair back from her face, then reached for a facecloth and handed it to her. 'You must've had too much to drink last night.'

'I didn't drink at all... I—I think it's a stomach virus. I've been feeling a little off for a couple of days.'

'Why didn't you tell me?'

Elodie stayed hunched over the toilet, not quite confident that her stomach was settled enough for her to move. 'Please, just leave me to deal with this. I don't need an audience right now.'

Lincoln flushed the toilet and then crouched down beside her, his expression full of concern. 'I'm not leaving you. What if you pass out and knock yourself out or something?' He put a hand to her forehead. 'You don't seem to have a temperature, but you're clammy.' He lowered his hand from her face and straightened to get another facecloth, this time rinsing it under the tap first. He crouched back down beside her and handed it to her. 'Here.'

'Thanks…' Elodie dabbed at her face, then handed it back to him. 'I think I'll be okay now.'

'Here, let me help you up.' Lincoln took her gently by the shoulders and guided her to a standing position. 'Do you feel up to having a shower?'

'Yes… I think so.'

'I'll stay with you.'

Elodie would have argued the point, but she was still feeling a little light-headed. Or maybe that was because he was naked and looking as gorgeously sexy as ever. She brushed her teeth and rinsed, relieved the bout of hideous nausea had passed.

Lincoln turned the shower on for her and helped her in.

'Aren't you going to join me?' she asked.

'Only to help you shower. Nothing else.'

He stepped under the spray of water with her, making sure not to take the bulk of the flow away from her. He shampooed her hair, gently massaging her scalp, then rinsed it and applied conditioner before repeating the massage. She was very conscious of his lean, athletic body so close to hers, wet and naked… and aroused.

'That feels divine…' She sighed and turned so she was facing him. Her hands settled on his slim hips and she moved closer to the jut of his erection. 'So does that…'

Lincoln placed his hands on her shoulders. 'I didn't get in the shower to have sex with you. You're not feeling well.'

'But I'm fine now.' Elodie pressed herself against him and he groaned. 'And you want me.'

'I can wait. I want to make sure you're feeling a hundred percent first.' He placed a soft-as-air kiss on the top of her damp shoulder.

Elodie stroked her hands down his chest, her heart skipping a beat at the tender look in his eyes. 'Thanks for making me feel better.'

He brushed her lips with his. 'Glad to be of help.' He turned off the shower and stepped out, picking up one of the bath sheets from the towel rail and holding it out for her. 'Come here and let me dry you.'

Elodie stepped into the warm folds of the towel and he proceeded to dry her. It was a thing he had never done, and it shifted something in their relationship. She had never allowed herself to be so vulnerable before. Seven years ago she would never have allowed him to see her hunched over a toilet bowl being sick, or bent double with period pain…

*Period pain.*

An invisible hammer swung against her heart, knocking it sideways in her chest. When was the last time she'd had a period?

She gave a jolt and Lincoln looked up from drying her feet.

'Sorry, was I too rough?'

Elodie stared down at him, kneeling at her feet, her mind whirling with dawning realisation. The nausea. The dizziness. The light-headedness. The sudden aversion to things she usually enjoyed, like champagne.

She swallowed and somehow got her voice to work. 'No…no… I was just getting a little cold.' She was, in fact, now shivering. Shivering with alarm. Panic. Despair.

How could she be pregnant? They had used condoms every time. Lincoln was pedantic about safety—it was something she admired about him. He would never intentionally put her or indeed any of his partners at risk.

Lincoln straightened and wrapped her in a fresh towel, warm from the towel rail. 'Go back to bed for a while. I can change our flights to London to a later time.'

'No, it's okay. I want to get back to work tomorrow.'

And get her hands on a pregnancy test as soon as possible.

# CHAPTER TWELVE

LINCOLN WAS AWARE of Elodie's silence on the way back to London. She kept assuring him she was feeling fine, but he wasn't so sure. In the past, he would have been fooled by her assurances, but this time he wasn't. She still looked pale, and she was huddled into herself as if she was in pain.

He knew from experience that a stomach virus could knock you sideways, leaving you listless and wan for days... He put his arm around her on the way to the car once they had landed in London. 'I think we should get you to a doctor for a check-up, just to make sure you're okay.'

Elodie pulled out of his embrace with a jerk that caught him off-guard. 'Will you stop fussing? I told you I'm fine. I'm just tired from all the travelling.'

Her tone was sharp and impatient, but her expression didn't match. There was a nervous flicker in her eyes and she didn't seem to want to meet his gaze at all.

He decided against pressuring her. That was another thing he knew from experience—she didn't take kindly to being told what to do.

The journey was mostly silent on the way to his house, but a few blocks before they got home Elodie asked if he would mind stopping while she picked up something at the local pharmacy.

'What do you need?'

'Just...female stuff.' Her voice was little more than a mumble.

For a young woman who had spent years parading on catwalks in the skimpiest underwear and swimwear, Elodie could be surprising prudish about her monthly period.

Lincoln pulled into the next available parking space and turned off the engine. 'Do you want me to go in for you?'

She reared back, as if he had suggested he walk into the pharmacy buck naked. 'No. I'll go. I won't be long.'

She scurried out of the car before he could open the door for her and shut it behind her.

Lincoln waited on the footpath, holding the door open for her when she returned a couple of minutes later. She was carrying a paper bag in her hand and her head was down, her cheeks filled with more colour than he had seen in them for hours. She slipped into the seat and flashed him a *thank you* smile that didn't make the full distance to her eyes.

Lincoln resumed the driver's seat and continued on the journey home. He parked outside his house and turned off the engine. 'I guess I should be feeling relieved you need those.' He glanced at the package she was holding.

'What?' She looked at him blankly, her forehead still knitted with a frown.

'Tampons and pads.'

'Oh…right…yes…'

He flicked her another glance, but she was looking out of the side window. 'Elodie?'

'What?'

Her voice was little more than a croak, and she still didn't look his way. But he noticed how tight her grip was on the package she was holding—the paper bag was crackling as if she was crushing crisps.

'You don't have to be shy about having your period. I did grow up with a sister, you know.'

The paper bag went silent and she turned to look at him. 'I'm not having my period.'

There was a strange quality to her voice…an empty, hollow sound that sent a ghostly shiver across the back of his neck.

'This is a pregnancy test.'

Lincoln stared at her with his mouth open, his heart beating like a drum set on some weird staccato rhythm. He could barely think about having a baby without a wave of panic coursing through him. He was to be a *father*?

He hadn't considered the possibility for years. Seven years, in fact. He had once wanted a family like the one he had grown up in, but Elodie jilting him had made him reset his goals. When she hadn't shown up at the church that day, everything had changed for him. He hadn't been able to imagine wanting a family with anyone else. He had taught himself to be content with the thought of being an uncle to his siblings' children rather than long for a dream he had lost and couldn't get back.

But if Elodie was carrying his child…

'You think you might be *pregnant*?'

'I'm not sure…' She swallowed and continued, 'I've got some symptoms. I've had some bouts of nausea and I'm late.'

'How late?'

'A few days…almost a week.'

Lincoln looked at the package in her hands. 'We'd better go in and do the test. The sooner we know, the sooner we can plan what to do.'

He got out of the car and came around to her side, opening the door for her. She alighted from the car and looked up at him with a frown.

'What do you mean "plan"?'

He closed the door with a snap and took her by the elbow. 'A pregnancy would change everything. We'd have to shift the goalposts on our marriage. We'd have to take out the six-months clause and make it permanent.'

Elodie tugged out of his hold. 'Will you stop railroading me, for God's sake? I don't even know if I'm pregnant. We've been using condoms all the time.'

There was a beat or two of silence. Lincoln could hear his heart thumping and his stomach dropped. 'Is there a possibility it's someone else's?'

Her face blanched of colour and she pushed past

him to go to the front door. Lincoln let out a curse and followed her. He opened the door and she stalked inside and made her way straight up the stairs.

'Elodie, you know I had to ask you that, right?' Even to his ears, his voice sounded hoarse.

She turned on the fourth stair to look at him. 'I know you did, but can we just wait until we see what the test says?'

'Sure.' He scraped a hand through his hair and sighed so heavily he was surprised the draught of his breath didn't knock over the hall table.

Elodie ran the rest of the way up the stairs to the nearest bathroom, closing and locking the door behind her. She stared at the package in her hand, her heart hammering as if she'd run up five flights of stairs instead of just one.

She ripped open the bag and the packaging and quickly read the instructions. She performed the test as outlined and waited for the result.

The first minute ticked by with agonising slowness, intensifying her distress.

If she was pregnant, Lincoln would want to stay married to her because of the baby—not because of her. Not because he loved *her*, but because he wanted his baby to have an active and involved father.

The second minute ticked past and her heart rate sped up.

She stared at the wand in her hand, not sure what she wanted to see.

The ambiguity of her feelings shocked her. She had

thought she wasn't the maternal type; her biological clock hadn't made a sound—ever. But now, as she waited for the lines to appear, she thought about the possibility of a baby. Lincoln's baby.

The third minute passed, and then the fourth.

Elodie was trying to keep the wand steady enough to read it. The instructions had said to give the test a good window of time—five to ten minutes at least. She didn't know how to deal with the suspense. Everything depended on the results of the test.

Finally, ten minutes passed and she held the wand up to the light. *Negative*. She waited another minute, her heart so tight in her chest she could barely take a breath. A wave of disappointment ambushed her. She wasn't carrying Lincoln's baby. There was no pregnancy. No need to change the terms of their marriage.

No need for her to stay with him…unless he loved her.

Elodie put the packaging in the bin but kept the wand, knowing Lincoln would insist on seeing it for himself. She didn't have to call him upstairs for he was waiting outside the bathroom door, with an unreadable expression on his face.

'How did it go?' His voice held no trace of worry, anxiety or fear.

'It's negative.' She showed him the wand.

He peered at it, his brow furrowed. 'Are you sure?'

'I gave it more than ample time to develop. It's negative. I'm not pregnant.'

He met her gaze. 'Are you relieved or disappointed?'

'To be honest, I'm a bit of both.'

She went back into the bathroom and put the wand in the bin. She washed her hands and gave herself a quick glance in the mirror, but it was like looking at a different person from the one she'd been just ten minutes ago.

The before-the-pregnancy-test Elodie had not been the earth mother type. A baby was something other people had. It wasn't on her radar. Her business was her baby. Her design label was still in its infancy. It hadn't had time to develop and grow and become successful.

But the post-negative-pregnancy-test Elodie wanted to carry Lincoln's baby in her womb, to give birth to it with him by her side, to raise it with him in a household full of love. But wasn't that little more than a foolish dream?

Lincoln was still standing outside the bathroom when she came out again. 'I think we need to talk.'

Elodie gave him a stiff smile. 'Yes, we do.' She let out a long breath and met his gaze once more. 'Why did you offer to make our marriage permanent if I was pregnant?'

'Because it would have been the right thing to do. I want any child of mine to have my name, and to bring it up like I was brought up—in a loving home. Even if the baby hadn't been mine, I would still have married you to give it a loving home.'

'But ours wouldn't be a loving home, would it? I mean, we would love our child, but what about each other?'

Lincoln's throat moved up and down. 'You have feelings for me, don't you?'

'It's not my feelings I'm most worried about. It's yours.'

'You know I care about you.'

'But you're not in love with me. Not now, and not seven years ago. So we've basically come full circle.'

There was a thick beat of silence.

Lincoln set his jaw. 'What do you mean by that? We have an agreement. There's a lot riding on it. Nina, your label, the funds I've put up for you... We have five months left.'

'For me to do what? Make passionate love with you but never hear you say the words I most want to hear? I want someone to love me—not for how I look or how good I am in bed or whether I'm pregnant or not. *Me*.' She banged her hand against her chest for emphasis. 'Me, with all my faults and foibles. That's what I want from you. But you can't or won't give it to me.'

He scraped a hand through his hair, his eyes flicking away from hers before coming back with glittering intensity. 'Are you saying you're in love with me?'

'Don't look so surprised!' Elodie gave a cynical laugh that was nowhere in the vicinity of humour. 'You make it so damn hard *not* to fall in love with you. But it's not enough for me to stay with you. I'm not wasting another five months of my life waiting for you to feel something for me other than physical attraction. That makes you no different from thousands, probably millions of other men out there who feel the same way about me.'

She dropped her shoulders on a sigh and then went on.

'I get it—I really do. You have bonding issues that probably go way back to infancy. You were adopted—and, while it was a good adoption, you still carry the wound of being relinquished at birth, even if it's only on a subconscious level. You don't let people get close to you. You don't let them in. You don't show your vulnerability.'

Lincoln's features were set in stone. 'If you leave, the deal is off. I'll withdraw my financial support for your label.'

Elodie brushed past him to go back to the master bedroom and collect her things. 'Do it. See if I care. I'll find someone else.'

'Where are you going? Talk to me, for God's sake.'

She swung around to face him. 'Tell me what you're feeling right now.'

He frowned so hard his eyebrows met above the bridge of his nose. 'I'm angry you're running away again without talking this through. You're acting like a spoilt child.'

'I'm not being childish this time. Last time I was running away from myself more than I was running away from you. I couldn't even face up to the truth about myself back then, so how could I tell you? But I'm telling you now. I can't be with you because we don't want the same things out of life. You essentially want a six-month fling with me. Do you think

I can't hear the clock ticking on our relationship? You put timelines on all your relationships because every woman you've cared about has left you. Your birth mother…your adoptive mother. And it's why you won't let your housekeeper go in spite of her appalling behaviour towards me in the past.'

'We can extend the time. I'm fine with that. We can keep it open and—'

'And what? A year on, two years or more, I'll still be waiting for you to fall in love with me. I'm not doing it, Lincoln. I want out. The pregnancy scare has jolted me into reality. *My* reality. Which is that I deserve to be loved for me. Just me.'

'Is this because I asked if the baby was mine?'

'No. You had an absolute right to ask that question under the circumstances. The press have made me out to be a female version of a playboy.' She sighed again, and added, 'I've spent years of my life pretending I don't care what people think of me, but deep down I do care. I've always cared. But I've buried those feelings so deep down they come out in other ways—such as in stupid and impulsive behaviour.'

'I don't want you to leave.' There was a raw quality to his voice. 'Stay a little longer. You might see things differently once you've got over the shock of thinking you were pregnant.'

Elodie went up to him and placed a hand on his lean jaw. 'Here's the thing that's shocking. A part of me wanted to be pregnant.'

He blinked a couple of times, his Adam's apple

rising and falling. 'Then you can get pregnant. We'll stop using condoms and—'

She placed her finger over his lips, blocking the rest of his speech. 'No. Listen to me. I've worked so hard to form my own label. It's almost within my grasp and I can't let anything stop me now. If I have a baby with someone it will be in a couple of years, not now.' She lowered her hand from his face and stepped back with a sad smile. 'It's time for me to leave. I know you don't want things to end this way, but I think it's for the best. Please send my best wishes to Nina. I'll pop a letter in the post for her.'

'This is crazy, Elodie. You're not thinking clearly and—'

'It's not just about the pregnancy scare. Elspeth and Mack's wedding really got to me as well. I'm so envious of what they have together. I fooled myself into thinking we could be like them, but it's not possible. I see that now. And I saw it seven years ago.'

'I suppose I should be grateful for the luxury of watching you pack up and leave this time.' The stinging sarcasm in his tone was unmistakable.

'You can watch me if you like. But I'd like us to part on better terms.' She took another few steps towards the bedroom before stopping and turning around again. She took off her wedding and engagement rings and handed them to him. 'Here—just in case anything goes astray again.'

He didn't even glance at the rings. 'I don't want them.'

Elodie closed her fingers over the rings. 'I'll leave them on the hall table, like last time.'

But he had already turned and walked away, and she didn't know if he had heard her or not.

Even if Lincoln hadn't heard the sounds of Elodie leaving his house, he knew he would have sensed the exact moment she'd gone. The house was different without her. The energy, the atmosphere faded away to a bland nothingness.

He considered moving to another bedroom, so he didn't have to be reminded of her, or going to a hotel for a while. He didn't want to smell the lingering trace of her perfume or picture her lying in his bed with her red-gold hair spread all over the pillow. To be tortured by every memory of their month together living as man and wife.

To say he was blindsided was an understatement, but the pregnancy scare had thrown him right out of kilter. He still couldn't get his still spinning head wrapped around the negative result. He'd got himself so worked up, so focussed on doing the right thing by Elodie and the baby, it had taken him a while to realise there was no baby.

But it wasn't only the pregnancy scare that had thrown him. He hadn't been expecting her to walk out—not before their time was up. He was the one who was supposed to call time on their relationship, not her.

There was no way of keeping Elodie married to him unless he said the words she wanted to hear. His feelings for her were complex, and messy, and he didn't like thinking too deeply about them. They got him tied up in knots—gnarly knots that pulled on his organs to the point of pain. She made him feel out of control—not just in terms of passion but in terms of vulnerability.

To openly confess to loving someone you had to accept that they could hurt you, leave you, sabotage you…humiliate you. And hadn't Elodie done all that? He had spent the last seven years trying to block every thought of her from his mind. She fancied herself in love with him, but how could he be sure it wasn't just because of the financial help he had given her for her label? A gift of money had a way of triggering all sorts of strong feelings.

He walked past the hall table and saw her wedding and engagement rings lying there. He picked them up, staring at them for a long moment.

How could one woman wreak such havoc in his life? What gave her the power to make his gut churn at the thought of never seeing her again? Or, worse, seeing her with someone else? Someone else who would father her future baby. The baby she'd decided she wanted in the not too distant future.

He tossed the rings back on the table and turned away. Maybe a month in a hotel would be a good idea.

A hotel a long way from London.

Elodie didn't want to spoil her twin's honeymoon, so left it another week before she called her about her breakup with Lincoln.

Elspeth was sympathetic and understanding of Elodie's decision to leave, and offered whatever support she needed.

'Have you seen or talked to him since?'

'No. I think it's best not to. A clean break is better.'

'I guess so...' There was more than a speck of doubt in Elspeth's tone.

'I *know* so,' Elodie said with conviction. 'He's never really forgiven me for leaving him the first time. I'm annoyed at myself for even considering it might work between us. What was I thinking? I should've had better sense. He didn't love me before. He doesn't love me now. I have to accept he's never going to.'

And the sooner she got on with her life without him, the better.

Lincoln came back to his London house after a month of working in New York. Well, trying to work... He'd come down with the same stomach virus Elodie had had in Scotland and it had only intensified his misery.

Like the last time Elodie had left, he'd given his housekeeper strict instructions to remove every trace of her from the house while he was away. But he'd more or less given up trying not to think about her. She was in his thoughts day and night, torturing him with memories of her touch, her smile, her playfulness. And coming home made it even worse.

His house was so empty without her. His life was so empty without her.

His coping strategy in life was always to keep

busy. He worked hard, played hard. He didn't have time for soft and fuzzy emotions. They didn't belong in his world of tough decision-making, wheeling and dealing and keeping an eye out for the next big challenge.

Elodie was the biggest challenge of his life and he had let her go.

He had lost her not once, but twice.

Lincoln wanted Elodie back and he hated himself for it.

He should have moved on by now. He should have moved on seven years ago. But he was stuck on her.

He would have to get unstuck soon, or he would be living the rest of his life as a monk. The thought of sleeping with anyone else made his stomach churn. He hadn't even looked at another woman while he was in New York. No one had turned his head or stopped his heart. The busiest city in the world hadn't held its usual appeal. He hadn't even enjoyed the deals he'd set up—in fact, the whole time he'd been bored. Empty and unfulfilled.

He wanted *her*. Only her.

Elodie was his nemesis—the one person who could make him feel things he had never wanted to feel for anyone. Was that love? Did he have this empty, aching feeling in his chest because he loved her and wanted her back so badly he couldn't think straight?

*He still loved her.*

Acknowledging the truth of those words was like suddenly remembering a language he had taught himself not to speak for years. But now he wanted to shout the words out loud.

*I love her. I love her. I love her.*

Morag appeared from the kitchen to greet him. 'How was your trip?'

'Awful.'

'I'm sorry...' Her gaze slipped away from his. 'Have you heard from Elodie?'

'No.'

Even hearing her name twisted a knife into his gut. What if she didn't believe him when he went to see her? He hadn't exactly given her a reason to harbour any hope that he might change his mind. The thing was, he *hadn't* changed his mind. His mind had finally revealed to him what he had been hiding from all these years.

He. Loved. Her.

'There's something I need to tell you about the last time Elodie left,' Morag said. 'I'm afraid you're not going to like hearing it.'

Lincoln frowned. 'Go on.'

Morag twisted her hands in front of her apron. 'She was telling the truth when she told you she left her engagement ring on the hall table. I found it.'

'Where is it now?'

Morag took something out of the pocket on the front of her apron and handed it to him. He stared at the ring box, his mind whirling. He hadn't believed Elodie about the ring. He had always thought she'd sold it and used the money to launch her career. He'd been so blind and prejudiced against her... Had he ever truly listened to her? Understood her? Believed in her?

He had kept her at arm's length, determined not to let her see how much he needed her, how much he loved her. How much it frightened and terrified him to love her, to openly admit it, to own it and say it out loud. He had always blamed Elodie for leaving him—but he had left first. In fact, he hadn't been there emotionally in the first place. Not totally, not unreservedly.

He looked back at his housekeeper. 'Why didn't you tell me she'd left it seven years ago?'

'I tried to, but you came back roaring drunk the night after she jilted you and you refused to have her name even mentioned in your presence. You told me to remove everything of hers from the house, just as you did this time.'

Lincoln could recall most of that conversation—most, but not all. Which wasn't something that made him particularly proud. 'Why didn't you tell me when I was in a better state of mind?'

'I thought about it that night, and the next day while you were sleeping off your hangover. I thought if I told you she'd left it behind you might go and find her, talk her into coming back to you.' Morag gulped back a broken sound. 'I didn't think she loved you, so I didn't tell you. But I was wrong. She did—she does. I think she always will.'

Lincoln's heart leapt right up to his throat. Could it be possible Elodie truly loved him? That it wasn't too late to undo the damage of his past mistakes and miscommunications? She had more to forgive of him than he ever had for her. Dared he hope she would find it in her heart to take him back?

'Does she know you have the ring?'

'She found it when she was looking for my insulin kit. She could've told you she'd found it that night, but she didn't. I think because she didn't want you to be hurt by my betrayal of your trust. And then, once I realised she knew, I begged her not to tell you. I shouldn't have asked her to do that for me. I'm worried it's contributed to your breakup.'

A rush of love and respect coursed through him for his beautiful Elodie. But she was no longer his—not unless he went to her and told her how he felt. How he had *always* felt.

'I need to see her. I was going anyway, so it has nothing to do with the ring.' He pocketed the ring and placed a hand on Morag's shoulder. 'You're not to blame for this. I am. I should've told her seven years ago what I felt for her.'

Morag's face lit up like a chandelier. 'You mean you love her?'

Lincoln smiled. 'You bet I do.'

Elodie was working late in her studio, doing some last touches on the collection of clothes she'd made for Nina. She had got Nina's measurements during a phone conversation with her, after she'd explained her reasons for leaving Lincoln. It had been a tough conversation to have—especially knowing of Nina's physical fragility—but Elodie had no longer been able to pretend. It was time to be honest about all things—most of all her feelings about the only man she had ever loved.

She was spreading out the last item of the collection on her work table when she caught sight of movement on the security camera covering the front door of the studio. She put the dress down and went closer to the security screen, her heart bouncing up and down in her chest like a yo-yo.

Lincoln was standing outside the studio, looking for a doorbell that didn't yet exist. His brow was furrowed and he kept reaching up to tug at his tie, as if it were choking him. He glanced up to the second floor, where she was working, but she wasn't near the window so he couldn't see her.

Elodie stepped away from the security camera and went over to the window. She unlocked it and opened it, bracing herself for an icy blast of the wintry night air. 'Lincoln?'

He looked up with relief flooding his features. 'I need to talk to you. Can I come up?'

His voice sounded rough around the edges, even from this height, and she could see the lines of strain and stress around his mouth.

'Sure. I'll unlock the front door.'

Elodie closed the window and went back over to the security panel, buzzed open the street door of the studio. The sound of Lincoln's firm tread coming up to her floor sent her heart thumping.

Was he here to pull the plug on her label? In spite of threatening to withdraw his support the night she'd left, he hadn't done any such thing. She hadn't been game to read too much into it, but she was grateful for the extra time to get her business up and running without having to seek another sponsor.

She was standing by her work table when he came in, looking windswept and tired and drained but as gorgeous to her as ever.

'I suppose you're here about the money?' She kept her voice calm and controlled. No mixing emotions and business, right? That was her motto, taken straight from his hard-nosed businessman's playbook.

Lincoln came over to her and took her hands in his. 'I have never said this to anyone before, so hear me out. I love you. I've missed you so much—not just this last month but for the past seven years. I've filled my life with work and activity, but the one thing that was missing was you. I'm sorry it's taken me so long to realise what was there all the time. My love for you.'

Elodie stared at him in shock, her heart beating so hard and fast it was making her dizzy. 'You're not just saying it? You really love me?'

'I'm not just saying it. I'm feeling it in every part of my body. I ache for you. I feel incomplete without you in my life. Nothing fills the emptiness you left behind. You're my centre, my anchor, my one true love, and I beg you to come back to me and be my wife. And one day even the mother of my children, if that's what you want.'

Elodie stared at him for a moment, struck dumb by his emotional openness. He had never shown her his heart, never opened it fully to her the way he was doing now. He had always kept a bit of himself back, and it had made it hard for her to believe he would ever toss away his armour and let her in.

She threw her arms around his neck and squealed for joy. 'Oh, Lincoln, darling, of course I will. I love you so much. I've been so sad about leaving you, but I convinced myself you could never allow yourself to love me. But hearing you say it...it's just so wonderful. There are no words to describe how I feel right now, knowing you love me.'

Lincoln framed her face with his hands and gazed into her eyes. 'You were right about the way I conduct my relationships. It struck a chord when you said the loss of my biological mother at birth and then the sudden death of my adoptive mother had made me shut down the possibility of loving someone in a romantic sense. The threat of losing that kind of love was too daunting, too terrifying. I realise now I rushed our first relationship. I didn't give you time or your own space for growth within it. No wonder you ran away. But I promise not to do it this time. We'll be true equals, working together on everything. I want you by my side for the rest of my life.'

Elodie rose up on tiptoe to kiss him. 'I want you by my side too. You are the only man I've ever loved. I truly was dreading going on with my life without you. I was considering a life of celibacy. I couldn't bear the thought of anyone else touching me.'

Lincoln gathered her close, hugging her so tightly it almost took her breath away. 'I'm the same. I spent a month in New York thinking only of you. I ached for you every night and every morning.' There was a catch in his voice and then he continued, 'I have another apology to make.' He released her a little so he could meet her gaze once more. 'I'm sorry I didn't believe you about the engagement ring.'

Elodie's eyes rounded to the size of baubles. 'Morag told you?'

He gave a grim nod. 'Yes—although I blame myself for the way I insisted on her removing everything of yours from the house. I even cut her off when she tried to tell me a couple of times, refusing to allow her to say your name in my presence. But the thing I find so touching is that you didn't betray what she'd done to me once you found out.'

'You're not going to fire her, are you?'

'Only if you want me to.'

'No, I don't. I think she got it wrong, but she did what she thought was best for you. She didn't realise I loved you back then. She thought I was a star-struck gold-digger. And her keeping the ring hidden from you more or less proved it to you.'

Lincoln gave a rueful twist of his mouth. 'The thing is, I think on some level I never believed you loved me. I'm ashamed to say I quite liked you being a little star-struck and infatuated with me. It fed my ego and allowed me to railroad you into marriage. But of course, that didn't go to plan. And I'm glad now that it didn't. I think we both needed time to let go of our baggage and come back to each other as fully mature adults who want to spend the rest of their lives together.'

Elodie smiled and tenderly stroked his jaw. 'I promise to always be little star-struck by you if you promise to be star-struck by me.'

'I'll let you in on a little secret—I've always been a little star-struck by you.'

And he covered her mouth in a kiss that left her in no doubt of his enduring love and adoration.

# EPILOGUE

*Eighteen months later...*

ELODIE LOOKED AT Lincoln, talking to Nina in the garden of their London home. He was smiling at something his mother said, and Nina's face was shining with love and happiness and, yes, even good health.

Nina's cancer had gone into remission, and so far things were tracking well. It was a miracle—one they were all so very grateful for. Elodie had grown increasingly close to Lincoln's biological mother, and had found Nina's support during her rising career as a designer invaluable. Her first show had been a phenomenal success, and she was feeling more fulfilled than she had ever dreamed possible.

And speaking of miracles...

Elodie's gaze drifted to her twin Elspeth, sitting beside her devoted husband, Mack, each of them holding in their arms a cute-as-a-button baby girl—identical twins called Maisie and Mackenzie. The besotted love on the new parents' faces said it all, and no one could have been happier for them than Elodie—especially since she and Lincoln had their own special news to share.

Lincoln came over to her and slipped an arm around her waist. 'Shall we tell them now, my love?'

'Oh, my God, you're pregnant?' Elspeth cried out in delighted joy. 'I just *knew* you were keeping a secret from me.'

Elodie's smile almost split her face in two. 'Yes—ten weeks. We wanted to wait until we were a little further along, but my tummy is already about to pop the zip on my jeans.'

Lincoln stroked a loving hand down the back of her head. 'We're expecting twins. Too early to know the sex.'

Nina didn't bother hiding the tracks of the tears pouring down her face. 'Oh, my darlings…you've made me the happiest person alive.'

Lincoln smiled down at Elodie, his expression so full of love it made her heart flutter. 'Our babies couldn't wish for a more beautiful and loving mother. And I couldn't wish for a more beautiful and loving wife.'

Elodie blinked back tears and grasped his hand, held it against her cheek. 'I love you.'

He bent down and placed a soft kiss to her lips. 'I love you too. Before, now and for ever.'

\* \* \* \* \*

# MARRIED FOR ONE REASON ONLY

**DANI COLLINS**

In this trying time, I'm so grateful I've been able to continue writing stories that lift my own spirits and hopefully lift yours. I couldn't have done it without the wonderful team at Mills & Boon, particularly my editor, Megan Haslam. My heartfelt thanks go out to all of them for their support and their dedication to delivering hope and happiness to readers everywhere.

# CHAPTER ONE

ORIEL CUVIER OPENED her hotel room door anticipating birthday roses and confronted a cleaning gent with a mop.

*Mon Dieu*, even the maintenance men were exceedingly attractive in Italy. Her startled gaze had gone straight to the yellow bucket, but as she dragged her attention upward, she arrived at eyes that were so dark they were nearly black. Much like the cup of espresso had awakened her senses an hour ago, she felt as though she was yanked from dull, mundane thoughts to a readiness to experience everything her day had to offer.

"*Mi scusi*. I heard you were out." His Italian was stilted, his smile a tense, flat stretch of his lips that apologized for his butchering of the language. "I was told to clean a wet." His voice was as deeply seductive as Italians were purported to be while his accent and dark coloring suggested he was South Asian.

Oriel had always felt an inexplicable kinship with people from that corner of the world, even though her parentage was supposedly a mixed couple from Eastern Europe.

"*En Français?*" she suggested. "Or English?"

"English. Thank you." His speech became as crisp and flawless as a graduate from a British boarding school. "I was told you were out for the day and I should clean a spill."

Honestly, he could be employed in her line of work with those sharp cheekbones, sensual mouth, mussed high-top haircut and devil-may-care stubble. He was substantially taller than her five-eleven, and his broad shoulders strained the seams on his blue boiler suit.

"I didn't request anyone," she said in bemusement.

"Who is it?" Her agent, Payton, spoke in her ear.

"Oh, one minute." She had forgotten her call and pointed at her wireless earbud so the hotel worker would know she wasn't speaking to him. "There's a man at the door, but there seems to be a mistake. I didn't call anyone."

"The maid texted me." The cleaner brought his phone from his deep pocket.

"The maids haven't been in yet," she said.

How was this godlike, educated man pushing a string mop? With that build, he could be laying bricks or bouncing clubs at the very least—which would also be a complete waste of a startlingly magnificent presence. The camera would love him.

*She* loved him. Oriel saw beautiful men all day every day, but none had ever emanated this sort of powerful energy that almost had her taking a step back in awe while wanting to bask in his presence at the same time. It was like an electric current that made her nerve endings tingle.

And even though handsome men rarely affected her, she had a nearly unbearable urge to twirl her hair and cock her head and wait breathlessly for him to speak.

"Send him away," Payton said in her ear.

She probably should have. Her career was her entire focus these days, providing the sense of achievement that otherwise eluded her. She would never admit to anyone the profound sense of inadequacy that stalked her, or that she had a hole inside her that craved approval and attention. It didn't even make sense. She had everything anyone could want—health, wealth, intelligence, and independence along with looks that ticked all the boxes for modern ideals of beauty.

She would be mocked to death if she revealed her feeling of being "less than," so she pushed her angst into climbing toward the very top of her field, allowing nothing to distract her, including men.

Suddenly she had nothing but time for watching how this stranger swiped his thumb across a screen, though. He studied it with an air of concentration. The strength of her fascination was embarrassing, but she couldn't help it.

He flicked his gaze up to meet hers, catching her giving him moon eyes like a love-struck adolescent. It caused a swoop in her stomach as though she'd crested a wave.

"My mistake. Wrong floor. And my colleague has dealt with the issue." He pocketed the phone while his penetrating stare kept hold of hers.

Her skin tightened and her bones grew soft. She knew when a man was interested in her. She rarely reciprocated such things, but here she stood. Involuntarily reciprocating with every fiber of her being.

It was disconcerting to be so overcome. To feel so helpless to do anything but stand there while he took in her snug, high-waisted corduroy trousers with matching suspenders over a low-cut floral top.

His mouth relaxed, and the angle of his shoulders eased. It wasn't all sexual interest, though. There was something else in his study. Not calculation, precisely.

Investigation? He liked what he saw, but he was delving into her eyes as though looking for answers to unasked questions.

She wasn't sure what that cooler side of his appraisal was about, but it was far more unsettling than if he'd worn a wolfish grin and said something suggestive. She could have handled that with flirt or frost. Whatever *this* was made her neck prickle with premonition. This man was going to change her life.

How silly, she scolded herself, trying to pretend she wasn't flushing with her reaction. But she was filled with anticipation and something else—her own curiosity. A far-reaching sense of possibility. Excitement.

"Was there anything else I could do for you while I'm here?" he asked in a bland tone.

The tension left the air with a withering dissipation.

She was reading him wrong, she realized with chagrin. He was an employee of the hotel waiting for her to dismiss him. That's all the lengthy, charged silence had been about. Could he tell she was drooling over him, wanting him to feel the same way she did? How mortifying.

"Yes, actually." As a hot, self-conscious blush stung her cheeks, she latched on to the first excuse she could think of to cover why she had kept him lingering. "The ceiling fan in my bedroom is rattling." It had driven her crazy all night. "I haven't had time to report it. I wondered if that was something you could fix?"

In the pause, she could have sworn she heard the gears in his head give a whir of computation. Then, "I can have a look."

Oriel's heart was pounding with nerves, but she pressed her back to the wall, allowing him to enter the small passageway.

He left the mop and bucket outside the door and briefly crowded her, seeming to steal all the oxygen from this tiny foyer.

Her instincts prickled another warning, not because she thought he posed a physical danger, but from awareness of the power that radiated from him. He could seduce her without even trying. Her blood was turning to molasses in the seconds that he loomed close and allowed one corner of his mouth to dent. Those dark eyes of his promised long, sensual nights.

She had never felt this way on meeting a man. It was pure magic, holding his gaze and feeling connected at a level that went far beyond what happened between strangers.

Then his expression hardened with refusal. He snapped his gaze forward and stepped into the room.

*He knows.* And had decided he didn't want to make a play for her.

Her whole body went into free fall, and her self-worth crumpled on impact. Oriel felt rejection *very* deeply. She had her theories as to why—being adopted and an only child. In her observations, people who had spats with siblings and were still loved afterward had more resilience to the small scuffs of life.

She hated that she allowed small rebuffs to strike such a deep place inside her, but they always did. The tiniest slights landed directly on that achingly tender center of her soul.

It was such a perverse reaction, because coming on to a guest could cost this man his job. She had no room in her life for romance, anyway. What did she care if a man she would never see again thought she was worth his time or not?

Nevertheless, she was so stung she thought about

asking him to come back later, but he was already trying the switch on the wall and looking at the fan over the coffee table. He wasn't wearing a ring and didn't have a tan line where one was missing, she noted. She was annoyed with herself for looking.

"The one in the bedroom," she murmured, waving across the small lounge.

"You didn't let him in." Payton's voice startled her again.

She seriously had to get her head on straight. "I did. It's fine."

"This is how scandals are created!"

"With me doing what? I live like a nun." She did more scandalous things in public, parading down runways in her underwear, than she did in private. She didn't travel with any jewelry worth stealing or have any secret predilections worth exposing, either.

She lowered onto the sofa, deliberately turning her back on the man flipping the switch inside her bedroom door. Trying not to think about how his shoes had looked far pricier than the kind she expected a man in his profession to be able to afford.

Perhaps they'd been left by a guest and happened to fit him. She occasionally left wine or clothing behind when she traveled. Most hotels had an arrangement in which the housekeeping staff could divvy up abandoned items as a small job perk.

"If someone saw you letting him in, it could ruin the interest from Duke Rhodes," Payton said.

Ugh. Right. The reason for his call. Oriel had been introduced to the aging action star at a cocktail party a few nights ago.

"Do you really think I should go to Cannes with him? He's twice my age."

"He likes you."

"We spoke for five minutes." He had tried to kiss her on the lips. "I honestly couldn't say whether I liked him or not." She hadn't. "Have *you* spoken to him? Caught a whiff of his breath?" she added with a wince of recollection.

"It's part of his image that he always has a cigarette in his hand."

"And a drink in the other? He smelled like scotch." The sour, lingering stench of heavy drinking had emanated from his pores.

"It's *good* scotch, angel. He smashes box offices. The cameras follow him everywhere. Do you want to take your career to the next level or not?"

"Of course, but that's my only week of vacation this year." And her parents were celebrating their thirtieth anniversary. "It will chop into the first two days of it."

"You can fly straight from Cannes to Tours. His people will pay for all of it."

Payton was the best in the business. One didn't move from runway to international ad campaigns without a man like him paving the way. Thanks to him, she no longer shared a room with other models and was given first-class suites like this one, with gorgeous views of the Milan skyline.

Even so, she found his strategy disheartening. What about working hard? What about advancing on merit? Why resort to timeworn gimmicks? Who would respect her if she couldn't respect herself?

"I'm concerned about what a man like Duke Rhodes would expect if—"

A dull thump and a sharp curse had her sitting up and twisting to see into the bedroom.

The maintenance man had draped a spare blanket

over the bed and was flat in the middle of it, pushing the fan off his chest while blood welled on his forehead.

"I have to go." She pulled out her earbuds and leaped to her feet.

"Be careful. Stay on the bed," Oriel Cuvier rushed in to say. "I'll call down for help."

Vijay Sahir sat up to set the contraption on the floor. "I'm fine."

He was rattled and bruised, but it was his own fault. He'd been scanning the room for clues about her, eavesdropping on her conversation while thinking less than honorable thoughts about her and the bed he was standing on.

He'd been paying no attention to the fan he'd been pretending to fix, giving the housing an absent wiggle. The damned thing had come down on top of him, ringing his bell hard enough to leave him angry with himself for being so careless.

"That could have come down on *me* last night." She eyed the wires dangling from the ceiling. "Your head is bleeding. You need first aid, and I need to make a proper complaint."

She stepped around the broken fan and reached for the cordless phone in its bedside charger.

"No!" He threw himself across the bed to catch her wrist. "They'll fire me."

They wouldn't. Couldn't. He didn't work here. Which would be even trickier to explain.

"Well…" Even wearing a frown of consternation, she was the most beautiful woman he'd ever seen.

Her profile said she was of mixed Romanian and Turkish blood, adopted at birth by a French couple. Vijay would be damned if she didn't look Indian with that natural golden tone in her skin and those strong brows. Hell, in person she looked even more like Bollywood legend Lakshmi Dalal with her big brown eyes, her delicate bone structure in an oval face, her near-black hair in an untamed disarray of wavy curls. Her mouth was naked, but still made a bold, full-lipped statement when she pursed it stubbornly.

"I won't let them fire you." She stood tall and wore the confidence of wealth.

*Don't be a hypocrite, Vijay. You're wealthy, too.*

Even more so very soon, but he had a well-earned aversion to spoiled heiresses.

"I'm still new here." Whether she took that as new to this hotel or this country didn't matter. Both were very weak versions of the truth. He unconsciously stroked his thumb against her incredibly soft skin in persuasion.

Her breath caught, and a confused spark flashed into her eyes, one that arced across to stab an answering heat into the pit of his belly.

Everything about her was slicing his brain into sections, making it difficult to remember she was the subject of an inquiry. Or possibly an innocent bystander chosen for her resemblance to a Bollywood icon. Either way, she was the key to ensuring Vijay's sister wasn't conned out of her fortune.

Vijay made himself release Oriel's wrist and rolled to his feet on the far side of the bed. "If you give me an hour, I'll have all of this sorted," he promised. "I need to fetch a few tools."

He wasn't a certified electrician, but he could rewire a fan.

"I actually have an appointment." She glanced at the clock.

"I can let myself in." That's what he'd been planning

to do with his ill-gotten, all-access housekeeping card. He had taken a chance, hoping she would already be out for the day. The mop had been a prop, the knock a precaution.

"I suppose." Her doubtful gaze dropped to the name tag on his borrowed coveralls, then came back to his eyebrow. "You're still bleeding. Did you realize that? Please sit down." She nodded at the edge of the bed and disappeared into the bathroom.

He touched the wet trickle that was winding its way down his temple. When he saw the blood, he swiped the sleeve of the coveralls across it, leaving a dark streak on the heavy blue cotton.

"I'll survive. Don't worry about it," he called.

"No, let me." She came back with a small bag marked with a red cross. "I asked you to fix the fan. This is my fault."

He hesitated, then sat on the bed and closed his eyes, trying not to picture the way the suspenders framed her breasts and cleavage so enticingly. He briefly thought about coming clean and saying, *Look, I need your DNA.*

A container ship of worms would open at that point, and for what? The chance that Oriel was related to Lakshmi Dalal was near zero. As far as Vijay could discern, a con man was leaping on Oriel's resemblance to Lakshmi to get his hands on the money Vijay and his sister would make as they merged ViKay Security Solutions with a bigger, global enterprise.

On the very slim chance that their "client" was telling the truth and Lakshmi did have a lost child out there, Vijay owed the man his utmost discretion. The mystery seemed too coincidental to be believed, though. When Vijay had booked this trip to Europe, he had seen an opportunity to get to the bottom of things. He'd tacked on this side trip to Milan so he could intercept Oriel. All he had to do was pretend to be a hotel worker for another few minutes, steal her toothbrush, and get on with his life.

There was a tearing sound, the pungent scent of alcohol, then a cool swipe on his brow that left a sting in its wake.

He couldn't help his small wince.

"Sorry." She blew on it, making his eyes snap open.

Her blouse gaped, and he was staring straight down the shadowed valley between her lace-cupped breasts. Lovely, abundant breasts that his palms itched to gather and massage.

He deliberately set his hands onto the blankets next to his hips, but he could still smell the fragrance of tropical body wash clinging to her skin and wanted to rub his face into her throat. He wanted to keep going, dislodging the edges of her shirt so he could find her nipples—

"There." She set a bandage over the cut, cupped his face in her cool hands, and *kissed* the injury.

He was so shocked, he snapped his head back.

"I'm sorry." Her hands fell away, but she was frozen, still leaning over him, as shocked as he was. "I didn't mean to—I have a little cousin who—Obviously, you're not a child. I'm so embar—"

"Do it again." The words shouldn't have left his chest, but there they were, rumbling up into the space between their lips. He didn't lower his attention back to her breasts. He kept his face tilted up and his gaze on her mouth.

For endless seconds, they were held in that state while she made up her mind. Then slowly, slowly she lowered her head. Her mouth pressed to his, delicate as a butterfly landing on a rose. He lost his sight. Impressions came to him in flashes as her lips slid against his—the softness of flower petals and the crushed scent of them filling his head. Velvety heat in her breath and the dark, sweetly sensual flavor of her as they both opened their mouths wider to deepen the kiss.

He skimmed his touch along her forearms, catching lightly at her elbows, inviting her closer. She braced her hands on his shoulders and leaned against him, slanted her head and sank into their kiss, stealing every thought in his head.

It was the most frustratingly delectable kiss of his life. He wanted to drag her in and take control, but he was too enthralled by letting her have her way. She sipped and experimented and decided what she liked before she pressed deeper. Tasted him more boldly.

He groaned and signaled more firmly on her arms, urging her to be more aggressive.

Her knees dug into the mattress on either side of his hips. The warm weight of her settled on his thighs. Gratification rumbled in his throat. He swept his palms to her shoulders and roamed his touch over the warmth of her body through silk. He followed the straps of the suspenders, enjoying the lithe flex of her back and the furrowed texture of her trousers where he made circles on the flare of her hips.

She sighed and inched her knees on the mattress, settling more deeply into his lap. She switched the slant of her head to the other side with barely a breath for either of them.

This boiler suit was a size too small. It pulled tautly across his back and shoulders and against his knees as he splayed his legs and looped his arms around her, trying to drag her even tighter into his lap. Her hair tangled in his fingers as he cupped the back of her head and gave in to the craving taking over him. He swept his tongue into her mouth and sucked on her lips, wanting to absorb her into himself.

She made a noise that was a helpless pang of pleasure, pure seduction, and shivered. Her arms folded behind his neck and she pressed even closer, so all he could think was how badly he wanted the heat of her sex scorching where he had hardened to titanium.

His hands cupped under her bottom and, purely on instinct, his arms hardened around her. He rolled, setting her beneath him on the bed. Now he could kiss her throat the way he'd been dying to, tasting the small hollow at the base. Her hands went into his hair and—

*"Mon Dieu. Stop."*

He lifted his head. Her horrified gaze was pinned to the ceiling. When she met his own, she pressed her head more deeply into the mattress, expression appalled.

Bloody hell. He wasn't a hotel employee, which would be bad enough. He had lied his way in here.

Vijay pushed himself off her, feeling as though he left a layer of his skin adhered to her. It *hurt*. He didn't dare look down to see whether these damned coveralls were disguising his arousal.

She was sitting up and smoothing her hair, ensuring her blouse buttons were secure. "That shouldn't have happened."

"No," he agreed. "It shouldn't. I'll leave." He did.

## CHAPTER TWO

It was a good thing Oriel's appointment this morning had only been a fitting. The main requirement of her had been to stand still and be quiet. She would have been useless at anything else. Her mind had been completely occupied by the most salacious kiss of her life.

Apparently, she harbored fantasies of making love to strange men who appeared at the door like the mythical pizza delivery hookup. What else could explain the way she'd crawled into his lap and practically offered herself? If she hadn't blinked open her eyes to see the bare wires in the ceiling, and been reminded where she was and that he was a complete stranger, she might have gone all the way with him!

Maybe it had been a dream, she tried telling herself as she looked around. The fan was back in place, the spare blanket gone, the bed made and the pillows fluffed. The suite wore the tidy polish of an efficient housekeeping visit.

When she tried the switch, the fan was perfectly silent, not rattling the way it had last night.

Should she call down and leave a message to thank him? Leave a tip with a note? What would she say? *You left me rattled. Can you fix that?*

The part that was torturing her most was, why? Why

had she lost any sense of decorum? Was she that starved for affection?

She did have yearnings for a serious relationship, but she also knew she had to love herself. She couldn't expect someone else to *make* her feel loved.

Maybe she should start dating herself, she thought, smirking around the mouth of the bottle of water she was drinking. Rather than seek outside validation, she could take herself out for dinner. It was her birthday, after all.

Actually, maybe she would do that, she decided, and started to search for a restaurant to make a reservation. She was distracted by an email from her agent. Payton had sent through a confirmation on her trip to Cannes in May. *Magnifique*, she thought dourly.

Her mother had also left a message about Oriel's gown for the anniversary party. Madame Estelle would be annoyed when Oriel told her she wouldn't arrive until the morning of, thanks to her red carpet appearance with Duke Rhodes.

She bit back a sigh and threw her phone down while she began to change, still irritated by this Cannes idea. She was trying to make her mark without riding her mother's famous coattails, but she would be riding the coattails of a one-time heartthrob who wanted to look as though he could still get off-camera action in the form of a twenty-five-year-old model. Payton would say it was how the game was played, but Oriel felt like a sellout.

She didn't have time to stand around brooding, though. She had a casting call for a luxury eyewear brand in an hour. Such things ran notoriously late, but she was always five minutes early. It was mid-March and the breeze still sharp, but she changed into a filmy summer dress that showed lots of her long, tanned legs.

She moved into the bathroom to brush out her hair and fix her makeup and found a note where her toothbrush ought to have been.

The scrawled handwriting took her a moment to work out.

> Apologies. I dropped your toothbrush while washing the dust from my hands. The fan is in order now. Call me if you have further concerns.

There was a phone number in place of a signature.

Hmm. Was he offering his number in a professional capacity or giving her his number?

She tucked the note in her bag while she applied a bold red to her speculative smile, pondering whether she would text him and what she might say.

After a quick check that she had a pair of heels, and a romance novel to read while she waited, she threw on her overcoat and hurried out.

Vijay ordered a beer while he waited for a table at an upscale restaurant a few blocks from the hotel. When he checked his phone, he saw a text from his sister, Kiran, asking how the merger discussions had gone and why he wasn't home yet. He replied,

Good. I was delayed. Will fly home tomorrow.

He didn't mention that the offer they'd received was so generous, he was more concerned than ever that she was being targeted for her fortune. He also skipped telling her that he'd stolen a toothbrush to prove it.

Vijay had sent the toothbrush overnight to a DNA lab. When he returned to Mumbai, he fully expected their client, Jalil Dalal, to refuse to give up his own sample to determine whether he was Oriel's uncle. Vijay was calling the man's bluff, dismantling the excuse Jalil was using to spend so much time with Kiran.

Jalil had seen Kiran speak in Delhi at a symposium about women in business where she had relayed how she and Vijay had grown their security company from a scrappy start-up to acquisition offers. Jalil had followed her to Mumbai, where he had asked her to help him with a "highly confidential, very personal assignment."

Kiran was beautiful and intelligent and successful enough for any man to want her on her own merit, but Jalil's request was not in their wheelhouse. Vijay and Kiran had started ViKay Security Solutions to protect themselves after taking a difficult stand that had destroyed the life they'd grown up in. A few years ago, they had accidentally developed a facial recognition system that accounted for skin tone, scars and makeup.

Their system was so accurate, global powerhouse TecSec wanted to acquire it. The owner was prepared to make Vijay the VP of his Asia division, and Kiran would have an executive role overseeing programming and development for the entire organization. They could finally put their past behind them and redeem their reputations.

This was *not* the time to run private investigations searching for imaginary children of deceased Bollywood stars.

That's what Kiran had been asked to do, though. Jalil Dalal had seen a model who resembled his dead sister and claimed Oriel must be his secret niece. Jalil didn't have proof Lakshmi had been pregnant. She had gone to Europe around the time of Oriel's birth and made a few remarks before she died—of a broken heart, according to Jalil—but that was all he knew.

It was the kind of tale that appealed directly to Kiran's soft heart, though. She had swallowed it hook, line and sinker.

Vijay sipped his beer, almost wishing the story was true. It would give him an excuse to see Oriel Cuvier again. He'd been in a state of low-key arousal all day thinking about their kiss. It shouldn't have happened, but he was not nearly as remorseful as he ought to be.

Oriel definitely possessed the same sensual allure as Lakshmi Dalal, he acknowledged sardonically, but it was beyond outlandish that she could be the screen queen's secret child.

For starters, the beloved actress wouldn't have such a scandal in her past. Lakshmi Dalal was India's *didi*, first charming her way into hearts with a portrayal of an older sister who was determined to give her kidney to her ailing younger brother. In a later film, she disguised herself as a young man, both becoming a symbol of feminism to girls and indelibly imprinting herself into adolescent male fantasies when she put on a sari and danced in the rain. From there, she became a mainstay in romantic musicals, a seal of wholesomeness that reassured all parents it was safe to allow their children to watch.

Jalil claimed that's why this had to be handled so delicately. He didn't want his sister's memory tainted, but Jalil lived off what remained of Lakshmi's earnings. That had to be running low by now. He was looking for fresh income, and Kiran was a convenient target.

That might be a cynical view, but Vijay didn't trust anyone except Kiran. And after his failed engagement, he would do anything to protect Kiran from similar disillusionment.

He flicked to the next email and saw his presentation to the hotel had resulted in an agreement in principle to move forward with the security package he had pitched to them.

Vijay was the king of multitasking. He'd detoured here on his way home from the merger meeting, booked himself into Oriel's hotel and wrangled a tour of the security system by pitching his own. That had given him the knowledge to break into a maintenance area undetected. He'd finagled himself a housekeeping card, talked his way into the room of a hotel guest, and retrieved what he needed to expose his sister's paramour as the fraud he was.

A man in his position should behave more honorably, he supposed. By misleading his sister and going behind Oriel's back, he was perpetuating the sorts of lies and betrayals he'd suffered.

As if karma wished to offer him a chance to make better choices, he absently lifted his gaze to the door and watched Oriel walk in. A jolt of electrical thrill went through him.

Dusk was closing in, but she looked as though she'd just left a beach with her hair windswept and her skin glowing. She wore makeup that emphasized her wide eyes and lush mouth. As she stood in the doorway, she unbelted her coat to reveal an airy dress with a ruffle across her chest. He leaned down slightly and caught a glimpse of her slender calves.

He was definitely in the throes of a sexual crush, but she had *climbed into his lap* this morning as though it was where she was meant to belong.

*Heiress*, his brain reminded him starkly, but his lap twitched with lascivious memory.

He watched her glance around uncertainly. Meeting someone? *Who?* The most intense aggression punched him in the gut, but he already knew that jealousy was a pointless emotion. If the person you were committed to wanted someone else, they were already gone.

Oriel smiled as the maître d' greeted her. She must have been informed the restaurant was full, because her smile fell away. Like him, she seemed to be invited to wait at the bar until a table became free. She sent a considering look his direction, and her eyes widened as she met his gaze.

*Don't*, he told himself, even as he stepped off his stool and nodded at it, inviting her to join him. Hot tension invaded his belly as he waited for her to decide.

Her dark red lipstick briefly disappeared as she rolled her lips together.

Oh, those lips. So soft. So hungry. How would they feel traveling other places?

With another faltering smile, she pointed and told the maître d' she would join him. She moved like a ballerina as she approached, hair bouncing as she seemed to float on air. Her coat fell open, and her dress seemed to be made of something delicate like gossamer. It clung subtly to her breasts, and he had to exert all his control not to ogle her.

"Hello again." Her cheeks might have stained with color, but it was difficult to tell in this light. "I should apologize for this morning."

"No, I was out of line." Way, way out of line. "It was excellent taste on my part, but poor judgment."

Her mouth twitched with reluctant humor. Her gaze

flickered over his collared shirt and tailored pants, then widened with startled comprehension.

"Are you on a date?"

"I had a meeting." He debated how much to tell her. "I pitched my security company. I'm Vijay." He offered his hand, deliberately withholding his surname.

"Oriel." Her wariness dissolved into a bright smile as she put her hand in his. "You didn't sign your note. Did you think I would get you in trouble if I knew your name?"

He practically fell into the dark, sensual pools of her eyes. The soft feel of her hand in his was the only thing keeping him from drowning.

"I'm quite sure you'll get me into trouble." It was supposed to be a joke, but the truth sent a skip through his chest. "Oriel."

She laughed, and of course it was the sparkling kind that was heady as champagne bubbles. "I'll try not to. Vijay."

Spending more time with her was a terrible idea, but as he held her hand, the noise around them dimmed, and all he saw was her. It was like taking a hit of a potent drug.

The bartender broke the spell, asking for her order. Oriel requested white wine and slid onto the stool Vijay had vacated.

"Thank you for fixing my fan. It seems perfect now."

He'd had to sneak around the maid's schedule, but as he subtly drank in her scent, he had no regrets about being inconvenienced.

"You didn't want to eat at the hotel?" Ironically, he had avoided the restaurant there out of concern he would run into her. He set his elbow on the bar, pleased that the crowded space meant he had to stand so close that her knee brushed his thigh.

"It caters to tourists. I wanted to treat myself to something more inspiring. It's my birthday. Are you also celebrating? Did your meeting go well?"

"It did, but I'm just having a beer." He would find somewhere else to eat. This was madness, even talking to her again. "Happy birthday," he said as her wine arrived.

They saluted with their drinks, and her spine softened as she sipped.

"Long day? What do you do?" He already knew, but he liked that she had to lean close to him to be heard over the din.

"Model. I've been at a casting call for hours. They were whittling it down, so I had to keep doing my thing as more higher-ups were called in." She lowered a pair of invisible sunglasses and made an O of her mouth.

He didn't care what the sunglasses looked like. He'd buy them and the car that went with it. "Did you get it?"

"Who knows, but it went well enough that it's another reason to celebrate. Only one, though." She tilted her glass. "I have an early call for a photo shoot tomorrow. Then I'm on a plane back to New York."

"You live there?"

"Paris, but I spend a lot of time in New York. Actually, I spend a lot of time on airplanes." She sipped again. "You? I assume your maintenance work is a side gig while you get your company off the ground? Why Milan?"

Damn. He had implied that he had moved here.

"It's a temporary thing." He considered how to stick as close to the truth as possible. "We're based in Mumbai, but hoping to expand. I came to Milan because my sister is involved with a man I believe is trying to take advantage of her."

"Oh?" Her expression cooled.

"I can see you judging me." He pointed the mouth of his bottle at her. "Brothers are allowed to be protective, especially when I raised her and she's all I have."

He hadn't meant to reveal that, only to keep her from labeling him as some sort of patriarchal, honor-obsessed throwback.

"You lost your parents?" Her expression softened. "I'm sorry."

"When I was fourteen, yes. She was ten." He drank the last of his beer, trying to rinse away the pall of anguish, old and more recent, that their deaths still left in his throat. "Our grandmother lived with us, but she was quite frail and passed a year later."

"That must have been a very difficult time." Her brow wrinkled with compassion. "No wonder you're so close and protective of her. Does your sister live here?"

"Mumbai. What about you?" He quickly flipped it so he wouldn't have to dissemble any more than he already had. "Do you have siblings?" Everything online said she was an only child, but he might as well have it straight from her.

"No. I always wished for a brother or sister, but my mother—" She hesitated. "Maman is very wrapped up in her career. She has every right to be. She's a famous soprano. Estelle Fabron?"

He shrugged, feigning unfamiliarity with the name. He only knew it from the mention in Oriel's profile anyway.

"Madame Estelle is beloved in the opera world. Especially here." She kept leaning in to speak against his ear. Her breath tickled, and he was damned close to turning his head and capturing her mouth with his own. "She casts a *long* shadow. It's refreshing to speak to someone who has never heard of her."

Her lips were right there, ripe and tempting. He looked into her eyes, and she was staring at his mouth. *Are we doing this, my beautiful goddess?*

The hostess appeared to say their table was ready. He was not ready to let her go, but his beer was finished.

"Join me," Oriel invited.

It was the moment when Vijay should have insisted he was only here for the one drink, but he couldn't make himself say good-night. Once he used the DNA test to vanquish Jalil, he would continue his life as programmed. It was highly unlikely he would ever see Oriel again. Surely there was no harm in buying her dinner and spending another hour in her company?

Now he was lying to himself as well as her. Or at least feeding himself weak rationalizations, but he waved her to follow the hostess and held Oriel's chair before he took the one opposite.

Oriel opened her menu, but glanced over it at him. "I'd like to buy you dinner. As I said, I'm celebrating, and you did suffer that injury from fixing my fan."

Her glance touched the nick above his brow, which was visible because he'd removed the bandage as soon as it stopped bleeding.

When her gaze dropped to the menu, she bit her lips again.

The prices were on the high side even for Italy. It struck him that she thought he might struggle to afford one meal, let alone two.

Wasn't this an awkward position to be in? Very few women he dined with had ever paid for themselves, let alone bought him a meal. Irrationally, he was insulted by her offer. There was a snobbery to the move that got under his skin—which was his personal baggage coming around on the carousel. He doubted she was *trying* to offend him.

"If one of us pays for the other, it makes this a date," he pointed out. "If this *was* a date, especially our first date, *I* would pay. Yes," he replied in answer to the way her brows lifted. "I'm that sort of man."

Her mouth pursed to hide a smile. "Split it down the middle then? Since we're sharing a table out of convenience? How do you feel about sharing dishes?"

"Depends what you like."

"I like everything." The look she sent him had to be from her stock of smoldering expressions for a camera. Even so, it went into him like a spear, straight to the tightening flesh between his thighs.

He was definitely paying for dinner.

Once they ordered, he said, "You seem to be traveling alone, but I should have asked. Is there anyone you usually dine with?" He had overheard her conversation about appearing with that action star. It had sounded like an innocuous photo op, and his research said she was single.

"I travel too much to date seriously. You?" She subtly braced herself.

"I would not have allowed you to kiss this mouth if it belonged to someone else. Yes," he said as her jaw went slack. "I'm also *that* sort of man." Blunt. Possessive in a reciprocal way. He offered monogamy because he expected it.

Her chin came up. "Did *I* kiss *you*?"

"You absolutely did."

"I didn't hear you objecting. Perhaps speak more clearly next time."

"Will there be a next time? I'm delighted to hear it."

She hid her smile with her wineglass, indignant but also amused. "Do all the hotel guests receive such personal treatment?"

"Definitely not. You're an exception."

"Hmm." She relaxed and recrossed her legs, bumping his shin beneath the table.

He reflexively caught her ankle between his calves, just long enough to have her startled gaze flash into his so he could watch that haze of sensual awareness come into it.

He released her as quickly as he'd caught her, leaving Oriel breathless.

She didn't believe in fate or destiny, but she was astonished to have bumped into him this way. She had glanced at the menu on the way to her audition, but hadn't had time to make a reservation. For a moment after she arrived, she had thought she would have to settle for room service after all.

Now she was enjoying an Indian-Italian fusion of tandoori duck, curried gnocchi, and tikka masala ravioli with a man she'd been thinking about all day.

He was an intriguing man. Educated and confident and quick-witted, but difficult to read. She wanted to ask him more about how he had come to be working at the hotel, but it sounded as though he was only doing it to make ends meet while he pursued bigger things, maybe paying for his expenses while he was here.

"Tell me about your security business," she invited.

"Most of the credit goes to my sister. She wrote specialty software, and I matched it to the right components. We literally began with one customer at a time, tailoring it to each client's needs. It's grown to the point that we're close to partnering with a bigger company. Those talks are highly confidential, so I can't say more."

"Sounds like a big break. Good luck. I hope it goes well."

"Thanks. How did you get into modeling? What was your big break?"

"Nepotism," she said wryly. "My mother hoped I would have more vocal talent, but she's a once-in-a-generation unicorn, and I'm adopted, so…"

His brows went up. Most people reacted with curiosity when she offered that information.

"It's public knowledge." She brushed away having revealed such a personal detail. "Maman's career was taking off. She didn't want to interrupt it with a pregnancy, but they wanted a family. Adoption was their perfect solution."

Perhaps *perfect* wasn't the best word. They had approached parenting wholeheartedly, but babies were demanding, and they never found the right time to adopt a second one. They claimed to be fulfilled by the single daughter they had, but Oriel had a twisted, illogical sense that if she'd been different, more winsome maybe, they would have wanted another.

"While I was growing up, Maman hired teachers for me in every type of classical instruction, but I was no prodigy. The closest I came was being scouted for a pop band."

"That suggests you have musical talent." He was looking at her the way he had when he'd stood outside her hotel room door. Penetrating. Collecting hidden data. "Have you tried acting?"

It was nice to have a man look beyond her face and want to know more about *her*, but this level of attention was disconcerting. She wasn't sure why.

"I can do many things reasonably well—dancing and singing and playing piano. I don't have Maman's level of talent, though, so I couldn't bring myself to go into performance arts. I would always be compared to her. Papa is an academic, very intelligent, but I'll never win prizes for literature or physics. I thought I was destined for mediocrity, but the summer I turned fifteen, one of Maman's costume designers asked if I wanted to model some of his designs at his show. It was the first thing I'd found where the bar wasn't already set impossibly high by someone in my family. With modeling, I've been able to grow into my own version of success."

That sense of carving out her own space and rising through the ranks soothed the part of her that struggled to feel good enough. She knew her angst stemmed from her adoption, and it wasn't entirely fair of her to harbor that sense of rejection. From what she knew of her birth mother, the young woman had been in a very difficult position. She'd had an affair with a married man of a different race and didn't feel she could keep the baby that resulted, not without losing all the other pieces of her life.

Oriel didn't resent her for giving her up. Her birth mother had chosen carefully, and Oriel lived an extremely privileged life, but it didn't seem to matter how often she reminded herself of that. She still suffered this bereft sense of having been cast off simply because she was mixed race.

They went on to talk about things. As they finished dessert, she asked the server to split the bill, but Vijay had taken care of it while she had visited the powder room.

"I thought—"

"It's your birthday," he said dismissively. "And you barely ate."

Oriel ran miles every day to keep her figure trim, largely because she had a healthy appetite. Even so, "That was a lot of carbs for a woman who is going to be in a bikini tomorrow."

"You'll be fine," he assured her with smoky admiration.

The potency of this man! She sold seduction for a living and had never experienced anything like his ability to make her swoon with a softly spoken word or a half-lidded glance.

"I…um—" *Control yourself, Oriel.* "I wouldn't have been able to sample all of these dishes if I'd dined alone, so thank you. This was a nice surprise." Beneath the table, she was aware of the toe of her shoe resting next to his. "I guess this is a date now?"

"I guess it is." His smile was only a tiny bit smug.

They finished their drinks and made their way outside.

"Do you dare be seen walking me to the hotel?" she asked.

"I dare anything." His mouth twisted with irony.

"Oh, you're *that* sort of man," she teased.

"And this." He offered his crooked elbow.

She tucked her hand through it as they ambled the few blocks that were bustling with tourists heading out to dine or enjoy the theater.

As they passed a recessed stoop, Oriel spun herself into it, tugging him in with her.

"Would you like to know what sort of woman I am?"

"If you tell me you're the sort who makes love in public, I may have to adjust what kind of man I am." He set his forearms on the door on either side of her head, caging her into the shadowed space created by his wide shoulders.

"Ha. Sorry to disappoint. I'm only the kind who doesn't like that awkward moment wondering if a man will kiss her. I'd rather make it happen. If it's going to."

"I noticed that about you already." He let the tip of his nose playfully brush hers.

"Are you still banging on about how I took advantage of you?" She let her hands rest on his rib cage. "Cry for help. See if someone will rescue you."

"Help," he said faintly, flashing his teeth. "I'm helpless to resist this woman." His lips touched a corner of hers.

She shivered and slid her hands to the backs of his shoulders. She tried to chase his lips, but he switched to kissing the other side of her mouth.

"I don't usually kiss strangers," she whispered.

"Nor I."

"You don't feel like a stranger, though," she admitted, perplexed by how true that was. "It feels like we're..." *Lovers.*

That's what she was thinking. Maybe she said it aloud, because he groaned and covered her mouth with his.

She had been waiting throughout their meal for him to kiss her again. Waiting and waiting.

She sighed with relief and stroked her touch across the landscape of his back, encouraging him to press her into the door, delighting in the way he devastated her with his kiss.

Had she thought she was in control this morning? He had been toying with her, letting her think so. This man knew how to ravage in the most tender way possible, claiming and plundering and pulling her very soul from her body.

At the same time, he gave. Oh, he generously venerated her mouth, silently telling her she was the most precious thing he'd ever tasted. The most exquisite.

Their lips made soft, wet noises while an ache panged in her throat. A sob of surrender. She softened under the press of his heavy body, wanting his weight. Wanting his hard, flat chest compressing her swollen breasts. She wanted to feel his steely thighs naked against hers, bracing hers open. She wanted the unforgiving ridge that was bulging behind his fly to fill her...

"Vijay..." Her hands went down his back, urging him to press into her mound. "Come to my room."

With the same attitude of superhuman strength he'd exhibited this morning, he dragged his head up and sucked in a breath. He straightened so he wasn't touching her at all.

"You have an early morning," he recalled with a ragged edge to his otherwise stern voice. "We should end this here." He looked away into the street.

"Should? Or is that what you want?" she asked through a tight throat.

He muttered something under his breath. "Believe me, Oriel. I want to come to your room. But it's not a good idea."

"Why not?" She hooked her finger in the waistband of his jeans to keep him from retreating further. "We're single. I don't know when I would have another evening free like this."

"And it's your birthday?" He spoke lightly, but there was a note of cynicism in his tone that made her drop her hand away from his jeans.

"What is that supposed to mean?"

"Nothing." He caught her hand. "Except you're flying to New York tomorrow. I won't be here by the time you come back. I have my own work commitments." His thumb stroked across the back of her knuckles. "I don't have one-night stands. I don't think you do, either."

"That's not what this would be, though, would it? I mean, you're right. I'm married to my career right now, but this isn't a hookup. It's... I've met someone I really like. I want to hang on to what little time we have together."

He swore again and gathered her up, swooping his mouth down to crash across hers. She tasted the conflict in him and poured herself into the kiss, enticing. Pleading, maybe.

When he lifted his head, they were both panting. His heart was pounding so hard in his chest, her fingertips felt as though they bounced where they rested on his pec.

She started to take his hand and lead him back onto the sidewalk, but hesitated.

"Would it be bad for you to be seen going into a room? I'll walk through the lobby and you can use the service elevator. You have a card, don't you? You don't have to knock when you come to my room."

His arms hardened to keep her in the shadowed stoop with him. "I'll knock. If you change your mind, no hard feelings."

"I won't change my mind." She slid her arms around him long enough to kiss under his chin. "But you're right. I never do this. I don't have anything. Protection, I mean. Can you?"

His breath left him in a jagged gust. "Yes. I'll take care of it."

"Thank you. I'll see you soon."

# CHAPTER THREE

*Don't go*, Vijay told himself.

That advice might have been easier to obey if he hadn't been staying in the same damned hotel. If he hadn't had to pass her floor to get to his own.

*I want to hang on to what little time we have together.*

Him too, for more reasons than the fact he was randy as hell after hours of flirting and footsie, then a kiss that had set his blood alight. He *liked* her. Enough that he felt like a heel for keeping secrets from her.

She wasn't looking for a relationship, though. Many things about their lives would remain a mystery from each other. Some people made this sort of relationship a habit, preferring to know as little as possible about their sex partners.

And some people waited until a few days before a wedding before revealing how shallow and faithless they truly were, he thought dourly.

Oriel was offering refreshing honesty, a night without the false promises that kept a person dangling on a string. If they were both law-abiding, consenting adults, did it matter why he'd knocked on her door in the first place?

Vijay collected the box of condoms from his luggage and, moments later, knocked on her door again.

"Your concierge request," he said dryly when she let him in.

She blushed, chuckling as she took it, and set it aside. She sobered as she noted he wasn't laughing. "Am I being too presumptuous?"

"Not at all. I want to use one. More than one, if we are so blessed."

That made her laugh throatily, and somehow they were close enough that he snagged his arm around her without thinking. She pressed into him.

He was lost. Any better thoughts went out the covered windows as he folded his arms around her and pressed her curves into his long-term memory. She was all softness and spice, hair spilling around her shoulders as she tipped her head back and showed him the glow of exhilaration in her eyes.

She had taken off her shoes, but was still tall enough that her nose was even with his mouth. Her long, dark throat was more than he could resist. He dipped his head and tasted her skin.

She gasped and shivered, and he automatically closed his arms tighter around her, holding her still for the swirl of his tongue against her skin. How had he thought he could resist her when she responded so immediately? So wantonly. She ran her hands into his hair and arched to rub against the erection straining against his fly.

*Slow down*, he ordered himself, but they only had tonight, and he wanted every inch of her. She seemed equally urgent, plucking at his shirt until he lifted his mouth and fused his lips to hers.

As they kissed deeply, his pulse throbbed so hard his entire body shook under the reverberations. His hands gathered and roamed over the filmy fabric of her dress, filling his palms with her heat, her lithe waist and her round, firm ass. He had never wanted to rip a woman's clothes off, but the impulse was there tonight. It took everything in him to seek the zipper against the indention of her spine.

"There's a hook," she said as he lowered the tab.

Maybe there was, but he had enough room in the opening to caress the smooth skin above and below the band of her lacy bra.

She flexed and her hand bumped into his, trying to finish opening the dress. She moaned with frustration. "Oh, just break it."

"Thank you," he said fervently, clutching the edge of the zipper and popping the hook. The delicate dress tore in a burst of barbaric satisfaction. He swept the ruined garment forward, peeling it off her front and brushing it down her hips so it landed as a puddle of blue around her feet.

*"Mon Dieu,"* she said on a pang of helpless laughter. "I've never felt like this."

"Me neither." When she began to untuck his shirt, he yanked it open, tearing the cuffs as he roughly pulled it free of his arms, all the while keeping his gaze fixated on the ice-blue lace of her bra and panties.

He may have spent a little too long studying her online photos in skimpy lingerie exactly like that, but reality was even more potent. As he freed his hands from his sleeves, he ran his touch from beneath her arms to her waist and down to her hips before coming back. The soft abrasion of lace against the downy warmth of her skin was a delightful contrast, as was the hint of pink rising beneath her golden skin. He wanted to bite at the dark circles of her areolas, barely visible through the lace in the cups, and *devour* the shadow behind the triangle at the top of her thighs.

"Kiss me." She ran her hands across his bare shoulders and cupped his head, drawing his mouth to hers.

He groaned as he covered her lips and gloried in how her mouth softened in surrender beneath his. He caught her hair and dragged her head back, kissing across her jaw and down to her throat. "I'm going to kiss every part of you," he promised.

Her collarbone, her shoulder where he brushed aside the strap of her bra, the place where her scent gathered between the swells of her breasts.

She opened her bra, and he nearly lost his mind as her breasts spilled into his hands. Her beautiful dark nipples were already pebble-hard as he circled his thumbs across them. He kept swirling his thumb on one while pulling the other deep into his mouth and stabbing at the little bead with his tongue.

A small cry left her, and her hands clutched at him while her weight sagged. His blood throbbed in the tip of his erection, hammering imperatives into his brain.

He ignored his own need and shifted his grip on her, bending her across his arm so he could consume her other nipple. She squirmed, and her helpless pants made him smile with dark satisfaction. When he slid a hand down to silk and discovered it was soaked with her response, he nearly lost it.

"Vijay." Her eyelids were fluttering, and she covered his hand, urging him to press harder.

"Are you going to come?"

"I don't know."

"Let's see, hmm?" He slid a finger under the lace and caressed between her slippery folds, so hot and welcoming. As he dipped his head and found her nipple again, he discovered the hard nub of her clitoris. She stiffened and trembled as he stroked, digging her nails into his scalp. He sucked harder and rolled his touch rhythmically across that little pearl, feeling her quiver and shake.

Her tension gathered until he thought she would break. Suddenly she cried out, shattering so completely, it was like holding a charge of lightning. She electrified him.

Then she went trustingly limp in his embrace, moaning with gratification.

"That was incredible." Vijay swung her up in the cradle of his arms.

"It was," she murmured, curling a heavy arm around his neck and nuzzling his throat. That orgasm had destroyed her in the most exquisite way. "I can walk," she claimed, even though she wasn't entirely confident in that statement.

"I could carry you to a cave on the top of a mountain right now. Somewhere that no other man will ever find you, so you would be mine forever. All mine. *Only mine.*"

She didn't normally find possessiveness sexy, but ooh. She sought his mouth and sucked on his bottom lip. She would be his if he would be hers.

He wouldn't. They only had tonight, she recalled with a catching sensation in her chest.

She might have descended into a fog of despondency then, but he stopped walking to give her a long, luxurious kiss, playing his tongue against hers. When he released her, his dark eyes held a feral glitter.

"Do you mind?"

It took her a moment to realize he wanted her to pick up the box of condoms.

*More than one, if we are so blessed.*

*Oui. Si'l vous plaît.* She did, and seconds later, he set her on the bed.

Her gaze snagged on the ceiling fan. She had a brief moment of unease as she recalled they had only met this morning. He had been correct in saying she didn't do one-night stands. Her first sexual experience had been a seduction at the hands of a young man trying to get close to her mother for career reasons. All the rest of her relationships had died of neglect.

Her last attempt at dating had made the complaint, *You're not a virtuoso like your mother. Why does your career mean so much to you?*

In this moment, as Vijay peeled her panties down her thighs as though savoring the opening of a Christmas gift, she realized the reason her career always took precedence was that no man had made her feel like this—cherished and wanted and *necessary*. She was both helpless and powerful, sated yet aroused. Self-conscious, but losing inhibitions by the heartbeat.

"Come here." He dragged her bottom to the edge of the mattress as he lowered to his knees on the floor beside the bed.

"You—I—" She lost her ability to speak as he set her legs on his shoulders and tasted her. No inhibition on his part, either. She groaned in tortured joy as he brought her replete flesh back to searing life.

He drew her to a height of tension, then slowed and soothed, then intensified his ministrations so her need for more became acute again.

"Vijay, please," she begged, and tangled her hands in his hair. "I need you inside me."

"The problem is, my beautiful goddess…" He stood and opened his belt, dropping pants and briefs in one swift skim. "I don't know how long I will last once I'm there."

Oh, he was beautifully made. From the tree of life that decorated his torso to the root of hair that gathered in a nest at the tops of his thighs to the thick spear of flesh dark with arousal. He reached for the condoms, and she watched as he rolled one on and squeezed himself in his fist.

Her body clenched internally with anticipation.

"Yes?" He touched her knee in a request that she open her legs for him.

"Oh, yes." She was dying and scooted herself into the center of the mattress.

He settled over her, bracing on an elbow as he traced the swollen, sheathed head of his penis around her wet entrance.

"Quit teasing." She nipped at his earlobe.

His crown nudged for admittance. He had girth to him. Her body instinctively tensed as his thickness began to invade. She made herself relax, and he pressed into her. All her sensations intensified as he slowly filled her.

"You're so hot," he breathed, backing off slightly before letting his weight settle so he sank to the limits of their flesh.

She had never felt anything like this. Perfectly full. She was so aroused and swollen and sensitized, she could feel his heartbeat in the steeliness lodged within her.

"Your heart is racing," he murmured as he cupped her breast and played with her nipple.

The small caress sent a tight jolt down into the place where they were joined, and she clenched in reaction. Sensations glittered through her, making her catch her breath.

"Like that?" He continued to roll his thumb around her nipple as he kissed her. Long, lazy kisses that drove her mad because her sex was growing wetter and needier, and he used his weight to keep their hips completely still.

She stroked her hands over the curve of his hard buttocks, then twined her legs up around his waist and dug her heels into his hard globes, inviting him to thrust with muted pulses of her hips. She blatantly thrust her tongue into his mouth and arched to encourage him.

He groaned as he rocked back and thrust in, seeming to pull sensations from her like the strings of a harp, then releasing them to send glorious vibrations shivering through her.

She couldn't help the strangled noise that left her. She twisted beneath him, almost overcome by the intensity of the sensations.

"Almost too good to bear, isn't it?" He worked his hand under her tailbone, tilting her hips so he could thrust with more power. As he invaded, he touched places inside her that made her vision go white.

Sharp spears of joy pierced her. It was inescapable, so she embraced it, clinging to him and moving with him, moaning unreservedly. His hand fisted in the sheet beneath her shoulder, and the slap of their hips was a primitive drumbeat beneath the song of their sobs and groans.

Climax licked and teased and tantalized.

"Not yet," he growled. "Wait."

She had never been held like this on the precipice of exaltation. It was exquisite torture. She clutched at him and said filthy things. "Deeper. Harder. Don't stop. I need more."

He kept to that rhythm that was driving her mad,

held them in that place of utter abandonment that was too sharp to be withstood, but oh, she wanted to be right here forever.

"Now," he commanded through gritted teeth. *"Come."*

He unleashed himself, pushing her toward the high, wide ledge with unconstrained thrusts. A viscously sweet sensation clenched within her, then released her into the universe, scattering her into pieces.

From a distance, she heard him roar with the force of his own orgasm. He fused his hips to hers and pulsed hotly within her. They stayed locked like that for long, euphoric moments, holding tight to that state of utter perfection before he collapsed upon her, sweaty and heavy and replete.

She sighed, drenched and drugged by a kind of pleasure she had never experienced in her life.

And never would again, she acknowledged with a pang of melancholy.

"Who was the thief?" the photographer asked as Oriel prepared for her photo shoot the next day.

"What do you mean?" She turned from hanging the robe she'd been wearing over her first bikini.

"The one who left fingerprints on your bottom. We'll have to call the constable to dust them." The photographer winked at his own joke and waved at the makeup artist.

The woman was grinning with amusement as she brought forward a tray of pots in an array of flesh tones from ivory to intense brown and began to mix them like a painter.

*Mon Dieu.* Oriel wanted to die. The poor woman had already spent an hour trying to disguise the dark circles under her eyes. Now Oriel had to stand here in all her ignominious glory while the sable hairs of a brush tickled the curves of her derriere.

"Don't be embarrassed," the woman said when she rose from her squat and saw Oriel's expression. "Unless he wasn't worth it?"

"Oh, he was," Oriel said ruefully. She had absolutely no regrets. That's what she'd been telling herself as she rose from the bed and had a quick shower a couple of hours ago.

Vijay had been gone when she emerged, but he'd left a note on hotel stationery.

Thank you for an amazing night.

She had his number from the previous note still tucked in a pocket of her bag. She'd been trying to decide if she should text something similar or let last night be a wonderful, stand-alone memory for both of them. Coming on as clingy was the last thing she wanted, but the yearning to keep him in her life was nearly overwhelming. It wasn't that she had felt "complete" with him, but for those hours from dinner through waking beside him, she had stopped feeling so deeply alone.

After several hours of shooting, when she was physically drained and about to change into her own clothes, she took a selfie in the full-length mirror. She was wearing a neon-pink bikini that was almost entirely made of loosely woven strings with a few tiny patches of solid nylon over the important bits.

At the last second, she cut her head out of the photo. Wasn't that the first rule of sexting? Keep it from being too incriminating?

She sent it with a message.

Miss me yet?

Almost immediately, she saw the three dots of a reply.

Niiiice. Who dis?

She texted back.

Not funny.

Then, as it occurred to her that she might have sent it to a wrong number, she asked with growing horror:

Who is this?

Erlich. Send more.

*Non, non, non.* With a whimper, she turned off her phone, resolving to get a new number the second she arrived back in Paris.

Oriel didn't text him. Which was *fine*. This wasn't his first rodeo, as they said in America. They had agreed their affair would only be the one night, and he'd crossed some ethical boundaries by accepting her invitation.

Vijay had struggled as he lay in her bed listening to the shower come on. He'd considered leaving his card, but decided that slipping away with only a thank-you note had been the most prudent course. If she wanted to reach out to him, she had his number from his earlier note. Leaving it had been a way to explain his stealing her toothbrush and to forestall any awkward involvement of hotel management, but at least she had it.

Three days later, he was still fading into lusty memories of their being all over each other, dozing off their sexual gratification before greedily demanding more. The third time, Oriel had instigated it, reaching for him in the predawn light.

"My alarm will go off soon," she had murmured. "Do you want to…?"

Her caress on the inside of his thigh had been all he needed to recover and harden despite the fact he should have been drained dry. He'd pulled her warm, silky body atop him and filled his hands with her smooth skin while their legs braided together. He'd done his best to memorize her with his touch, letting her set the pace since he imagined she was tender after so much lovemaking.

Her damp mouth and cool hair had drifted a tickling sweep across his chest all the way down to his stomach and lower, anointing him in a way that had him forgetting why breathing was a thing anyone bothered to do.

When she had risen to straddle him and guided herself onto his hardness, he hadn't had a condom on yet, but after that much lovemaking, he had known he wouldn't come right away. He had let her lazily ride him and enjoyed the way she crested with a broken gasp and shivers of ecstasy. Her rippling pleasure on his supremely aroused, sensitized flesh had nearly taken him over the edge, but he'd managed to hold back.

After she calmed, he had slipped out of her, put on a condom and taken control. He'd aroused her with his mouth, making her squirm and writhe. He'd tried to be gentle because they'd been at it for hours, but by the time he was moving inside her, the beast had been gripping him with insatiable talons.

He had known it would be their last time. Each stroke

had been bittersweet. Powerful. They had completely abandoned propriety, both moaning and encouraging the other until the people in the next room had banged on the wall and yelled, "Give it a rest!"

He couldn't. He had wanted to meld them into one being for all time. Parting from her was going to leave a piece of himself behind. When the culmination arrived, he'd nearly blacked out from the force—

"Vijay!"

His sister's voice snapped him back to his office. He shifted in his chair, arousal dying a quick death as he leaned to see her across the small courtyard they shared. They left their doors open for exactly this, so they could call across whenever they had a question.

Kiran was glaring at him.

"Are you worried about the language around the patent? Me too." They'd both been studying the offer from TecSec. At least, that's what he was supposed to be doing.

"Why is Jalil texting from the coffee shop, asking me if I want a chai latte and whether I'll be sitting in on his meeting with *you*?" Kiran demanded.

"Is he here? We can do it in your office if you like."

He rose and walked through the courtyard. It was really just a short hallway with a skylight and a water feature against the back wall to provide some cooling and atmospheric noise.

The rest of their company offices were on this same ground floor of a four-story, glass-fronted commercial building. It looked onto an abstract sculpture and a collection of taller buildings. At the far end was the café where Jalil bought Kiran coffee. Above them was an architecture firm, a publishing agency, and a call center for a company in America.

They hoped to take over all of that once the acquisition went through because this was such a good space for Kiran's wheelchair, but they would also open a center in Delhi before looking to Singapore, Hong Kong and Shanghai over the next few years.

"What is this about?" She watched him close the courtyard doors with a glower of suspicion.

"Just a quick hand of poker."

"Is this why you disappeared for a few days on your way home from Europe?" She narrowed her eyes. "Look, just because I haven't found proof that Lakshmi visited a clinic while she was away, doesn't mean anything. A clinic like that would be very discrete about how they handled their records. Twenty-five years ago, they might have still been using paper."

Vijay didn't have to respond. There was a knock, and Jalil was shown in. He was a healthy widower of fiftysomething with strands of silver in his otherwise thick black hair. He held a cardboard tray of three disposable cups.

As he and Kiran saw one another, the pair lit up and smiled and shared a look of tangled emotions that was so intimate, Vijay had to look away.

He had thought he had that once, the feeling of someone else's emotions being his own. It had been a lie, and he was not looking forward to picking up the pieces when Kiran realized Jalil was toying with her.

Actually, he had thought he might have something like it with Oriel, too, but her silence spoke volumes. Sexual connection was simply that, a trick of biology, and he wouldn't allow Jalil to use it on his sister.

He couldn't wait to expose the man and kick him out of their lives once and for all.

"Vijay, Kiran said you like black coffee." Jalil's

warm smile turned stiff. He set the tray on the corner of her desk and pulled out each cup.

Kiran and Vijay provided a well-stocked break room full of coffee, tea and soft drinks for their staff, but Jalil liked to impress Kiran by overpaying for takeaway.

This was what annoyed Vijay about the man. He could have kept his pursuit of his "niece" entirely professional, but he hadn't.

*Did* you?

*Oh, shut up*, Vijay told the irritating voice in his head.

"It was kind of you to think of me," Vijay said as politely as he could. "And thank you for coming in." He waved at a chair in invitation, waiting until Jalil had seated himself before saying, "I have good news." Jalil wouldn't see it that way, but Vijay certainly did. "While I was in Europe, I was able to intercept Oriel Cuvier and get a DNA sample—"

"You *told* her?" Kiran cried.

"No. I stole her toothbrush and sent it to the lab we use. I didn't put her name on the paperwork. It's Sample X, but Jalil can offer his own sample, and we can put an end to speculation." Vijay leaned on Kiran's desk, facing Jalil. He crossed his arms and ankles and conveyed a silent and ruthless *checkmate*.

"I can't believe you would jeopardize Jalil's confidentiality." Kiran rolled out from behind the desk to move next to Jalil. "I am *so* sorry I told him what you had asked me to do."

"Don't be," Jalil said, patting Kiran's arm in a placating way. "Your brother has gone to a lot of trouble on my behalf."

Vijay had absolutely not done it for Jalil's benefit,

and they all knew it. He was trying to get rid of a man who was playing his sister.

"I know it must seem as though I'm grasping at straws," he said to Vijay. "You have every right to be skeptical of my motives, but this is something I've wondered every day since Lakshmi returned from Europe. When I saw those photos of Ms. Cuvier and read up on her details, I couldn't stop thinking about this possibility, but I didn't know how to ask her without tipping my hand. I would be devastated if Lakshmi's reputation was tarnished by false rumors. This is perfect. Thank you. How do I proceed?"

"You want to give a sample?" Vijay tried not to let his jaw hit the floor.

"Of course."

Vijay had just had his own bluff called.

# CHAPTER FOUR

Worst. Idea. Ever.

Duke Rhodes hadn't booked her into a hotel. He'd added Oriel to the roster of guests on a yacht. Granted, it was a billionaire's superyacht and was full to the gunwales with entertainment industry movers and shakers as well as artists and designers. Oriel even knew a handful of them *and* she'd been given her own stateroom—not that she was in it.

Payton had instructed her to use this to her advantage. *See and be seen.* Easier said than done when Duke wanted her by his side like a security blanket.

At least he wasn't being a creep about it. He had looped his arm around her as they walked the red carpet, keeping it colleague-friendly, not pervy, but she had still hated it.

She was so burnt out, she felt like charred bacon. She had been working nonstop for weeks, putting in long days and getting most of her sleep on airplanes crisscrossing the Atlantic. She was beyond ready for vacation, but she had to paste a smile on her face and pretend to be thrilled with Duke's latest film—which struck her as a paint-by-numbers rehash of every action flick ever made. The audience's tepid response seemed to agree.

By the time they arrived back on the yacht, the after-party was in full swing.

Oriel wished she had confessed to the headache that was intensifying behind her brow. It was growing bad enough to make her nauseous.

Duke was holding court, though, drinking and smoking and making off-color jokes. He wasn't a terrible person so much as a man in denial of his age. He wanted to be twenty, so that's how he was acting. He loved his cigarettes, which he lit with a shaking hand, making her suspect he had social anxiety, but the smell was turning her stomach.

Either way, all her years of practicing aloof, unbothered looks were being severely tested as Duke blathered on about his glory days.

"I need the powder room," she murmured and excused herself.

She needed to find a tender to run her to shore. She was flying home to her parents' in the morning and had overheard someone say the yacht was hauling anchor at first light. Why had she agreed to this wretched stunt?

She texted Payton as she moved into the crush of the saloon, telling him she was done with this pageantry, and asked if he knew of any rooms she could book at this late hour.

What happened? I told his people this was only for publicity. If he's crossed a line, tell me. I don't put my clients in harm's way.

Oriel didn't feel like explaining that pretending to be with Duke made her feel cheap. It made her think about everything he wasn't. About *who* he wasn't and who she really wanted to spend her time with.

Not that the man she *did* want had reached out in the nearly two months since they'd spent their rapturous night in Milan. Granted, she'd been on the move, but she wasn't hard to reach. She could be contacted online fairly easily.

Maybe he'd given her the wrong number on purpose. That's what she kept thinking. He could have given her his number again with that second note, but he hadn't. She was the ultimate feminine stooge who had fallen for a player's game, and it made her feel like an absolute neophyte.

She caught up to a steward, who told her she only needed to go down to the lower deck in the stern where she had come aboard. A tender was making regular trips to shore all night.

She moved down a staircase to the passageway that led to her room and halted. A man in a dark suit stood outside the door to her room.

*Mon Dieu*, he looked just like Vijay.

Her heart screeched to a stop in her chest while such a rush of joy exploded in her, she had to reach back and grasp the rail to stay upright. At the same time, her mind blared an alarm at how *not normal* it was that he would be here.

It had been nearly two months to the day since she'd met him. Slept with him. He'd been on her mind every day, but when the number he'd given her turned out to be wrong, she'd decided they weren't meant to be.

Or that he had never really wanted them to be. How had he known where to find her? Bumping into him in a restaurant a few blocks from her hotel had been unexpected, but a reasonable happenstance. Of all the yachts in the south of France right now, however, he was on this one? Standing outside her door?

No, he must have come to find her, but how had he gotten on board? Given all the celebrities in attendance, security was very tight. He had some sort of security company, she recalled vaguely, but it still seemed very odd.

As she stood there trying to assimilate his presence, he turned his head.

"Oriel." His voice pierced as sharply as his flaring gaze.

His innate energy leaped down the long passageway to catch at her, threatening to overwhelm her the way he had the first time. It was so visceral, it alarmed her. She hadn't properly gotten over him, and here he was about to make it worse.

Acting purely on instinct, she whirled around and fled up the stairs like Cinderella from the ball. She didn't know why she needed to get away. She just did.

She tried to, anyway.

"Sweetheart. Where you going?" Duke lurched in front of her, swaying, eyes barely open.

Oriel tugged Duke out a door so they stood at the rail and dredged up a lame smile.

"This has been so much fun." *Lie.* "But I have an early flight tomorrow. I'm going to get a room on shore."

"What's the problem, sugar? Feeling neglected?" Duke splayed a hand on her waist. "I can't help it if I'm popular. C'mon. We'll go to my room."

"What? Ew. *No.*" She tried to brush his hand off her, but he caught hers and wouldn't let her shake him off. *"Duke."*

People further along the rail turned their heads.

He crowded into her, cajoling, "Don't make me look bad, sweetheart."

Good heavens, was he begging? What a poor, desperate man.

She looked him straight in the eye and said, "You need rehab. Do you want me to ask my agent to arrange it if yours won't?"

He dismissed that with a tired curse, hissing, "I need good press, darling. Come to my room. Let people think what they think. That's all I want. Swear."

*"No."* She pressed his chest, but he kept her trapped against the rail. "Seriously, Duke. Back off. Let me go."

"Come *on*. I got you a room so you'd at least *pretend* we're having sex."

"I'll see that you're given a full refund," she muttered and pushed harder. *"Let me go."*

Duke was suddenly yanked back a few steps.

"I will cut you up and throw you to the sharks," Vijay said in the most frightening tone Oriel had ever heard.

"Vijay!" She shot out a protesting hand.

Before she could react further, security guards emerged from the shadows and closed in on all of them. They clapped their hands on Vijay, forcing him to release Duke.

"I know him," she blurted, still holding up her hand as if she had some kind of magical powers to stop men from acting like barbarians. *"Tout va bien."* Was it fine? Maybe Vijay was some sort of stalker who had followed her here. She didn't know.

"I'm Vijay Sahir. I work for TecSec. Let me go." Vijay tried to shrug off the men holding him. "I'll show you my card. You can call in for my credentials."

Confusion ensued. Duke spat venom in her direction about bitches being crazy, and staggered off. Oriel and Vijay were invited to quit ruining the party and wait in her stateroom until Vijay's identity was confirmed.

Oriel could have balked at being left alone with him. His presence here was growing more bizarre by the second. Her parents used TecSec. Were they okay?

He was the only one with answers, so she led him into her stateroom. It was a midrange one with built-in shelves, recessed lighting, and a double bed. The shades were pulled over the windows, and she hadn't bothered to unpack, so her suitcase was open on the rack.

Somehow, she had wound up with one of Vijay's cards in her hand.

"This says Vice President of TecSec Asia Division." At least one mystery was explained. She had mistaken a five for an eight when she had texted him her bikini photo. "You made it sound as though you were barely scraping by." Why else would he have been working in maintenance at the hotel?

"I told you we had a deal in the works that I couldn't talk about. Are you all right? Did he hurt you?" He noted she was massaging her wrist and carefully took her forearm in his two hands.

His touch. It was as beguiling as ever, sending little tingles of awareness all through her.

She made herself pull away and step back. It took everything in her not to let him see how thrown she was by his turning up this way. How defenseless he made her feel. Her whole body felt electrified. *Awake*. Which undermined her confidence, because she didn't want to be this sensitive and reliant on anyone, least of all a man who had stripped her down to her most elemental self and seemed like he could effortlessly do it again.

"I'm fine." She might bruise later, but only because when Duke had released her, she had snapped her hand back so hard she'd bumped her wrist on the rail. "Why are you here?"

"They wouldn't let me near you at the premiere, but fans of Rhodes tipped me off to the fact you were staying on board with him here. I swear, the best security system in the world is no match for autograph seekers," he said ironically. "This yacht is leaving for Italy in the morning, though. I didn't want to miss you."

He was different than she recollected. His hair was a little shorter, his tailored suit on par with those of the movie stars and producers continuing their gaiety beyond these walls. His expression was forbidding, though. Nothing like the easygoing man she'd taken him for.

Or the humble maintenance man he had pretended to be.

"How did you know I was in Cannes? Are *you* some kind of super fan?" Worse? "Have you been spying on me? Tracking my phone?" She glanced around for it as if it would be glowing with a beacon.

"Nothing that high-tech." He was still using that dry tone. "I overheard your conversation in Milan. You said this trip would cut into your vacation. I thought it would be a good idea for you to have personal time after we talk."

"That's very arrogant."

"Which part? Assuming how you'll react to what I have to say?" His voice hardened. "Or that you would speak to me at all?"

That took her aback until she recalled that she had run the minute she'd seen him.

All this time, she had been telling herself she was fine with not hearing from him. It was what they had agreed on, but deep down, she'd taken it as a rejection, one that stuck like a thorn in her heart.

As sophisticated as she'd tried to be about their night

together, she'd also been more uninhibited with him than she'd ever been in her life. That knowledge kept hitting her in ever stronger waves as she remained in his presence, like a tide coming in. Her self-consciousness was deepening by the minute, and her feet were stuck in the sand. She wanted to get away, but couldn't.

Meanwhile, he stood there with his Just The Facts Ma'am attitude, suggesting he barely remembered they'd clung to each other while moaning with abject passion.

"I was surprised to see you," she said with as much dignity as she could scrape together. "Why didn't you reach out through my website or my social profiles?"

"You had my number but didn't reach out," he said with a negligent shrug. "I wasn't sure you would take my call, and this is important."

She wanted to say, *You gave me the wrong number*, but if this card was anything to go by, he'd given her the wrong everything.

"Why were you working for that hotel in Milan? Were you actually in their security department?"

He licked his lips, the first sign of him not feeling completely in control of this moment. "We hope that hotel will join our roster of clients. I presented to them while I was there, but no. I was not working for them in any capacity when I met you."

"Then why…?" She was growing deeply uneasy, pinching his card so hard her thumbnail went white.

"I told you the truth when I said I was trying to prove something to my sister." His detached air cracked enough that his cheek ticked. "As it turns out, she was right and I was wrong."

*How much did it cost him to admit that?* she wondered with a twinge of grim amusement.

"What is that supposed to mean? What are you doing here? What were you doing there?" She could feel hysteria edging into her psyche. It made her sick that he'd had some sort of ulterior motive when they'd made love. It sullied her memory of a night that was otherwise pure and wonderful. It made her feel used. Not desired for herself.

*Unwanted.*

He flicked open his jacket as if he was overheating.

Despite how fractious this moment was, she became acutely aware of his flat stomach and had a flashing vision of kissing across his muscled abdomen while her breasts nestled his erection. He'd tangled his hands in her hair and groaned as if she was torturing him in the most exquisite way possible.

A searing mix of arousal and embarrassment poured through her. She had been utterly shameless with him. It had felt right at the time, as if they were both revealing something no one else had ever reached, but now her gaze pinned itself to the floor, mortified.

A sudden knock rapped before the door swung open, making her gaze fly up in a panicked *What now?* One of the ship's security guards strode in and handed Vijay the passport he'd taken from him a few minutes ago.

"Thank you for your patience, sir. You're free to go anytime. Please let me know if I can assist in any way."

"Thank you." Vijay pocketed his passport and nodded at the door in arrogant dismissal. The man left, closing the door behind him.

Oriel stared at the closed door, wondering if she should be reassured by the deference that man had shown or intimidated. She clung to her elbows.

"Are my parents okay? Does this have something to do with them?"

"Not in the way you think. To the best of my knowledge, your mother and father are completely fine. But you should sit down." Vijay pulled out the chair tucked beneath the built-in desk. "What I'm going to tell you will shock you. It's about your birth family."

Oriel instinctively backed away. She was already against a wall, though. Some kind of knob was trying to puncture her kidney. She barely felt it. Her hair scraped against the wood as she shook her head.

"I know all I need to about them."

His face blanked with shock. "You do?"

"Yes." Oriel repeated what she had always known. "They were a mixed race couple, and that was a problem for my birth mother's family, so she gave me up." Which cut Oriel to the bone, obviously, but not everyone enjoyed the advantages she and her parents had. She tried not to judge her biological mother too harshly, not when she didn't have all the facts. "I've never wanted to cause problems to resurface for them, so I've never tried to find them. Plus, it would hurt my parents if they thought I was looking for my birth family. So, no thank you. Keep whatever you know to yourself."

Despite her dignified refusal, her heart pounded so hard she thought her ribs would crack. Her stomach was seriously trying to turn itself inside out.

Vijay set his hands on his hips. He started to speak a few times before finally saying, "I've been thinking about this from every angle, trying to work out how to phrase things. It never once occurred to me you wouldn't want to hear it. But okay." He nodded with bewilderment. "That's your choice." He rubbed his jaw, casting about the room as though completely at sea. "You have my card if you change your mind."

He looked at the card she held. In her agitation, she

had twisted it beyond recognition. He removed a fresh one from his pocket and set it on the folded clothes inside her suitcase.

He stood there a long moment, staring at her.

A million images flashed into her mind, from his first sexy side-eye when he had entered her suite to his quick smile at the bar. The way the touch of his leg against her own had filled her with melting heat, and with a cocky brow, he declared they were on a date. His kisses and caresses and deeply generous lovemaking and his note that had claimed it had been an amazing night.

She waited for him to acknowledge any of that, but he only nodded once and said, "Good night." He started for the door.

"That's it?" she cried, panic-stricken that he would walk away so easily. *Again.* "You can't just stroll back into my life with a baited hook and dangle it like that! What were you trying to prove?"

"To my sister? You just said you don't want to know."

She pressed back into the wall again. "If you tell me you and I are related..."

*"No,"* he choked out. His mouth twitched, but he added firmly, "Absolutely not."

She hugged herself, searching his eyes for clues. Until this moment, she would have sworn that she had no interest in learning about her birth parents. She had long ago made peace with the fact she would never know more about where she came from than she'd always known.

She suddenly discovered she did have questions, though. Thousands of them, each one making her burn with curiosity. There was a scorch of guilt that came with it. This desire to hear more felt disloyal to the people who had always treated her as though they'd made her themselves.

"I love my parents," she blurted.

"I'm sure you do." His voice gentled. "This is my mistake, Oriel. It's been a busy few weeks for my company. I got it into my head that I had to have all of that wrapped up so I could catch you here in Cannes before you went on vacation, but you're right. This is something you should learn in your own way on your own timeline. It's just…" His gaze flickered down her silver gown, which was covered in sequins that caught the light. "Well, it was good to see you again. Call if you want to talk to me."

"Why didn't they just write to me? What about an email?" She threw up a flailing arm. "Have they *always* known where I was?" The thought of that nearly broke her into pieces. Who kept something like that from someone? "Why didn't you warn me that you were planning to come back into my life with news like this? Why are *you* the one delivering this news? *Mon Dieu*, is that why you sought me out in Milan?"

It was. She knew it as she said it. Her heart hardened into a stony lump in her chest. She had thought she was special, that they had shared something extraordinary. But she had never been special. Not special enough. Not good enough to keep.

"The situation is delicate." His cheeks hollowed. "Best handled personally so things can be managed on both ends. I don't want to say more than that because you've just said you don't want to know."

"Who do you think you are?" she cried, charging forward a few steps. "You've come all this way. I'm not going to let you torture me with it. *Tell me*."

He stiffened as though bracing for a physical attack.

His head went back and he looked down his nose, but otherwise he was very still.

"Are you sure, Oriel? There's no going back—"

*"Vijay."* A pulsing charge was running through her, burning painfully in her arteries, throbbing and stinging and making her stomach swish around and around. She thought she might throw up, but fought it back, glaring at him. Daring him to speak or walk out. She didn't even know what was worse right now, looking into his eyes knowing he didn't care about her, or letting him walk away with her deepest secrets still unlocked.

He seemed to hold every part of her in his wide hand. Did he realize that?

After an interminable silence, he nodded at the chair. "You look like you're going to snap in half."

Sitting down felt like lowering herself onto a bed of nails. Her whole body was prickling with confusion, wanting to react to something big without knowing what it was. She clutched her hands together and pressed them to her trembling lips, probably most infuriated by the fact he was witnessing her react this nakedly.

"My adoption is supposed to be *my* information," she told him resentfully. "*I* should decide who I share it with and how much is known. You're not supposed to come here and tell me things I don't know about myself. Not things that are so..." the word *intimate* wasn't strong enough "...*integral* to who I am."

"You're right."

She instantly hated him for that ultra-reasonable tone. It told her how badly she was betraying herself if he thought she was in danger of a breakdown and had to neutralize her emotions by sounding all calm and agreeable.

Bitter tears stood in her eyes as she watched him

lower to the corner of the bed. He set his elbows on his knees and linked his hands loosely. His expression was very grave.

"It's not much of a defense, but I didn't believe this theory would prove true. It seemed too outrageous. I went to Milan thinking I would prove to my sister she was being fed a fabrication."

"Kiran," she recollected. "You thought someone was trying to take advantage of her."

"Yes. Because reuniting lost families isn't something we even do, but this man had seen your photo and thought you looked like his sister. The timing of your birth matched a trip she'd taken to Europe a few years before she passed away."

"She's dead." A cold wind buffeted her, pushing her back into her chair. She had to take a measured breath to absorb what a blow that news was. She really had been carrying a lot of unacknowledged maybes and somedays. Tears of grief and loss gathered in her throat.

Vijay waited until she lifted her gaze.

"I'm sorry." He offered his hand. "Do you want me to give you a few minutes?"

"No," she choked and tucked her cold, bloodless hands between her knees.

"I'll tell you up front that I have no idea who your birth father is. He remains a mystery, but our client saw your photos and recalled some remarks his sister had made. He became convinced you were his biological niece. I thought he was using the mystery to spend time with Kiran, and the sooner I proved him wrong, the sooner he would leave her alone." He paused as though giving her a chance to brace herself. "I went to your room in Milan so I could steal your toothbrush. I sent it to a DNA lab."

"You're not allowed to do that," she hissed, sitting up straighter. "You're supposed to get a person's consent."

"It was expensive," he allowed with a tilt of his head. "I didn't attach your name to it. I thought the man was a fraud, Oriel. I thought I would force him to admit he was blowing smoke and make him disappear. Or he'd go through with the test, it wouldn't match, and I could tell him to go to hell for sending us on a wild goose chase. I didn't expect it would lead back to you. And I never once took for granted what I was doing was crossing a line. I am sorry."

"It matches?" Of course it did, or he wouldn't be here.

Her stomach tightened, and she pushed herself deeper into the chair. On some higher plane she was appalled that Vijay had gone behind her back. She would never forgive him for interfering in her life in such an underhanded way, but her eyes were fixated on his mouth, her ears straining for every word.

"He's...my uncle?"

"It came back with a high statistical likelihood that you're related, yes. You look a *lot* like his sister, Lakshmi Dalal. She was a very famous Bollywood star around the time you were born."

"No." Oriel dismissed it on reflex. "My birth parents were from Romania and Turkey. I was born at a private clinic in Luxembourg."

"Lakshmi went to Europe with her manager about four months before you were born, supposedly to record some songs at a private studio. When she came back, she was different. Her brother could tell she was grieving. He believes her manager pressured her to give up her baby for the sake of her career."

"Is he still alive? The manager? Has anyone *asked* him?"

"Jalil is being very careful. He's afraid the manager, Gouresh Bakshi, will attack you and smear Lakshmi's memory. Or he'll lie or line his own pockets by selling some version of the story. Jalil would love more answers, but he doesn't believe he would get the truth from that man. He hoped you or your parents might have some piece of the story. Would you be willing to speak to him?"

"Go to India?"

"Or video chat. Take as much time as you need to think about that."

"I don't need to think." She shook her head and rose. Adrenaline was pouring into her system, and her mind fixated on one thing. "I need to go home. I need to see my parents."

She needed to go to ground like a wounded animal. Her mind was too shocked to form any other thought. She began to gather her few items scattered around the room as though she could outrun the crazed hurt and anguish breathing on her neck and sending trickles of apprehension down her spine.

She couldn't make sense of what this might mean and wouldn't even try. Better to carry on with her original plan.

"Oriel." Vijay tried to catch her by the hands. "You're in shock."

"Oh, don't pretend you care!" She shook him off. "Really, Vijay? Really? This is the reason you slept with me? To steal a toothbrush and ruin my life? Go to hell!"

# CHAPTER FIVE

SHE SWEPT AROUND him with a rustle of her sparkling gown. The graze of her sequined skirt against his leg was an absent caress that wafted a tortuous sensuality through him.

How had he forgotten how truly beautiful she was? He'd let his memory of her harden and dull, telling himself he was better off because she hadn't tried to stay in contact. They were too far apart in more ways than geography. If she was the kind who resorted to publicity stunts to advance her career, she wasn't that different from Wisa. He definitely didn't need anyone like that in his life again.

Despite that very sensible conclusion, from the second he had confirmed Jalil was her blood uncle, Vijay had been anticipating seeing Oriel again. Jalil had still been speechless and pale when Vijay had urged him not to make any moves without discussing it with him. He'd confessed to having dinner with Oriel, not the rest, but insisted on being the one to inform her.

He had told himself he simply wanted to come clean about his part in this discovery, that it was the decent thing to do, but he'd been impatient to see her again. His heart had leaped into his throat when he'd seen her at the end of the passageway. The animal within him had finally scented his mate.

He didn't know what he had expected, but not that she would turn and *run*.

His gut tightened at that memory of her dress swirling and disappearing up the stairs. It had stung, damn it. But had he really thought she would be happy to see him? She was probably mortified she had slept with a commoner.

Moments later, when he'd found Duke cornering her, he'd been overcome with rage. The actor was lucky he hadn't been thrown into the sea.

That sharp swing of emotions had been so unsettling, he had steeled himself to stick to the facts once they were alone.

Then she had astonished him by refusing to hear him out. It hadn't computed when he'd spent weeks thinking, *I have to get to her. I have to explain*.

He had expected her to be shocked. Anyone would be, but as someone whose beliefs about his own parents had been shattered when he had least expected it, he should have realized she would be shaken to her core.

The way she was trembling and seemed greenish-gray beneath her natural tan alarmed him.

"Will you sit down and give yourself a minute?"

"No." She clapped her case closed and thumped it onto the floor, then yanked up the retractable handle with a snap. She scooped up her shoulder bag, checked its contents, then slung it across her body before snagging her case and starting through the door.

Vijay caught the door and followed her through it.

"You're really leaving?" He set his hand on the handle of her suitcase.

She held on and crashed her furious gaze into his.

As their knuckles sat against one another's, a deeply

vulnerable glint edged into her eyes. It slid like a knife between his ribs, parting his lips on a sharp inhale. He had made a grave error. She was more than shaken. She was devastated.

"Oriel." He didn't know what else to say.

Her brow flinched, and she snatched her hand away, saying caustically, "Fine. Be my valet. Saves me the trouble of carrying it." She swished ahead of him. "But then you can go to hell."

"So you already suggested."

The throng of party guests in a small bar turned their heads as he and Oriel strode through, trading barbs. Vijay paused to get his bearings, then redirected her down some steps to water level.

"Transport to shore, please," Oriel said to the deckhand when they arrived.

"The tender just left." The young man nodded at the running lights disappearing toward the glow of the city. "It will be back in thirty or forty minutes."

"My boat is right here." Vijay moved to where his rented speedboat was tied and set her suitcase inside it.

Oriel was a Victorian queen in that stunning dress with her hair teased up in loops. Earrings like chandeliers dangled, while she was nude from her chin down her long neck to that plunging point between her breasts. She stood with her arms straight at her sides, likely hiding clenched fists in the folds of her skirt while she glared at him in a way that declared, *Off with his head*.

Waves were hitting the yacht from all sides, causing sucking and slurping noises. The deck lifted and fell. He saw her swallow uncertainly.

"Wait for the tender if you want. I'll wait with you." It wasn't a warning, more of a promise.

"Oh—" She strung together some very un-regal

words and gathered her skirts. "I'm only going with you because it's the quickest way to get to shore and away from you."

He helped her into his tender and handed her a PFD.

"You can't get me to dry land without drowning me along the way?"

"You're wearing chain mail. If you fall overboard, you're sinking straight to the bottom. It's dark out." He didn't even want to contemplate trying to make such a rescue. "Is the gown rented?" He would have to make arrangements to return it.

"It was a gift."

"From Duke?"

She shoved her arms into the vest and closed the tabs, then lowered herself onto the seat nearest her suitcase, chin high, nose turned to the water.

Very well, then. Vijay shrugged into his own vest and started the engine, nodding at the deckhand to cast him off while he sent a quick text to ensure his car would be waiting.

Was he jealous of her wearing something another man had given her? He was so green he was septic with it. He had been from the moment he had learned she wasn't staying in a hotel but was on this yacht with the dissolute actor. At least there'd been no evidence of Duke sharing that stateroom with her, but what did he know?

What right did he have to care? None. Oriel had made clear she had no further interest in him when she hadn't reached out to him after their night. *Which was fine.* They had agreed it was a one-time thing. She didn't belong to him.

Oriel made a noise behind him, and he glanced back to see her grasp at the side of the boat as they hit a patch of wash that made for a bumpy ride. He eased off the throttle.

A metaphor for how he ought to handle her?

What was left to handle? He'd gone behind her back, and she was furious with him. The fact that he was still sexually enthralled by her meant nothing.

They arrived at the marina, and he helped her onto the dock once the boat was secured. He could feel how her hand was shaking. Her expression looked anguished.

"Are you all right?"

"Fine." She spat the word like it was poison.

He returned the keys for the boat, and she paused next to him to ask the man in the rental shack if there was a shuttle service to a hotel.

"I have a car waiting," Vijay told her.

"Good for you. I'll make my own way." She wrested the handle of her suitcase from him and rolled it toward the bottom of the ramp that led up to the parking lot.

"Do you have a room booked? Because the entire world has checked into the city for the film festival." He was staying in a middling three-star place well back from the bay where the only window looked onto the pool.

"Do you know what's funny?" She whirled to face him. "The day we met, when I let you into my room, my agent said that was how lives were ruined. I should have listened to him."

She spun away and started up the ramp. Her suitcase caught on the lip. She turned and roughly gave it a yank, trying to make it come with her, but it was well hooked. She released a noise of helpless fury and shook it harder.

Vijay moved to help, but she released it so abruptly, it tumbled back onto his legs. He barely managed to keep from losing his footing and falling into the water.

"Look," he said shortly. "We need a reset before one of us—"

Oriel grasped the rail on the ramp and leaned over it, moaning with pain.

"Oriel!" He left the suitcase on the dock and hurried up the ramp to set his arms on either side of her. "Are you going to faint? What's wrong?"

She lost her stomach over the rail into the shallow water below.

Ah, hell. He smoothed a few tendrils of her hair away from her face and neck and rubbed her back until she finished retching.

*"Mon Dieu,"* she moaned, sagging against the rail. "How is this night getting worse?"

He offered the black silk of his pocket square. "You get seasick." Or was this a visceral reaction to him and his news?

Vijay had a pigheaded view that ignorance was not bliss. Once he'd learned about his father's crimes, he'd been eaten up by guilt that he hadn't at least made enquiries sooner.

He had twisted his contempt for himself and his own willful blindness into thinking Oriel not only had a right to know about Lakshmi, but that she *needed* to know. If Lakshmi's manager forced Oriel's adoption, he couldn't be allowed to get away with it!

He was conveniently forgetting the hours of ruminating and soul-searching he'd done getting to the decisions he'd made and the actions he'd taken.

Oriel wiped her mouth and straightened, still trembling.

"Let me take you to my hotel," he said gently. "If they don't have a room, we'll ask them to phone around. Either way, you'll be comfortable while we sort things out." He went back for her case, then set his arm around her to guide her up the ramp. "I didn't mean to cause you this much distress."

"What did you think would happen?" she asked with disbelief.

"That it would go slightly less poorly than this."

"You lied to get me into bed."

"No—" As they arrived in the parking lot, his car slid to a stop at the curb. He opened the door. She sank into the back seat, still pale and subdued.

He closed the privacy screen as the limo worked its way into the knot of bumper-to-bumper traffic.

"Oriel." He squeezed his thighs so he wouldn't reach for her. "I honestly thought it wouldn't be true. Everything we said about not having another opportunity to be together was real. I never expected to see you again."

"So you took advantage of the one chance you had to nail me? That makes it all better, then." She helped herself to a miniature bottle of water.

"I didn't seduce you."

"You *lied*."

"I kept one detail from you because I wasn't at liberty to reveal it." He held up a finger, aware this angry defensiveness was the diametric opposite from the way he'd planned to handle this. He was supposed to be giving her the sincere apology she rightfully deserved, but clipped excuses were spewing out of him instead. "If you hadn't been Lakshmi's daughter, I couldn't risk starting rumors that she potentially had one. I didn't know you would come to that restaurant. You invited me to eat with you. You invited me to your room after. Remember? *Bring condoms*, you said."

"Well, I regret that now, don't I?"

"Only now?" he asked with more bitterness than he meant to reveal.

She snapped her head around. "What is that supposed to mean?"

"The second you saw me tonight, you turned and ran."

"Because I was *embarrassed*. You ghosted me."

"No, I didn't." He frowned. "You had my number."

"You have terrible handwriting," she spat, then looked toward the window. "I sent a bikini pic to a stranger because of you, thanks very much. I had to change my number."

She was speaking contemptuously, blaming him, but he was grimly thrilled to hear she had made an effort to reach out.

"I was completely sincere with my second note." He spoke more calmly. "The attraction I felt was real. I enjoyed being with you that night."

"I hate to break it to you, Vijay, but a lot of men are attracted to me. That doesn't mean they get to sleep with me under false pretenses."

His temperature skyrocketed, but he bit his tongue because the car was arriving at his hotel. There was no doorman, so the chauffeur slipped around to open her door while Vijay climbed out his own. As he came around to her side, he saw Oriel grasp at the edge of the door. She had gone white and looked like she was going to throw up again.

He hurried to get his arm around her.

She pressed a weak hand against his chest, obviously resenting that she had to lean on him, but she needed his support.

He managed to tip the driver and take charge of her

case, but as the car drove away, he kept her in the fresh night air.

"Is this something more serious? Bad shellfish? A bug?"

"I don't know," she said plaintively. "I thought it was Duke's cigarette smoke and being on the boat that was making me feel so awful. I haven't eaten much today."

"I'll order room service." He guided her into one of the pockets of the revolving door, saying facetiously, "You're not pregnant, are you?"

They both halted.

The door bumped them from behind, nudging them into the bustling noise of the lobby.

He looked down at her sallow face. Her eyes were swallowing up her features.

A dry lump formed in his throat. A nest of cobras arrived in his stomach.

"Are you?" His lips felt numb. A vivid memory came to him of the exquisite sensation when she'd been riding his naked flesh. He hadn't come, though. Even if he had, surely he'd have been shooting blanks by then!

"No. That's—no, of course not." She didn't sound sure. She looked aghast, but who wouldn't after the last few hours? "No. That would be ridiculous."

*I hate to break it to you, Oriel, but "ridiculous" was left behind long ago.*

He didn't say it. He led her to the elevator and walked her to his room, experiencing a twinge of embarrassment when he let her in. The room was clean and secure, but it was no superyacht or even the classy place they'd stayed at in Milan.

"It's all I could get at the last minute." And he'd thought it would be only him.

"It's fine." She dropped her shoulder bag on the bed

and moved to the window, where she hugged herself while staring down at the guests partying alongside the pool.

"Do you…" He pushed his hands into his pockets. "Do you want me to go to a pharmacy?"

"No." Her fingernails were digging into her upper arm. "But I think you should." Her gaze flashed over to his, swiping through him like a blade when he saw the deeply apprehensive shadows lurking there. "Just to be sure."

He tried again to swallow the lump in his throat. His lungs felt tight. He nodded, glad to have an excuse to catch a breath of air and organize his thoughts.

"Order something," he said, nodding at the card on the nightstand. "Maybe you just need to settle your stomach."

Her eyes widened with persecution, as if food was one decision too many.

"I'll ask downstairs, have something sent up," he offered.

"Thank you." She was staring at the pool again.

The fact she was not throwing sarcasm and defiant looks at him said a lot. She was worried. Which worried him.

Did it? He didn't know what to think or feel.

He moved like a robot, asked for directions at the registration desk, and almost forgot to request two bowls of soup be sent to his room.

What if Oriel was pregnant? Was it even his? If it was, what would he do?

At one time he had assumed without question that he would eventually marry and become a father. His parents had been indulgent, his broader family of aunts, uncles and cousins a warm network of affection, endless food and constant laughter. The expectation of a similar life had been very natural—if intimidating when his grandmother had dubbed him "man of the house" after his parents' death. Vijay had had her and Kiran to look after, though, and his father's business to take over. He had focused on growing into the role and had been determined to do it well.

When the foundations of the business proved to be rotten and his fiancée's fidelity was revealed to be equally compromised, Vijay had put aside aspirations of marriage and parenting. Staying clothed and fed had become his priority.

Over time, as his fortunes improved, he'd become aware that women looked on him as a prize worth winning. His ability to trust was so eroded, however, he hadn't been willing to commit to anything serious. He didn't want to set himself up for another gross betrayal. Besides, he hadn't met anyone he couldn't stop thinking about.

Until Oriel.

It had been two months since he'd seen her, and he'd thought of her constantly, checking his phone like an adolescent hoping for a "like."

Surely she would have had a sign by now if the baby was his? He cautioned himself not to get caught up in a sense of duty toward her, but uneasily recognized he wouldn't cut all ties if it wasn't his. He had delivered the shock of her life. She was in a vulnerable state and could be even more so, depending on what this test told them. He couldn't wish her a nice life and go back to his own.

Damn it, why were there so many brands? He scanned the array of boxes, brain nearly exploding at the advertising flashing that promised "results in one minute" and "estimated weeks." He grabbed the two priciest ones and half expected her to be gone when he returned.

She had changed into plaid pajama pants and a T-shirt, washed off her makeup, removed her earrings, and gathered her hair into a low ponytail. She was as fresh-faced as when he'd met her that morning in Milan, except far more somber.

The soup had arrived. It sat untouched and covered on the tray on the small table.

She eyed the bag choked by his fist.

"Listen." He was too restless to sit. "Whether it's mine or not—"

"Of course it would be yours," she snapped. "Don't be rude!"

A sharp wave hit him at that declaration, one that winded him so thoroughly, it took him a second to find his voice again. A smart man would be cautious about taking her word for it, but a very primitive part of him was already aligning with this news, accepting it as truth.

He made himself say, "I thought you would have had some sign by now if that was a possibility?"

"I have really low body fat. I never have regular periods," she said stiffly, then pinched the bridge of her nose. "I've been feeling run-down, though. I threw up a few times. I thought it was a bug from travel. I've been exhausted for weeks, but I've been working nonstop. I thought it was burnout."

"I see." That sounded plausible. "Well, I'm here. No matter what." He spoke before he'd fully contemplated all that might entail, but he couldn't turn his back on her, not if he was responsible for what she was going through.

He held out the bag.

"I don't have to go yet," she said sullenly and looked out the window.

"Oh." He set the bag on the bed. "Should we watch TV while we eat?"

"Do whatever you want."

He lifted the cover off the soup, hoping the aroma of leeks and potatoes and fresh rolls would tempt her, but she didn't even look at him.

He replaced the cover. "Do you want an apology?"

"For what? Producing, single-handedly, the absolute most stressful hours of my life? For completely overturning everything I thought I knew about myself while potentially wreaking havoc on my future?"

Vijay had had a few weeks to digest the news of her parentage and it was purely incidental to his own life, not rooted in his foundation. He was reeling under the idea that he might become a father, but he wouldn't let that sink in until he knew for sure she was pregnant and intended to keep it. For her, this meant her *body* would be taken over. He couldn't make assumptions about how she would proceed.

What remained constant through all of this, however, was his fascination with this woman. He was trying to keep his head and think about facts and next steps, but learning about her birth family had only meant something to him because it was about *her*. He was angry with himself that he hadn't handled this better.

"You have every right to be angry. And scared."

The corners of her mouth went down. "I have to go *so bad*." She looked to the bathroom. "But I'm afraid of what I'll find out. Then it will be real."

He couldn't stand it. He closed in on her, moving slowly so she had plenty of time to rebuff him, but he didn't know how else to express the conflicting emotions gripping him, the remorse and concern.

When he gathered her in, she shuddered and slid her arms around his waist, tucking her nose into the nook of his neck.

It was surprisingly powerful to hold her again, to feel this sense of interlocking his life with hers. Her scent filled his head and her breasts pressed his chest and her hair tickled his chin. He wanted to press his lips to her skin, but made himself speak against her hair.

"What *we* find out," he managed to say. He was taking her word for it that he was the only possible father, but he wanted to believe it, which was its own sort of terrifying. It wasn't just a latent desire to be a father, either. He wanted to be the father of *her* child.

And no matter what was going on in his head, it must be a thousand times worse for her. He knew that because she was trembling.

"You're not alone." He rubbed her back reassuringly. "I'm here."

She nodded and withdrew, biting her lip as she picked up the bag and moved to the bathroom.

Her silver gown was hanging on the door. She unhooked the hanger from the edge and threw the whole thing toward the bed, where it slithered to the floor. She didn't seem to care and closed the door behind her.

Vijay hung the gown on the curtain rod, then took her place staring at all those mindless people going on with their mindless lives around the pool. Didn't they know that life-altering discoveries were being made right now?

He reminded himself to breathe.

This was too much.

Oriel shakily did her thing, then set the test on the

empty box on the back of the toilet without looking at the result. She stared into her ghoulish reflection as she washed her hands, fighting back a hysterical cackle. Her birth mother was a Bollywood icon? Her one-night lover was an undercover DNA thief? Her career was about to be derailed by an unplanned pregnancy?

*Non.* She might have been able to handle one or two of those things, but not all of them. Not all at once. It was too much. Way too much. Her vision was fading at the edges, she was working so hard to keep from breaking down.

Especially because, deep inside herself, she knew what she wanted that test to say, and it went against everything she had ever told herself. She had long ago decided that when she was ready for children, she would adopt. She understood how important it was to offer a good home to a child who needed one, and she had a lot of love to give as well as many advantages.

A man had not been a necessary part of that picture, deliberately. Of course, she had always hoped to find someone who would make a life and family with her, but her mother was an icon who had molded the life she wanted rather than waiting around hoping for it to manifest on its own. Seeing how Estelle had managed to have it all—career, marriage, family—had made Oriel open to the idea of having children on her own timeline, by herself, without waiting for a committed relationship if that was what felt right when the time came.

Pinning her future on a man was very last century, yet here she was, secretly hoping that test would tie her to Vijay forever. He didn't even want her! Not the way she longed to be wanted and loved. He might be nice enough to give her a hug when she was falling apart, but he'd also gone behind her back and *he hadn't called.*

As she turned off the taps, she heard a knock at the door. "Can I come in?"

"I haven't looked at it," she said flatly.

He came in uninvited.

She really should learn to lock him out of rooms she was in.

She ought to bash him in the chest and make him leave her alone, but that was the problem. She was feeling very, very alone right now. Who could she explain this to? Her agent? Her parents? She had cousins and friends, but they were scattered all over, and no one had any shared perspective. They would say the wrong things. You found your birth mother? Wonderful! But it wasn't. Her birth mother was already gone. You're pregnant? Exciting! But no. It meant the career that was finally taking off would fizzle.

You were treated badly by a man? Tell him to go to hell.

She couldn't. Because rather than lean around her to see the result, rather than take her by the shoulders and babble some unhelpful platitude, Vijay stood before her, quiet and calm, as though whatever happened next couldn't shake him. He was solid and demanded nothing. He was here for her, and that meant the world.

"Why didn't you want Jalil to date your sister?" she asked.

His brows went up at what must have sounded like a random question, but she'd been wondering ever since he'd mentioned it in Milan. Plus, she was putting off facing whatever that test was going to tell her.

What if she *wasn't* pregnant? Would she announce she hated him and send him on his way? She doubted she could do that, and that was the most disturbing discovery of all.

"Jalil is much older than Kiran. I thought he must be showing interest in her because of her youth or the money we stood to make in the acquisition."

"A nurse or a purse," Oriel murmured. "That's what one of my mother's friends says older men are looking for when they date younger women. I kept thinking of that when I was with Duke. That I was resuscitating his career for him. Administering oxygen so I could gain something for myself. I felt like a fame whore."

"Oof. Is this where the self-bashers meet? Because I feel like an ass for not believing my sister possesses sound judgment and knows her own heart. I interfered in her life and have overturned yours, all out of an arrogant belief that I know best."

She gave him a chiding look, but appreciated his acknowledging how much he had tripped her up. She appreciated his humor, too. She had liked that about him from the first.

"I can't tell Jalil anything about my birth mother," she pointed out. "The information I had was wrong."

"I think he just wants to know that a part of his sister lives on. I wouldn't want to be in his shoes, but if I was, I can imagine how much it would comfort me to discover Kiran had a child."

Oriel felt her mouth twisting at his sharing such a personal detail. She looked at her reflection—that remnant of a woman who was gone.

She noted the anxiety around her eyes, the lack of color in her lips. She had always known she was the result of an unplanned pregnancy, but she suddenly felt deep affinity for that mysterious person who had given birth to her. This was how Lakshmi must have felt. Overwhelmed. Frightened. Head pounding with the question, *What do I do*?

She couldn't imagine how much more difficult this would be if Vijay or someone else were pushing her around, telling her what to do. The way it was sounding, Lakshmi might have had to fight just to give birth to her.

A ferocity rose in her, an instinctual, angry determination that arrived in her like a gleaming light of truth.

"If I'm pregnant, I'm keeping the baby." Her eyes grew damp. It felt good to acknowledge that, even though it turned her crystal-clear future into a blurred vision through a fogged glass.

She looked straight at Vijay, letting him see that she would never be swayed on this.

He nodded thoughtfully, while his eyes narrowed with intensity.

"And if you're pregnant…it's definitely mine."

The way he said it made her heart lurch unsteadily in her chest. She wanted to set her chin with indignation, but it didn't sound as though he was questioning her. At the same time, she realized this was her chance to firmly eject him from her life if she wanted to.

She couldn't.

She swallowed the hot constriction in her throat. "Today I learned that everything I thought I knew about my birth parents was a lie. I wouldn't do that to my own child. You are definitely the father."

"Then, if you're pregnant—" he spoke with steady resolve "—I'll propose."

The impact of that was so monumental, her ears rang. Her chest felt as though it was pierced by a stinging arrow.

"You don't owe me anything." *Us*.

"I owe any child I make everything I am capable of providing."

Not about her, then. She realized how intently they'd been staring into each other's eyes when she dropped her gaze. A giant brick seemed to settle between her lungs.

"I'll refuse," she warned through her tight throat. "I'm still angry with you. I don't trust you."

"Trust is difficult for me, too." His mouth twisted. "But this isn't about us, is it?"

"I don't know," she said, voice nearly nonexistent. "Maybe we're arguing over nothing." They weren't. Her intuition told her exactly what that test would say.

"Shall we see?"

Biting her lip, she nodded jerkily.

When she didn't turn to retrieve it, he crowded close. One of his arms went around her waist to steady her as he leaned past her.

She tensed, ears straining. She felt the jolt that went through him. He sucked in a breath and his chest expanded.

A shower of sparkling lights filled her vision. She closed her fists into his shirt, afraid she was going to faint.

He made a small space between them and showed her the stick. She had to blink and blink to see its bright blue, unmistakable cross that indicated a positive. In a voice husked with reverence, Vijay said, "We're having a baby."

# CHAPTER SIX

ORIEL'S PHONE BEGAN emanating soft harp strings that gradually increased in volume.

As Vijay reached across her to turn it off, she reached for it herself.

She must have still been mostly asleep, because as their hands bumped and their bodies shifted against one another's, a startled gasp tore out of her throat. She sat up in a tangle of blankets, hair spilling across her face. She impatiently shoved it out of her eyes.

As she stared at him, recognition arrived with comprehension and memory. She sagged and pulled her knees up to hug them, giving a little choke of helplessness.

The angels in her phone grew more insistent. She grabbed it and stabbed to silence it.

"What's the alarm for?" His voice sounded like a garbage disposal. He cleared his throat.

"I'm flying home to spend the rest of the week with my parents. I told you that."

"That's your vacation? Do you have a flight booked?" He rolled toward the nightstand on his side, picking up his own phone, but ignored the notifications.

"Yes." She fell back onto her pillow and flicked through her messages.

His eyes were so gritty with lack of sleep, he could barely see his screen.

Last night, they'd eaten and she'd gone to bed while he had stood at the window, trying to assimilate the fact he was becoming a father. He might not trust easily, but after her indignant declaration about learning her birth history was a lie, he believed her about that much.

Family was an extremely complex knot of emotions for him. He had grieved the loss of his parents and grandmother with the support of his extended family. Then he lost his parents again when he realized what they'd been covering up. The people he had thought he knew had never existed. When he exposed that, he was called an ungrateful traitor and worse. The loving safety net he'd believed would always be there for him had been yanked like a rug. None of those relations would take his calls, and he was still angry and hurt enough that he wouldn't pick up the phone, either.

Only Kiran had stood by him, and he would give his life to protect her. He'd gotten used to thinking she was all he would ever have.

Now he had this nascent, fragile idea of a person beginning to take up space in his heart. There was no question in him that he would claim his child with every part of himself and ensure his child's life was intrinsically interwoven with his own.

So that meant doing the same with Oriel.

She was a far more complicated person to weave into his life. He still wanted her physically. Desire for her was simmering beneath all his best efforts to ignore it. He recalled her as an amusing, interesting companion over dinner, but real life was not a few hours of casual conversation. Real life was *real*. He knew very little about the real Oriel Cuvier.

He had thought he did. When she hadn't called, he had convinced himself she was too stuck-up to reach out to a blue-collar boy toy.

Beneath her animosity and shock about her birth parents and the baby news, she was angry with him, though. Hurt. Because she thought he'd deliberately given her the wrong number. Because she thought he had only come to her room for a toothbrush, not *her*.

As he'd stood at the window wondering if it was time for him to quit being so damned suspicious of everyone around him, he'd heard her sniffle and realized she was giving in to the volume of emotions drowning her. He had crawled into bed fully dressed and curled himself around her.

She'd cried herself to sleep, and maybe he had dozed. Mostly he'd stared into the darkness, working through the thousand paths forward, trying to find the best one. His entire life needed to be reshaped around her and their child. They had a lot of decisions to make.

"Are you flying into Tours?" he asked her, recalling where her parents' home was located. "What time does your flight leave?"

"Nine thirty."

"Nine thirty-eight?" It was the only one aside from another in the late afternoon. "It's not giving me a seat selection. I don't think we'll be able to sit together." He booked it anyway.

"I can't take you home with me." She sat up. "What do expect? That you'll just sleep with me in my old bedroom?" She gave their shared blankets a disdainful look.

"If there's no room in your parents' *chateau*..." He wondered how she would react when he told her where *he* came from. "Then I'm sure I'll be able to find something online."

"I'm not being a snob," she said impatiently. "I'm saying I don't know what to tell them. Who am I supposed to say you are?"

"Your fiancé?" he suggested pleasantly.

"Oh, was I asleep when you proposed? I didn't hear it."

"Because you told me you would refuse." He sat up and swung his legs off his side of the bed, not wanting her to see that her rebuff had landed and left a bruise. "I'm saving my breath until I've answered a few questions for myself."

"Such as?" She dropped her feet off her side of the mattress, but twisted to look at him.

He looked over his shoulder at her. "You travel for work and I'm president of the Asia division. How will we address that? Where would we call home?"

She held his gaze. Swallowed. Then she gave him her back again. "You're right. I don't want to talk about it. I'm planning to tell my parents about…" Her voice grew muffled as she looked down and spoke to her lap. "About my birth mother. But that's all. For now."

Did it sting that she didn't want to tell her parents she was pregnant with his baby? Yes, but he accepted that the news about her birth family was delicate enough.

"I haven't told Jalil that I've spoken to you." They were still sitting back to back with the width of the mattress between them. "If you're not ready to speak to him, I'll tell him you need time to break it to your parents. He'll understand. I can say your work schedule is very demanding, and you'll be in touch when you have a break."

She gave a humorless choke of laughter. "I'll have

to tell my agent that I'm pregnant. Once I do that, I anticipate my work schedule will become much less demanding *very* quickly."

"Oriel." He twisted to set his hand in the middle of the mattress. "I—"

"Don't say you're sorry." She rose abruptly. "I know I'm sounding bitchy. I'm not blaming you. The timing could definitely be better, but I'm not sorry I'm pregnant."

Nor was he, which was a very strange realization to absorb.

He rose and opened the curtains, letting in a blast of morning sunlight that made him wince.

When he turned to look at her, she was staring at him. She stood in bare feet and rumpled pajamas with unbrushed hair. Her face was naked, her brow crinkled.

He decided this was how he liked her best, even though she was so lacking in defenses, it made his chest tighten.

"Were you planning to have kids at some point?"

She gave a confused shrug. "My career hasn't left a lot of room for thinking about starting a family. When I did, I didn't worry too much about whether my fertile years were passing me by. I've always assumed I would adopt because I was adopted."

She chewed her lip, and her brow wrinkled even harder as she continued. "I've always felt loved by all my family, but there's no ignoring the fact that everyone looks and sounds like at least one other person. They have odd quirks that mark them as related. I tried not to let it bother me that I didn't have that because it couldn't be changed, but I've always had this sense of…missing out. Or…missing someone?" Her mouth trembled, and she firmed her lips.

The sun caught on the dampness in her lashes, making his lungs burn.

"I'm so sorry I'll never meet Lakshmi. That's what I was crying about last night. I do want to meet Jalil, sooner than later. And I want to meet this baby." She set her hand on her belly. "I'm really excited to see..." Her smile wavered with emotion. "A little bit of myself?"

His heart caved in. He moved around the bed, reaching for her.

She threw her hand up to hold him off. "I'm still angry with you."

"Fair." He caught her hand and used it to reel her closer. "But know that I feel the same. That baby is a part of me, and I can't imagine not being in our child's life every day."

Her gaze searched his, and the question was on his lips. *Will you marry me?* Even the bright sunshine and dancing dust motes became too much to have between them. He drew her closer, softly crashing her curves into his hardening body.

He wanted to kiss her. Hell, he wanted to take her to bed and reestablish the connection they had shared in Milan. Her lashes fluttered, and her mouth trembled. Her grip tightened on his fingers where their hands were clasped.

He had been waiting for this, the warmth of her, the scent in her hair, the feel of her as he drew her closer. He tipped his head and started to lower his mouth across her parted lips—

"I don't think that's a good idea." She jerked back and pulled herself free of him.

The chill of her absence was an abrupt bucket of ice water splashing over him. He pushed his hands into his pockets, hoping to disguise that he was aroused.

"I did try to text." She was hugging herself again. "But you didn't. You've only ever sought me out for... investigative purposes."

"That's not true." If she only knew how obsessed he'd been all these weeks. "I had dinner with you because I wanted to. I shouldn't have come to your room without telling you everything, but I couldn't stay away. That's the truth, Oriel." He ran his hand through his hair, agitated at being forced to reveal himself this way. "When you didn't get in touch after, I accepted that you didn't want to pursue anything beyond what we'd agreed to. But once Jalil's theory panned out, I had to see you again. I wanted to see if we still react to each other like this. And we do."

Lust was a churning furnace within him, waiting to explode at the first breath of oxygen she blew across it.

She hugged herself and eyed him warily.

"Wanting to kiss you and make love to you isn't an *idea*," he said. "It's attraction. I wanted to see you again. Jalil's news gave me the excuse. Now we've learned we're having a baby, and our lives are going to be linked forever. I can understand if you're worried sex will cloud things or you simply don't feel up to it, but seducing you isn't some master plan on my part. I'm reacting to being near you, same as you are to me."

"That's exactly what I'm doing—reacting! I can't keep a lucid thought in my head or figure out what comes next. My hormones are saying, 'Have sex. Then you don't have to think at all.' That's not going to solve anything."

"I don't know," he drawled. "My hormones would love a sidebar with yours. Maybe we should give it to them, see what they accomplish."

"Pfft." She dissolved into the prettiest laughter he'd ever heard. "Nice try."

He shrugged. "Worth a shot."

The air crackled with awareness and possibility and the panting breath of a wolf circling his mate. Her eyes widened, and she licked her lips. He started to close in on her, but her phone released a more aggressive sound of church bells.

"I always set two, in case I sleep through one," she said, moving to silence it. "And I can't miss this flight. My parents are expecting me." She glanced warily at him.

"I'm coming with you," he reminded her. "We have a lot to talk about."

She started to say something, but her gaze focused with annoyance over his shoulder, and she tsked. "I forgot the garment bag for this on the yacht."

She circled around him to ruffle the gown he'd left hanging from the curtain rod.

Vijay ran his tongue over his teeth.

"I'll call the concierge. I'm sure they can send something up." He moved to pick up the hotel phone, then paused. He had to know. "*Was* it a gift from Duke?"

"Maman." She splayed the skirt to look for flaws. "For their anniversary party. She'll be annoyed that I haven't been caring for it properly. It will have to be cleaned and steamed. Repaired." She touched a loose thread at the hem. "You can have my bed at the chateau, because I'll be in the doghouse."

He snorted, but her smile faded. She seemed to remember that a less than perfect gown was the least of the things that could potentially upset her mother.

He wanted to tell her it would be okay, but he didn't

know that. All he knew was that she'd just conceded to his going to Tours with her. That was enough for now.

He called down for a garment bag and ordered breakfast at the same time.

Oriel didn't protest Vijay coming home with her. He was the father of her unborn baby. Whether she married him or not, he ought to meet her parents.

They arrived to chaos. Caterers and decorators and workmen were overrunning the place, erecting marquee tents and unloading tables, chairs, linens and dishes.

Her mother would be in her element. It was the sort of orchestration she loved best. She was not only the center of attention—her rightful place—but she was director, producer, and critic, providing a swift review if a flower head sagged or a bulb on a string failed to light.

"When you said the gown was for your parents' anniversary party..." Vijay said as they climbed from the car at the bottom of the steps.

"Um, yes. It's tonight." She grimaced as she realized she hadn't exactly prepared him. "It's just an intimate affair with three hundred of Maman's closest friends and colleagues. I did mention that she is beloved? The spare room in my suite please, Tauseef," Oriel directed as her mother's chauffeur retrieved their luggage.

Vijay lifted a brow at her. She lifted a shoulder at him. She was angry and wary of trusting him again, but she kept thinking about him saying, *I shouldn't have come to your room without telling you everything, but I couldn't stay away.*

She was equally compelled to keep him near. The way he'd held her last night had been deeply comforting. He was right that they had a lot to talk about, and she couldn't help wondering if they might have something beyond what looked on the surface to be a complete disaster.

Maybe she was kidding herself, but there was only one way to find out.

She led him into the house, where it was easy enough to locate her mother. She was nearly always in the music salon even when she wasn't singing.

They went through the oval-shaped foyer with its curved staircase and domed ceiling, then passed the large sitting room with its grand fireplace and row of arched windows that looked onto the grounds. Abundant furniture was arranged in pockets for her parents' frequent houseguests and evening soirees. On their other side, they passed the formal dining room with its long table and westward-facing windows that caught the sunset on the pond, and finally arrived at the octagonal-shaped room where her mother spent most of her time.

The music salon was no less exquisitely built than the rest of the modern chateau, but it was kept free of carpets and pollen and other dust-producers so as to preserve Madame's voice. Like her bedroom, the windows were triple-paned and the humidity carefully monitored and controlled. The grand piano was played every day while she exercised her vocal cords.

Today Estelle was surrounded by her entourage of assistants, agents, and designers along with some of Oriel's favorite aunties and cousins.

"Chou. At last." Estelle came forward to embrace Oriel, kissing each of her cheeks.

Madame Estelle was only five and a half feet tall, but she was such an imposing presence she seemed to be at least six and a half. Her hair was wrapped in a silk turban unless she was performing or making an appearance. Today, she wore one of her colorful caftans in bright yellow and magenta. It made her dark brown skin glow. She had been born with an assertive personality and tremendous operatic talent. As her voice had developed and her status rose, she had become a powerhouse in the entertainment business and a diva everywhere else.

Introductions were made, and Oriel gave and accepted all the kisses. Her mother eyed Vijay with curiosity. "A fellow model?"

"No," he dismissed with a self-conscious twitch of his mouth. "It's flattering you think I could be, but I'm in security technology."

"Vijay is the President of TecSec's Asia division," Oriel provided.

"Oh? We use them ourselves. I imagine you have many secrets about your private clients that you will refuse to let me worm out of you, but I shall enjoy the challenge of trying. I'm so glad you brought someone interesting." Estelle tapped Oriel's arm. "I feared you would bring that tired actor. I didn't know much about him, but what I did know made me certain I didn't need to know more."

Madame Estelle could get away with speaking her mind like that. Oriel would have chuckled along with everyone else, but she was too anxious over what she had to reveal.

"Where is Papa?" she asked.

"In his citadel, taking refuge from the chaos. Go along and say hello. Come down to visit after you've settled in."

"Will you come with me, please? There's something I need to discuss with you both."

"Cherie, I have so much to do, and our darling family

is here." She waved at all the faces that had grown avid with curiosity. "You'll be here all week. Can it wait?"

"It can't." Oriel smiled an apology, but let her mother see her firmness.

Estelle gave Vijay another sidelong look. "Are you here in a professional capacity, Monsieur Sahir?"

"I'll let Oriel explain," he said with equanimity as he fell into step alongside her down the hall.

Moments later, they entered the library where Oriel's father, Arnaud, wrote his papers and studied his historical research.

Arnaud was the perfect foil for Estelle. He was a quiet, patient man who could sit for hours in dressing rooms and concert halls or amid the babble of creative people who were his wife's constant companions. If he wasn't actively reading, he held a book with his finger notched between the pages. He had absolutely no desire for a spotlight, but was sincere and effusive in his praise of his wife for earning her place in hers.

Oriel had always felt completely loved and supported by him, but also as though she was a creature he didn't quite understand. Today, her sense of being an alien was stronger than ever. She worried they would both feel slighted by what she was about to tell them.

Her hands were so clammy, her father frowned with concern when he took them. He kissed both her cheeks, then shook Vijay's hand, studying him enquiringly as Oriel nervously closed the doors.

"Are we to have an engagement announcement at our anniversary?" Estelle asked with obvious delight as she perched herself on the arm of her husband's chair. "There would be some lovely symmetry to that."

"No, Maman." Oriel glanced at Vijay, silently begging him to say nothing about the baby.

He lowered himself to sit beside her on the sofa, and she took strength from his unflinching gaze and supportive silence.

"Vijay is an envoy from my birth family."

Estelle was rarely taken aback. Her breath went in as though she was doing her most aggressive breathing exercises. She rose with quiet grace and moved to her husband's sideboard, where she poured brandy with heavy liquid gurgles.

Oriel waited until her mother had handed out all the glasses and had perched on the chair again, taking Arnaud's hand in her own.

Oriel set her own drink aside and kept to the facts, skipping over absconded toothbrushes and a dinner-turned-dalliance. She simply relayed what Vijay had told her about Lakshmi, and that Jalil wished to meet her.

"I don't understand," Estelle said. "The clinic told us Oriel's birth parents were from Romania."

"I can only presume that was a red herring meant to protect Lakshmi's identity," Vijay said. "We've been trying to learn more about the clinic itself, but it closed two decades ago."

"Are you concerned there was impropriety? They came highly recommended. The lawyer who handled our side of the paperwork will be here tonight. He's above reproach," her mother insisted. "We had our name registered with several organizations at the time. This clinic was the first to contact us. They said the young woman liked our profile. We weren't attempting anything shady."

"I'm not suggesting you were. We may never know the complete truth about how Lakshmi came to give Oriel up. The important thing is that nothing we do learn could change the fact that you and Oriel are a family." Vijay looked at Oriel as he spoke, reinforcing that he wasn't here to take anything away from anyone. "Jalil has concerns the manager may have behaved unethically, though. If he did, he would like to see justice served."

"Of course." Estelle touched her throat. "Oriel isn't in any danger, is she?"

"Not to my knowledge, but if and when this news becomes public, you should expect a great deal of attention." Vijay sent Oriel a grimace of apology. "There is one other detail I haven't made clear to you. Jalil regards Lakshmi's estate as rightfully belonging to her child. In euros, it's worth over a hundred million."

"What? Non!" Oriel would have leaped to her feet, but her bones dissolved. "Please stop giving me these shocks. I'll need defibrillator paddles!"

He chuckled and reached across to squeeze her hand. "Whether you accept it or not is between you and Jalil. I'm telling you so you can plan security. You'll need it." He glanced at her parents. "I suggest you keep this news to yourselves until you have a full contingent of bodyguards in place, especially for the initial excitement. If you don't mind, I'll introduce myself to your security team while I'm here, purely as a courtesy."

"Of course." Arnaud nodded.

*"Très bien."* Estelle rose from the arm of the chair in her take-charge way. "We will discuss details tomorrow, but tonight the show goes on." Her glance bounced off where Vijay still had his hand over Oriel's. "We don't want you to *look* like a bodyguard, Monsieur Sahir. Did you bring a tuxedo? Our party is white tie. Oriel, Max is in the pool house if you need assistance." She clapped her hands. "Four hours to curtain, my dears."

\*\*\*

"Max" was Madame Estelle's personal designer. He tailored the entire family and had a full team offering an array of spa services from the cabanas around the pool.

Vijay was led there by the head of security after he and Oriel had made their rounds together.

Oriel had retired to her room by then, and Vijay hoped she was resting. He had thought her parents had taken the news as well as possible, but she'd seemed very withdrawn after.

He was concerned about her, but after walking the estate and getting a true sense of her family's net worth, he was concerned about *them*.

Back when he'd proposed to Wisa, he'd thought they were on the same level of wealth and privilege. As it turned out, his family's wealth had been ill-gotten. The fallout of discovering that had contributed to their extremely ugly breakup.

Vijay had had to start over. He was extremely comfortable now, but even though he was evolved enough not to feel threatened by the idea of a woman making more money than he did, he couldn't help being aware he would never catch up to Oriel if she stood to inherit all of this *and* all of Lakshmi's wealth. It shouldn't matter in a relationship, but it would always have the potential to.

Despite that, he kept coming around to their marriage being inevitable. He wasn't so rich in family that he could afford to let his own child be raised away from him. Oriel seemed equally devoted to being a full-time parent. That meant at least living together.

He wanted marriage, though, and not for entirely logical reasons. Wisa had proved to him that a ring didn't ensure fidelity, but the vows and formality of marriage were something *he* would take seriously. He wanted that stability for their child, but he wanted it for himself, too. And he couldn't help thinking that making those promises to each other would go a lot further in earning each other's trust than keeping their options open.

Could they make a marriage work, though? The differences in their backgrounds became even more obvious as Max asked him to remove the tuxedo he'd just tried on so it could be altered on the spot.

While he waited, Vijay's beard was sculpted and his hair trimmed. He was given a manicure for the first time in his life, even though he was also given gloves to wear. His shirt required cuff links, and gold ones appeared. The points of his white vest were a precise quarter-inch beneath the edge of his split-tailed jacket. The jacket's lapels matched the satin stripe down his trouser seams. New shoes in his size fit perfectly over his fresh silk socks. His bow tie was snow white.

Vijay might have felt overdressed and pretentious, maybe even resentful of being forced to fit in, if he hadn't looked so damned good.

He was directed to join the flock of penguins in the drawing room, where he noted that not all of the tuxedo-wearers were men. Vijay wasn't sure what they were waiting for, but they were all offered a signature cocktail with cognac lemon from sugar-rimmed glasses. Arnaud introduced Vijay to everyone and explained how each person was related to Oriel.

Vijay wasn't intimidated by titles or political power, but this level of society underscored even more how different he and Oriel were. They could negotiate how and where they would live, but at some point he would have to tell her about his father. How would she react to that?

"Monsieur," the butler said to Arnaud. "If you would

like to assemble your guests in the front hall, the rest of the family will descend."

Vijay moved with the group into the entranceway.

Madame Estelle certainly enjoyed her pageantry. A trio of strings began to play as a name was announced. A woman floated down in an evening gown of peacock blue. She was met at the bottom by a man who brought her to a spot near the door, where they would form the head of the procession out to the marquee.

Cars were bumper to bumper on the drive. Guests had been queuing up on the red carpet for nearly an hour.

Vijay politely added his glove-muted applause for each person who came down in their glamorous and sophisticated evening wear, enjoying the drama of it.

"Mademoiselle Oriel Cuvier," the butler called.

His heart unexpectedly rose into his throat as he waited for her to appear.

He'd already seen her in the gown. The sight of her shouldn't have affected him, but she was entirely too beautiful for him not to feel his breath punched right out of him as she moved into the light at the top of the stairs.

Her hair was up again, but she wore a tiara that cast sparks of light between her piles of curls. Her earrings were matched by a stunning necklace that dripped ice down her cleavage. Her elbow-length gloves were silver to match her gown, and she wore a cuff of diamonds over her left wrist.

He had not appreciated her ability to command attention purely by the way she moved, but the gown and jewels all became secondary to the enigmatic mystique she projected as she descended, seemingly oblivious to everyone watching her.

Her eyes found him, though. Her gaze beckoned him

to the bottom of the stairs. The smoldering sensuality in her expression stoked a fire in him. When he offered his arm, she bestowed a smile on him that sent a rush of pride through him. Pride that she found him pleasing. Pride that he was the escort for this stunning woman whose touch on his arm became a hot ember in his chest.

They moved into their place in the procession and turned as her mother was announced.

"Thirtieth anniversary is pearl," Oriel whispered.

Madame appeared in a gown covered in luminescent seed pearls. It rustled softly as she came to a halt at the top of the stairs and waited for the clapping to subside.

The music changed, and she began to sing. Her voice climbed and fell with deep emotion, filling the high-ceilinged space with every octave of love imaginable as she slowly made her way down.

Vijay didn't understand a word, but he felt his own heart rising and wrenching. The way Estelle never removed her eyes from her husband told him she meant every syllable. It was magnificent.

After his broken engagement, Vijay had convinced himself love was a sentiment sold by greeting cards and Bollywood musicals, but as he watched Arnaud cross to the bottom of the stairs and hold up his hand for his wife, with his face flushed and his eyes aglow, there was no denying the pair shared something beautiful and precious. It made Vijay feel small to be so cynical when, for some, love was absolutely real.

As the song ended and the final notes faded, Arnaud said, *"Mon coeur."*

The pair kissed, and everyone applauded once more.

Oriel's expression was gleaming with fierce love for them, but Vijay thought he glimpsed envy there, too.

When her naked gaze lifted to his, his heart lurched. He read her question plain as day.

She wanted what her parents had.

He needed to be completely honest with her from here on out. He'd been burned deeply by love, not just by his fiancée's infidelity, but also by his own father's betrayal. He didn't trust lightly anymore and wouldn't give up his heart easily to anyone.

When she looked at him like that, however, he wanted to promise her the world.

# CHAPTER SEVEN

"Would you like to dance?"

Oriel was spellbound by the romance of the evening. The marquee was strung with fairy lights, the air laden with the scent of roses and jasmine. A twenty-piece orchestra played between courses and speeches. Several songs and recitations had been performed by close friends of the celebrating couple. She herself had given a final, heartfelt toast to her parents, and her mother had left everyone in tears with one more song that had earned her a standing ovation.

Now Estelle and Arnaud, had started the dancing and Vijay was standing over her, offering his gloved hand.

She was losing her mind over how sexy he was, and it had nothing to do with the tuxedo. It was all him. His sensual mouth and half-lidded eyes were pure seduction, his air of alert watchfulness and quiet command delicious.

She almost wished things had gone worse with her parents. Then she could hate him and use her resentment to hold him off. As it was, she was falling under his spell as easily as she had that night in Milan. Had she learned nothing? He was a destroyer of worlds.

"You waltz?" Her heart tripped as she placed her hand in his and he helped her rise.

Of course he waltzed. He was a man of infinite capabilities, hidden depths and fascinating angles.

"I know the basics. Don't expect…that," he said with a wry look at her cousin, who had married her fellow champion and partner from the professional ballroom circuit. They were swirling around the floor with airy grace.

"We're a family of overachievers." Oriel swooned as he took her in steady arms and confidently led her into the steps. "That's why it was so hard to find my niche and why I still feel only moderately successful." She was babbling out of nerves and felt like she had said too much when he frowned with perplexity.

"You seem pretty successful to me."

"Well, yes. I am. I mean, most women would kill for the opportunities I enjoy, but my work is based on genetic luck and tricks like attending high-profile premieres with attention-starved actors. It's not the same as rising through practice and mastering of craft."

"Your work is still a performance. You have to distill a mood down to a single snapshot. I saw you do it tonight when you came down the stairs. I was captivated."

"You don't have to build me up," she said with discomfort. "Maman and I made our peace with our differences a long time ago. I'm just saying…this is a lot to live up to," she ended on a mumble.

"I was being sincere, but okay. How are things between you and your mother now? Is she upset by the news?"

"Unsettled. She came to my room earlier. We had a heart-to-heart." And enough tears they had had to use cool compresses after or risk looking like puffy-eyed newts at the ball. "She said she always knew this could happen, and she only wants whatever I want. She asked about you. She wanted to know if you were more than my sort of bodyguard."

"And you said?"

She didn't know! She had first been drawn to him because he had sparked a more intense attraction within her than she'd ever experienced before. Since then, he'd made her feel *all* the emotions in the most intense ways. She couldn't help but be wary of what more could come.

"I told her I'm trying to keep my distance since I have enough to worry about."

*"Trying,"* he mused, mouth curving. "That sounds like you're having to work at it."

*My hormones would love a sidebar with yours.*

If her presence here for her parents' celebration hadn't been so important to her, she might have allowed them to fall into bed at the hotel. Vijay was an incredibly compelling man, confident and handsome and still capable of waking her senses with a glance. The fact he knew what she was going through and was actually facing her unplanned pregnancy *with* her made her gravitate to him even more.

She'd been starkly honest when she'd told him she was tempted to lose herself in the same wild excitement they'd shared in Milan so she didn't have to think about the more mundane and difficult details of how they would proceed. Maybe there was something very basic to her desire, too. Her body recognized he was the father of her child and yearned to pair-bond with him as a way of reinforcing their connection, ensuring he would look after both of them.

No matter what it was, she was breathless and dizzy as he steered her from the cloying scent of cigar smoke and gave her a small twirl as the song ended.

He caught her close. "How are you feeling? It's been a long day."

"I had a nap before I dressed." She was giddy from being in his arms, smiling even after he eased his hold and started to lead her off the floor. "I'm glad for the distraction of this party. Thank you for being my date. I know this is a lot."

"What I find most fascinating is that I have the feeling this sort of evening is not unusual for you." He nodded at the mime performing for a table.

"Not at all. Maman adores setting a stage and creating an experience. She began planning this two years ago, after Papa's sixtieth birthday."

"When I tell Kiran that tumblers served dessert *while it was on fire*, she will die."

Oriel laughed. "I can't wait to meet her. Will she be on the call with Jalil tomorrow?" They had agreed they would call in the morning for a brief introduction.

Vijay's expression froze.

Her heart stopped. "No? You don't want me to meet her?"

"No, of course. I hadn't considered how much I have to tell her. I won't say anything about—" He dropped his gaze to her middle. "Not yet. But…"

"I know. It keeps hitting me at odd times, too." Aside from avoiding more than a sip of champagne when she toasted her parents, Oriel hadn't been letting herself think too much about the fact she was carrying his baby.

His hand came to her upper arm in a small caress. "Tell me if you need anything."

She nodded. He stood close enough that she could feel the warmth of his body. Her shoulder was still tingling from his touch, and his mouth was right there.

*Seducing you isn't some master plan on my part.*
Wasn't it, though?

His gaze touched her mouth, and his lips twitched. "Bodyguard, you said?"

"*You* said it. We all went along with it even though you were holding my hand."

"I was, wasn't I? I'm thinking about doing it again."

"Holding my hand?" She tried to suppress her grin, but her heart was soaring with excitement. Why? It was only hand-holding, for heaven's sake! Even so, she gave him a coquettish bat of her lashes. "Perhaps while I accompany you on a patrol of the grounds?"

"I'm sure I'm overdue for that." As he let his knuckles brush against hers, he dipped his head to speak in her ear. "I know you dislike that awkward moment of wondering whether a man will kiss you, so I'll warn you now. I intend to."

Her skin tightened with anticipation, and she opened her fingers for the weave of his.

It was a chilly night, something she felt as soon as they were away from the marquee. The music faded and the stars opened above them.

They weren't the only ones seeking a moment of privacy. They passed two other couples tucked into shadows before they found a pocket among the hedges where the cool scent of cedar closed around them.

Oriel slid her arms over his hard shoulders and curled her hands behind his head, expecting the crash of his mouth onto hers.

He barely grazed her mouth with his own, running his lips across her jaw and blowing softly against her ear, making shivers rise up her arms and into her nape before he came back to lightly nibble on her bottom lip.

With a frustrated sob, she pressed herself tighter

to him and slanted her mouth with invitation. He reacted by sealing them into the swirling darkness of a deep, passionate kiss, one that made them both groan in gratification.

His hands roamed her back and hips, pulling her tighter into the hardness behind his fly. When his tongue brushed hers, she sucked delicately. His whole body hardened and his fingers dug into her backside, holding her tight as he rocked her against his aroused flesh.

Oh, why be coy? She had known what she wanted in Milan, and she knew it just as clearly tonight. She dragged her head back.

"Let's go inside."

His nostrils flared. "For?"

"You need me to spell it out? I want to continue the affair we started. See where it might have gone."

His gaze was flinty, his caress on her jaw light. "An affair is something you can walk away from. We're beyond that."

She couldn't argue, not with his baby growing inside her, but lust had its talons dug into her. "You don't want to see what our hormones can accomplish?"

He snorted and said in a graveled voice, "I'm quite sure they can level a city." His mouth tightened. "You realize this is all I think about? I don't have much room left in my head for being noble. Be sure, Oriel."

"I am." From a physical standpoint, at least. She led him into a side entrance up to her rooms.

Her suite was a pair of bedrooms off a shared sitting room, all with tall windows overlooking the pond. The curtains were already drawn, the only light a stained-glass lamp casting red and blue streaks across the walls and ceiling.

"Have I told you that you are the most beautiful woman I have ever seen?" He leaned against the door as he locked it.

"Have I told you that you are the sexiest man I have ever seen?" With slow deliberation, she bit one finger of her glove and began to draw it off, making a show if it.

"Is that how we're playing?" He loosened his bow tie and opened one collar button. "Strip tease?"

"It seems a shame to waste the costumes. I was barely going to undress at all." She sent him her most beguiling look and came across to press the hand that was still gloved against his fly.

He looked down at her diamond bracelet, which flashed and sparkled. His breath hissed in, and his whole body went taut.

"I can definitely work with that," he said with a slow, wicked smile.

His gloved hand cupped her neck, and he ran his hot mouth into her throat. His other hand worked a finger beneath the neckline of her gown. The cool silk of his glove scraped erotically across her nipple, making tight golden wires shoot heat into her loins.

She fumbled at his fly and got her gloved hand into his pants. As she caressed and fondled, his teeth took hold of her bottom lip, and they stared into one another's eyes. His pupils were huge and glazed with feral passion right before he slid his arms around her and plundered her mouth with his own.

This was what she had wanted to feel again—*alive*. Connected. She was still angry at his subterfuge, but this incredible desire had pulled her toward him from the first, and it was still here. *He* was. Kissing her as though he would consume her. Wrapping his arms around her as though she was everything he needed in life.

She was so lost to the passion of their kiss, she didn't realize he had backed her to the bed until he tilted her onto it. She gasped and braced her hands on the mattress, but he was already lifting her gown, caressing her legs.

"The number of times I have thought about doing this again…" He went to his knees, and the heat of his mouth scorched the inside of her knee. He took soft, playful bites of her inner thigh, swirling his tongue against her skin until her legs trembled. Then the warmth of his mouth settled against the silk covering her most tender flesh. He began to lick around the edges of lace.

"Vijay," she moaned helplessly and sank onto her back in surrender.

He shifted the silk aside to anoint her until she was molten with need. She dove her fingers into his hair and arched, abandoning herself to the pleasure he bestowed, but he didn't take her over the edge.

When she was sobbing and tense and lifting into his caress, he rose and said, "Do you mind?" as he gently rolled her onto her stomach. "I just want to see how you look with the shoes and this icicle dress up around your waist—"

His voice faded into a guttural curse as she accepted the challenge and owned it. She planted her feet apart and braced her elbows on the bed, then arched her back to lift her bottom. She cast him a provocative look over her shoulder.

Did he think she didn't know how to use her sex appeal to achieve a desired result?

His breath was rattling unevenly as his hands moved over her buttocks and thighs, caressing everywhere but the place she ached most. He told her how sexy she was. How much he wanted her as he slowly, slowly drew her panties down her legs.

When he crouched to draw them free of her ankles, his teeth scraped the tendon at the back of her thigh where her leg met her cheek.

She shook in reaction, hands fisting in the blankets as she waited in agony while he caressed her calves and kissed the back of one knee, then stood. She heard the rustle of his pants as he freed himself.

"Do you want to roll over?" His voice was deep and far away, buried in layers of carnal hunger.

"No. Like this…"

"Naked?"

"Yes." She could hardly speak as his hot tip began to trace and slide, seeking, then pressing for entrance.

She was so wet and aroused, he entered her in one smooth, steady thrust that made them both groan with abandon. His hands splayed to brace her hips before he slid his palms up to her waist, exposing more of her.

"You're exquisite." His powerful thighs shifted hers apart a little more, feet planting firmly between hers. He took hold of her hip and shoulder and began to thrust with lazy power.

She pressed her face into the mattress, moaning unreservedly. It was base and hot and no one else had ever broken her down this way, pushing her past inhibition into a state of pure animalistic pleasure. No one could hold her on this pinnacle of acute near-climax for what felt like hours, so she was lost to all but the exquisite sensations rolling through her in waves.

Only him. Only him.

Then, just as she thought she would break from the agony of resisting satisfaction, his hand roamed to where they were joined. His long finger caressed across the swollen bud of her clitoris, strumming and sending her shooting past the limits of her control. She exploded, crying out at the sudden power of it.

He gave a final deep thrust and joined her with a ragged shout.

"We may not have thought this through." Vijay could hardly speak, let alone find the strength to shift his weight off her back. He grunted with profound loss as he pulled free of her and collapsed on the bed beside her, legs dangling off the mattress.

It had taken everything in him not to hammer into her the way he'd longed to. Somehow, that controlled, exquisite lovemaking had been even more intense and left him utterly shredded.

"I have nothing left to get undressed." Speaking was an effort.

"Same." She turned her head on the mattress to blink at him. Her eyelids were heavy with gratification, adding a layer of smugness to his satisfaction.

"Was I too rough?" He had managed to hold back until the very end, but he'd lost some control as they'd hit their peak. This woman completely dismantled him every single time. He'd known it in Milan and had known it when they stood outside, necking in the hedges. He'd known coming in here that she would pull him apart in ways that weren't comfortable, but he'd done it anyway.

That bothered him, yet here he was.

"I liked it." Her smile kept the erotic memory glowing between them like a golden light of promise. "But you're right. This won't be my most graceful moment."

She stole his pocket square and asked, "Can you get my zip?"

He did, stealing a caress of her spine before she pushed up from the mattress. As she straightened, she let the gown fall to the floor in what was actually a very supple, unselfconscious display of glorious nudity before she disappeared into the bathroom.

With superhuman strength, he tucked himself back into his fly and rose to pick up her gown. He was still looking for the hanger when she appeared in a pink silk robe.

"That poor gown." She tutted. "*Never* tell my mother what it's been through."

"You think I'm going to tell your mother that I bent you over the bed and made love to you in it?"

She found the hanger and came across with it, offering him a lingering kiss as she took the gown. Her hair was still up, her jewelry on, her makeup smudged in the most libidinous way.

He could get used to this, he decided as he began to undress. The fog of sexual satisfaction was particularly delicious while watching her move around her personal space, seeing her in a way that very few others were allowed to.

She slid a knowing smile at him when she caught him admiring her. A hunger that wasn't purely sexual nestled in the pit of his gut. It was desire for all of her. Her thoughts, her laughter, her moments of doubt. He imagined her belly swelling and being at liberty to press his hand there anytime so he could feel their baby kick.

At some point she would go into labor, and that thought was enough to send a cold rush of protectiveness through him, one that propelled him across to still her hands from fiddling with the gown. He gathered her in and kissed her, holding her close, trying to convey the myriad emotions gripping him.

Her arms came up around his neck, and for long moments they were lost to lazy, sexy kisses. When they broke to catch their breath, her hands slid down to his vest.

"Careful," she said with an unsteady smile. Her gaze skittered from his as though she was as unsettled by the intensity of the moment as he was. "We'll wind up forgetting to get undressed again."

He stole a last fondle of her bottom through the silk of her robe and released her.

"Who do I return this to and how do I pay for borrowing it?" He unbuttoned his vest. "Max wouldn't say."

"Because I bought it for you."

Vijay bristled.

"Oh, don't look at me like that." Oriel began to remove her jewelry and set it in a crystal bowl on the dresser. "You didn't expect or particularly *want* to attend this party."

He'd managed to put aside their different backgrounds and enjoy the evening, but it came around hard enough to slap him now.

"I can afford my own tuxedo, Oriel." Aside from tonight, he had no use for one and had no doubt this one was priced at a premium, given this had been a last-minute alteration, but he wasn't a pauper. He'd recently inked his name onto a deal that gave him a lot more disposable income than he'd had when he had bought her a gourmet dinner in Milan.

"My father can afford his own Maserati and rarely drives," she said, "but my mother still bought him one for his birthday. Don't worry about it."

"They're married," he pointed out. "If you're buying me clothes, does that mean you intend to marry me?"

"You haven't asked, have you?" she shot back. "But consider this before you do." She held up a finger like a scolding schoolteacher. "The reason my parents chose to adopt me was that my mother values her career. She has always had to work very hard to balance her personal aspirations with being a wife and a parent. Papa has a decent income from his books and papers, but Maman is the one who can afford a custom-built house like this. Yet she is constantly judged for not being maternal enough. For emasculating her husband by earning more and holding the spotlight while he takes a supporting role and arranges his life around her touring schedule. If the shoe were on the other foot, no one would bat an eye."

"You're warning me I will have to play second fiddle to you and the riches you stand to inherit? I'm well aware, Oriel." His voice hardened along with every muscle in his body. All his sexual afterglow was gone.

"I'm saying that if you're already threatened by it, you should definitely save your breath on proposing, because I won't marry you if you expect me to apologize for who I am or what I have." She waved at their surroundings. "I'm proud of my mother for all she has accomplished. I won't reject this or her to appease your ego."

Vijay removed his cuff links and dropped them into the dish with her own jewelry. The sound was very loud inside their thick silence.

"Those were a gift, too," she said frostily. "I thought it would be a nice keepsake from a special night. Most people were very honored to be included, but apparently this evening isn't something you consider worth remembering. Good to know. Sleep in the other room." She turned her back and started into her bathroom.

"My father was corrupt," he bit out, loath to talk about it, but it had to be addressed. This fight wasn't about whether their lovemaking was memorable—it was imprinted on his soul never to be forgotten—or whether he would keep a pair of cuff links. He probably should have mentioned this blight in his history before he started talking about marriage. "I was complicit in his crimes."

"What?" Her jaw went slack.

"Unknowingly." He ran his hand into his hair. "But it went on way too long. I'm deeply ashamed, but it's something you should know about me, whether or not we marry, given we share a child."

She moved to lower herself onto a velvet stool and blinked somber eyes at him. "What happened?"

"I told you my parents died when I was in my teens."

"And that you raised Kiran, yes."

He nodded abruptly. "She was in the car when they died. She uses a wheelchair now, which I only tell you to help you understand how I could have been so oblivious to what was going on beneath my nose. After we lost our grandmother, we still had possession of the house we grew up in. Technically our aunt had care of us, but she had a family and a busy medical practice in Delhi. We stayed in our home with some staff. I was Kiran's de facto guardian. She still required surgeries and other therapies. We were grieving and trying to move forward with our lives, going to school and making what felt like a normal life. My father's construction business continued to run under his top managers. I met with them once or twice a year, but I didn't involve myself in it.

I was grateful I didn't have to worry about money on top of everything else."

"You were a child," she said, as if that might excuse his ignorance.

"I was fifteen when I started meeting with them. I was twenty-two before I took a proper interest in how the company turned such a healthy profit." He still hated himself for trusting so blindly. "When I did, I realized our success was built on bribery and backroom deals. Intimidation, in some cases."

"Are you sure those weren't the tactics of the people who were left in charge after your father passed?"

"I'm sure. They were following the playbook he had created when he took over a handful of broken-down machines from his own father. He had been bribing officials to win contracts for roads and bridges from day one. Sometimes he failed to meet the building requirements. At one point, a bridge had collapsed and they'd paid to cover up their deliberate watering down of material. Thankfully, no one was injured or killed, but it was only a matter of time. The level of corruption was astonishing."

"What did you do?" Her eyes were wide with muted horror.

"I took the evidence to the police. Records and assets were seized, arrests made. They were lenient with me because I cooperated, but we lost the house, the business. Everything of value. It was social and financial suicide. All of my friends were connected to the relationships my father had built. To avoid going down with the ship, many turned on us and tried to smear our name. When that happened, even our family turned their backs on us, especially my father's side."

"Because you were trying to make reparations for

a wrong that wasn't even your crime? Since when is integrity worse than living off ill-gotten gains?" Oriel asked crossly.

"Since it affected their own social standing and ability to keep their jobs. But thank you for that." He pushed his hands into his pants pockets. "Kiran was the only one who stood by my decision to come clean. Everyone else said I should have kept my mouth shut and wound it down quietly if I didn't like it. Instead we had death threats. That's why Kiran started our security system, to protect us. Many people tried to undermine our success with it, retaliating by suggesting I employed my father's methods to win the few installations we were hired to make. Our success has been achieved honestly," he stressed. "Killian, the owner of TecSec wouldn't have touched us with a ten-foot pole otherwise. So it's not ego that makes me reluctant to accept your gift, Oriel. It's my conscience. I need to earn what I have."

What a terrible betrayal. She couldn't fathom how hurtful it would have been for him and his sister to lose everything, including their friends and family, after suffering so much loss already.

"I'll have Max invoice you if it's important to you."
"It is."
She nodded, compulsively running the silky tail of her robe's belt between her fingers. "I won't take that money from Jalil. It's not mine—"

"Don't let my feelings color yours." Vijay moved to crouch before her. His big hand stilled her fidgeting fingers. "Whether you accept that fortune or not is between you and him. Just as what you do with this…" he lifted his gaze to the ceiling of the chateau "…and the rest of what you inherit from your parents is completely up to you. I don't expect you to renounce any of it. Just know that if we marry, people are going to suggest I came after you for your money. That will get under my skin sometimes, and now you know why. But I know what I'm worth. And it's not insubstantial."

Nothing about him was insubstantial. He would be a lot more easy to dismiss if he was.

"Okay, but I hope you won't think what you just told me, or the fact I will inherit all of this, has anything to do with my concerns about whether or not we marry. We barely know each other, Vijay. I always imagined that if I married, it would be because…" Why did it make her feel so gauche to admit it? "That I would be in love."

He didn't laugh. He accepted that with a nod of understanding and stood.

"Did you know that something like ninety percent of marriages in India are still arranged?" he asked. "The couples aren't usually strangers anymore, but they don't always know each other well. Even so, our divorce rate is really low. People wind up very content. Why don't we approach it that way? Tell me what you're looking for in marriage beyond love."

What else was there?

"I always thought love was the key," she said. "My parents have very different personalities, but they're in love, and that seems to be what makes their marriage work."

"I'm not going to promise you a life of love, or even that I'm capable of falling in love. But looking at your parents as an outsider, I see a couple who seem to have friendship, respect, affection. Loyalty. We could have those things."

It was a fair offer, but seemed like a pale knockoff version of the connection she really yearned for.

"What do you want?" she asked, playing her fingers into the space between his shirt buttons. "Don't say 'someone who cooks.' I promise you, I will disappoint."

His mouth twitched. "I like that you make me laugh. I want that." He ran his hands over her waist and hips. "Passion is a 'nice to have.'" He nodded at the wrinkled impression they'd left in the blankets on the edge of her bed.

"Not a deal breaker?"

"It's not." He sounded surprised by his own admission. "Don't get me wrong, I definitely want it. My mouth is watering thinking about all the ways I want to make love with you." His mouth twisted with self-deprecation while his hand drifted down to fondle her bottom. "But if that was all we had, if I thought I couldn't trust you, then no. *That* would be the deal-breaker. Trust is hard for me. It's going to take time."

She could understand that, given what he'd just told her, but she drew a slow breath that felt as though it spread powdered glass all through her chest.

"Given the way we started this relationship, I have to question how much I can trust you, too."

He acknowledged that with a stiff nod and moved his hands to her hips.

"Where does that leave us, then? With me sleeping in the other room?"

"No." The word escaped her as a barb of loss caught at her heart. She flashed her thick lashes up at him. "We're not going to learn to trust each other if we put walls between us."

"Or oceans," he said pointedly and started to draw her closer.

"No," she said, pressing away. "We have such different ideas of what a marriage means. I don't want to think about it anymore. I am washing off my makeup before you distract me again."

"Fine. I'll go brush my teeth. But Oriel." He caught her wrist. "If you want to sleep, tell me to stay in the other room."

She gave him her smokiest smile. "We'll sleep. Eventually."

Oriel had a rough start to her morning. They had slept, but not much. They might still be tentative about trusting one another, but between the sheets, she felt completely safe with Vijay. When she was with him like that, she felt, well, *loved*. It was kind of addictive.

When she woke and rose, however, she was tired and a bit achy and had to face the reality that sex hadn't solved anything. She was still pregnant by a man who was a bit of a mystery. Her life had still been cracked wide open by her birth family.

She barely swallowed her breakfast and was worried about it staying down by the time Vijay was placing the call to India.

"Do you want me to put it off?" he asked, frowning with concern.

"I think it's nerves." She had never felt so many caterpillars spinning cocoons in her middle.

His sister Kiran answered with a cheerful hello that immediately put Oriel at ease.

Thankfully, she had the excuse of a late night at her parents' party to explain any colorlessness on her part. It was also such an emotional call for both her and Jalil, bringing sharp tears to her eyes when she heard the break in his voice, that they could both hardly speak.

They kept it short, and she promised to be in touch soon to let him know when she might book a trip to meet him in person.

Afterward, she had a reactive cry in Vijay's arms, then pulled herself together and asked him to drive her to her childhood physician, where she was pronounced healthy and definitely pregnant. If her morning sickness became debilitating, she was advised to seek further medical attention. Otherwise, she should take her prescribed vitamins and consider scaling back her workload.

Oriel already knew she would have to do that, and it was eating at her.

"I know I don't *have* to work, but I've put in so much effort to get this far. Now my entire life is a row of dominoes that are falling over, one after another," she complained as Vijay drove her home. "I'll have to tell Payton to break my contracts. He'll want to tell the clients why, because some will say it's okay if I'm pregnant. Sometimes that works for their show or campaign. But I can't leak my pregnancy to the whole industry without telling my mother first. If I tell her, she'll want to know who the father is." She rolled her head on the headrest. "And what our plans are. Then there's your sister. I don't expect you to keep this from her, but will she tell Jalil? How will *he* react?"

"There is one more domino to consider."

"*No*," she said petulantly and turned her face away. "I don't want to hear it."

He pulled the car off the road to a spot that gave them a view of the river. The fronds of a willow dangled to play with the lily pads at the edge of the water.

"At some point your connection to Lakshmi will become public. You can put that off, but I doubt you can keep it hidden indefinitely, especially once you're in India. Her face is very well known. I recommend staying in front of the story to control how it rolls out. Once it's known, much will be made of the fact that Lakshmi was an unwed mother. Do you want to be judged for being the same?"

"That shouldn't matter! Not in this day and age."

"I agree." He held up a hand. "And to many it won't. To some it will be an affront. Unfortunately, those are the voices the media will amplify because that's what gains them clicks and revenue. I wouldn't want our child to suffer because we wished to make a point about free will."

"Ugh. What kind of a world are we bringing this baby into?" she muttered, bracing her elbow on the door and covering her eyes with her hand.

"Come. Let's walk a minute. Clear our heads. Is this the park your cousin teased you about last night?"

"Yes." She couldn't help a small laugh. She had forgotten about their childhood game in the pavilion of pretending to be a princess locked in a tower, taking turns rescuing the other.

"Show me." Vijay left the car and came around to open her door.

"I will not re-enact it," she warned, but enjoyed the short walk along the river's edge to the structure that overlooked the river. A family of tourists left it as they arrived.

"I don't know what I thought a knight in shining armor was supposed to save me from. My life was very simple and happy back then." She moved to the spot with the best view and curled her arm around the post. "Honestly, my life is not that difficult right now, just very unclear. I wish I knew what to do first."

"Oriel."

She looked over her shoulder.

Vijay was on one knee. He opened a ring box and offered it. "Will you marry me?"

She slapped her hand over her mouth, but a muffled squeak of shock came out. Inexplicably, tears came into her eyes. She wouldn't have expected to be so moved by a proposal from a man she had really only known a few days, but she was.

"How did you…?" She came closer. The ring was lovely. Modest, but eye-catching with its center diamond surrounded by smaller ones in a daisy pattern, all set in yellow gold. It looked like an antique. "Is that a family ring?"

"I went shopping while you were with the doctor. The jeweler said it came to him through an estate sale. It was likely made in the middle eighteen hundreds, but its provenance is mostly unknown."

As she had been for much of her life.

Her throat closed and her eyes grew hot. She could hardly speak.

"You're a romantic," she chided.

"I am not," he said with indignation. Then, with gentle affection, he added, "But I think you are, given your games here. I don't know what sort of white horse or dream castle I can offer you that you can't buy or make or achieve for yourself, but we're going to be a family. I think we can make a strong one if we go all in. I think we can make it work, even though it won't be ideal."

That was really what a family was—wholehearted, unconditional commitment. She knew that. It was how she already felt toward their child, and she believed he felt the same. It only made sense that they would close that final link between them.

The hollow pang that had sat in her heart all her life said, *But he doesn't love you, and he's said he won't be able to love you too.* It hurt quite a lot to acknowledge that, especially when that same ache made her fear she would never be loved, that there was some flaw in her that made it impossible for her to be cherished the way she longed to be.

That was something she had to resolve within herself, though. She had to believe she was worth being loved and not put it on others to prove it. Besides, maybe Lakshmi hadn't been given a choice about giving her up. By revealing that, Vijay had already gone a long way to helping her heal all those old insecurities inside her. She was grateful to him for that.

The even starker truth was, even if he never loved her, she knew she could love him. She was already halfway there. Maybe he hadn't been completely honest when they first met, but in the time since, he'd been considerate and protective and open in a way that must have been difficult for him. She admired the man he'd made of himself and knew she wasn't done learning who that man was.

It was terrifying to let her heart make such a huge decision for her, but she moved to perch on his bent leg and cupped his stubbled jaw. Her voice shook with unsteady emotion.

"Yes, I will marry you, Vijay."

He closed his arms tightly around her. His hot mouth captured hers. It was sweet and so intense it would have been frightening if he hadn't been so tender about it.

As tears of joy and trepidation burned behind her closed eyelids, she heard a faint cheer go up.

They broke away to see the family of tourists had been watching from a distance.

She and Vijay tipped their heads together in embarrassed laughter. Then he grasped her close to balance her while he got them both upright on their feet.

As he slipped the ring onto her finger, he said, "I'd prefer to marry as soon as possible."

"I have a few days of vacation left." She wrinkled her nose. "How do you feel about eloping?"

"Done."

# CHAPTER EIGHT

THEY MARRIED IN a brief civil ceremony in Gibraltar. Oriel wore a cream-colored skirt with a pale rose top that set off the golden tones in her skin. Vijay was in a gray suit and tie. Their wedding was short, solemn and profound. Vijay hadn't approached his marriage lightly, but he hadn't expected such a depth of pride and satisfaction once their rings were on their fingers, either.

It felt like a beginning, a fresh one that held more promise than he'd allowed himself to believe in for a long time.

They returned to the chateau, where they called Kiran. She happened to be with Jalil, so they told them their news at the same time they told Oriel's parents. Everyone was ecstatic to hear a baby was on the way.

"I'm going to be an auntie." Kiran clapped with delight. "I can't wait to hug my very own sister!"

"I'm excited for that, too, but I have commitments in New York," Oriel said with an apologetic glance at Vijay. She had told him that as they'd been on their way to the registry office. "I have to meet with my agent, tell him everything that's happened. Figure out what my career will look like moving forward."

"Oh, but... Vijay, I thought you were coming home?" Kiran asked.

"I am." He had barely finagled this week in France as it was. The building up of the Asian division was fully underway, and he'd been paid to ensure it went smoothly.

He didn't like starting their marriage apart, though. It felt like they were getting off on the wrong foot, and his worst niggling doubts had resurfaced. He was trying to tell himself this was the sort of test that would be good for them in the long run—provided they passed it—but the separation still annoyed him.

"Vijay is bringing copies of everything my parents have on my adoption," Oriel said. "Perhaps you and Jalil can find something that ties back to Gouresh Bakshi. My parents are happy to make inquiries on this end, but we don't want to misstep and tip him off that you're investigating how he might have behaved with Lakshmi."

Jalil was pleased with that lead, and they soon signed off.

The rest of the day was relaxed, and Vijay tried not to think about the fact that they were flying in different directions the next morning, but when they made love that night, they were both more aggressive than usual. Oriel laid claim to him with her mouth and hands. He did everything he could to imprint on her that they were one.

They were both sweaty and near comatose after, but she woke him in the night, kissing him with a frantic urgency that lit his fire all over again.

He pried her nails out of his hair and pressed her hand to the mattress, pinning her with his weight. "What's wrong?"

"I'm afraid something will happen and I won't see you again."

"This won't be like last time." He sucked flagrantly

on her earlobe and settled himself with proprietary ease between her soft thighs. "You're my wife."

He was an absolute Neanderthal because he loved saying that. *My wife. Mine.* "I would travel the world to come after you now. Don't you know that?"

"I've always been fine traveling on my own. I *like* not answering to anyone, but it suddenly seems very lonely."

"You're not alone, *priyatama*." He shifted so he could roam his hand across her stomach. He circled her navel with his thumb, then caressed up to her breast, cupping the warm swell. They kissed long and slow.

When she reached between them and guided him, he pressed into her heat.

They stayed locked like that a long time, shifting here and there, mostly kissing and caressing and reinforcing their bond. When he heard the sweet moan reverberate in her throat and her sheath clenched hungrily around his erection, he gave them both what they were aching for. He began to thrust with tender power.

As the storm brewed, he felt her growing tense beneath him.

"Wait," he commanded raggedly, wanting them to hit the peak together. His lower back tingled, and a feral noise gathered in his throat. *"Now."*

Her voice broke on a scream of agonized pleasure. They seemed caught in the stasis of orgasm for eternity. Wave after wave rolled through him while her body milked at his. He lost track of which one of them convulsed or moaned, which sobbed or made wordless noises of bliss. He knew only that they were in this singular place together.

And when they parted the next day, he went home with an empty ache inside him far bigger than the one she'd left in him last time.

* * *

A morose cloud descended on Oriel the minute she left Vijay. By the time she was in New York, she was struggling harder than she ever had in her life to find a smile.

Her priorities had completely shifted. Her mind was around the other side of the planet, wondering what her husband was doing. Her most important goal had become a need to put down roots so her baby would have a home when they arrived. All of her work commitments became obstacles to what she really wanted.

She sat down with Payton two days after arriving and told him everything.

His jaw went slack, but he was very understanding.

"I wouldn't be doing my job if I didn't point out that you could capitalize on the connection," he said in the middle of their discussion.

"No," Oriel said firmly. "I know how many doors a famous mother opens, but I don't want to do that to Lakshmi. I have a feeling she's been exploited enough. No, the baby will be my priority for the next year, at least. I want to scale back. Cancel everything you can. If that means I have to start from scratch when I'm ready to work again, so be it."

"You will never have to worry about that, but I hear what you're saying." He promised to begin making calls.

She phoned Vijay from the car afterward.

"You sound upset," he noted. "I thought you were going to try to work while you were pregnant, not choose the nuclear option."

"Yes, but as I sat there, I knew this was what I wanted. I'm teary because it was a big step, but it feels right. This way I can come to India and properly settle in. I haven't stayed in one place for years."

"You can get to know this part of yourself before India knows who you are," he teased.

"Exactly. Has Jalil made any progress?"

"My sister, the frighteningly brilliant strategist, suggested Jalil send out letters to people who worked on Lakshmi's films, claiming he wants to make a biopic and request interviews. It's been a slow process tracking them down. A lot have retired or moved on to other things, but as word gets out in that community, Jalil expects more people will come forward."

"That's actually a great idea even if he didn't have an ulterior motive. I would love to watch something like that. Could her estate fund it?"

"I'll call him tomorrow and mention it."

"Okay— Oh. I'm having lunch with an old friend, and I've just arrived at the restaurant." The car pulled up to the curb. "He wants me to—"

"Tell me you're making my dreams come true." The silver-haired man who had been formulating exclusive skin care products for four decades opened her door.

"I'll text you later," she hurried to say to Vijay and ended her call.

She let Yosef help her from the car and kiss both her cheeks. He had hired her for her first magazine ad five years ago, and she wanted to tell him herself. "I'm sorry, but I'm going to break your heart. I'm going on hiatus from modeling. If you want me to pay for lunch, I completely understand."

Six days later, Oriel was exhausted. She had one more shoot tomorrow before she could finalize things with Payton and leave New York. She was in the middle of modeling skiwear, trying not to sweat makeup onto the furred hood, when one of the hovering assistants said, "There's an urgent call for Ms. Cuvier."

Her mind immediately went to her parents. Oriel unwound from awkwardly grasping a pair of skis while standing in fake snow and took the phone.

"Bonjour?"

"It's me," Vijay said in a hard, flat tone. "Payton is on his way with someone from TecSec. Don't leave until they get there. The news is out that Lakshmi was pregnant when she left for Europe."

"What? *How?*"

"A cameraman from one of Bakshi's film crews received Jalil's letter about a biopic. He decided to cash in and sold the story that she was pregnant in *My Heart Sings for You*. It was her last film before she went to Europe, and it came out when she got back. He said she was sick on set, and everyone suspected. He assumed Bakshi was the father."

They had already debunked that. Oriel's DNA test had said she had forty percent Scandinavian heritage. "Has Gouresh made a statement?"

"No one can find him, but Kiran has set up a bunch of alerts, and your photo is already turning up in subthreads remarking on the resemblance."

"No." She looked for somewhere to sit and sank onto a closed trunk that held equipment. "How is Jalil?"

"Worried about them finding you before we have a chance to put protections around you. So am I. Payton said he can get you out of your last shoot if you want to. I'd like you here where I can see to your fences and firewalls myself. The alternative is the chateau, but…"

"Maman is starting a new tour. I'd rather be with you."

"Good. I'll start making your travel arrangements. Watch for a text."

She ended the call and handed the phone to the assistant.

"Is everything all right?"

"Not really," she said in a daze. "Let's get what we can before I have to leave."

Vijay's new partner and the founder of TecSec, Roman Killian, arrived with Payton. Payton finalized the cancellation of her last contracts, and Killian escorted Oriel to her mother's apartment, where she hurriedly packed. Then he brought her to the TecSec jet. His wife, Melodie, and their two children were already aboard.

Melodie was excellent company, and the toddlers provided a lovely distraction on the flight to Paris, where the family disembarked. Each of the children gave her a big hug that jump-started all of Oriel's maternal instincts.

From there, she traveled with only a security detail and slept most of the way to Mumbai. By the time she was asked to sit up because the plane was descending, she had almost forgotten why she'd left New York in such a scampering hurry. She hadn't found much online about Lakshmi's possible pregnancy except a few sensationalized posts on gossip sites.

Oriel had been reading up on her biological mother every spare moment, absorbing the details of Lakshmi's life with greedy fascination, and had watched a few films with subtitles. Everything reinforced that Lakshmi had been very popular and treasured as well as a talented singer and performer, but she seemed mostly a South Asian phenomenon, not known well internationally.

Watching her was a surreal experience. She seemed familiar, yet everything about her was completely different from the life Oriel had lived or the person she had believed herself to be.

Now Oriel was landing in a country that, under different circumstances, would have been her nation of birth. Her identity. She was eager to discover if it felt like home, but a greater uncertainty confronted her.

It was hitting her that she had completely overturned her life to be with a man who was still very much a stranger. As an only child, and one who had begun traveling for her career when she'd still been in school, she had a very independent spirit. It would be one thing to reshape her future around the love of her life. It was quite another to do it for passion. What if she'd made a horrible mistake?

Landing under low, soggy clouds that looked cold and unwelcoming did not reassure her. Where was the undo button for life? She had a sudden urge to backspace all the way to Milan and make different choices.

*Not true*, she assured the baby, patting where apprehensive butterflies were taking flight in her belly. She peeked out the window and saw Vijay on the tarmac below, stepping from an SUV with a practiced pop of a wide black umbrella.

The air hostess pressed a button to lower the hatch that formed the stairs, and a dozen impressions hit her at once.

The temperature wasn't cold, merely rain-fresh cool. A gust brought in the fragrance of washed tarmac and wet earth. The patter of the rain was steady and musical, the humidity so tangible, her deep inhale rehydrated her, filling her with buoyant excitement.

And here was Vijay, taking the stairs in an easy

stride, arriving in the opening with the umbrella so he provided a shelter to step into. Masculine scents radiated off him with the warmth of his body—spice and coffee and the damp cotton of his shirt as she stepped out of the plane.

She paused there, drinking in everything about this moment so she could remember it forever. She memorized the lights in the puddles and the green in the distance and the way her husband looked down at her, face filled with intriguing angles.

He took her breath away when he looked at her in that hooded way, holding his sensual mouth so tense and serious. His dark lashes flickered as he stole a very swift, proprietary glance to her toes and back, revealing nothing about his thoughts.

Even so, as she stood close to him, spatters of rain pelting them with the changeable wind, she felt as though she had arrived home—not because this country was in her blood, but because he was.

She had missed him. This was the place she *had* to be. It was a profound realization and yet one more way she was losing a piece of herself to the unknown.

If he had kissed her then, she would have laughed with joy, but a gust caught the umbrella and tipped it, sending a cold drizzle down her bare arm, startling her.

"Monsoon," he said. "Welcome to India."

She was so wrapped up in wanting him to show some sort of affection, she briefly thought the word was an endearment. As she realized her mistake, she ducked her head and wiped the trickle from her arm, embarrassed that she was behaving like a pubescent child wishing for a paper valentine.

The truth was, she wanted a lot more. She was falling in love with him, she realized with a catch of alarm.

It was too soon, too spontaneous, too *new*. It made her terrifyingly vulnerable when she had already sacrificed everything, but her heart had opened itself to him of its own accord. She had quit her old life because she wanted to be here, with him.

And his reception to all of that seemed very lukewarm.

*Why don't you want me? Why don't you love me?*

She tried not to be crestfallen, but she was.

"You are a true Mumbaikar if you're willing to stand in the rain instead of running to where it's dry." He nodded an invitation for her to move ahead of him down the narrow steps.

She dredged up an uncertain smile to cover her disappointment. "I am ruining an expensive pair of shoes."

Rain hit her ankles beneath the cuffs of her snapping wide-legged pants as she descended. Her sleeveless, light-knit mock turtleneck left her arms bare to the spits and spats that whipped off the breeze and stung her skin.

"Jalil has arranged a press conference at a hotel near here," Vijay said as they settled in the SUV. "You're up for it?"

No. She wanted to go somewhere private to reevaluate all her life choices, but she didn't think she had the option to refuse.

"Of course." She had already approved the press release and memorized the statement she would make. "I warned my parents what was happening, but do you really think people will care that much? I mean, beyond reporters."

He looked at her as if she was very naive. "I do. Yes."

He didn't say anything else, but it wasn't far to the hotel. Their car was met in the parking garage by four burly, expressionless men. *Four.* Plus two people wearing hotel security badges.

They were shown through a private corridor and past an open door to a kitchen, where a curious silence fell as they walked by. An excited babble rose in their wake.

She looked to Vijay and noted that his whole demeanor was on alert.

"Kiran wanted to be here, but I asked her to stay at the office so I can give my full attention to you and your safety."

She began to realize he was actually *working*, wearing the role of protector in the most basic way. It was sweet, but she grew intimidated as they approached what sounded like a thousand voices beyond a wall. She unconsciously tightened her hand on the crook of his elbow.

As they reached a pair of doors where a handful of people were waiting, one looked up and made a noise of surprise.

Jalil turned and did a double take. He covered his mouth, and his dark eyes filled with tears. *"Beti,"* he breathed as he held out his hand to her. "You look just like her."

"Please don't make me cry." She caught his hand in both of hers. "Not yet."

They both laughed emotively, and he squeezed her hand so hard her rings dug into her fingers, but the pain helped her keep hold of her composure.

Someone offered to touch up her makeup while Jalil went into the room. The babble of voices nearly knocked her over, but they abruptly went silent as he was introduced.

Jalil began to speak in Hindi.

"He's explaining that he had suspicions Lakshmi had

a child," Vijay translated for her. "And that she gave up the baby to protect her career, that she feared she and her baby wouldn't be accepted if she kept it."

"I can only speak English or French," Oriel whispered in belated panic.

"English is fine. When Jalil called this, he said most of it would be conducted in English. Now he's saying he's confident Bakshi was not the father."

"Has Bakshi been found?"

"No, he's still in hiding." He cocked his head. "He says he has confirmed that Lakshmi had a daughter because he has found her. You're up."

Oriel's knees wanted to give out. She swallowed the worst stage fright of her life. *It's just a runway.*

Walking for an audience had never bothered her beyond a few twinges of nerves, but her entire body became encased in ice. Her limbs felt disjointed as she allowed Vijay to escort her into the ballroom.

A collective gasp rippled over the hundred or so assembled reporters. Cameras flashed in a violent strobe. A babble of incomprehensible questions assaulted her ears.

She wore a resemblance, she told herself, in the same way she often wore an haute couture gown. That was what people were looking at, not her.

Her training came to her rescue, and she managed an aloof confidence as she joined Jalil at the podium and flashed her warmest smile.

"Good afternoon," she said as Vijay's men stepped in front of the microphone.

The room fell silent again.

"If you were surprised to learn that Lakshmi Dalal gave birth to me, you know exactly how I feel."

It was exactly the right note of humor and humanity

to win them over. The flashes continued, but she felt the shift in the room. The acceptance.

She read her statement and took a few questions. Then Jalil's people ended the conference by providing contact information for further questions. As she walked out, someone was asking the reporters to please respect their privacy.

Jalil came with them in their car so they could have a few more minutes to chat. He knew she had been traveling for nearly a full day and needed time to take all of this in, so they made a date to have dinner with him and Kiran in a few days' time.

As she and Vijay were dropped off, Jalil said he would continue on to "make a report to Kiran."

"Make a report," Vijay scoffed as they entered the elevator with the doorman who brought her luggage.

"Does it still bother you that they're involved?" she asked.

"No," he allowed. "Jalil is insisting they take their time because he worries about the age difference."

"So did you," she reminded him.

"True, but I've since seen that their personalities are well-suited. If they wished to marry, I would support their decision."

He was speaking very objectively, reminding her of the night he'd asked her what her expectations of marriage were. Passion wasn't a deal-breaker, he had said, but she had hoped it was still alive between them. So far, desire seemed the furthest thing from motivating his urgency in bringing her here.

Doubts were digging claws ever deeper into her as he opened the door into a penthouse and thanked the doorman, instructing him to leave the luggage in the entranceway.

"Oh. Wow."

Vijay had told her over their daily video chats that he had found an apartment they could live in right away, with the option to buy. From the outside, the building had looked unremarkable, but this was a tasteful, modern oasis with endless views of the sea.

"It was renovated last year by one of our clients. It was actually two units and he combined them." Vijay pointed at the loft to indicate it had two floors. "I made him an offer on condition you approve."

If she hadn't been feeling as though there was an invisible wall between them, she would have thrown her arms around him and squealed with delight.

The decor was understated, the furniture chic but comfortable. Sliding walls of glass were the only separation between indoors and the wide terrace that overlooked the Arabian sea. The dining, living and kitchen area were all one airy space with plenty of room for Kiran's wheelchair if she decided to come live with them.

Oriel and Vijay had discussed it, and Oriel had no problem with sharing their home with Vijay's sister. She had often roomed with complete strangers at different times and always made it work. Once the baby came, she would probably be very glad for an extra pair of hands. Besides, judging from the way things were going with Jalil, Kiran wouldn't be with them for long.

For now, Kiran had chosen to stay in the lower level of a duplex that she and Vijay had called home for several years. The neighbors all treated her like family, and the home itself was fitted for her chair. Plus, Kiran said she wanted to give the newlyweds their privacy.

For what? Oriel had to wonder uneasily.

There was an elevator to the upper floor, but they walked up the floating staircase to a loft with a small sitting area beneath a skylight. They passed two spare bedrooms and a home gym before entering a master suite fronted by a wall of glass. It opened onto a private terrace that had a small landscaped garden as well as another stunning view of the sea.

Oriel moved to the part of the rail that was protected by an overhang and instantly imagined walking out here every single morning, drinking coffee, tasting the day.

"You're not saying anything." He was still wearing that watchfulness. She was beginning to think it had less to do with his security persona and more to do with whatever was going on in his own head. But what was *that*?

"It's incredible," she said with a reluctant smile. "You know it is."

"The security system is first class," he said dryly as he joined her at the rail. "The location is excellent. One of the best maternity hospitals in the city is nearby."

"That's good," she murmured.

They both stood there watching the rain.

"Oriel—"

"Do you want me here?" she asked over him.

"What?" He angled to look down his nose at her. "Of course." His voice was brisk, though, and his gaze went out to the gray horizon, where low clouds hung against chopping waves. "Why do you ask?" His demeanor was as cool and colorless as the rain.

She felt callow admitting it. Defenseless because she couldn't hide the fact she was hurt. "You didn't…kiss me when I arrived."

Thankfully, he didn't laugh at her. She might have gone straight back to the airport if he had. Even so, as he looked at her with vague bewilderment, a scorched self-consciousness rose behind her breastbone.

"We're not like Europe. Public affection isn't customary here."

"Oh." She hadn't even thought of the cultural differences she would face with this move. She might look like she had been born here, but she was French. Being demonstrative in public was very natural to her. "I have a lot to learn."

"We're a nation of people who live in multigenerational homes, so it's kept behind closed doors out of respect for our elders. I honestly don't recall ever seeing my parents kiss, not because their marriage was arranged. It just wasn't done."

"Oh." She started to relax, but realized, "You still haven't, though." Fresh shyness struck, and her cheeks stung with a painful blush. "Kissed me, I mean."

"I know." His voice had returned to being clipped. He moved back to the door into the bedroom.

Her heart lurched at the way he was putting that distance between them.

He lightly tapped his loose fist on the frame. "I hate myself for asking, but I have to." He pinned her with his steady gaze. "Who was he?"

She was taken aback. "Who?"

"The man whose dreams you were making come true."

She shook her head. "I honestly don't know—"

"Lunch. You left Payton's office and you were going to meet an old friend for lunch."

"Yosef!" she recalled, then stood tall with instant outrage. "He's nearly seventy, Vijay. He gave me my first magazine shoot, and yes, I wore a negligee back then, but he never once made me feel cheap about it. Unlike *you*. Do you really think I was stepping out on you days after we married? *Mon Dieu*, when you said you didn't trust easily, you should have explained you meant there was none at all."

She tried to brush past him into the bedroom. He put out a hand to stop her, and she thrust his arm away. She glared at him, daring him to touch her again.

"I don't want to be like this," he said through his teeth.

"Then don't," she threw back at him and stalked toward the bed. "Should I feel the sheets?" She patted the blankets. "See if they're still warm from whoever *you've* been with?"

His mouth tightened. "I haven't been with anyone since you. There was no one between meeting you in Milan and finding you in Cannes, either," he clarified.

"Same." She flipped her hair over her shoulder. "Do you believe me?" Let him try and say he didn't.

"Damn it, Oriel, I had someone cheat on me. I know it's weak of me to be suspicious, but I can't stand the idea that I might not be seeing what's right under my nose." He rubbed his stubbled jaw before dropping his hands onto his hips. He stared out the open doors as though seeing a past he couldn't change.

She was still angry, but an even more insidious sense of threat crept into her.

"Who? How long were you together?"

"Her name is Wisa. We met at university and wanted to finish our degrees before we married."

"So you were..." She had assumed he would have a romantic history, but, "You were *engaged*?" She covered the sick knot that arrived in her middle.

"Yes. The wedding was days away when we called it off. She was sleeping with my best friend. I found out as the rest of my life fell apart over my father's crimes. The worst part is—"

That wasn't the worst part? She dragged her gaze up to his shuttered expression.

"I realized later that she had likely been steered toward me in an attempt to have influence over me when I took control of my father's business."

"Oh." She touched the night table for balance. "That is awful."

"I don't think she knew what was going on any more than I did." He brushed a tired hand through the air. "On the surface, we seemed very compatible, nothing to raise my suspicion. I was the heir to a successful company, and she was the daughter of a local politician. I took my degree in business with a minor in electronical engineering. She thought I should plan to go into politics. That was our only bone of contention."

Oriel was still reeling. He'd been days away from a wedding. Relationships didn't get that far unless hearts were involved.

Vijay shrugged out of his jacket and threw it onto a chair in the corner.

"After Kiran, Wisa was the first person I told about my father's business dealings. Initially she supported my going to the police, but as our friends began to distance themselves, and she realized her uncle might be implicated, I caught her on a call with Madin. It was obvious they were involved. She said it was my fault, that I had ruined our future. *Everyone's* future. That I *drove* her to Madin. We canceled the wedding, and she stuck me with the bills as a final slap in the face."

"Were you in love with her?" The question came out before she had fully braced herself for the answer.

He met her gaze unflinchingly. "I was."

Her heart plummeted like a shot bird. "Are you still?"

"No," he dismissed firmly. "But I'm suspicious of

that emotion, as you saw with my reaction to Jalil's interest in Kiran." He pushed his hands into his pants pockets. "I can't help thinking it's a smoke screen that people use to get whatever it is they really want."

That's why he had asked her what she wanted from marriage. He didn't intend to give her his heart. It was a surprising blow. He didn't want to love her. Wouldn't.

She pressed a hand over the spot where she felt as though a knife was lodged in her chest. When she tried to speak, she had to gulp in air first.

"Love can be used like that," she acknowledged, hugging herself. "My first boyfriend was only using me to get close to my mother's theater connections." It still made her feel like the worst naive fool for not seeing it. "I fell for it because..." She worked to keep her mouth from turning down. "Because I wanted that *big* love. You know? *The one.*"

He flinched and looked away guiltily.

"Don't. This isn't about you and your limitations. This is something I want you to understand about me." She hunched up her shoulders defensively. "I've always struggled with not feeling that I was loved enough. Otherwise she would have kept me. Right?" Tears rose in her eyes.

"That's not true." His shoulders sank, and he came toward her, reaching to cup her elbows.

She pressed her hand to his chest, holding him off.

"Even if it was, you've seen how much my parents love me. They would do anything for me, which makes me feel even worse for having these fears. But it's a normal thing a lot of adopted children struggle with. We worry that we were at fault somehow. It's irrational and complex and confusing, but that's how I realized I was susceptible to letting that feeling take over. Ever since that boyfriend treated me that way, I've been cautious about giving up too much of myself. I don't like getting hurt, either."

He pulled his head back slightly as if her words had shaken him at some level. Then he gave a jerky nod of understanding. His hands tightened on her elbows.

"I was only asking a question. It wasn't an accusation. I don't think you're cheating on me. I just needed to hear from you that it was nothing."

"It was nothing."

"Thank you." His hands twitched as though he wanted to pull her close while still trying to give her space. "But Oriel, look at the lengths Jalil has gone to find you. He wouldn't have done that if his sister hadn't seemed tortured by losing you. You were wanted. You were loved."

Her composure crumpled, and she went into his arms.

He held her secure, stroking her and saying, "I wanted to kiss you the second I saw you today. I want you all the damned time. Never doubt that."

She gave a small sob and looked up at him. "Even like this? All weepy and messy?"

He framed her face in his warm, broad hands. "All the damned time," he repeated.

"Then kiss me." She lifted on tiptoe and offered her tear-dampened lips.

He closed his arms around her and opened his mouth across hers. As his flavor seeped into her senses, all her reservations eased.

Then, as their kiss deepened, sharp need twisted inside her. Vijay slanted his mouth for a deeper seal, and between one breath and the next, their kiss yanked her into a maelstrom of want.

For one moment, he let her feel the ferocity of his desire as he plundered her mouth, arms tight as he crushed her hips into the aroused shape behind his fly.

He seemed to exert all his will as he made himself ease his hold and lift his head.

"You should get some rest. You must be tired."

"What happened to 'all the damned time'?"

With an agile twist, he had them both on the bed.

"Oh!"

"Yes, oh." He tucked her beneath him. "If you are too tired, now would be a good time to say so."

"I'm a little bit tired. You might have to do all the work."

"That, my beautiful wife, would be my pleasure."

A few nights later, Vijay took Oriel to meet Kiran and Jalil at one of Mumbai's most exclusive restaurants. The pair had been over to visit twice already, and Vijay had been going to work, but Oriel had been staying in the penthouse while she acclimatized.

They'd also been making love nonstop because they couldn't seem to help themselves. He had no complaints about that, but he did suspect they were expressing themselves physically because they didn't know how to do it verbally.

He was still disturbed by what she'd said about wanting the "big" love. *The one*. He had known there was a romantic hidden deep inside her, but he hadn't appreciated how fragile her heart was. Her amazing front of confidence hid any hint of insecurities. He was glad she had spelled out for him where she struggled, but he was also—very hypocritically—frustrated that she had developed her own inner guards to protect herself. It made it that much harder for them to be sure of one another.

It would all come with time, he assured himself. For now, she was feeling cooped up, and he was eager to show her his city and show the world his wife.

Of course, she caused a stir the minute they hit the street.

It was more annoying than anything. They had a security detail. He wasn't concerned about her safety to any serious degree, but he suspected this would wear on her long-term.

At least the restaurant was used to catering to Bollywood celebrities and other high-profile clientele. It was candlelit with glinting reflections dancing off glossy floors and mirrored tiles in the wall mosaic. Partial walls of wooden slats absorbed sound and formed partitions that created pockets of privacy.

Heads turned as they were shown to their table, but Oriel seemed unfazed.

"You're taking this in stride," Vijay remarked as they settled at their table.

"The attention? I forgot it was for me," she said with a blink of bemusement. "The same thing happens when I go anywhere with Maman. I've learned to ignore it."

They all chuckled, and it turned into a pleasant, relaxing meal. They were finishing dessert when Kiran's smile stiffened.

"Someone must have posted that we were here. Why else would *she* show up?"

"Who?" Oriel asked.

Vijay knew without looking and stiffened, watching for Oriel's reaction as his past literally caught up to him.

"Vijay, Kiran." Wisa's voice was a smug purr. "What are you two doing in this part of the city?"

"Wisa. Madin." Vijay rose to greet his ex-fiancée and his ex-best friend, determined to be nothing but polite. "Please meet my wife, Oriel. And our good friend, Jalil Dalal."

"Ah, yes. Such a colorful story. It's everywhere." Wisa's gaze widened on Oriel as though she was an exotic animal, a curiosity, but something to be dismissed. "You do have a way of making headlines, don't you?" she said pithily to Vijay.

It was exactly the sort of sly, denigrating remark she and everyone else had made when he had refused to look the other way over his father's transgressions. Anything to put him down.

He was about to set her in her place once and for all when Oriel spoke up.

"Would you like a photo?" She sent a friendly nod to someone beyond Wisa.

They all glanced to see that an elderly woman in a saree was watching Oriel with a delighted smile of recognition.

"I'll come there." Oriel rose and brushed past Wisa, saying, "I don't want to offend her." She paused and set a delightfully possessive hand on Vijay's shoulder. "This would be a good time to make an escape, or I'll be here all night. You should buy their dinner, though." She nodded at Wisa and Madin. "Make it up to them that we can't stay."

"I'd love to."

The look on Wisa's face was worth whatever they charged to his credit card.

"That was savagely brilliant," he said when he and Oriel were in the back of his car on their way home.

"It's from my mother's bag of tricks. I felt petty resorting to it."

"You shouldn't. The family at the other table was happy." They'd been over the moon that their grandmother had been singled out and fussed over by a celebrity. "Wisa will think twice before driving across the city to make things awkward for us ever again."

"Holding on to a grudge like that suggests she still has feelings for you." She glanced across at him, eyes wary and watchful.

"Her uncle had to pay a fine and narrowly missed going to jail. I imagine she believes I still deserve punishment for that."

"Why? Her uncle was the one who broke the law," she muttered impatiently.

"Thank you." He reached across to squeeze her hand, so moved that his chest felt tight and he had to swallow a lump from his throat. "Anytime I have to revisit that episode in my life, I feel sick. I thought I was a law-abiding, principled sort of man and had to decide if I really was. It was sobering to be put to the test, and when I stood by what I thought was right, I was vilified and abandoned. It means everything to me that you didn't give her a chance to spit poison in your ear."

"I should have thanked her," she mused. "If she hadn't been so self-interested, you'd be married to her, and I wouldn't have you or our baby or know any of this about myself."

Neither would he, Vijay realized with a catch of fierce possessiveness for her, their baby, and the life they were starting.

Recognizing that flashed a fresh light on all he'd been through, searing away much of his resentment and anguish. His ever-present shame died a final death, becoming cold, flaky ashes. From now on, it would be a bitter and sooty memory, but not one that still had the ability to scorch and burn him.

"But honestly?" Oriel said with annoyance. "She

was kind of a bitch. 'What are you two doing in this part of the city?' Like she owns it. I don't actually feel bad for snubbing her."

He chuckled and tugged her across the seat, into his arms. "I felt great about it." In fact, he felt as though he was falling in love, and he wasn't that unsettled by the prospect.

# CHAPTER NINE

As the days turned into weeks, Oriel had to concede that she and Vijay were very well-matched. Sexually, their compatibility continued to be an A-plus, ten out of ten. They could hardly keep their hands off each other.

They also complemented each other in broader ways. They began adding personal touches to their home by way of art and sculptures and were always in agreement. They hired a housekeeper and cook with minimal discussion and already knew what they wanted in a nanny.

She and Kiran got on as if they'd known each other all their lives, laughing and enjoying each other's company whether Vijay was in the room or not. He even brought her into the office to introduce her around. Everything was in disarray due to merging with TecSec, but she was fascinated and enjoyed seeing that side of his world.

In the hours when the rain let up, Vijay drove her to different parts of the city to help her get her bearings, and into the mountains, where everything was lush and green. They took a day trip to see the caves with rock carvings on Elephanta Island, and because it was mostly tourists there, they enjoyed one of their most relaxing, incognito days ever.

He worked a lot, which made her conscious of the

fact she didn't, but he chided, "Your job is to build our baby. That's work."

So far being pregnant wasn't that hard. Her nausea had passed once she'd caught up on her sleep. Today they were having a scan, but it was purely routine.

"I have to go to Delhi for a few days," he said, reading his phone while they waited.

"When?" She instantly felt a pang of separation anxiety. It wasn't that she was emotionally dependent on him. She was genuinely falling in love with him and hated to be apart from him.

"Tomorrow."

"Can you tell me why? Or is it something confidential?" She was getting used to the fact that he sometimes couldn't talk about certain things.

"Dangerously boring reasons. There's a problem with wiring in the building we've leased and some HR issues that need massaging. I'd ask you to come, but I won't have time to show you around. You'd be stuck in a hotel room."

"And I would miss my language class." She was going three times a week and practiced diligently with Kiran and their housekeeper. The classes were more than a determination to explore her roots, though. It was a nice reason to get out of the house, something she did for herself that wasn't wrapped up in her husband, and she was making some pleasant friendships with the eclectic expats she was meeting.

The ultrasound technician arrived, greeting them cheerfully. As Oriel stood, the young woman made a noise of amused surprise, then consulted her notes.

"Eighteen weeks? Is that a typo?" She made a perplexed face at Oriel's still flat middle.

"I'm very tall," Oriel pointed out defensively.

She had already had a small lecture from one of Kiran's well-meaning friends about ensuring her calorie intake was high enough. No one seemed to realize how thin she'd been when she'd gotten pregnant. The amount of weight she'd gained was right on target, and she was actually thickening around the waist and showing fullness in her breasts and face.

Plus, "My waist is long. There's lots of room for a baby to hide in here."

For one second, Vijay's expression seemed arrested, but he shook it off so quickly, Oriel wasn't sure if that had really been a moment of suspicion coming into his head.

"We'll confirm your dates," the woman assured her.

*I know when I conceived.* Oriel bit back the words.

A short while later, her affront was forgotten as the blurry image of their baby appeared with its heart pitter-patting.

Her eyes filled with tears, and so did Vijay's. As they touched their trembling smiles together, she was so happy at having this little miracle inside her, she almost told him she loved him. Because she did. And she didn't know which made her heart overflow more, their baby or him.

New Bride with an Old Flame?

Vijay stared at his screen, annoyed by the unsavory headline, but more bothered that his team was taking this seriously enough they'd forwarded it.

They had a team who filtered through all the false sightings, many of them easy enough to disprove when they claimed Oriel was in New York and she was clearly here, but this one was from the days shortly after Vijay had met her in Milan.

It was a photo of Oriel at a restaurant table with a man who had a healthy head of dark hair and the shoulders of a thirty-year-old.

The shot was actually a screengrab from a selfie video posted by someone visiting New York and dining at an upscale restaurant. As Oriel's notoriety had risen, this tourist had realized she had inadvertently caught a celebrity in the background of her vacation vlog. Now the woman was claiming her ten minutes of adjacent fame by circulating the shot on the gossip sites.

In it, Oriel was leaning in, smiling playfully while delivering a flirty look through her long, thick lashes. It was unmistakably her. Vijay knew that curve of her cheek, the ripple in her hair that caught the light. He knew that adoring expression and had started to believe she only ever showed it to him.

He checked the date stamp and was further irritated to see it had been taken in the days after they'd been together in Milan. He told himself he had no right to the soul-eating jealousy that was trying to consume him, but he had a right to the truth. She had told him she hadn't been with anyone except him since Milan. And that the "old friend" she had lunched with had been a man in his seventies.

There was also that niggling moment at the ultrasound the other day, when the technician had remarked on Oriel not looking pregnant *enough*.

Back in Cannes, Oriel had been offended when Vijay had suggested the baby might not be his. *Of course it would be yours. Don't be rude!*

But she had gone back to New York after Milan. Had

she seen—he read the caption—Reve Weston, New York billionaire, while she was there?

"Sir—"

"I need a few minutes." He abruptly closed the door of the empty office he stood in, cutting off the babble of voices down the hall.

He wanted to jump on a plane back to Mumbai, but things were still in disarray here in Delhi. He couldn't wait and wonder, though. He called Oriel for a video chat.

"Hi!" She was in her yoga clothes, hair bundled messily atop her head. "How's it going there?"

"Terrible. I'm sending you a photo."

"Of?"

"You. Having lunch with a man. In New York."

She frowned. The screen briefly went black. "What? *Mon Dieu*, that's not me." She came back onscreen. "Or it's been altered to make it look like it's me." She was frowning with concern, but not guilt, as far as he could tell.

"You don't know him?"

"I know who Reve Weston is. Every straight woman or gay man in New York does. He's one of those wealthy tycoons everyone dreams of catching. Is that what I'm up against now?" Her mouth twisted with annoyance. "People putting my image into photos to manufacture clickbait?"

"I ran it through Kiran's program, Oriel. It hasn't been edited. It was taken a few days after we met in Milan."

"Vijay." There was enough shock and hurt in her tone to cause him a trickle of compunction. "I thought we were past this."

"I'm not angry." He was trying not to be. He was trying to give her the benefit of the doubt. "I just want you to be honest about it. Tell me if you had a relationship with him and saw him again when you went back. Either time."

"Either…? Are you asking if I went on a date with an old boyfriend after you and I were married? No, I did not. I have never had lunch with Reve Weston. Ever. Or dinner. Or breakfast the morning after a night before. Please tell me you are not accusing me of getting pregnant by another man and passing it off as yours!"

"I'm just trying to get to the bottom of this."

"We are definitely hitting rock bottom if we're here," she snapped. "I'm sitting here eating my heart out, missing you because I love you so much, and you call to accuse me of *that*?"

His heart lurched. *I love you.* They were words he had told himself he didn't want or need to hear. His scorned self from years past warned him she might only be saying it to throw him off her affair, but his gut told him that was wrong. She meant it.

"You're punishing me for Wisa's infidelity," she accused, expression contorted with hurt.

The last thing he ever wanted was to hurt her, but he said, "I'm simply asking for an explanation for what is right in front of my eyes."

"I can't explain it," she cried with frustration. "But the fact you jump to the worst possible explanation tells me what you think of me, doesn't it?" She ended the call.

It was as though she'd stabbed clean through the screen and jabbed a hole in his chest. Vijay swore and pocketed his phone.

Oriel hadn't spent much time looking herself up online. She knew that way lay madness, and Vijay had people screening all of that, but in her hurt and fury, she began going down rabbit holes on Lakshmi fan forums. She found threads by dozens of people claiming to also be the product of Lakshmi's illicit liaison and therefore entitled to her fortune. Some of the posts were clear fakes, others credible look-alikes.

Some of it was very unsavory, but so was being accused of infidelity by her husband. She kept searching and came across another photo that claimed to be of her, this one more recent. It showed three frames in which she supposedly had an altercation with a photographer that ended with the man clutching his bleeding nose.

Cuvier Clocks Cub Reporter for Catching Her Canoodling

"With who?" she cried.

The woman in the photo was a really good double. She had a streak of pink in her hair, but her face and body were uncannily similar. The shocked, fear-filled look on her face was what really got to Oriel. She felt that other woman's emotions as if she was staring at her own reflection in a mirror.

Disturbed, she went back to the photo of the woman with Reve Weston and started searching for more of the couple together. She didn't have much luck until she stumbled across a list of guests from a gala that said Reve's plus-one had been someone called Nina Menendez.

When Oriel searched Nina's name, she discovered the woman's social profiles had been locked down. The only thing she was able to turn up was—weirdly—from a fashion degree program at a college in New Mexico. Nina appeared in a video from four years ago.

Oriel's skin broke out in goose bumps as she listened to Nina speak. She sounded just like her!

"I go for my first job interview on my twenty-first birthday next Thursday. No matter how that goes, I plan to have my first legal drink after. Wish me luck."

Oriel glanced at the date, and her heart nearly came out of her mouth. Nina's birthday was the day after Oriel's, but Oriel had been born a few minutes before midnight. She knew because she'd been going through all the paperwork on her adoption with Jalil.

She and Nina were essentially the same age.

*"Mon Dieu, mon Dieu..."* she heard herself muttering, her skin going hot and cold as she hurriedly read the rest of Nina's bio on the college website.

She was barely able to make sense of it. Nina mentioned her father's military career as inspiration for some of her designs, adding that her father had been stationed at one of the bases in Germany when she had been born.

Oriel shakily opened another tab on her browser and punched in the distance between the air force base and the small village in Luxembourg where she'd been born.

One hour and seven minutes by car.

*Impossible.*

For a long time, she sat without any coherent thought in her head. The words *I should call Vijay* drifted into her head, but faded before she could act on them. She had the sense that Kiran could do some intensive digging, but Kiran would feel compelled to tell Jalil. Oriel didn't want to cause the older man any further upheavals if she was being delusional.

Was she? The truth seemed as plain as the identical nose on Nina's face. She didn't know if she wanted to laugh or cry or check herself into a hospital for possible hallucinations.

When Oriel realized it was the middle of the afternoon in France, she called Max, barely stammering out, "Do you have access to any sort of database that would give you background information on a designer in New York?"

"It's called gossip, *chou*. Give me a name and I'll have all the dirt within the hour."

She told him, and he called back forty-eight minutes later.

"Well, that was interesting," Max said cheerfully. "Mademoiselle Nina is an upstart who began working for Kelly Bex a year ago. The party line is that she showed promise, but was ultimately a disappointment. The truth is, she stole a hunky billionaire, Monsieur Reve Weston, from the maven Bex herself. *That's* why she was fired, thrown onto the street, told never to darken their doorway again."

"Not so much a lack of talent, then."

"*Oui*. Because she does have talent. This was much harder to pry from one of my nearest and dearest, but he claims to have seen some of her work. He expects it to be, and I quote, 'priceless when the designer is revealed.' I've looked her up. She looks just like you. Beware, *chou*. She may try to trade on that."

"She's still in New York?"

"No. Apparently, she flew to Paris on Weston's supersonic jet yesterday. He has a pied-à-terre—which is a monstrous two-story penthouse—on Avenue Montaigne."

"*Merci, Maximus. Tu es mon héros.*" She hung up

and, with her heart racing out of her chest, called her mother's assistant. If anyone could charter a flight to Paris within the hour, she could.

Every time Vijay reached for his phone, he became infuriated by their fight, by his vacillating trust, by the seesaw of wanting to believe her and not wanting to be a fool.

He set aside his phone and closed his eyes, but all he saw was Oriel looking at that other man with the love she had claimed to have for *him*.

Jealousy was such a lowering emotion. So insecure.

That photograph wouldn't bother him so much—that was a lie, but he told himself it wouldn't bother him this badly—if Oriel had owned up to the affair and assured him the relationship was over. Instead, she had denied the association even though she had been in New York after Milan and again after they'd married.

He wanted to ask Kiran to search the online archives for more photos of this bastard billionaire, to see if Oriel had been photographed elsewhere with him, but he was too ashamed. Ashamed of his suspicions, ashamed of what might turn out to be true.

Ashamed that he might have allowed himself to be taken in. Again.

He was trying to believe Oriel's word—another lie, but not entirely. He wanted to believe her. He did. But there was a piece of himself that couldn't let go of the past. He had failed to see reality when it had been deliberately obscured from him, so he had learned to keep his eyes open. There was *photographic evidence* to refute what she claimed.

What else could he think but that she had feelings for someone else? Feelings she wouldn't admit to?

The mere idea of it scraped out his chest far worse than Wisa's betrayal. He didn't want to believe Oriel would do that to him. They were far too close, closer than any relationship he'd ever had.

He *loved* her. He wouldn't be this tortured if he didn't. He loved her and he was anguished at the thought of her with a stranger, but he was being a fool. She was here in India, making a life with him, wearing his ring and having his baby.

What did he care what she had done in the past if she was here with him now? If she wanted another man, she would be with that other man. He shouldn't push her away with his rotten suspicions. Instead, he should be looking for another explanation.

He glanced at the clock, unwilling to wake Kiran to help him, but in the morning he would ask her to come to Delhi and take over for him. He would go home, make up with his wife, and figure out what the hell was going on.

His phone pinged, and he picked it up to see a text from Oriel.

Her name is Nina Menendez. She's in Paris. I'm going to see her.

# CHAPTER TEN

ORIEL HAD SLEPT a little on the flight. Mostly her mind had been cracked in half by a thought that was even more outlandish than her being the secret daughter of a Bollywood star—that she might be the twin of one.

Vijay had texted her back, asking her to wait for him, saying he would go with her.

I'm in the air. I have my guards. I'm not leaving you, but I have to meet her. She might be my twin. Please trust me to come back. I love you.

There was no response to that, but she really hoped he would trust her. She was devastated by his accusations and didn't know how they would move forward if she was forever trying to prove herself to him.

Was she running away from him as impetuously as she had married him? A little. She'd been trying so hard to become a part of his world, which was her own world too, she supposed. But she had constructed a life with him because everything she had known about herself had been shattered. Now she might have yet another layer to unpeel, and she didn't know how to deal with it.

She entered her old flat with a desperate need for a sense of homecoming, the way it had always felt when she had returned from breaks between modeling gigs. Her parents had helped her buy this place when she had begun traveling for modeling, and she had been making the payments since. She had rarely spent more than a few weeks at a time here, but it was hers, and it was where she had always been able to relax and feel like herself.

It was also in a nice, secure building in the same arrondissement as Reve Weston's. She was only a short distance from him, she realized. A half-dozen blocks from Nina.

Oriel was so worked up, she only spent five minutes in her flat, just long enough to freshen up before she had her security detail drive her to Avenue Montaigne.

The paparazzi had posted photos of the building where "Oriel" was supposedly staying with Reve, so her driver found it very easily. She had one of her men escort her past the photographers, who snapped to attention as she left her car.

In the lobby, the doorman greeted her in English. "Mademoiselle Menendez. I understood you were away with Monsieur Weston."

For a moment, her heart pounded so hard she thought she might faint. Blood rushed in her ears and she recalled that she hadn't eaten since before she had landed.

*I want Vijay*, she thought.

*"Elle n'est pas là?"* She didn't realize she was speaking in French until the man grew alert with confusion at her native accent. "I'm Oriel Cuvier. When will they be back?"

He blinked with astonishment. "I'm sorry, but I couldn't say. Would you like to leave a message?"

She left all her contact details, and the paparazzi followed her home. She ignored them. She crawled into bed and noted that Kiran had texted.

I spoke with Vijay. I'm here if you want to talk.

Oriel thanked her and said she needed time to think. Then she called her mother, who was going on stage in Vienna shortly. Estelle was flabbergasted to hear there might have been two babies.

"I don't know why anyone would do something so hurtful as to separate a pair of twins. Our application would have said we wanted a single baby, but if they had told us you had a sister, we would have taken you both."

"I knew you would say that, but I needed to hear it."

"Can Vijay not help you learn the truth? He seems resourceful. He found *you*."

"We had a fight." She didn't get into the painful details of his accusations.

"A disagreement or a fight?" Her mother's tone grew serious.

"We're having trouble trusting one another. I'm worried we rushed into things."

"Of course you did, *chou*. It's always been your way to move quickly. You walk away just as quickly if something isn't right. Is that what happened? You've discovered he's not right for you?"

"Marriage isn't piano lessons," she said grumpily.

"This is true. But you know yourself, and if you have realized these piano lessons do not make you happy, then leave him. I'll support you."

Oriel laughed, but it was more an anguished sob, because her stomach clenched hard with rejection of that suggestion.

"No," she murmured. "He's the father of my child."

He was *the one*. For her, at least. She didn't know how he felt. "We'll have to make it work." She only wished that she knew *how*.

"And that is also your way," her mother chided gently. "When you do find what feels right, you *commit*."

Oriel's heart swerved. Her mother was right. She had locked herself into a life with Vijay that would be nearly impossible to unravel. She didn't want to! But he didn't love her. Didn't trust her. She didn't know how to fix that.

"I'm about to go on, *chou*. Would you like me to sing for you?"

"It's been a long time since we've done that. Yes, please, Maman. I love you. Break a leg."

Estelle hadn't done this since Oriel was very young and missing her when she was away on tour, but she had her assistant keep the line open and prop the phone in a suitable place so Oriel could hear her while she performed.

Oriel fell asleep with her phone on the pillow and tears on her cheeks.

She awoke with a melancholy knowledge that Paris was no longer her home. She belonged in that other place, the one with a spicy fragrance in the air and sheets of rain falling from the sky. The place where a man stretched naked beside her in the morning and played with her hair when they watched TV in the evening.

Could they have that again? She didn't know, but not if she was here and he was there.

She texted Vijay.

I'm going to stay and list the flat.

It seemed a neutral enough means to open communication, but he didn't respond. It was the middle of his workday, though. He had a lot to get done in Delhi.

She called a property agent, then had boxes delivered and began sorting through her personal things. One of her guards was helping her take down a box of keepsakes from the closet shelf when her door buzzer rang, indicating someone was waiting outside.

The paparazzi had been pestering her periodically, so she asked him to leave the box on the kitchen table while he ran down to tell them to shove off.

She absently filled the kettle as she acknowledged that all this culling of her possessions was a time-filler while she contemplated the bigger unknowns in her life. How would she mend her marriage? What would happen when she returned to India?

The knock on the door sent her heart leaping.

It was probably the guard returning, she cautioned herself, but she hurried across the room. Had Vijay come? She didn't actually want him to come after her. She wanted him to trust her to return to him so they would have a foundation to build on.

She flung open the door with anticipation anyway and confronted a mirror.

Her reflection wore a different outfit, something in denim. Oriel wasn't taking in superficial details when there was so much else that was exactly *her*. The wave in her dark hair, her arched eyebrows, the shape of her nose and the flecks of greenish gold in her eyes. The way her jaw hung slack and her mouth worked to find words.

Oriel's mouth was doing the same. No coherent thoughts were coming to her. Her throat had closed, her chest was tight, and her whole body began to tremble.

There was a rushing sound in her ears, so a man's voice in the distance barely made sense. "I thought I should bring her up since you went looking for her yesterday. She was going to be mobbed downstairs."

She and Nina stared at one another for twenty-five years and nineteen weeks and three days and however many hours and minutes and seconds had passed since they had exited the womb they had shared.

Oriel didn't know how she knew that to be fact, but it was. This was her sister.

They took a step at the same time, hugging themselves back together again.

A whistling kettle broke them apart.

A different man's voice said, "I'll get that. You two sit down."

He nudged them inside and closed the door, then snagged a box of tissues from a table and held it between them.

That's when Oriel realized fat tears were dripping off her cheeks. She took a few of the tissues and sniffled, beginning to mop up. She watched her sister—*her twin*—do the same. They were both gasping and shaking in the same way.

They both smiled through all of it as they moved to the couch and sat. Still neither spoke. Each time one of them tried, each time they looked at the other, they welled up again. Oriel knew exactly how Nina felt. Her heart was too big for her chest. Her emotions were so expansive, her shoulders ached. There was a lump in her throat too sharp to swallow.

After a few minutes, Reve came back with two cups and set them on the table. Oriel couldn't have said what was in them, but Nina looked at him with naked love that she blinked away when he raised his gaze.

Oriel felt that agony of unrequited love inside herself, too. Amid this upheaval, her heart throbbed with want for Vijay. He wouldn't be able to do anything, but she wanted him here anyway, sharing this monumental moment with her.

She wanted him to squeeze her shoulder the way Reve did Nina's as he asked, "Do we need introductions? I'm Reve. This is Nina. I presume you're Oriel unless there's a third one?"

"*Mon Dieu*, can you imagine?" Oriel laughed into her handful of damp tissues.

"There's not," Nina said. "There are only two of us." She looked around, and Reve came from the door, where she had dropped her bag. She smiled her thanks at him again with that same glimmer of adoring love. "Reve and I were in Luxembourg, trying to find some answers about... Well, everything. Me. I didn't actually know my parents weren't my birth parents until you were making headlines and people started calling me by your name. I thought you'd think I was a crackpot if I didn't have some proof that we could be... It's weird to say it. Twins," she said with a teary laugh. "We raced back here when Reve's doorman sent the message that you were here in Paris and had come looking for me."

"Did you find the clinic? What did you learn?"

"We found some records from the doctor who delivered us." She sent Reve a look that held a scold, but started digging into her bag. "And we met a woman who was a maid at the house where Lakshmi stayed. I showed her a photo of Lakshmi's manager. She said it was him, that they claimed to be married, but she said they fought all the time. They spoke in Hindi, but she could tell he wanted her to give up the baby. Lakshmi didn't want to. She said Lakshmi wrote letters whenever he went out and threw them in the fire when he came home. The maid pulled this out of the grate one day. She wanted to know what was going on, but she didn't know what to do once she'd read it. Then Lakshmi delivered and they were gone."

"And she kept it all this time?" Oriel carefully unfolded the paper. It had been folded in four and was scorched where the corners had come together. Only the middle of the page remained, but she'd written in English.

> …know we promised we wouldn't write. I hope your boy is improving…
> …never wish to separate you from him, but want you to know…
> …could marry him, but he says the baby will be white…
> …midwife assures me all is well, but I sense she's hiding…
> …and when it's time insists I must give it up…
> …know what else to do. I wish you were here to…

"To our father?" Oriel bit her lips to keep them from trembling. It meant so much to know there had been love between them, even if it had been an impossible one. "This is so sad. My heart is absolutely broken for her."

"Me, too." Fat tears sat in Nina's eyes, and her voice cracked. "I don't think she got to see us or hold us or even know there were two of us."

They searched each other's eyes, anguished for the mother they hadn't known and the memories they had missed making as a family.

"My parents would have taken both of us if they'd been told. They're actually really excited to meet you," Oriel said with a small, quavering smile.

"Oh, my gosh, when I tell you how I came to be with my family..." Nina sent the heel of her hand across her cheekbone and glanced at Reve, seemingly at a loss. "We're going to need something stronger than coffee."

"We have more paperwork that we want to give to Lakshmi's family, too," Reve said.

"It's okay," Oriel said, waving Nina off from reaching into her bag again. "That can wait a few minutes. I want to know everything about you. I already know you're a fashion designer."

"And you're a model. It's like we're twins."

They laughed in a way that was eerily similar and that might have made them dissolve into fresh tears, but an abrupt knock on the door had them both twisting to look at it.

Reve ambled over.

"Ah," he said as he saw who was behind it. "The husband."

# CHAPTER ELEVEN

It wasn't Vijay's worst nightmare, precisely, but he really wasn't thrilled when a man—*the* man—opened the door of his wife's flat.

Reve Weston was handsome, rich. At home. Smug.

"Vijay!" Oriel leaped to her feet.

Reve stepped aside, and Vijay saw Oriel's double stand and smile in a tentative greeting.

The resemblance was eerie and an easy mistake in a photo. In person he knew immediately which one was his wife. There were small, obvious differences. Nina's teeth were not quite perfect, and was that a streak of pink in her hair? She was a tiny bit shorter, but she was every bit as beautiful as Oriel.

Even so, rather than inciting a spark of sexual attraction in him, he only felt endeared toward her for her close resemblance to someone he loved. He didn't feel a gut-deep hunger and overwhelming need to connect or a stark, protective urgency to touch and reclaim intimate space the way he did toward Oriel.

"This is a plot twist, isn't it?" He moved into the sitting area and greeted Oriel with a light kiss on her cheek.

*When in France*, he conveyed when her lashes flicked up at him.

He hovered close enough to inhale her scent and absorb the light brush of her body against his.

She dipped her chin and rolled her lips together, indicating their conflicts were not resolved, but she stayed in the arm he looped around her waist. Her gaze up at him was not hostile, merely vulnerable and deeply uncertain.

He had hurt her. The knowledge squeezed his guts in a cruel fist.

"Vijay, this is Reve Weston and Nina Menendez." He heard the catch in her voice. Her joy was so visceral, it cracked something open in him. "My twin."

"That's what the birth records would suggest, at least," Nina said with shaken laughter as she took his hand.

"And anyone with eyes," Reve drawled.

"Still." Nina glanced back at him. "I imagine Lakshmi's family has been inundated with people claiming to be her daughter. I'm happy to do a DNA test."

"It looks like it will be redundant, but I've already connected with the lab we use here," Vijay said. "They have someone who can take the samples and rush the results. I'll make that call shortly, but…" He looked at Oriel, and whatever was in his face made her pupils expand and her lips tremble. "I need to speak with my wife."

"You should speak to your family, Nina. Things are going to get very chaotic when the jackals at the door downstairs realize there are two of you." Reve sounded grim enough that Vijay was put on high alert to threats he couldn't see.

Nina bit her lip and nodded with agreement, maybe remorse, but she smiled as she reached for Oriel. "I didn't mean to impersonate you. I've been trying to stay under the radar, but they're relentless."

"Vijay, you should arrange protection for her," Oriel said, looking to him.

"Already in the works," he assured her.

Reve shot him a glare that warned him to stay in his lane.

Vijay didn't flinch, and only said, "Do you think I'm going to let anything happen to my wife's sister?" He reached for his phone. "I'll have one of my guys lead you out through the maintenance entrance that I used to come in. Tell your car to meet you on the south side."

While he and Reve exchanged information, Nina asked, "Will you come for dinner? Now that I've found you, I don't want to miss another minute."

"Me, either," Oriel said emotively, but she looked to Vijay as if she knew they had things to talk out, too. "I'll text you in a little bit?"

"Perfect." They hugged each other so tightly, it added another layer of ignominy to Vijay's guilt over suspecting she'd lied to him.

The pair left, and Oriel stayed at the closed door, chewing her bottom lip as she regarded him. The space between them was a cavern of vipers and land mines, and the valentines of love she had sent him, which he had crumpled and stepped on.

"I apologize," he said sincerely. "I should have trusted you. I knew you wouldn't hurt me like that. In here I knew it." He tapped his chest. "Up here…" He tapped his temple. "But I won't let that happen again. I love you, Oriel."

He saw her jerk and heard her breath hiss in, but her expression only grew more anguished. His heart lurched as he realized he might have done irreparable damage to something that was becoming increasingly precious to him.

He took a step toward her, and she put up a hand.

"I'll give you a pass because there's no way you could have known I had a twin, but the fact is, you *don't* trust me, Vijay. And I can't fix that." She shrugged with despair. "And I can't spend my life worried about how you'll interpret everything I do, especially when there are people out there who will use my image and cast doubts and—"

"Shh. Stop."

He came forward a few more steps, but she kept her hand up to hold him off.

"I promised to come back and I *will*. Look around. I'm packing!" She waved at the full boxes on the floor, and at the bare walls. "I'm selling this flat. I'm going to live with the father of my child. I hope we can repair this marriage of ours, but you didn't even trust me to come back. Instead you've chased me here, and what did you think when Reve opened the door? That he'd just left my bed?"

"I thought I should have been here," he said fervently. "Because I made a promise to you when we learned you were pregnant that I would be here for you through all of this. I meant *all* of it. Not just the baby, but this. Learning who you are. You told me once that you always wished for a sibling. The minute I realized that's who she was, I knew you would be so excited, but also rocked to the core. *I* have questions, Oriel. You must be…"

His heart hurt for her, for all the anger and confusion she must feel at having been torn from the woman who gave birth to her *and* the sibling she should have had in her life all this time.

"Somewhere in there, you're wondering if you should have known that Nina was out there, aren't you? You think you should have found her long ago, on instinct or something."

"I think she knew before I did, but she didn't reach out. She said it was because she thought I wouldn't believe her, but…"

"I know." He came close enough to gather her in. "You feel cheated. And also guilty for wishing you'd had that other life where you grew up with her and Lakshmi."

She nodded while tears tracked down her cheeks.

"See? I know you, Oriel. More importantly, I *love* you. It kills me that I hurt you so badly, you felt you had to come here and face this alone."

Her eyes were leaking more tears. "I'm used to doing things on my own. I've told myself it was the way I liked it, but from the moment I left Mumbai, I've been thinking that I want you here with me, even though you can't do anything."

"I can do this." He folded his arms around her and held her, just held her and rubbed her back as she trembled.

Slowly she wound her arms around his waist and leaned on him, sighing out a lifetime of pent-up grief. He closed his eyes in gratitude.

"I love you, Oriel. I should have said it the first time you did. I've been sick with myself that I didn't. I know my heart is safe with you. *I know that*. It wasn't you I didn't trust. It was love. It hurts to love. It bloody *hurts* to love someone this hard. But I forgot that it heals, too. It gives a reason to hope and to push on when the rest of life is too bleak to face."

* * *

Vijay's hand stroked her hair, and his stubbled jaw rested against her cheekbone. A bubble of hope was trying to crack open her breastbone.

"Can I also say," his voice rumbled next to her ear, "that even though I understand your sense of urgency to meet Nina, and that you were hurt and angry with me, if you had trusted me just a tiny little bit more, you might have held the plane and let me come with you?"

She sniffled back her tears and looked up at him, chagrined. "Guilty."

"You probably would have had more faith in me if I'd told you I love you." He slid her hair behind her ear.

"I do. So much." He looked at her as though he was beholding something magical. "I've had to beat and claw my way into the life I have. It didn't seem like being this happy should be this easy, but I won't give you a reason to doubt my feelings again."

"Me, either."

He touched her chin, and their mouths flowed together in the simple, inevitable way they had between them. Perfect and tender and now an expression of that wider, deeper, heart-expanding emotion.

He took great care as he tightened his arms and swept his mouth across hers, but his love was so tangible in that kiss, she shook under the force of it.

"Come," she invited him, taking his hand and drawing him into her bedroom.

They settled on the bed fully clothed, sharing soft, soothing kisses that held no urgency because this was love in its purest form. It was touch and acceptance of their human flaws and celebration of their perfection. Of their divine connection.

They were a special combination, though. One that

couldn't help but create passion when they were together. Soon it was snapping like flames around them, burning away a fold of collar so kisses could extend down a throat. Demanding layers be removed so they could rub their bodies together in the exquisite friction of animal desire.

But even when he slid into her with a carnal groan and her body responded with a sensual clench, their coupling was imbued with the intense love that emanated from their pores. She petted his spine and he sucked on her earlobe, but sweet light shone behind her eyes. His voice was hoarse with joy as he moved, telling her raggedly, "I love you. We belong like this. Always. Together."

That was how they crested the final peak. Together. Shattering in unison. Destroyed, yet rebuilt with pieces of the other embedded within their souls.

# EPILOGUE

"I LOVE THAT she thinks I'm you, but she's hungry, so…" Nina spoke ruefully as she handed Lakshmi, whom they all called "Lucky," to Oriel.

The six-month-old began to nuzzle and root at Oriel's cheek. Thankfully, Oriel's sister, the genius designer, had been immersing herself in their roots by studying the construction of traditional Indian clothing. She had sewn Oriel's celebratory saree and included nursing snaps in the blouse. Oriel adjusted her *pallu* and settled her squirming daughter to latch on.

"Also, I have somewhere to be."

"Oh?" Oriel was teasing her, and Nina knew it. Her sister was an open book at the best of times, but they had a wonderful ability to read each other very well.

"Don't ask me," Nina pleaded with exasperation and beckoned someone from across the marquee tent.

Oriel chuckled. "Don't worry. I don't know what Maman has planned, only that it will be spectacular."

For anyone else, the bringing together of all these people for Oriel and Vijay's wedding reception would have been enough, but Madam Estelle was determined to outdo herself and make it a memory that would be talked about for years. Nina's family were here, along with Jalil and Kiran and other treasured connections from around the globe, all dressed in a mix of Western and Indian garb.

The courses of French and Indian cuisine had been amazing, and the tribute to Lakshmi had been heart-wrenchingly sweet. The marquee was draped in silk and strings of flowers. Everywhere there were tropical plants, a wild abundance of color, and spices lending fragrance to the air. There had been speeches, a song from Estelle, and a toast from Oriel's father that would live in Oriel's heart forever.

It was already a night of pure enchantment.

"Did you need me?" Vijay asked, his warm hand descending on her shoulder.

"No, I—"

"Yes," Nina corrected her. "Sit." She nodded at the spot on the love seat that had been Vijay's for most of the evening. Nina had stolen it when he had moved to the bar with Reve.

"She's more and more like my sister every day," Vijay remarked to Oriel as he retook his seat and brushed a light greeting across their daughter's curled fist.

Nina laughed, then poked her tongue out at him before she disappeared.

"What's happening?" Vijay asked.

"I have no idea, but I suspect we'll need…"

He was already fishing into the diaper pack for the baby earmuffs. He slipped them onto Lucky's head as the lights began to swerve all over the tent, gathering everyone's attention.

A firm thump-thump sounded on a *tabla* drum. A flute and sitar strings drew people in colorful sarees from all sides of the tent.

As Madam Estelle began to sing in Hindi, the dancers settled into a precise formation on the dance floor, beginning a slow, undulating walk. They were Oriel's cousins and Nina with her sisters, and there was Kiran among them, spinning her chair and raising her arms in a graceful ballet, giving her shoulders a shimmy before clapping her hands to pick up the tempo.

Vijay's arm closed around Oriel's shoulders, and he drew her tight into his side. She felt his chest expanding with laughing emotion, but they both had tears in their eyes.

"I could not feel more loved," he told her sincerely.

"Me, either," she admitted, deeply touched that her mother would go to all this trouble to celebrate this side of her daughter's life.

The energy picked up, and the dancers moved into more of a hip-hop style until the music abruptly cut off with a group clap.

A dozen people in suits abruptly stood. They wore serious expressions as they popped their collars, then pretended to spit on their palms before they smoothed their hair back on both sides. The music resumed in plucked strings as they sidled onto the dance floor.

"Will there be a rain machine?" Vijay asked.

"Don't put it past her."

It was a dance-off between gowns and suits, full of push and pull, defiant head tosses and waved scarves, straight out of a Bollywood musical.

Dying with delight, Oriel fell into her husband. "This is too much, but I never want it to end."

"It won't," he promised her. "The credits will roll, but we'll continue to live happily ever after."

"Promise?"

"I do."

She believed him.

\* \* \* \* \*

# COMING SOON!

We really hope you enjoyed reading this book.
If you're looking for more romance
be sure to head to the shops when
new books are available on

## Thursday 26th March

To see which titles are coming soon, please visit
**millsandboon.co.uk/nextmonth**

MILLS & BOON

# FOUR BRAND NEW BOOKS FROM
# MILLS & BOON MODERN

Indulge in desire, drama, and breathtaking romance – where passion knows no bounds!

## OUT NOW

Eight Modern stories published every month, find them all at:

**millsandboon.co.uk**

# TWO BRAND NEW BOOKS FROM
# Love Always

Be prepared to be swept away to incredible worldwide destinations along with our strong, relatable heroines and intensely desirable heroes.

## OUT NOW

Four Love Always stories published every month, find them all at:

**millsandboon.co.uk**

# OUT NOW!

Available at
millsandboon.co.uk

MILLS & BOON

# OUT NOW!

Available at
millsandboon.co.uk

MILLS & BOON

# LET'S TALK
# *Romance*

For exclusive extracts, competitions and special offers, find us online:

- **f** MillsandBoon
- **X** @MillsandBoon
- **◉** @MillsandBoonUK
- **♪** @MillsandBoonUK

Get in touch on 01413 063 232

For all the latest titles coming soon, visit
millsandboon.co.uk/nextmonth

# MILLS & BOON

## THE HEART OF ROMANCE

---

### A ROMANCE FOR EVERY READER

---

**MODERN** — Prepare to be swept off your feet by sophisticated, sexy and seductive heroes, in some of the world's most glamourous and romantic locations, where power and passion collide.

**HISTORICAL** — Escape with historical heroes from time gone by. Whether your passion is for wicked Regency Rakes, muscled Vikings or rugged Highlanders, awaken the romance of the past.

**MEDICAL** — Set your pulse racing with dedicated, delectable doctors in the high-pressure world of medicine, where emotions run high and passion, comfort and love are the best medicine.

**Love Always** — Celebrate true love with tender stories of heartfelt romance, from the rush of falling in love to the joy a new baby can bring, and a focus on the emotional heart of a relationship.

**HEROES** — The excitement of a gripping thriller, with intense romance at its heart. Resourceful, true-to-life women and strong, fearless men face danger and desire - a killer combination!

 — From showing up to glowing up, these characters are on the path to leading their best lives and finding romance along the way – with plenty of sizzling spice!

To see which titles are coming soon, please visit

**millsandboon.co.uk/nextmonth**

# MILLS & BOON
## MODERN
# Power and Passion

Prepare to be swept off your feet by sophisticated, sexy and seductive heroes, in some of the world's most glamorous and romantic locations, where power and passion collide.

Eight Modern stories published every month, find them all at:

**millsandboon.co.uk**

# MILLS & BOON
# Love Always

Celebrate true love with tender stories of heartfelt romance, from the rush of falling in love to the joy a new baby can bring, and a focus on the emotional heart of a relationship.

ur Love Always stories published every month, find them all at:

**millsandboon.co.uk/LoveAlways**

# MILLS & BOON
## HEROES
### *At Your Service*

Experience all the excitement of a gripping thriller, with an intense romance at its heart that will keep you on the edge of your seat. Resourceful, true-to-life women and strong, fearless men face danger and desire – a killer combination!

Eight Heroes stories published every month, find them all at:
**millsandboon.co.uk**

# MILLS & BOON
## HISTORICAL

## Awaken the romance of the past

Indulge your fantasies of delicious Regency Rakes, fierce Viking warriors and rugged Highlanders. Be swept away into a world of intense passion, lavish settings and sumptuous details as you awaken the romance of the past.

Four Historical stories published every month, find them all at:

**millsandboon.co.uk**

# MILLS & BOON
## MEDICAL
*Pulse-Racing Passion*

Set your pulse racing with delectable doctors, hot-shot surgeons and fearless first resonders. Escape to a world where life and love play out against a high-pressured medical backdrop, where emotions and passion run high.

Six Medical stories published every month, find them all at:
**millsandboon.co.uk**